PRAISE FOR THESE
nationally bestselling authors:

D1318317

Jayne Ann Krentz is one of today's top contemporary romance writers, with an astounding twelve million copies of her books in print. Her novels regularly appear on the *New York Times,* Waldenbooks and B. Dalton bestseller lists. First published in 1979, Jayne quickly established herself as a prolific and innovative writer. She has delved into psychic elements, intrigue, fantasy, historicals and even futuristic romances. Jayne lives in Seattle with her husband, Frank, an engineer.

Christine Rimmer is a third-generation Californian, who held jobs as an actress, salesclerk, janitor, model, teacher, waitress, playwright and office manager before she settled down to write about the magic of romance. It's work that suits her perfectly, and Christine is grateful not only for the joy she finds in writing, but for what waits when the day's work is through: a man she loves who loves her right back, and the privilege of watching their children grow and change day to day.

Lynne Graham was born in Ireland and at the age of fifteen submitted for publication her first romance novel— unsuccessfully. Then, a Christmas visit home resulted in her having to make a choice between career or marriage to a man she had loved since her teens. Her understanding husband has learned to cook since she started to write! They are the parents of three, and live in Ireland in a household overflowing with dogs, plants and books.

ONE MORE TIME

JAYNE ANN KRENTZ

CHRISTINE
RIMMER

LYNNE
GRAHAM

HARLEQUIN®

TORONTO • NEW YORK • LONDON
AMSTERDAM • PARIS • SYDNEY • HAMBURG
STOCKHOLM • ATHENS • TOKYO • MILAN • MADRID
PRAGUE • WARSAW • BUDAPEST • AUCKLAND

HARLEQUIN BOOKS
225 Duncan Mill Road, Don Mills,
Ontario, Canada M3B 3K9

ISBN 0-373-83536-1

ONE MORE TIME

Copyright © 2002 by Harlequin Books S.A.

The publisher acknowledges the copyright holders
of the individual works as follows:

LADY'S CHOICE
Copyright © 1989 by Jayne Ann Krentz.

MIDSUMMER MADNESS
Copyright © 1992 by Christine Rimmer.

TEMPESTUOUS REUNION
Copyright © 1991 by Lynne Graham.

This edition published by arrangement with Harlequin Books S.A.

® and TM are trademarks of the publisher. Trademarks indicated with ® are registered in the United States Patent and Trademark Office, the Canadian Trade Marks Office and in other countries.

Visit us at www.eHarlequin.com

Printed in U.S.A.

CONTENTS

LADY'S CHOICE
Jayne Ann Krentz

CHAPTER ONE

"I LOVE YOU, Travis. Hold me, hold me."

"*Juliana.*"

Travis Sawyer heard his own muffled shout as he shuddered heavily over the flame-haired woman in his arms. The last of his white-hot passion spent itself in a blinding, driving storm of pure release. He lost himself in his lover's arms, surrendering to her fire even as he exulted in his victory. She clung to him with all her sleek strength, drawing him into her until he felt as though he'd stepped into another universe.

It had never been this good with anyone else. Travis Sawyer was thirty-eight years old. He'd never been a womanizer but he considered he'd lived long enough to make the judgment. This was special. Nothing had ever been this good before in his life.

It was everything he had instinctively sensed it would be with this woman. Hot, wild, powerful. He had never felt so alive, so strong. Satisfaction swept through him in the wake of the slowly dissipating passion.

She was his now. Reluctantly he disengaged himself and rolled to one side, his hand trailing heavily over the gentle curve of Juliana's breast. She smiled up at him from the pillow, the expression as dazzling as always, even here in the darkness of her bedroom.

The thick, untamed mass of her hair was an elegant, pagan crown framing her vivid features. Travis stared down at her, captivated by huge, long-lashed eyes, a noble nose, an arrogant, yet surprisingly delicate chin and a luscious mouth. Her long leg slid between his in a languidly sensual movement. Then she closed her eyes and snuggled into his warmth.

He had done it, Travis thought triumphantly as his arm tightened around her. He had claimed his red-haired, topaz-eyed queen.

And then, in the next moment, reality settled back into place around him. What the hell was he doing here, holding her like this? He'd never intended to take his revenge this far; never intended to wind up in bed with Juliana Grant.

He stared deeply into the shadows of the bedroom, searching for answers that weren't there. He felt dazed now that the fiery passion had receded.

Vengeance led a man down strange paths. Juliana Grant had been an unexpected detour in the long road he'd been walking for the past five years. But he could not, would not allow the detour, no matter how exotic, to deflect him from his chosen course. He had come too far. There was no turning back now, even if he wanted to do so.

Travis Sawyer was very good at what he did, and when he had set out to orchestrate his revenge he had left no loopholes. There was no escape for anyone, not even for himself.

THE CLEAR, BRIGHT California sunshine danced across the bay and slammed cheerfully through the condominium's bedroom windows. Juliana opened her eyes slowly and watched the early-spring light as it bounced around the dramatic white-on-white room. It sparkled on the thick white carpet, bounded off the white walls, struck the chrome and white leather chair and tap-danced over the gleaming white lacquer dressing table. It sizzled when it struck the only color accent in the bedroom, an egg-yolk-yellow abstract painting that hung on the wall over the chrome and white bed.

Mesmerized, Juliana followed the trail of sunlight as it ricocheted between the mirror and the painting and splashed across the foaming white sheets of the rumpled bed. There, in a final burst of dazzling brilliance, the morning sun revealed the alien male being who had invaded her room last night.

A man in her bed. That, in and of itself, was a rare enough event to excite wonder and curiosity, but in this case it was an even more notable occurrence. Juliana hugged herself with her secret knowledge.

Because she knew beyond a shadow of a doubt that this partic-

ular man—this hard, lean, sexy man named Travis Sawyer—was
the man. The right man. The one she'd been waiting for all her
life.

She savored the delicious secret and held herself very still so
as not to awaken the exotic creature lying next to her. She wanted
a moment to luxuriate in the thrilling certainty that she had finally
encountered her true mate.

He was not exactly as she had fondly imagined over the years
when she had indulged in a little harmless fantasizing. He wasn't
quite as tall as he should have been, for one thing. She, herself,
was just a sliver under six feet and she had always envisioned her
true mate as being somewhere in the neighborhood of six feet,
four inches or so. Tall enough so that she could wear high heels
comfortably around him. Travis was barely an inch over six feet.
In two-inch heels she was eyeball to eyeball with him. In two-
and-a-half-inch heels she was taller than he was.

But whatever he lacked in height, he more than compensated
for in build, Juliana assured herself cheerfully. Travis was sleekly
muscular and as solid as a chunk of granite. Last night she had
been in no doubt of his strength. The masculine power in him had
been totally controlled and all the more exciting for that sense of
control. This was a man who exercised a sure command over
himself, a man who had learned the techniques of self-mastery.
She admired that kind of control in a man. It gave a woman a
sense of security—an old-fashioned, primitive assurance that his
greater physical strength need never be feared but could be relied
upon for protection.

Travis did not quite match Juliana's inner image of her perfect
man in a few other minor respects, either. His eyes were the wrong
color. Juliana preferred sensual, warm brown or hazel eyes in
those of the male persuasion. Travis had cool, crystal gray eyes
that did not betray his emotions except in the most intense situations. Last night had been intense, however, she recalled with
delight. She'd seen the passion blazing in his eyes and it had sent
shivers of excitement through her.

This morning she was quite prepared to drop her old standards
regarding eye color in view of the fact that Travis's eyes were not

only capable of reflecting his passion, but also an intelligence that complemented her own and a rare sense of humor that delighted her when it showed itself.

His hair was a bit off, too, unfortunately. It was a far darker shade than she'd fantasized. Juliana had always liked men with tawny-colored or blond hair, but she had to admit that Travis's severely trimmed, night-black hair seemed to suit him. The hint of silver at the temples was not at all unattractive.

There were a few other minor discrepancies between the real Travis Sawyer and Juliana's fantasy version of her true mate. If she were inclined to be picky, for example, she could have carped about the undeniable fact that his rough, grim looks would probably forever keep him from gracing the cover of *Gentlemen's Quarterly* magazine. Ah, well, it was GQ's loss, she told herself. He looked perfect here in her bed.

Then, too, there was Travis's apparent total lack of interest in style and clothes. She had known him for almost one whole month now and she had never seen him in anything but a pair of dark trousers, an austere white shirt, a conservatively striped tie and wing-tip shoes. His jackets were all muted shades of gray. But Juliana figured she could fix the problem. After all, she had more than enough style for both of them, she told herself. She glanced at her closet and smiled as she pictured the rack of expensive, high-fashion clothes and the boxes of shoes inside. Shopping was high on her list of hobbies.

All in all, Juliana was more than willing to make allowances for the few areas in which Travis Sawyer fell short of her idealized image of Mr. Right. She was used to working for what she wanted, and she was quite prepared to put in whatever time and effort was required to polish her very special diamond in the rough. Last night she had received ample assurance that the effort would be worth it. She still tingled from head to toe with the hot memories.

Having finished her perusal, Juliana stretched slowly, deliberately stroking one toe down the length of Travis's muscular calf. When there was no response, she sighed and accepted the fact that the man probably needed his sleep after last night.

Juliana grinned with amused regret, pushed back the sheet and got to her feet. She was mildly startled to discover she ached pleasantly all over. Travis had been a demanding as well as a bold and generous lover. He'd taken everything he could get but he had given back passion with equal intensity. If she closed her eyes she could still feel his strong, sensitive hands on her this morning. She felt as if she'd been imprinted with his touch.

Standing in the middle of her bright white room Juliana allowed herself one last, fond gaze at the man in her bed and then she headed for the bathroom with a long, exuberant stride.

She would welcome her true mate with a proper display of feminine domesticity, she decided. Might as well give the man a little foretaste of the wonders that were in store for him.

HALF AN HOUR LATER, showered, her mass of red curls caught up in a dramatically cascading ponytail and dressed in a pair of fashionably cut, high-waisted slacks and wide-sleeved painter's shirt, Juliana made her way back into the bedroom. She was carrying a black enameled tea tray. Perched on the elegant tray was an art deco teapot and two cunningly designed, bright red cups.

"Good morning." She smiled brilliantly when she saw that Travis was awake. He sprawled on his back, watching her through half-closed eyes.

"Good morning." His voice was husky with sleep and very sexy.

"Beautiful day, isn't it? But, then, it always seems to be beautiful here in Jewel Harbor. That's one of the things I had trouble getting used to when I first moved here four years ago. It's the perfect California seaside town, and perfection always makes a person a little suspicious, doesn't it?" Juliana busied herself with the tray. "Even the fog, when it shows up, is different here than it is anywhere else. Soft and romantic and eerie. You don't take milk or sugar in your tea, do you?"

"Uh, no. No, I don't." Travis sat up slowly against the pillows.

"Didn't think so. You're not the type."

"There's a type?" He watched her, as if deeply intrigued by the whole process of pouring tea.

"Oh, definitely. But I knew you wouldn't be one of those."

She handed him a red cup. "Just as I knew the day you walked into my shop that you drank just plain coffee, not espresso or latte or cappuccino."

Seemingly bemused, he glanced down at the strong, dark tea and then up to meet her expectant gaze. "No offense, but it is a little surprising to discover that the queen of the local coffee empire serves tea in bed."

Juliana laughed and helped herself to the second cup. "I'll let you in on a little secret," she said as she sat down in the white leather and chrome chair. "I really don't like coffee, especially all those fancy French and Italian variations I serve at the shop. The stuff upsets my stomach."

Travis's mouth curved faintly. "I know most of your secrets but you've hidden this one well. I would never have guessed you're a closet tea drinker. What would the patrons of Charisma Espresso say if they knew?"

"I don't intend for them to ever find out. Until, that is, I get ready to open up a chain of tea shops."

Travis frowned, shaking his head in an automatic, negative gesture. "Forget the idea of tea shops. Your goal is to expand Charisma, remember? There are a lot more coffee drinkers than tea drinkers around here."

"Never mind about my tea shop idea. I don't really want to talk about it this morning, anyway." Juliana eyed him with great interest. "Did you think you knew all my secrets just because you've been looking into my business affairs for the past couple of weeks?"

"Most of them." Travis shrugged, his bare, bronzed shoulders moving with masculine grace against the white satin pillow. "I'm a business consultant, remember? I'm good at what I do. And I've learned that once you know someone's financial secrets, you usually know all the rest of his or her secrets, too."

"Sounds ominous." Juliana shuddered elegantly and took a sip of her Darjeeling. "I'm glad that in our case there are still a few surprises left. More fun that way, don't you think?"

"Not all surprises are pleasant ones."

The warning was soft. And, predictably enough, it went unheeded. Juliana figured Travis was still a bit sleepy.

"Oh, in our case I'm sure the surprises will all be at least interesting, if not downright pleasant," she said with assurance. "I'm looking forward to each and every one." A rush of happiness sizzled through her as she studied him. He looked so good lying there in her bed. She loved that mat of dark hair on his broad chest. To think she had ever wasted time fantasizing about fair-haired men. She shook her head in disbelief at the recollection of her own foolishness.

"Something wrong?" Travis asked.

"Not in the least."

"I thought you might be having a few regrets—" he paused carefully, his eyes meeting hers "—about last night."

Juliana's stared at him in astonishment. "Of course not. If I'd worried about having regrets, I wouldn't have gone to bed with you in the first place. I knew exactly what I was doing."

"Did you?"

"Absolutely. I'm sure you did, too."

"Yes," he said, looking contemplative. "I knew what I was doing. You look pleased with yourself this morning, Juliana."

"I am." She smiled widely, vastly pleased indeed, with him, life and the world.

"I'm glad you weren't disappointed."

"Disappointed?" She was shocked. "How could I possibly have been disappointed? It was glorious. Perfect. Everything I imagined. You are a fabulous lover, Travis Sawyer. Magnificent."

An unexpected telltale red stained his high cheekbones. For a few seconds Juliana could have sworn Travis looked embarrassed by the expansive praise. She was instantly touched by his lack of ego in that particular department.

"No," Travis said, concentrating on his tea, "I don't think it was anything special I did. We just sort of clicked, I guess. It happens that way sometimes. Two people meet, find each other attractive and, well, things work out in bed."

Juliana's brows rose and she pursed her lips thoughtfully. "Has it happened that way a lot for you in the past?"

Travis blinked and his crystal eyes gleamed behind his lashes. "No," he admitted quietly. "It hasn't happened that way a lot for me."

Juliana relaxed immediately, satisfied to know for certain that the emotions in this situation were not one-sided. "Good. I knew last night was special."

"I take it that it hasn't happened that way a lot for you, either?" The question was reluctant, as if Travis did not want to know the answer but was unable to stop himself from asking the intimate question.

"Never in my whole life," she assured him with perfect honesty.

He grinned slightly. "Maybe you just haven't had enough experience to judge."

"I'm thirty-two years old and along the way I've had to kiss a few frogs to find my prince."

"But you haven't slept with too many of those frogs have you?"

"Of course not. Frogs can be very slimy, you know. A woman has to be cautious."

"Ummm. These days it works both ways."

"I'm aware of that. And I know you're not the kind of man who jumps into bed with any willing body that comes along." Juliana wrinkled her nose with distaste. "I could never fall for a man who didn't have enough sense to be extremely discriminating when it came to his sex life. More tea?"

"All right." He held out the red cup, watching with amusement as she leaped out of the chair to pour from the stunning little art deco pot. "I could get accustomed to this kind of service."

She laughed. "You've caught me in a good mood. Either that or the novelty of the situation has inspired me." She handed him back the cup, enjoying the brush of his fingers against hers. "Well?" she asked, barely able to conceal her impatience. "Would you like to talk about it now or later?"

"Talk about what?"

"Our future, of course." She was aware of Travis going very still against the pillows, but she ignored the implications. "When did you plan to ask me? I wouldn't want to spoil the surprise, but it would be helpful to know what date you had in mind so that I could start making plans. So much to do, you know. I want everything to be just perfect."

Travis stared at her, his tea forgotten. "Plans? What the devil are you talking about?"

"Are you always this dense in the morning?" She smiled at him indulgently. "I'm talking about our marriage plans, of course."

"Our *what*?" The red tea cup slipped from Travis's hand, spilling its contents on the white sheets. It rolled off the edge of the bed and landed on the white carpet with a soft thud.

"Oh, dear. I'd better get something on that right away. Tea stains, you know." Juliana jumped to her feet again and scurried into the white-tiled bathroom to fling open a cupboard.

"Juliana, wait. Come back here. What the hell did you mean a minute ago? Who said anything about marriage?"

She turned around, sponge and carpet cleaner in her hands and marveled at the sight of Travis standing fully nude in the doorway. For a few seconds she forgot about the risk of tea stains in the other room. "Who cares if you're a little on the short side?" she asked softly. "You're just perfect."

"Short?" He scowled at her. "I'm not short. You're too tall, that's the problem."

"It's not a problem. We can work it out. I'll wear flats or short heels most of the time," she vowed. Her eyes traveled wistfully down the length of him. "And certain parts of you are not very short at all."

"Juliana, for Pete's sake." Travis snatched a white towel off the nearest rack and wrapped it around his lean hips.

"You're blushing. I didn't know men could do that."

"Juliana, put down that sponge and start talking sense. What did you mean about getting married?"

She remembered the carpet with a start. "Hang on a second, I have to get that tea out right away. That's the trouble with a white carpet. You can't let anything sit on it very long or the stain sets." She brushed past him and hurried over to where the brown stain was slowly sinking into the beautiful white fibers. "This thing is supposed to be stain resistant, but unfortunately that doesn't mean it will take just any sort of abuse. I probably shouldn't have put in white but it looked so terrific in here I couldn't resist."

Travis stalked slowly across the room to stand towering over her while she knelt and began to scrub industriously. "Damn it, Juliana, I'm trying to talk to you."

"Oh, right. About our marriage. Well, I've been thinking about it and I've decided there's no real reason to wait, is there? I mean, we're hardly kids."

"No, we are not kids," Travis shot back. "We are adults. Which means we don't have to start talking marriage just because we went to bed together on one occasion."

"You know me well enough by now to realize I like to get going on things right away," she reminded him airily. "Once my mind is made up, there's no stopping me. Just ask anyone."

"Juliana, stop scrubbing that damned carpet and pay attention."

"But while it's true there's no real reason to wait, maybe we shouldn't move too quickly on this." Juliana chuckled. "I mean, you're always telling me that I should take my time and plan major moves carefully, right?"

"Damn right."

"And I do want to plan this wedding carefully. I think I'd like to have a big, splashy one with all the trimmings including an engagement party first. After all, I only intend to go through this once, you know? I'd like to do it right. I'd want the whole family present, naturally. My cousin Elly and her husband live just a few miles down the coast and my parents will be able to come down from San Francisco quite easily. Uncle Tony lives in San Diego so that's no problem, either. Then there are all my friends here in Jewel Harbor. There are also several good Charisma customers I'd like to invite."

"Juliana…"

"We could use that lovely little chapel that overlooks the harbor."

"Does it occur to you, Juliana," Travis interrupted in a grim voice, "that you're rushing this a bit?"

She paused in her scrubbing and looked up curiously. "Rushing?"

"Yes, rushing." He seemed gratified to have her full attention at last. "I recall everything that happened last night as well as every detail of everything we've discussed for the past three and a half weeks and I know for a fact that nothing, I repeat *nothing*, was ever said about marriage."

"Oh, dear. I've gone and ruined your big proposal scene, haven't I? You were probably planning a romantic evening with wine and caviar topped off by a stroll along the harbor front and a formal proposal of marriage." Juliana bit her lip contritely as she got to her feet. "I'm sorry, Travis. But there's really nothing to worry about. We can still do all that tonight or tomorrow night. That restaurant where we ate last night, The Treasure House, makes a great location for marriage proposals. We can go back there this evening."

"How would you know it makes such a great location for proposals? Oh, hell, what am I saying? Forget it." Travis's gray eyes glittered with anger and exasperation. "Damn it, Juliana, I have no intention of asking you to marry me."

There was a heartbeat of silence while Juliana absorbed that information. For a moment she was convinced she must have misunderstood. "I beg your pardon?"

"You heard me," he said, rubbing the back of his neck in a gesture of irritation and frustration.

"But I thought…I assumed…" Juliana ran out of words, a stunningly unusual event. Vaguely she waved her hand, the one with the sponge in it, in a helpless little gesture. "I mean, last night we…"

Travis's mouth twisted wryly. "You think that just because we'd been dating for the past couple of weeks and we went to bed together that it automatically followed that I intended to marry you? Come on, Juliana, you're not that naive. In fact, you can be pretty damn savvy when you choose. You're one heck of a sharp businesswoman. You now how to take care of yourself and as you pointed out, you're thirty-two years old and you've kissed a few frogs. So don't give me that wounded doe look."

The accusation stung. Juliana instantly narrowed her eyes as a slow anger began to simmer through her veins. "I will have you know, Travis Sawyer, that my intentions were honorable all along. I knew the minute I met you that I was going to marry you."

"Is that right? Well, maybe you should have warned me. We could have avoided this whole silly, embarrassing scene. Because I have no plans to marry anyone at the moment."

"I see." She drew herself up proudly. "You were just using me, is that it?"

"No, I was not using you and you damn well know it. We are two adults who happened to be very attracted to each other physically. We have professional interests in common, we're both single and we're working together because you hired me as a consultant. It was perfectly natural that we start an affair. But right now, that's as far as things have gotten. We're involved in an affair, nothing more."

"You're not prepared to make a commitment yet, is that it?" she challenged.

"Do you always hit your dates over the head like this the morning after?"

"As we've already discussed, there haven't been that many morning afters and no, I don't generally hit them over the head like this. But, then, I haven't wanted to marry very many of my dates."

"How many have bothered to ask you to marry them?" Travis asked sarcastically.

"Lots of men have asked me to marry them. I get asked all the time, as a matter of fact. Usually at The Treasure House. That's how I know it's a perfect setting."

"If you've had all those opportunities, why haven't you taken one of the poor jerks up on his proposal?"

Juliana was furious. "Because none of them have been the right man. I've turned them all down. Except for one that didn't work out, anyway."

"So I'm one of the lucky two you've considered suitable, huh? What happened to the other sucker?"

Juliana felt hot tears gathering. She blinked furiously to get rid of them. "There's no need to be so rude. He wasn't a sucker. He was a wonderful, charming person. A caring person. He was also a real hunk. Beautiful hazel eyes and tawny blond hair. He was a handsome, golden god. And he was a lot taller than you."

"I don't care what he looked like. I just want to know how the guy escaped."

"Why? So you can escape the same way? All right, I'll tell you how he escaped my clutches. He turned tail and ran, that's what he did. Straight into the arms of someone else. Someone who happened to be very close to me. Someone petite and blond and sweet natured. Someone who never argued with him. Someone who never presumed to question his judgment. Someone who didn't overwhelm him the way I did. There. Satisfied?"

"Hell, Juliana, I didn't mean to rake up old memories." Travis rubbed the back of his neck again. "I was just trying to make a point."

"Consider it made. Go ahead, take the same way out my fiancé took three years ago. Run away if you're that skittish. But I have to tell you, Travis, I expected more from you. I didn't think you were the kind of man who was intimidated by a woman like me. I thought you had some guts."

"I am not going to run anywhere," Travis bit out. "But I am also not about to let you pressure me into marriage. Do I make myself perfectly clear?"

Juliana dashed her hands across her eyes, nodding sadly. "Perfectly. It's obvious there's been a terrible misunderstanding here. I guess I misread all the signals." She sniffed back the incipient tears. "I apologize."

Travis's hard face softened. He stepped closer and lifted a hand to stroke the side of her cheek. "Hey, there's no need to upset yourself over this. I've known you long enough to realize you're the impulsive type."

"My cousin Elly says I'm very spontaneous."

Travis smiled, and the rough edge of his thumb traced the line of her jaw. "That, too."

"This is so embarrassing."

"Forget it," Travis said magnanimously. "Last night was very

good. I can see where you might have read more into it than...
uh..."

"More than you intended?"

"Let's just say more than either of us intended."

"Speak for yourself." She turned away, ducking out of the
range of his hand. "It's getting late. You'd better get dressed. I'm
sure you've got a lot to do today."

"Nothing that can't wait until Monday." Travis watched her
closely. "What do you say we spend the rest of Sunday at the
beach?"

"No, thanks." She bent down to take one last swipe at the
carpet. Then she picked up the empty red cup. "I've got a million
chores to do today," she added grimly. "You know how it is. I
think I'll start with washing my hair and move on to the laundry.
These sheets definitely need to be cleaned."

Travis didn't move. "Are you going to sulk?"

"I never sulk," she assured him grandly.

"Then why the excuses? Last night we both made plans to
spend today together."

"Everything's changed now. I'm sure you can comprehend
that." She moved into the white-tiled bathroom and replaced the
carpet-cleaning materials in the cupboard. "I wish you would
hurry up and get dressed, Travis. It's disconcerting having you
standing around in my bedroom wearing nothing but a towel."

"I could take the towel off."

She glared at him through the open doorway. "You're not suggesting we go back to bed together, are you?"

"Why not? We both agreed last night was very good."

"I don't believe this." She braced one hand against the door
frame. "Travis, you surely do not expect me to jump right back
into bed with you now that I know your intentions are not honorable?"

"Will you stop talking like a nineteenth-century heroine who
thinks she's been compromised?"

"You don't seem to understand," Juliana said with seething
patience. "I am throwing you out. Now. Get dressed and get out
of my condo. Everyone makes a mistake now and then, but I do

not cast pearls before swine twice. And I have no intention of wasting any more of my valuable time with a man who is as muddle-brained and stubborn as you are.''

''Is that a polite way of calling me stupid?''

''You got it. I'm the right woman for you, Travis Sawyer. I was made for you. And you were made for me. If you're too dumb to see that, then there's no point taking this relationship one step further. Get out of here.''

His eyes were narrow slits as he snagged his trousers from off the dresser. ''Does this mean you're going to try to terminate your contract with Sawyer Management Systems?''

Juliana was startled. If she actually fired him she might never see him again. The thought was too terrible to contemplate. ''No, it does not. SMS is the best business consulting firm in this part of California and the future of Charisma Espresso is too important to jeopardize by getting rid of you. Unfortunately.''

''Is that right?'' Travis yanked on his pants and reached for his white shirt. ''Nice to know I'm still appreciated in some respects. But aren't you afraid of mixing business with pleasure? That's how we got into this situation in the first place.''

Juliana lifted her chin. ''No, I am not the least worried about it. I am quite capable of separating my business from your pleasure.''

''Yeah? Well, we'll see just how good you are at it, won't we?'' He finished buttoning his shirt and grabbed his wing-tips.

''Are you threatening me, Travis?''

''Wouldn't think of it.'' He tied his shoe strings with short, savage movements of his fingers and stuffed his tie into a shirt pocket. ''But we both know you're the emotional one in this equation. And you want me. Hell, this morning you woke up convinced you were in love with me.''

''I never said that.''

''Yes, you did,'' Travis countered coldly. ''Last night when you were lying under me, hanging on to me as if I was the only man left on earth. I heard every word.''

Juliana felt herself grow very warm with humiliation. Her chin lifted defiantly. ''All right, so I said it. I won't deny it. I wouldn't have wanted to marry you if I wasn't in love with you. But you brought me back to reality this morning. Love is probably no worse than the flu. I'll recover just like I did three years ago when my engagement ended. Now go on and get out of here before I lose my temper. You are becoming very annoying.''

Travis stalked toward the door. ''You'll be sorry you're kicking me out like this.''

''Hah. Not a chance. Life is too short for foolish regrets. Like I said, I'll recover. But I warn you, Travis, someday you're going to look back on this whole thing and call yourself a fool.''

''Is that right?'' He was in her turquoise and apricot living room now, his hand on the doorknob.

Juliana hurried down the hall behind him. He was practically out the door she thought with horror; practically gone. ''Yes, that's right. I'm the perfect woman for you, and one of these days you're going to realize it.''

He swung around to confront her, the door open behind him. ''I already realize we're good in bed together. What more do you want from me?''

She skidded to a halt a couple of feet away from him, breathless. ''I want you to realize you love me. And then I want you to ask me to marry you.''

''You don't ask much, do you?''

''I never do anything by half measures. You should know me well enough by now to realize that. But—'' she paused, gathering her courage ''—maybe I should make allowances for the fact that you're a man and therefore not as in touch with your own needs and emotions as you should be.''

''Gosh, thanks for all the deep psychological analysis and understanding, lady.''

''I'll tell you what, Travis. I'll give you one month. One month and that's all. If you haven't come to your senses by then, I won't give you any more chances.''

His brows rose in an intimidating fashion. ''One month to do what?''

''One month to figure out you're in love with me and ask me to marry you.''

"One month, hmm? I'm surprised at you, Juliana. You should know me well enough by now to realize that I don't react well to ultimatums."

"Don't think of it as an ultimatum," she urged. "Think of it as a breathing space in which you can sort out your options."

He shook his head, amazed. "You never give up, do you?"

"People who give up don't often get what they want."

Travis went through the door. "I don't need a breathing space. I already know what I want. I've known all along."

"Just exactly what did you want from me?" she demanded, moving to stand in the doorway. "A night in bed?"

"No, Juliana. Getting you into bed wasn't the important thing. Believe it or not, it wasn't even part of my original plan. Just icing on the cake, I guess you could say."

He walked away into the bright, sunny morning. Juliana stood on the brick steps of her Spanish-style white stucco and red-tiled condominium. She watched with dismay as the man she loved climbed into his tan, three-year-old, nondescript Buick.

How could she have been such a nitwit as to lose her heart to a man who drove such a wretchedly dull car and wore such old-fashioned ties, she wondered.

CHAPTER TWO

THE WHOLE THING had gotten far too complicated, unbelievably complicated, disastrously complicated.

Revenge should have been a simple, straightforward matter filled with strong, clear, uncomplicated emotions. There were just two sides to this thing, Travis reminded himself—his side and the other side. And anybody with the last name of Grant was on the other side.

He sat behind the wheel of his car and stared broodingly out over the Pacific. From the top of this bluff the view was postcard perfect. The town of Jewel Harbor sparkled down below, an artistically charming mixture of Spanish-Colonial-style homes and the latest in California Coast modern architecture. There was an air of trendy prosperity to the whole place that was a bit unreal at times. It would make a good setting for the headquarters of Sawyer Management Systems.

The streets were lined with swaying palms and every yard was lush and green. A lot of the backyards had sapphire-blue swimming pools and orange trees. The cars parked in the wide drives tended to be of German manufacture with the occasional Italian or classic British model thrown in for variety.

The downtown business section of Jewel Harbor looked as casually upscale as the rest of the town. Strict ordinances kept the shops and office buildings low in height and architecturally reminiscent of the Spanish look. White stucco and red tile predominated, just as they did in Juliana's condominium complex. Travis narrowed his eyes momentarily, searching the vista. From here he could just make out the busy shopping plaza where Juliana had opened Charisma Espresso.

He thought about the fateful day nearly four weeks ago when

he had walked into the trendy watermelon-red and gray interior of Charisma. He had told himself at the time it was a simple reconnaissance move. He was like a general with a carefully arranged battle plan and he wanted to be sure he had covered all the angles. He had timed everything else involved very carefully, right down to making sure that his trap would close while he was here in Jewel Harbor setting up the newest office of Sawyer Management Systems.

Juliana Grant was the one member of the Grant family he hadn't met five years ago, the one unknown quantity in his equation. She had not lived in Jewel Harbor back then. He vaguely remembered being told that she was working in San Francisco at the time.

Travis wasn't quite certain what he'd been expecting when he pushed open the glass doors of Charisma Espresso, but he had been immediately struck by two powerful forces. The first was the heady aroma of freshly ground coffee and the second, far stronger force, was the vivid, red-haired, incredibly dressed, six-foot-tall goddess behind the counter. The electric-blue jumpsuit she'd been wearing should have looked tacky or at least overpowering, and on anyone else it probably would have. But on Juliana it looked just right. It was as bold and animated as she was.

Juliana Grant was unlike any of the other Grants, and that was probably why he had allowed the situation to get so complicated. Travis remembered the men of the family as being of average height, the women petite and delicate.

Juliana, by contrast, was almost as tall as Travis. Hell, he thought wryly, when she put on heels she was as tall or taller than he was. Her flaming red hair might have been inherited from her father, but it was difficult to be certain because Travis remembered Roy Grant as being gray. The same with Tony Grant, Roy's brother. She had probably gotten her eyes from her mother, Beth. But there was no one in the family with quite the same combination of coloring and height that Juliana had. In her, the genes had obviously come together in a whole new, exotic mixture.

But it wasn't Juliana's looks that had caught him off balance; it was Juliana, herself. She was different. Not only different from the other members of her family, but different from every other woman Travis had met in his life.

Too much, he thought, seeking the right words to describe her. That was it. Juliana was a little too much of everything. Too colorful, too tall, too emotional, too dynamic, too assertive, too smart. The kind of woman who, a thousand years ago, would have carried a spear and ridden into battle beside her chosen mate. The kind who would give everything and demand just as much in return.

She was, to put it bluntly, the kind of woman most men found overwhelming except in very small doses. Travis knew his own sex well enough to realize that the average male would find Juliana riveting for about fifteen minutes. Shortly thereafter, that same man would be frantically searching for an exit, running as fast as he could in the opposite direction.

No question about it. Women like Juliana could be downright intimidating to the average male.

Travis didn't consider himself average and he refused to be intimidated by Juliana, but that didn't mean he was prepared to jump through hoops for her, either. The lady was a handful but he had no real doubt he could handle her. That was not the problem.

The problem was that he wanted her and, given his current situation vis-à-vis the Grant family, he had no business getting any more involved with her. It had gone far enough. How in hell had he let himself get hired by her as a consultant? He must have been temporarily out of his mind. He hadn't taken on a tiny client like Charisma Espresso for over ten years.

Travis exhaled deeply, trying to think his way through the mess. In the beginning it had seemed simple enough. Juliana was a Grant and he had vowed revenge against the entire clan of Grants. He had told himself that seducing Juliana would add a nice fillip to the masterpiece of vengeance he had concocted. And it was obvious Juliana wasn't going to object to being seduced.

But looking back on it now, Travis wasn't quite sure who had seduced whom. It was Juliana who had paved the way for the affair when she had talked him into taking her on as a client. The moment she had discovered what he did for a living, she'd started bombarding him with questions about how to successfully expand Charisma Espresso.

Travis had taken what seemed an obvious opening and proceeded to play it for all it was worth. One more Grant scalp for his belt.

His mouth twisted grimly at the thought. He didn't need Juliana's scalp. She'd had nothing to do with what had happened five years ago. She didn't even know who he was. It was her misfortune, however, to be related to all the other Grants, and three and a half weeks ago when he had first met her, he'd told himself he might as well make use of her.

Last night he'd stopped thinking in terms of using her for revenge and started thinking in terms of satisfying the craving that had been building up inside him.

This morning he had been too bemused by events to think at all until Juliana had breezed into the bedroom with her chic little art deco teapot and started making marriage plans. That had brought Travis back to reality with a thud.

Juliana was taking over, threatening his plans for vengeance. After all the planning and hunting and patience he'd been obliged to exert during the past few years, Travis was not about to lose control of the situation now.

He rubbed the back of his neck and switched on the Buick's ignition. He should have seen it coming, he told himself. Juliana had fallen in love with him sometime during the past three weeks. He'd known that for certain last night when she had given herself freely, without any reservations. That was the way she did things. And if he was honest with himself, he had to admit he had taken everything she had to give.

He had to keep reminding himself that she was a Grant, Travis thought as he headed back toward his apartment. And he would be damned if he would let any Grant give him an ultimatum.

One month to figure out he loved her? One month to come to

his senses? Who did she think she was? Before the month was out he was going to have reaped his revenge on all the Grants.

He would be lucky to have a week with her, at the most.

Because when the manure hit the fan, as it surely would very soon, everyone would have to choose sides. Travis didn't need to be told which side Juliana would choose. Her choice was preordained by the fact that she was a Grant. Travis faced this reality with stoic acceptance. He was used to being the outsider, to being the one not chosen.

But all he could think about as he drove back down the winding road into town was that last night had been something else. The memory of it would haunt him as long as he lived and he knew it. He could still feel the imprint of her nails in his back. Juliana Grant was the kind of woman who left her mark on a man.

Suddenly the prospect of stealing even one more week with her was more than he could resist.

"HEY, HOW WAS the big date, Juliana?"

"Saw you having dinner down at The Treasure House last night. You two looked so involved I didn't want to interrupt. Thought maybe the man was about to pop the big question."

"How about it, boss, you wearing a ring this morning?"

Juliana glowered fiercely at the expectant faces of her staff as she came to a halt in front of the long gray counter. "Don't the two of you have anything better to do this morning than stand around asking personal questions?"

"Uh-oh." Sandy Oakes, her gelled hair sleeked back behind her ears to show off the three sets of earring she was wearing, eyed her co-worker. "Looks like all is not well with our supreme leader this morning. Best go grind a little coffee, Matt."

Matt Linton, whose hair was even shorter than Sandy's and who wore only one earring, frowned in sudden concern. "Hey, we were just teasing. Is everything okay, Juliana?"

"Everything is just fine. Absolutely peachy. Fabulous." Juliana hurled her oversized leather tote into her cubbyhole of an office and then reached for one of the watermelon red aprons that bore the Charisma logo. "I couldn't be happier if I had just found out

I had won the lottery. Satisfied? Now get busy. The morning rush will be starting in a few minutes. Sandy, why aren't those *biscotti* in the display case?''

''The bakery just delivered them five minutes ago,'' Sandy explained in soothing tones. ''I'll have them out in a sec.'' She slid a speculative glance at her boss as she arranged the *biscotti* in a glass case near the cash register.

''Matt, try to look useful. The counter needs straightening. And where's the cinnamon shaker?''

''Ouch.'' Matt shook his hand as if it had just been bitten by a savage dog.

Juliana groaned. ''Look, I apologize for being snappish this morning. But the truth is, I am not in a good mood.''

''Funnily enough we could tell that right off,'' Sandy said. ''I take it the turkey didn't ask you to marry him as planned?''

''Not only did the turkey not ask me to marry him, he was apparently stunned to find out I expected him to do so,'' Juliana informed her. ''The whole thing was a complete misunderstanding. I made an absolute fool out of myself. If I ever show any signs of wanting to get involved with anyone else of the opposite sex ever again, I want you to promise to remind me of what happened this time. I refuse to repeat my mistakes.''

Matt grinned. ''You're going to swear off men forever just because Mr. Right turned out to be Mr. Wrong?''

''He isn't Mr. Wrong. He just doesn't know he's Mr. Right.'' Juliana turned her back to the door and busied herself with grinding an aromatic blend of beautifully roasted Costa Rican beans. She raised her voice to be heard over the roar of the machine. ''But I guess if he doesn't have enough sense to know he's Mr. Right, then he really is Mr. Wrong, isn't he? I mean, the real Mr. Right wouldn't be that dumb, would he?''

She was so busy working through that train of logic that she failed to hear the shop door swing inward.

''Uh, Juliana,'' Matt began nervously, only to be cut off by Juliana's diatribe.

''But I have to tell you, I think my heart is broken. And what does that say about my intelligence, I ask you? How could I let Mr. Wrong break my heart? I'm too smart to do that.''

"Juliana, uh, maybe you'd better…''

"What's more,'' Juliana plowed on forcefully, "if Travis Sawyer is so stupid he doesn't even realize I'm the right woman for him, then he's probably too stupid to be planning the future of Charisma Espresso. This morning I told him I didn't intend to fire him, but now I'm not so sure. I've had time to think about it and I really don't believe I want to put the future of my company in Sawyer's hands…''

"Juliana,'' Sandy broke in hurriedly. "We've got a customer.''

"What?'' Juliana finished grinding the last of the beans and the machine stopped.

"I said,'' Sandy repeated very clearly, "we've got a customer.''

"Oh. Well? Why make a big deal out of it. Go ahead and see what he wants.''

"What he wants,'' Travis Sawyer said calmly from the other side of the counter, "is the one month you promised him in which to come to his senses.''

"*Travis.*'' Juliana couldn't believe her ears. Relief and happiness rushed through her. She swung around to confront him, knowing she was smiling like the village idiot, but not caring in the least. Her heart was not broken after all. "You came back.''

"I never left. At least, not willingly. You're the one who kicked me out.''

"I knew you'd see the light. I knew you just needed a little time to get your head screwed on straight.'' Juliana tossed the sack full of ground coffee toward Matt and dashed around the counter to hurl herself into Travis's arms.

Travis braced himself as she landed against him with an audible thud. He only staggered back a step. "I'm touched by your faith in my intelligence.'' Travis looked straight into her glowing eyes. She was wearing two-inch heels today. "Does this mean you're not going to try to find a way out of our business contract, after all?''

Sandy spoke up firmly from the other side of the counter before

Juliana could respond. "I don't think he's groveled enough yet, Juliana."

"Give the man a break, ladies," Matt growled. "He's here, isn't he? How much more can you ask?"

"Thank you," Travis said gravely, nodding at Matt. "I agree completely. How much more can you ask?" He turned his attention back to Juliana who was smiling with delight, her arms around his neck. "Would you mind very much if we conducted the rest of this grand reconciliation scene in private? I like Matt and Sandy, but once in a while I find I like to operate on a one-to-one basis with you."

"Don't mind us," Sandy said quickly. "We're only too happy to help out."

"Right," said Matt. "We're just like family."

"Not quite," Travis said, taking a firm grip on Juliana's arm and leading her toward the door.

Juliana was bubbling over with laughter by the time Travis had led her to the outside seating area. Morning sun poured warmly through the decorative wooden lattice overhead, dappling the white tables and French café-style chairs.

"They mean well, you know," Juliana said easily as she sat down across from Travis.

"I know they do but I feel like I'm in a goldfish bowl every time I go into the shop. Do you tell them everything?"

"No, of course not," Juliana assured him quickly. "But they've been sort of monitoring our relationship right from the start. They were there that first day when you walked in and ordered a cup of coffee, remember? They knew how I felt about you at the beginning. They guessed right away this morning that something terrible had happened."

Travis sighed and leaned back in the small chair. It creaked under his weight. "You're a full-grown woman, Juliana. Not a starry-eyed teenager. You'd think by now you would have learned to be a little less, well, less obvious about your personal feelings."

"I'm a very straightforward person, Travis." Juliana grew more serious as some of her initial euphoria subsided. "People always know where they stand with me and I like to know where I stand with them. Life is easier that way. Keeps the stress level down a little.''

"You're an odd combination of ingredients, you know that?"

"You mean, for a woman?" she asked dryly.

"For anyone, male or female. When it comes to business you're as shrewd a small-businessperson as I've ever met. The success you've made out of Charisma speaks for itself."

"But?"

Travis's mouth kicked up at the corner and his eyes glinted. "But when it comes to a lot of other things, you're a little outrageous. No, that's putting it mildly. You're more like a keg of dynamite. I can't always predict when and how you'll go off. And you always do it loudly."

She shrugged. "You don't know me as well as you think. And I obviously don't know you as well as I thought I did or I wouldn't have put my foot in my mouth the way I did this morning. But that's okay. We've got plenty of time to learn all we need to know about each other, don't we?"

Travis studied her for a long moment. "I'm not going to make any promises, Juliana. I want that clear this time right from the start."

"Are you one of those men who can't make a commitment? If so, just say it straight out because I really don't want to waste any time messing around with a male who's uneducable."

"Damn it, I'm one of those men who won't be rushed into anything, including a commitment. And I just want that fact on the table before we try this relationship again. Knowing that, are you still willing to give me my month?"

Juliana thought about it but not for long. "Sure. Why not? I'm willing to take a risk or two if the prize is worth it."

Travis shook his head in silent wonder. "So reckless."

"Only when I'm going after something important."

"I guess I should be flattered that you consider me a worthwhile prize."

"That remains to be seen. At this point, you're just a potentially worthwhile prize."

"Yeah. Well, as long as we're dealing in warnings, I guess I ought to inform you that you've had yours. No promises from me, Juliana, implied or otherwise. No commitments. We take things a day at a time. I won't be pushed into anything."

"I've had my warning," she agreed smoothly. "But you haven't had yours."

His brows rose. "What warning is that?"

"Since you are unable to see your way clear to make a commitment, I am unable to see my way clear to go to bed with you until we've resolved all the issues between us."

Travis's eyes narrowed coldly. "I didn't think you were the kind of woman who used sex to get what you want."

"I'm not. Just as you're not the kind of man who could be manipulated with sex." She smiled brilliantly. "Therefore, I wouldn't dream of trying to hold you that way."

"Very thoughtful of you," he muttered.

"By not going to bed with you I will leave your brain free of hormonal clutter," she added. "You'll be able to think much more clearly about our future."

"Juliana," Travis said with elaborate patience, "last night we discovered we happen to be very good together in bed. Remember?"

"Of course I remember. So what?"

"So why deny ourselves that element of the relationship?" he asked gently. He reached across the table and covered her long, copper tinted nails with his big palm.

"Simple. I happen to view the act of going to bed with a man as an act of commitment. And when it comes to this relationship of ours, I'm not making my commitment again until you've made yours and that's final. I have no intentions of sticking my neck out twice. Still want to use your month's grace period?"

He stared at her for a long, charged moment. "What the hell. Why not? Maybe it's better this way. This relationship doesn't stand a snowball's chance, anyway. I must have been crazy to think I could have my cake and eat it, too.''

''What are you talking about? What's all this about a cake?''

''Nothing.''

''But, Travis...''

He got to his feet. ''I'd better get back to the office.''

Juliana looked up at him anxiously. She reached out to catch hold of his arm. ''Travis, wait. I don't understand what's going on. Do you want to see me again or not?''

He touched her hand as it rested on his sleeve. His gaze was diamond hard in the sunlight. ''Yes, Juliana. I want to see you again.''

She relaxed. ''Even under my terms? You don't look too thrilled about the prospect.''

He looked down at the bright copper-colored nails on his sleeve. Then his eyes met hers. ''I thought you knew what I wanted better than I did.''

Juliana gnawed on her lower lip. ''Once in a while I guess wrong, just like everyone else. I can make mistakes. It's happened before.''

''With the fiancé who ran off with the petite blonde a few years ago?''

''Like I said, I'm not infallible. Up until last night, I was very sure about you and me. As you said, things clicked between us and not just in bed. But if I'm wrong, I'd rather call it quits right now.''

''Would you?''

Juliana drew a deep breath. ''You're a very hard man, aren't you?''

''And you are a very volatile woman.''

''Maybe that's not such a good combination after all. Maybe all we'll ever succeed in doing is striking sparks off each other. That's not enough, Travis.''

''Getting cold feet already, Juliana?''

She reacted to that instinctively. ''No. I'll give you your month.''

"Thanks." Travis leaned down to brush her mouth with his own. "I'll pick you up for dinner tonight. Six o'clock okay?"

"Yes. Fine." She smiled again, pushing aside the dark second thoughts that had crept into her mind. "I'll be ready. How about the new Thai place on Paloma Street?"

"It's a date." He walked out to where the tan Buick was parked and got inside.

Juliana sprang to her feet and hurried after him. "And do you still want to go with me to my cousin's birthday party next Saturday?" she asked anxiously. "It will mean meeting a lot of my family, including Uncle Tony."

Travis looked up at her through the open window, his expression so startlingly, unexpectedly harsh that Juliana instinctively stepped back a pace.

"Wouldn't miss it," Travis said and turned the key in the ignition.

Juliana smiled uncertainly and waved as he drove off. It was nice to know Travis was the kind of man who didn't mind getting involved with family, she told herself. And immediately wondered why she was not particularly reassured by that information.

THE FOLLOWING SATURDAY evening Juliana sat in the passenger seat of her snappy, fire-engine-red two-seater sports coupé and reveled in the balmy sea air coming through the open sun roof. Travis was at the wheel, and under his guidance the little car hugged the twists and turns of the coast road with easy grace. The blackness of the ocean filled the horizon, merging with the night. Far below the highway, moonlit breakers seethed against the rocks. It was a perfect Southern California evening, Juliana reflected, feeling happy and content. The past few days had been good with Travis, even if there were a lot of uncertainties hovering in the air between them.

"You're wasting your talents behind the wheel of that Buick," Juliana declared as Travis accelerated cleanly out of a turn. "One of these days you'll have to get yourself a real car."

"The Buick suits me. We understand each other."

"Don't you like driving?"

"Not particularly."

"But you do it well," Juliana observed.

"It's just something that has to be done and I try to do it efficiently so that I don't get myself or anyone else killed in the process. That's the extent of my interest in the matter."

Juliana sighed in exasperation. "You've been in a rather strange mood ever since you appeared at Charisma to tell me you wanted your month. And tonight you're acting downright weird. Are you sure you want to go to Elly's birthday party?"

"I've been planning on it for weeks." He braked gently for another curve.

"Yes, I know, but I don't want to force you into this. I mean, a lot of men are not real big on family get-togethers."

"It's a little late to change my mind now, isn't it? We'll be at the resort in fifteen minutes."

"True. You'll like my family, Travis. I would have introduced you to Elly and David before this but Elly's been out of town for the past three weeks. She's been visiting other resorts to get some ideas for Flame Valley. My folks flew into San Diego earlier today to pick up Uncle Tony and drive up the coast to the resort. They should be there by the time we arrive and I know they'll want to meet you. David is—"

"Juliana?"

It worried her more and more lately when he spoke in that particular tone, she was discovering. She did not understand him when he was in this mood. "Yes, Travis?"

"You don't have to sell your family to me."

"Okay, okay. Not another word on the subject. I promise."

He smiled fleetingly, with visible reluctance. "And if I believe that, I ought to have my head examined."

"Hey. I can keep a promise."

"Yeah, but I'm not sure you can keep your mouth shut."

"You got any serious objections to my mouth?" she demanded.

"No, ma'am," he said fervently. "None." He paused. "Has your cousin been married to this David Kirkwood long?"

"Almost three years. They make a wonderful couple. Perfect

together. Elly was involved once with someone else about five years ago. I never met the man and she refuses to talk about him, but I know he traumatized her. For a while I was worried she wouldn't let herself love anyone again. And then along came David.''

"And they're happily running this resort?''

Juliana smiled. "Flame Valley Inn. One of the most posh on the coast. Wait until you see it, Travis. It's beautiful and it's got everything. Golf course, tennis courts, spa, fantastic ocean view, first-class luxury rooms and a wonderful restaurant. My father and my Uncle Tony, that's Elly's father, built it over twenty years ago. They wanted to cash in on the spa craze.''

"And now your cousin and her husband run it.'' It was a statement, not a question.

Juliana slanted Travis a quizzical glance. "That's right. My father sold a lot of his stock in it to Uncle Tony four years ago but he still holds a minority interest. Uncle Tony was supposed to take over running the place full-time but about three years ago he developed some heart problems and the doctors insisted he start taking it easy. Elly and David took over and they've been running the place ever since. They love it.''

"So your cousin's husband has been making most of the decisions about Flame Valley?''

"For the past couple of years, yes. David has a lot of big plans for Flame Valley.'' Juliana propped her elbow on the door sill and lodged her chin in her hand. "Unfortunately I think he moved a little too quickly on some of those plans, though.''

"Too quickly?''

The small show of interest was all Juliana needed. Her brows snapped together as she frowned intently. "David and Elly have a lot of ambitious plans for Flame Valley. If they work out, the place will be one of the premier resorts in the whole world. But if they don't, Flame Valley could be in real financial trouble.''

"I see.''

"Travis, I've been meaning to ask you something. I know your company consults for a wide variety of businesses. Do you know anything about the resort business?''

There was a beat of silence. Then Travis said softly, ''Yes. I know a little something about resorts and hotels.''

''Hmmm.'' Juliana mulled that over. ''I wonder if I could get David and Elly to talk to you. I've been a little worried about them lately.''

''How much trouble are they in?''

Juliana drew a breath and settled back in her seat. ''I really shouldn't say anything more until I've talked to them first. David is very touchy on the subject of his business ability, and Elly gets defensive. But if I could talk them into hiring you for some consultation, would you be willing to take them on as clients?''

''I've got my hands full at the moment, Juliana. I managed to squeeze Charisma into my schedule but I'm afraid that's the limit. Taking on a project the size of Flame Valley would be impossible.''

''Oh.'' Juliana swallowed her disappointment. ''Well, in that case, I guess I'd better not say anything to David or Elly.''

''That would probably be best.''

Juliana brightened. ''But maybe you'd have room in your schedule in another month or two?''

Travis gave her a brief, sharp glance. ''You never give up, do you?''

She grinned. ''Only when the situation is clearly hopeless.''

''The question is, would you recognize a hopeless situation when you saw it?''

''Of course I would. I'm not an idiot. Slow down. There's the sign for Flame Valley. Turn right toward the ocean at the next intersection.''

Travis obeyed. He was silent as he navigated the narrow strip of road that wound its way toward a glittering array of lights perched on a hill overlooking the ocean.

He continued to say nothing as he parked the red coupé in the lot below the resort. Then he switched off the ignition and sat quietly as Juliana unbuckled her seat belt. He watched as she turned quickly, kneeling on the seat to reach into the back of the car to retrieve a bundle of brightly wrapped gifts.

"Juliana?"

"Yes, Travis?"

"I want you to know something."

"What's that?" She was bent over the back of the seat, fumbling with the biggest of the presents and wondering if she'd made a mistake buying Elly the huge Italian flower vase. Not everyone liked two-foot-tall pillars of aerodynamically shaped black glass.

"When it's all over tonight, try to remember that I never meant to hurt you."

Juliana froze, the packages forgotten. She whipped around in the seat, eyes widening quickly. "My fiancé said exactly those words three years ago just before he announced his engagement to someone else. What are you trying to tell me, Travis?"

"Forget it. Some things cannot be changed once they've been set in motion." He cupped her face quickly between his strong hands and kissed her with a fierce possessiveness. Then he released her. "Let's go." He opened the car door and got out.

"Travis, wait a minute. What's going on here?" Juliana scrambled out of the car, clutching the gifts. The glass beads that trimmed the scoop-necked black velvet chemise she was wearing sparkled in the parking lot lights. "You owe me an explanation. You can't just go around making bizarre statements like that and expect me to overlook them."

"You're going to drop that if you're not careful." He put out a hand and took the biggest package, the one containing the vase, out of her arms. Then he turned and started walking resolutely toward the main entrance to the resort.

Juliana hurried after him, hampered by the remaining presents, the tight chemise skirt and the two-inch heels of her black and fuchsia evening sandals. "You can't get away with this sort of behavior, Travis. I want to know what you meant. If you're seeing someone else, you'd damn well better tell me up-front. I won't be two-timed. Do you hear me?"

"There is no one else." He walked under the dazzling lights that illuminated the entrance.

The massive glass doors were opened by a young man uniformed in buff and gold. "You must be here for the owners' private party," the doorman said with an engaging grin. "Right straight through the main lobby and out to the swimming pool terrace. Can't miss it." He nodded at Juliana. "Good evening, Miss Grant."

"Hi, Rick. How's everything going?"

"Just fine. You should enjoy yourself tonight. The kitchen's been working overtime for the past three days getting ready. A real blowout."

"I believe it. See you later." Juliana smiled distractedly and dashed ahead to catch up with Travis who was still moving forward with the purposeful air of a man heading into battle.

"Honestly, Travis, you're getting weirder by the minute."

He stopped at the doors at the far end of the elegant lobby and paused to hold one open for her with a mocking gallantry.

Juliana scowled at him and then peered through the glass at the throng of people gathered around the turquoise swimming pool. She caught sight of her mother and father, her Uncle Tony and then she spotted her cousin, Elly.

As Juliana looked at her cousin, a tall, fair-haired, good-looking man moved up behind Elly and draped an arm around her shoulders. They made a handsome couple, no doubt about it. Elly, petite, blond and delicate looking, was a perfect foil for her tall, charming husband. When Elly glanced up at David and smiled, it was easy to see the love in her eyes.

Juliana jerked her gaze away from the sight of Elly and David just in time to catch Travis staring intently at the couple. There was something in his expression that sent a frisson of genuine alarm through her veins.

"Travis?"

"We'd better go out and join the others, hadn't we? Wouldn't want to keep them waiting. It's been long enough as it is."

Confused, Juliana walked through the door, conscious of Travis right behind her. Several faces in the crowd turned to smile in a friendly fashion. Juliana paused to say hello a few times before she reached the small group composed of Elly and David and three of their acquaintances.

Elly turned, David's arm still resting affectionately on her shoulders. She smiled with genuine pleasure when she saw her cousin. Her short, silvery hair gleamed in the light.

"Juliana, you're here at last. Uncle Roy and Aunt Beth got here with my father a couple of hours ago. We've been waiting for you."

"How did the spa survey go?" Juliana asked.

"Great. I picked up all sorts of terrific ideas. Now, who is this mysterious date you told me you were bringing tonight?" Elly's gaze switched to the man standing behind Juliana. Her blue eyes widened with shock and the words of greeting died on her lips.

She looks as if she's just seen a ghost, Juliana thought. She watched in sick fascination as her cousin struggled to conceal the panic that had so clearly blossomed at the sight of Travis Sawyer.

Travis did not move but Juliana felt the tension in the atmosphere between him and her cousin. It was the kind of tension that signals powerful emotions and dangerous secrets.

In that moment Juliana's parents came forward with her Uncle Tony, and Juliana saw Elly's shock mirrored on the faces of the other three Grants.

And suddenly Juliana understood it all. Travis was the man from Elly's past, the one she'd been engaged to five years ago, the one no one talked about.

CHAPTER THREE

"THE MOST AMAZING thing is how calm, cool and collected every-one is behaving," Juliana muttered to Elly twenty minutes later when she finally managed to corner her cousin in a remote section of the terrace. "I thought you were going to faint from shock when you first saw him, but then, two seconds later, there you were, greeting him as if he were just another casual acquaintance. Uncle Tony was just as cool. Just an old business associate. And Mom and Dad acted as if they could barely remember him."

"Well? What did you expect us to do?" Elly demanded. "Scream hysterically and fling ourselves over the balcony? It's been five years, after all."

"Yeah, but we both know his showing up here at this point is not just one of those strange little coincidences that sometimes happen in life. Nothing that man does is a coincidence. Believe me."

"You know him that well, do you?" Elly gripped the railing and faced the sea. The evening breeze ruffled her graceful white skirts.

"Let's say I'm getting to know him better by the minute. He's the one, isn't he? The one you were going to marry five years ago. The one who saved Flame Valley Inn from bankruptcy."

Elly bowed her head. "Yes. He wanted me and he wanted the resort, and Dad and Uncle Roy needed his help desperately."

"Nobody ever told me the whole story. All I knew was that you'd been shaken to the core by the whole incident. I thought he'd seduced and abandoned you or something, but it wasn't like that, was it?"

"No." Elly sounded thoroughly miserable. "I'm the one who broke the engagement."

"But not before you'd played the role of Judas Goat, right? You led him on, making him think that you were going to marry him and that he would get a share of the inn that way? But first he had to do everyone the little favor of saving Flame Valley from its creditors."

Elly turned to Juliana, her expression anguished. "It wasn't like that. I honestly thought I was in love with him at first. And everyone encouraged me to think that way, including Travis. It was only as time went on that I began to realize I was not in love with him, that what I had felt was just a sort of fascination, a crush. You ought to understand crushes. Men are always having them on you."

"Sure. And they last all of a day, if that. Within forty-eight hours they always come to their senses and back off as fast as they can. But this was more than a crush, Elly. You got engaged to the man."

"It was a mistake," Elly cried.

"What brought about that great realization?"

"You don't know what it was like. He...he frightened me in some ways, Juliana. He was always one step ahead of everyone else. Always plotting and scheming. Always had his eye on the main goal. Always willing to do whatever it took to reach that goal. I decided he was just using me to get a share of Flame Valley. I didn't think he could really be in love with me. A man like that never really falls in love with a woman."

"So you used him? You didn't tell him the engagement was off until after he'd accomplished the job of saving Flame Valley, did you?"

"I didn't use him," Elly protested. "Or if I did, you'd have to say I was evenly matched, because he certainly used me, too. In any event, the reason I didn't tell him the engagement was off was because Dad wouldn't let me."

"Oh, come on, Elly." But Juliana believed her. Anthony Grant had his faults but he had been a good father and utterly devoted to Elly, having raised her alone since the death of his beloved wife years ago. Elly returned that devotion in full measure. She was fiercely loyal to Tony Grant. It would have taken a great deal to make her go against her father's wishes. Obviously whatever she had felt for Travis had not been enough to counter the loyalty she felt toward her father.

Elly swallowed heavily, slanting an uneasy sideways glance at Juliana's angry expression. "It was wrong, I know it was, but I was afraid. I couldn't bring myself to tell Travis the truth and wind up being the reason the inn went into bankruptcy. And make no mistake about it, Travis would have walked out and let the whole place go under if he'd found out the wedding wasn't going to take place. Dad explained to me that Travis had only taken the job in the first place because he wanted a piece of Flame Valley Inn. They had an understanding. A sort of gentleman's agreement. Travis would collect his fee—a partnership in Flame Valley—the day he married me."

"So you continued to wear Travis's ring until he'd pulled Flame Valley out of the red."

"I had to wait until Dad and Uncle Roy were sure everything was stable financially. I felt a responsibility to the family. You should understand that. They'd all worked so hard to build this place. It was a part of them. It still is. I couldn't let them down in the crunch."

"You must have felt something for Travis. You've never wanted to talk about the time you were engaged to him. You've never even mentioned his name to me since I moved here four years ago."

"No one in the family talks about him. No one wants to remember the whole mess, least of all me. It was embarrassing and traumatic and painful. And rather scary, to be perfectly honest. Especially at the end when Travis found out I was calling off the engagement."

"How did he react?"

"Like a chunk of stone. I'd never seen anyone look so cold. It was terrifying, Juliana. I'd expected him to yell or fly into a rage or threaten a lawsuit. But instead he was utterly quiet. No emotion at all. He stood there in the middle of the lobby and just looked at me for what had to be the longest minute of my life. Finally he said that someday he'd be back to collect his fee. Only next time, he said, he wouldn't take just a share in the inn, he'd take the whole damned place. Those were his exact words. Then he turned around and walked out the door. We never saw him again.''

"Until tonight. Oh, Elly, what a mess.''

"I know.'' Elly closed her eyes. Teardrops squeezed through her lashes.

"Why do you think you were in love with him in the first place? Why did you develop the crush, as you call it? He's not your usual type.''

"I know. But please try to remember that I was a lot younger then. Only twenty-four years old. Travis was older, successful, powerful. It was exciting to realize he was attracted to me. And everyone kept saying what a wonderful match it would be. Dad and Uncle Roy and Aunt Beth all wanted him in the family because they knew they could safely turn Flame Valley over to him. He'd know how to run it. It was easy to think I was in love with him at first and by the time I realized I wasn't, it was too late. Everything was very complicated.''

"I'll bet.'' Juliana went to stand beside her cousin. "Too bad I wasn't here at the time. I could have told you instantly that you and Travis were all wrong for each other.'' She hesitated and then added, "Does David know who he is?''

"No.'' Elly shook her head quickly, her eyes shadowed with worry. "I've never told him about Travis. I'd rather he didn't know. He might not understand. Juliana, what are we going to do?''

"We?''

"Don't torment me. You have to help us.''

Juliana shrugged. "I don't see that there's anything we can do. At least not until we find out why Travis has gone to all this effort to stage his big return scene.''

"There's only one reason why he'd appear like this out of the blue,'' Elly hissed. "He's here to get his revenge. He must have found a way to take Flame Valley away from us. Or ruin the place."

"Elly, be reasonable. How's he going to do that?"

The soft sound of shoe leather on flagstone made both women turn their heads.

"I'll tell you how I'm going to do it," Travis said, materializing out of the pool of darkness cast by a clump of oleander bushes. "In the simplest way possible. I'm going to watch Flame Valley Inn go straight into the hands of its biggest creditor."

Elly's hand flew to her throat. "Oh, my God."

Juliana glared at Travis. "Must you creep up on people like that?" But she didn't think he even heard her. His whole attention was on Elly. Juliana felt very much a fifth wheel and she did not like the sensation at all. She'd felt this way once before when she'd stood near her beautiful cousin and another man.

Elly stared at Travis's harshly shadowed features. "You know, don't you? You know everything."

He moved his hand, and ice clinked in the glass he was holding. "I know. I've known from the beginning."

Juliana's gaze flicked from one face to the other. "What are you two talking about?"

"Don't you see, Juliana?" Elly's voice was thick with unshed tears. "He's here because he knows Flame Valley is having financial problems again. He's here to watch everything fall apart the way it would have five years ago if he hadn't rescued it."

"You and your husband have certainly managed to make a hash of things with your big expansion plans, haven't you?" Travis observed. "If Tony and Roy Grant had kept their hands on the reins, they might have been able to pull it off. But once they turned things over to you and David Kirkwood, it was just a matter of time."

Juliana was incensed. "What do you plan to do, Travis? Sit around like a vulture watching the inn collapse under a mountain of debt? Is that your idea of revenge? If you can't have it, nobody else can, either?"

He glanced at her. "Who says I can't have it?"

"What do you mean?" Elly demanded, sounding even more panicked than she had a moment ago.

Travis took a slow swallow of his drink and then smiled a grim, humorless smile. "I'll spell it out for you, Elly. Five years ago I was promised a one-third interest in Flame Valley Inn. I was cheated out of my share, as I'm sure you recall. So this time around, I'm going to take it all."

"But how?" Elly's voice was no more than a faint whisper of distress.

"You and Kirkwood, in your eagerness to get on with your grand plans for remodeling and expanding Flame Valley, have been borrowing from a lot of sources, but you're in debt most heavily to a consortium of investors called Fast Forward Properties, Inc."

"But what does that have to do with you?" Elly asked.

"I am Fast Forward," Travis said softly.

"*You.*" Elly looked stricken.

"I put together that group of investors and I make all the major investment decisions for them," Travis explained coldly. "When Flame Valley falls, as it surely will sometime during the next six months, it will fall right into my hands. I timed things so that I'd be here to step in and manage everything from the new Jewel Harbor headquarters of Sawyer Management Systems."

"Travis, you can't do this," Elly pleaded.

"You're wrong, Elly. It's as good as done. Everything is in place and all the fuses have been lit. It's too late for anyone to do anything about it. Nothing can stop what's going to happen to Flame Valley."

"Oh, my God." Elly burst into tears. They streamed down her face, sparkling like jewels in the moonlight. She made no effort to brush them away. "I should have known that sooner or later you would come back. I should have known."

"You knew. I told you I'd be back, remember?" Travis took another swallow of his drink.

Elly's tears flowed more heavily.

Juliana had had enough. She scowled at her beautiful cousin.

"For pity's sake, Elly, are you just going to stand there crying? Haven't you got any backbone? Don't let him bully you like this."

Travis snapped another quick look at Juliana. "Stay out of this," he said. "It's got nothing to do with you now."

"I've already played my part, right? I helped the big bad wolf stage his grand entrance. Now I know what you meant that morning you left my apartment saying I was just icing on the cake. You wanted the entire Grant family to pay for what happened five years ago, didn't you? Even me, the one member who hadn't been around when you got aced out of your share of the Inn."

"That's enough, Juliana," Travis said, so cold, so quiet.

"Enough?" she yelped furiously. "I've got news for you, Travis. I haven't even started. If you think you're going to get away with destroying Flame Valley as an act of revenge, you're crazy. I'll fight you tooth and claw."

Travis's eyes glinted. "The inn belongs to the other members of the Grant family, not to you. Stay out of it."

"The hell I will. This is a family matter and I'm family. We'll find a way to fight you, won't we, Elly?"

Elly shook her head mournfully, the tears still flowing copiously. "It's hopeless," she whispered.

"Don't say that, Elly." Exasperated, Juliana caught her cousin by the shoulders and shook her gently. "This is your inheritance we're talking about. It belongs to you and David. Surely you're not going to just give up and surrender like this. You've got to fight back."

Travis wandered over to the edge of the terrace and leaned one elbow on the teak railing. "You're wasting your time, Juliana. Elly's not like you. She doesn't know how to fight for what she wants. She's used to having someone else hand it to her on a silver platter."

Elly's head came up abruptly. "You...you bastard. Thank heaven I didn't marry you five years ago. I would have been married to a...an inhuman monster." Elly choked audibly on her tears and broke free of Juliana's grip. Without a backward glance she ran toward the relative safety of the crowd near the pool.

Juliana gritted her teeth in disgust as she watched her cousin dash away like a graceful gazelle fleeing the hunter. Then she whirled to confront Travis. "Satisfied? Are you proud of yourself? Do you enjoy hurting things that are softer and weaker than you are?"

"There's nothing all that soft or weak about your cousin. She may not know how to fight a fair fight, but that doesn't mean she's not very good at getting what she wants. She uses her softness, trades on it."

"She's a gentle, loving creature by nature. And you've got a lot of nerve talking about a fair fight. Is that what you call this nasty bit of vengeance you're after? A fair fight? So far all I've seen is a lot of low-down, sneaky, underhanded, manipulative, back-stabbing tactics."

"Believe me, everything I know about that kind of fighting, I learned from your family."

"Don't you dare use them as an excuse. My guess is you were born knowing about that kind of fighting."

"It's not an excuse. After what they did to me five years ago, I've got every right to fight as dirty as I have to in order to get even."

"You make it sound like you're involved in some sort of vendetta."

"I guess you could call it that," Travis agreed. "I told Elly the day she called off the engagement that I would come back and when I did, I'd take the whole damned place out of Grant hands. I always follow through on my promises, Juliana."

"Really?" She lifted her chin. "Is that why you were so very careful not to make any promises of marriage to me? You wanted to feel you'd maintained your high standard of business ethics even in bed? How very noble of you."

"I know you won't believe this, but I'm sorry that you got caught in the cross-fire. You're different from the others. I should have left you out of it. I can see that now."

"You couldn't have left me out of it. I'm family, remember? I'm a Grant."

"I remember. And that automatically puts you on the other side. I've known how it would be from the beginning. But, like I said, I'm sorry, all the same."

"Stop saying you're sorry. I don't believe that for a minute."

He swirled the contents of his glass. "No, I don't suppose you do." His gaze was on the darkness of the sea.

"If you were truly sorry," Juliana said suddenly, knowing she was clutching at straws, "you'd call the whole thing off, walk out of here tonight and never bother my cousin and her husband and the rest of the family again."

His teeth were revealed in a brief, macabre grin that vanished as quickly as it had appeared. "Not a chance in hell of that happening, Juliana. I've come too far, waited too long and planned too carefully. Nobody gets away with making a fool out of me the way your family did five years ago."

"Sounds to me like you made a fool out of yourself."

"It's true I made a few mistakes. I let the personal side of my life get mixed up with the business side. I don't make that kind of mistake these days."

"Yes, you made a few mistakes." For an instant Juliana was overwhelmed by the sense of loss that swept through her. "Damn it, Travis, how could you be so blind? We could have had something wonderful together, you and I. I was so sure of us. So certain we were meant for each other. But you're going to throw all the possibilities away for the sake of your revenge. You are a fool."

His face was a taut mask of controlled anger. "You know something, Juliana? I don't expect you to accept the situation and I don't expect you to forgive me. I knew from the start that you'd have to end up on your family's side of this thing. But I think that, given your own talent for straightforward action, you might at least understand my side."

"If you're talking about your desire for revenge," she said, impatient with him now, "I might be able to understand it. But I don't approve of it. How can I? This is my family you're going to hurt."

"Yeah, I know," he said, watching her with what looked like resigned regret. "That's the way the chips had to fall."

"Just for the record," Juliana said, "it isn't your notion of vengeance that has convinced me you're a fool and a muddle-brained, stubborn idiot." She turned on her heel and started toward the crowd near the pool.

"Juliana, wait." The words came roughly through the darkness, as if they had been wrenched out of him.

She refused to turn around. Head high, two-inch heels clicking furiously on the terrace stones, she walked swiftly away from the man she loved.

"Juliana." Travis came up behind her. "Look, I know you're angry and I know you probably won't ever be able to forgive me. But I had my reasons and I did what I had to do. Maybe if I were confronted with the same situation today, I'd handle it differently."

"Don't give me that bull." Juliana didn't pause. She was nearing the long buffet table.

"Okay, so I'd probably do it the same way a second time if I had to do it all over again. That doesn't mean I'm not sorry about involving you the way I did."

"Stop whining. I don't want your apologies. Things are bad enough as it is."

"Damn it, I am not whining. And I'm not apologizing. I'm just trying to explain—" He broke off with a muttered oath, moving quickly to keep up with her. "Juliana, what did you mean a minute ago when you said it wasn't my plans for revenge that convinced you I'm a fool?"

Juliana paused beside the buffet table long enough to pick up a huge glass bowl full of guacamole. She swung around, the bowl held in both hands. "Revenge I can comprehend. Being the magnanimous, liberal person that I am, I could even understand your using me to further your scheme. I don't condone it, mind you, but I can understand your doing it. Given a similar situation, I might have been tempted to do something very much like what you're doing."

"I knew you'd be able to see my side of it." Travis looked bleakly satisfied. "I realize you can't side with me, but at least you understand why I'm doing it."

"What I cannot and will not forgive," Juliana continued fiercely, "is the fact that this whole mess occurred because you thought you were in love with my cousin."

"Now, Juliana, listen to me. That was a long time ago. I was a lot younger then."

"Oh, shut up. I don't intend to ever listen to you again. Why should I listen to a fool? How could you have been so dumb, Travis? She's too young for you. Too soft. You would have run roughshod over her and then gotten angry because she didn't stand her ground. You would have been climbing the walls after six months of marriage. Can't you see that?"

"Uh, Juliana, why don't you put down that bowl?" Travis eyed the guacamole uneasily.

"She's not your type. I'm your type."

"Juliana," Travis said very firmly. "The bowl. Put it down."

"I'll put down the bowl when I'm good and ready. You asked me why I thought you were a fool. I'm telling you. You're a fool because you fell in love with the wrong woman. You still don't even realize that I'm the right one. I could forgive just about anything but that kind of sheer, unadulterated masculine stupidity."

"Juliana." He put out his hand, as if to catch hold of her.

"Don't touch me."

"Damn it, Juliana. *Juliana.*"

Travis released her and leaped back but it was too late. The avocado-green contents of the bowl were already sailing through the air toward him. He held up a hand and instinctively ducked but the guacamole was faster than he was. It spattered across his white shirt and jacket, a good deal of it hitting him squarely on his striped tie.

Juliana surveyed her handiwork with some satisfaction and put the bowl back down on the table. "Now, at least, you're the right color for a frog."

She swept away from the buffet table, moving through the stunned onlookers like a queen through a crowd of stupefied courtiers. She had never been this infuriated, this hurt before in her life. Not even when her fiancé had told her he wanted to marry another woman.

She had been so sure of herself this time; so sure of Travis. How could she have been so certain and yet be so wrong? It wasn't fair.

Her mother, petite, silver-haired and quite lovely at fifty-nine, was suddenly hovering anxiously in front of her. "Juliana, dear, what's going on? Are you all right?"

"I'm fine, Mom."

"Your father and Tony are worried. That man..." Beth Grant's voice trailed off as she glanced helplessly past her daughter to where Travis stood covered in guacamole.

"I know all about it, Mom. Excuse me, please. I'm going home."

"But, Juliana..."

Juliana patted her mother reassuringly on the shoulder and hurried around her. She took several deep breaths as she went through the lobby and out into the parking lot. She would have to calm down a little before she got behind the wheel of her car.

Travis stood staring after her, as riveted in place as everyone else around him. He could not quite bring himself to believe what had happened. No one he knew did things like this. Not in front of a hundred people.

"Welcome to the dangerous hobby of escorting Juliana Grant." Like the good host he was, David Kirkwood waded through the shocked crowd toward Travis. He grinned wryly and picked up a napkin off the buffet table. "If you plan to hang around her very long, you'd better get used to being taken by surprise," he advised as he handed Travis the napkin. "She's got a way of keeping a man off balance."

Travis snatched the napkin from his host and took several furious swipes at the guacamole. He could tell instantly that the tie was ruined. "You sound as if you speak from experience. I take it you've seen other men buried under guacamole?"

"Oh, no. Juliana rarely repeats herself. She's too creative for that. But I've sure seen more than one man with that particular expression on his face."

"What expression?"

"That of a poleaxed steer. If it's any consolation, I know exactly how you feel."

"How would you know?" Travis looked with disgust at the avocado stained napkin.

"I was engaged to Juliana for a short but very memorable month almost four years ago."

Travis crushed the napkin in his fist, his gaze slamming into David Kirkwood's amused eyes. Sympathetic, lively hazel eyes. Six foot three, at least, Travis estimated. Fair-haired. Smile like something out of a toothpaste commercial. An expensive Italian pullover sweater over a designer sport shirt and pleated slacks. A massive gold ring on one hand that went with the massive gold watch on his wrist. Travis's instincts warned him of the truth. No doubt about it, this was Juliana's golden god, the one who'd left her for the petite blonde. The blonde was Elly.

"You were engaged to her?" Travis wiped off more guacamole.

"I know what you mean. Hard to believe, isn't it? She's definitely not my type. I'm not quite sure how it happened, myself. She sure dazzled me for a while, though. Something about her makes a man look twice. Then run."

"What do you mean, she dazzled you?"

"Hey, give me a break. You've been around her long enough to know what I mean. She's a lot of woman. But maybe a little too much woman for most of us poor mortal males. Who wants to marry Diana the Huntress? You always get the feeling you're one step behind Juliana. Say, you want to wash the rest of that stuff off in the men's room?"

Travis shook his head, feeling oddly numb. Before he could think of what to do next, Juliana's father and uncle hove into view, planting themselves squarely in front of him. Just what he needed, he thought. They'd been coolly ignoring him for the most part until now. Apparently Juliana's exit scene had prodded them into staging a confrontation.

"What the hell do you think you're doing, Sawyer?" Roy Grant demanded. He glared hostilely at Travis through the lenses of his bifocals. "What did you say to my daughter to upset her that way?"

"Why don't you ask her? I'm the one wearing the guacamole," Travis muttered. Roy Grant hadn't changed much, he reflected briefly. The younger of the two Grant brothers by two years, he was still in good shape for his age. He'd always been the quieter, calmer one but he wasn't playing that role tonight.

"The real question," Tony Grant interrupted, his florid face turning red with anger, "is what are you doing here tonight, Sawyer? I know you. You've got something up your sleeve. Whatever it is, you'd better watch your step, mister. Roy and I are going to keep an eye on you."

"I'll bear that in mind." Travis wondered if his tie was salvageable. Then a sudden thought struck him, galvanizing him back into action. Juliana was in a mood to walk out of here tonight and effectively strand him thirty miles from his apartment. "Oh, hell. The car."

"If she's got the keys, she's probably long gone by now," David assured him cheerfully.

"I've got the keys." Travis shoved his hand into his pocket and found them. "But I don't know if she's one of those women who keeps a spare in her purse."

"She always did when I dated her," David remarked. "Like I said, she's usually one step ahead of a man. That's our Juliana. Gets on the nerves sometimes, doesn't it?"

"The *car*." At the thought of being left without transport, Travis launched himself toward the lobby doors.

"Now hold on just one damned minute," Roy Grant called after him.

Travis ignored the warning. He flew through the lobby doors, raced past a startled desk clerk and dashed outside to the resort's brightly lit entrance.

The roar of an angry sports car engine was already reverberating through the night air. Travis came to an abrupt halt in the drive and watched in furious dismay as Juliana's red coupé hurtled toward the main road.

"That blasted, redheaded witch." Travis stood with his hands bunched into fists on his hips and watched the coupé headlights disappear around a curve in the highway. "She did it. She went and left me here."

"The thing you have to keep in mind about Juliana," David said as he ambled casually over to stand beside Travis, "is that she tends to be a mite impulsive even under normal circumstances. The only thing she's ever really levelheaded about is business. On the other hand, she's generous to a fault. Can't stand to see someone suffering. There's a chance she'll get ten miles, remember you don't have a ride home and come racing back to rescue you."

"Sure there's a chance of that happening. A fat chance."

David nodded. "You're probably right. She did look a little annoyed with you. Hey, but not to worry, mate." He clapped Travis familiarly on the shoulder. "I'll run you back to Jewel Harbor. No problem."

Travis cursed softly, fluently, and with great depth of feeling. The thought of accepting a friendly lift from the man he fully intended to ruin was enough to make him a little crazy. And on top of everything else, Kirkwood was Juliana's ex-fiancé—her golden god.

Travis wondered if Juliana had deliberately abandoned him just so he'd be faced with this bizarre social situation. He was certain the awkward irony of the whole thing would appeal to her warped sense of humor. The woman was a menace.

"Maybe one of your other guests is going to be returning to Jewel Harbor later this evening," Travis suggested tightly.

David frowned consideringly. "Can't think of anyone right off."

"Maybe I can rent a car from your front desk."

"We don't have any car rental service."

"An airport van service?" Travis tried, feeling desperate.

"The kid who drives the airport run has gone home for the night." David grinned. "Afraid you're stuck with me."

Travis flipped another puddle of guacamole off his sleeve and said very carefully, "I think I'd better tell you who I am."

"Why don't you do that?" David said quietly. "I've been wondering just who you are since you walked onto the terrace and caused my wife to nearly faint. And Roy and Tony have been looking as if they'd seen a ghost."

Travis looked at him with a tinge of reluctant respect as it sank in that there was more to David Kirkwood than appeared on the surface. He should have been prepared to find the man had hidden depths, Travis reminded himself. After all, Juliana had once thought herself in love with him.

"I'm the head of Fast Forward Properties, Inc.," Travis said.

David exhaled slowly. "So my time has run out, has it?"

"That's about it. I'm running a business, Kirkwood, not a charitable foundation."

David ran his fingers through his hair. "No, you don't look like the charitable type. But that doesn't answer my question. What else are you besides the big, bad wolf come to blow the house down?"

Travis sighed, not particularly enthusiastic about telling him the rest but knowing it would all be coming out eventually. "I'm the guy who saved this place five years ago when Tony and Roy Grant were teetering on the brink of bankruptcy."

David's gaze sharpened. "The consultant they stiffed? The one who thought he was going to get a third of the resort as his fee for services rendered?"

"You know about that deal?"

"Not all of it. No one talks about that incident. No one talks about you or what happened five years ago. But there were some papers and records left in the office when I took over after my marriage. I think I pieced most of the story together. Including the fact that you were once engaged to my wife."

"Yeah, well, if it's any consolation, I'm not here to claim her. All I want is Flame Valley."

"You don't just want your fee. You're here to get revenge, aren't you?"

Travis shrugged. "I just want what's due me."

"Juliana wasn't a part of what happened five years ago, was she?"

"No." Travis stared out into the darkness. "I shouldn't have involved her."

"No way you could avoid it." David fished a set of keys out of his pocket. "Come on, Sawyer. I'll drive you back to Jewel Harbor."

"Why would you want to do me any favors?"

"I don't see it as a favor," David said as he led the way toward a white Mercedes. "I see it as a final, desperate struggle of a drowning man. I intend to use the time between here and Jewel Harbor to get you to listen to my side of this thing."

"You might as well save your breath, Kirkwood. I've already told you, I'm not running a charity." But Travis reluctantly walked toward the Mercedes. He wasn't going to argue with a free ride at this time of night.

"And you've already told me you wished you hadn't involved Juliana." David opened the door of his car.

"That's right. As far as I'm concerned, she's out of it now. Financially, at least."

David smiled coolly. "I've got news for you, wolf. Juliana is in this up to her big, beautiful eyes."

Travis looked at him sharply over the roof of the car. "How?"

"A year ago she loaned Flame Valley Inn a sizable sum of money."

"She did *what*?" Travis felt as if he'd been punched in the stomach.

"You heard me. It was a very large loan. I was planning to repay her at the end of this year. That won't be possible if you foreclose, of course. If the inn goes under, all Juliana's big plans for Charisma Espresso will probably go with it."

CHAPTER FOUR

JULIANA WAS IN BED, but she was far from being asleep when someone began leaning on her doorbell and did not let up. The famous notes of the opening passage of the William Tell Overture clamored throughout the condo, over and over, endlessly repeating themselves until Juliana's head was ringing. She wondered when the Lone Ranger would arrive.

It didn't take her intuitive mind long to figure out who among her acquaintances was most likely to be standing on her doorstep making a nuisance of himself tonight. It also did not require great mental endowment to figure out that the offender was probably not going to give up and go away anytime soon.

Travis Sawyer was not the type who gave up easily, as he had already demonstrated by waiting five years for his vengeance.

Juliana got out of bed and reached for her peach satin robe. She ignored the dueling chimes long enough to pause beside her dressing table mirror and gloss her lips with a shade of lipstick she thought went well with the robe. She was considering adding blusher when the endless chimes finally got to her. Unable to stand the torture any longer, she stepped into a pair of silver high-heeled lounge slippers and stalked into the living room and threw open the door.

"Whatever you're selling, I'm not buying," she announced. "But you can try."

Travis, who was leaning against the chime button, straightened slowly, his eyes chips of ice. "Why didn't you tell me you had dropped a chunk of your personal savings into Flame Valley Inn?"

"Why should I have told you? It was family business and I

only hired you to consult on Charisma. Besides, I had no idea of your deep, personal concern for the inn until a few hours ago.''

His gaze swept over her and his cold expression grew even harsher. "You can't stand around out here dressed like that. Someone's likely to drive past any minute. Let's go inside.''

"I don't think I want you inside my apartment. Maybe you secretly hold the mortgage on this whole building or something. Maybe you're getting ready to foreclose on the condominium association and kick all us poor owners out into the street.''

"Stop talking nonsense. I am not in the mood for any more of your warped humor tonight. Stranding me at Flame Valley was the last straw.'' He shouldered his way past her, heading for the living room.

"How did you get back to Jewel Harbor?" Juliana closed the door slowly and followed Travis. She noticed that he had removed his tie and there were several green splotches on his white shirt. A niggling sense of guilt shot through her. She quelled it quickly.

By the time she caught up with Travis he had already lodged himself on the salmon-colored leather sofa. He sprawled there with negligent ease, one foot prodded on the black and chrome coffee table.

"What do you care how I got back?''

"It wasn't a question of caring exactly,'' Juliana explained as she sank into a turquoise chair and crossed her legs. The silver slippers gleamed in the light from a nearby Italian style lamp. "I asked out of simple curiosity.''

"I flew.''

"On your broomstick?''

"No, you used the broomstick, remember?''

"Ah,'' said Juliana. "Feeling peevish, are we? I'll bet David gave you a lift home. He would. David's always the perfect host. Did you tell him who you were before or after he went out of his way for you?''

"Before.''

"How very upright of you. Your sense of business ethics is

certainly an inspiration to the rest of us.'' The silver sandals winked again as Juliana recrossed her legs and smiled blandly.

"Don't give me that superior look, Juliana. My temper is hanging by a thread tonight."

"Shall I fetch a pair of scissors?"

Travis closed his eyes and leaned his head back against the leather cushion. "No, you can fetch me a shot of brandy. Lord knows I need it."

"Brandy is expensive. Why should I waste any of my precious supply on you?" Juliana asked.

Travis's eyes opened and he looked straight at her. "One of these days you're going to learn when to stop pushing," he said very softly.

"Who's going to teach me?"

"It's beginning to look like I'm stuck with the job. It's obvious there aren't a lot of other candidates and one can certainly understand why. Go and get the brandy, Juliana. I want to talk to you."

She hesitated a few seconds and then, hiding a smile, got to her feet and went into the kitchen. She opened a cupboard, found the expensive French brandy she saved for special occasions and carefully poured two glasses.

"Thank you," Travis said with mocking courtesy as she returned to the living room with the balloon glasses balanced on a clear acrylic tray. He picked up one of the glasses.

"Okay," Juliana said as she sat down again. "What do you and I have to talk about?"

"How the hell could you get yourself engaged to David Kirkwood?"

Juliana had thought she was prepared for whatever bomb Travis dropped, but this salvo took her by surprise. "My, you and David certainly got chummy on the drive back to Jewel Harbor, didn't you? The old male bonding routine, I suppose."

Travis scowled. "Answer me, Juliana."

"How did I get engaged to him? Well, let me think a minute. It's been nearly four years now and my memory isn't totally clear on the subject, but as I recall it was in the usual manner. He took me out to dinner at The Treasure House, the same place you and I ate the night you tricked me into going to bed with you, as a matter of fact, and…''

"I didn't trick you into bed and you know it. Stop trying to sidetrack me with a guilt trip. It won't work. And I don't give a damn about where Kirkwood put an engagement ring on your finger. I want to know why in the world you manipulated the guy into asking you to marry him in the first place. Anyone with half a brain can see he's all wrong for you."

Juliana's temper flared at the accusation. "I didn't manipulate him. He asked me and I accepted for all the usual reasons."

"Don't give me that. Nothing happens around you for the *usual reasons*. Damn it, Juliana. How could you even think of marrying a guy like that?"

"David is a very nice man as you witnessed tonight. There aren't a lot of other people in his position who'd give you a lift knowing you planned to ruin them."

"You don't need a very nice man," Travis said through his teeth. "You need someone who can hold his own with you. Someone who won't let you get away with murder. Someone as strong or stronger than you are."

"You may be right." Juliana smiled and gave him a pointed look. "But a woman can't afford to be too choosy these days. Sometimes we have to lower our standards a trifle."

Travis's smile was as well chilled as hers. "Meaning you lowered your standards when you picked me for your second fiancé?"

"You said it, not me. But now that you mention it—"

"Juliana, that's enough. I've already told you I'm not in the mood for your backchat. All I want tonight are a few straightforward answers. I always thought straightforwardness was your specialty. You once told me you like everyone to know exactly where he stands with you and you like to know where you stand with others."

"I've answered your questions. I got engaged to David because we had a lot in common and because I thought I loved him and he thought he loved me. We both realized our mistake within a month. Actually, to be perfectly truthful, I realized it within a couple of days. At any rate we ended the engagement. No hard feelings.''

"You mean David ended things when he realized he would drive himself crazy trying to keep up with you. Elly probably looked like a restful, sweet, golden-haired angel to him after a month of being engaged to you."

"Are you implying I'm a witch?"

"No, ma'am, although I'll admit I called you that earlier tonight when I watched you drive out of that resort parking lot. You're what Kirkwood said you are, a lot of woman. Not every man wants that much woman. Kirkwood sensed he couldn't handle you. You'd have run him ragged and then gotten irritated with him for letting you do it."

"Rather like you and Elly." Juliana felt goaded and warned herself not to let Travis trap her into losing her self-control.

"Like Elly and me? Possible." Travis took a swallow of the brandy and gazed broodingly at the black stone gas fireplace. "You're probably right, as a matter of fact. It doesn't matter anymore, though. Whatever was between Elly and me five years ago is nothing but ashes now."

"I'm not so sure of that," Juliana said coolly. "I saw the way you two looked at each other tonight. There was a lot of old emotion in the air."

Travis waved that observation aside with an impatient movement of his hand. "Old anger on my part. Old fear on hers, probably. Five years have passed and she had convinced herself I'd forgotten all about Flame Valley Inn. She practically had an anxiety attack tonight when she realized that I hadn't forgotten anything."

"Revenge is powerful stuff, isn't it, Travis?"

"It'll keep you warm when you haven't got much else," he agreed. His gaze switched back to her face. "Tell me what happened when you found out Kirkwood was calling off your engagement because he was in love with your cousin."

"That's personal. Why should I tell you?"

"I'll bet there was a hell of a scene. Fireworks and mayhem. Blood and guts everywhere. You wouldn't easily surrender something you wanted. Did you fight like a she-cat to hold on to your handsome tin god?"

Juliana wrinkled her nose. "Golden god, not tin god."

"Let's compromise on papier-mâché god. Did you fight for him, Juliana?"

"Why do you care?"

"I want to know, damn it. I want to know if you fought for him. I want to know how hard you fought for him. Maybe I want to know if you're still fighting for him. Just answer the question."

"I don't owe you any answers. Did you fight for Elly? How hard? Are you still fighting for her? Is taking over Flame Valley your way of trying to reclaim her?"

That appeared to startle him for an instant. Travis looked honestly taken aback. "I don't do things the way you do."

"You just turned around and walked out, huh? Vowing revenge, of course."

"I think," Travis said, "that we had better change the subject."

"You started this conversation."

"Your logic is irrefutable, madam." He saluted her with his glass. "You're right. I started it."

"I love it when you use big words. So professionally macho."

He shook his head. "You're in a real prickly mood tonight, aren't you?"

"I have good cause."

"You're not the one who found himself stranded in the middle of nowhere without a ride home." Travis's crystal cold gaze locked on hers. "Why in hell did you sink your personal cash into Flame Valley, Juliana? You're a better businesswoman than that. You must have realized it was a high-risk investment."

She blinked at the quick shift of topic. "We're back to that, are we?"

"Yes, we're back to that and we're not letting go of it until I get some answers."

Juliana sighed and sipped her brandy. "I've already given you the answer. It was a family thing. I knew David and Elly were in trouble. I made them a loan. So did my parents, for that matter. And Uncle Tony. Everyone in the family has tried to help David and Elly save the inn. We've all got a stake in it.''

Travis set the brandy glass down on the table with a snap. ''Damn it, Juliana, you're too smart to have let yourself get sucked into that mess. I've been working with you long enough to know you're anything but a fool when it comes to business. You must have known how bad things were with the inn.'' He slanted her a quick, assessing glance. ''Or did Kirkwood lie to you about how precarious the situation was?''

''No, he did not lie. I knew exactly how bad things were.''

''And you loaned him the money, anyway.''

''He and Elly are fighting to save the resort. I wanted to give them a chance. Of course, the one thing I didn't know at the time was that you and Fast Forward Properties, Inc. were waiting to pounce on the wounded victim at the first sign of blood. We all assumed Fast Forward would be reasonable when David approached them in a month or so and asked for an extension. Obviously that was a false assumption.''

''Obviously,'' Travis agreed dryly. ''You're going to lose a hell of a lot of money because of David and Elly Kirkwood.''

''If I lose my money, Travis, it will be because of you, not David and Elly.''

Travis swore and surged to his feet. ''Oh, no, you don't. You're not going to blame this on me.'' He began to pace the length of the gray carpet. ''Don't you dare try to blame this on me,'' he repeated huskily. ''You should never have put money into Flame Valley and you know it.''

In a way he was right and Juliana did know it. She lifted one shoulder carelessly. ''Win some, lose some.''

Travis swung around at the far end of the room and leveled his finger at her. ''You can't afford to lose that much cash, Juliana. Not if you want to expand Charisma Espresso. No one knows your financial situation better than me, and I'm telling you that you can't take this kind of loss. All your plans for Charisma will be set back three or four years at the very least.''

''Okay, okay. You've made your point. I can't afford the loss. Not much I can do about it now.''

Travis shoved his hands into his back pockets. ''Is that all you can say?''

''No point crying over spilt espresso.''

''You're looking at the end of all your plans to finance Charisma's expansion this year, and that's your reaction?'' Travis asked, staring at her in disbelief. '''No point crying over spilt espresso'? I don't believe I'm hearing this.''

''Be reasonable, Travis. There's not much I can do now, is there? The damage is done.'' She took a swallow of brandy and gazed forlornly into the dark fireplace. ''I'm ruined.''

''Let's not get melodramatic. We've got enough problems as it is.''

''You don't have any problems. I have the problems. And frankly, Travis, if you can't offer anything helpful to the discussion, I'd just as soon stop talking about my dismal business future. It's depressing.''

''Helpful?'' he snarled. ''What kind of help do you expect from me?''

She slanted him a sidelong glance. ''Well, Travis, you are the problem, in case you've forgotten. That means you're also the solution.''

''I didn't get Flame Valley Inn into this mess,'' he growled furiously. ''Kirkwood and Elly did it all on their own. With a little help from you and your parents and good old Uncle Tony, of course. Don't expect me to solve everything by paying you back after I take over the resort. I've got investors to pay off first, remember? A half dozen of them, and they'll all be standing in line waiting for their money. I've made commitments to them. And I can personally guarantee that none of them are going to be feeling charitable.''

''You're right. I don't expect you to pay me off when you and your investors take over the inn.''

"Well, what do you expect out of me?" Travis roared.

She pursed her lips primly. "You're my personal business consultant," she reminded him. "You are paid to keep me out of hot financial waters. You are paid to guide and advise me. I'm putting my complete faith, total trust and all my hopes for the future in your hands. I feel certain you'll save my hide."

"Juliana, what the hell am I supposed to do?"

"Save Flame Valley Inn from the clutches of Fast Forward Properties, Inc."

Travis looked thunderstruck. For a moment he just stood there in towering silence, staring at her as if she'd lost her mind. Juliana held her breath.

"Save the inn?" Travis finally repeated blankly. "From myself?"

"From yourself and that pack of hungry wolves you're leading."

"Am I supposed to do this for you?" He looked as if he was having trouble following the conversation.

"I'm one of your clients, aren't I? I hired you to help me put together a workable plan to expand Charisma. As far as I'm concerned, we still have a valid consulting contract. And the bottom line is that we can't expand my firm unless you rescue Flame Valley from Fast Forward Properties. Therefore, yes, I'm expecting you to do this for me."

"You," Travis announced softly, dangerously, "are crazy."

"No. Desperate." If only he knew how desperate, Juliana thought. She wasn't fighting to save the inn or Charisma's future. She was fighting to save the love of her life. But she did not think now was the time to point that out to him. "Will you help me, Travis? Will you salvage the resort from bankruptcy?"

"I already did that once, remember? And I didn't get paid for my efforts. What makes you think I'd repeat that mistake?"

"This time I'll be paying your fee. And you already know I pay my debts."

"Lady, you can't afford my fee."

She frowned. "I'm paying you already, remember? For the consulting work on Charisma. And so far I haven't had any trouble meeting the tab. I paid your retainer right on time and I'll meet the monthly fees, no sweat.''

"Oh, Lord. What an innocent.'' Travis rubbed the back of his neck in a gesture of pure exasperation. He stalked to the end of the room and back again. "Juliana, let me make this crystal clear. The fee you are paying me for consulting work on Charisma is only a fraction of what I would normally charge for that kind of job. In fact, under normal circumstances, I would never even agree to take on a job the size of Charisma. Your operation is far too small for Sawyer Management Systems. Do I make myself plain?''

"You're telling me I got a special deal?''

"You got a hell of a deal.''

She caught her lower lip thoughtfully between her teeth. "Why? Because I was a Grant and you were out to punish all the Grants? You wanted to get close to me so that you could hurt me by destroying Charisma?''

"No, damn it, I never intended to destroy Charisma. I don't know what happened. Not exactly. All I know is that I walked into your shop that day last month because I was curious to meet the one member of the Grant family who hadn't been around five years ago.'' Travis's palms came up in a gesture of total incomprehension. "The next thing I knew I was having a cup of coffee and agreeing to consult on your expansion plans.''

"You mean you took on my project out of the kindness of your heart?''

"I don't do business out of the kindness of my heart,'' he said grimly.

"Well, that's neither here nor there now, is it? We've got a contract. You're my business consultant and I am facing a financial disaster. It seems to me you're duty bound to save me.''

"Is that right?'' His gaze was unreadable.

"Looks that way to me.''

"Since you've got all the answers,'' he said, "Maybe you'll be kind enough to tell me just how I'm supposed to save you?''

"I don't know. That's your business, isn't it?"

Travis shook his head. "You are really something else, you know that?"

"So I've been told. Well? Will you do it?"

He sighed. "It can't be done. I'm too good at what I do, Juliana, and I've set this up so that there aren't any loopholes. Even if I thought I might be able to save the inn and even if I was idiotic enough to agree to try, there's still the little matter of my fee for the job."

"Name it. I'll tell you whether or not I can afford it," she challenged softly.

He looked at her through dangerously narrowed eyes. His gaze moved from the toe of her silver lounge sandals to the top of her red mane. "What if I told you my fee was an all-out affair with you? What if I said that the price of my services, win, lose or draw, no guarantees on saving the resort, was access rights to your bed?"

Juliana stopped breathing for a few seconds. Then she sucked in a dose of air and sat very still to conceal the fact that she was trembling. "My fabulous body in exchange for your services as a consultant? Don't play games with me, Travis. If you don't do business out of the kindness of your heart, you certainly wouldn't do it for sex."

He didn't move. When he spoke his voice was very, very soft. "But what if I said that was the fee, Juliana?"

She shivered, aware that he was deliberately tormenting her. "I'd tell you to take a long walk off a short pier."

He turned away and stood looking out the window into the darkness. "Yeah, I figured that's what you'd say. All right, smart lady, I'll tell you what my fee for trying to salvage Flame Valley Inn and Charisma's future would be. It would be the same as it was five years ago, a piece of the action."

Juliana gasped, not in shock this time but in outrage. "You expect David and Elly to make you a partner in the business if you save it from your own investors? Talk about gall." She thought quickly. "Still, I suppose something along those lines might be worked out. It would have to be a very small piece of the action, however. You simply can't expect David and Elly to give you a half interest or anything like that.''

Travis slanted her an assessing look over his shoulder. ''No. You don't understand, Juliana. I don't want a piece of Flame Valley Inn. If, by some miracle, I do manage to save the resort, it's going to need a lot of cash and a lot of work and even then there's a good chance it will still go under within a couple of years. I want a piece of a sure thing this time.''

She watched him closely, the way she would a predator, and felt her stomach tighten. ''What sure thing?''

''Charisma.''

Juliana nearly dropped her brandy glass. Her mouth fell open in amazement. She sat staring at him, unable to comprehend what he was saying. ''A piece of Charisma? You want a piece of my business? But, Travis, Charisma is mine. All mine. I built it from scratch. No one else in the family is even involved with it. You can't be serious.''

''Welcome to the real world. I am very serious. I told you my usual fees are always very high, Juliana. And if you agree to the deal, you'd better understand going in that there's a big possibility I won't be able to save the resort. But I'll expect to be paid, even if I fail to salvage Flame Valley.''

Juliana was reeling. She struggled frantically to collect her thoughts. She hadn't been expecting this, although looking back on things, she probably ought to have expected it or something equally outrageous. Travis Sawyer was a formidable opponent. ''But Charisma is mine,'' she repeated, dazed. ''I made it what it is all by myself. I learned the ropes managing an espresso chain in San Francisco for years while I saved my money to buy my first machines and find a good location. I've done it all, all by myself.''

''And all by yourself you put Charisma's future at risk by making that loan to Kirkwood and your cousin.'' Travis started for the door. ''Think about it, Juliana. I'll drop by your shop Monday morning to get your decision.''

"Travis, wait, let's talk about this. I'm sure we can find some reasonable compromise if we just—"

"I don't make compromises when it comes to insuring my fee. I learned my lesson on that five years ago. And I learned it from dealing with people named Grant."

"But, Travis..." Juliana leaped to her feet but the door was already closing behind him. She raced to the window in time to see him get into the Buick he'd left parked in front of the apartment earlier in the evening. The headlights came on, blinding her. In another moment he was gone.

"You sneaky, conniving, hard-hearted, sonofa...Charisma is mine, damn it. *Mine*. And I'm not going to let you or anyone else have a piece of it." Juliana halted in the middle of her tirade as a thought struck her with the force of a lightning bolt.

If she gave him a chunk of Charisma Espresso Travis would be financially bound to her for what might be years. Their lives would inevitably be deeply entangled. It was easier to get rid of a spouse these days than it was a business partner.

And if she had him around to work on all that time, Juliana told herself, spirits soaring, she just knew she could convince him to see that they were meant for each other.

TRAVIS WAS AWARE of the tension that gripped his insides as he parked the Buick in front of Charisma Espresso on Monday. He should be used to the unpleasant sensation, he told himself. He'd been awake two nights in a row because of it.

He could see the lights on inside the espresso bar, and he thought he caught a glimpse of Juliana's red hair as she ducked into the back room. His hands tightened on the steering wheel. He still could not quite believe he was doing this. But he supposed he shouldn't be too surprised. This whole deal had been skewed from the moment he had met Juliana. Nothing had happened the way he had planned it since then, so why should anything straighten out now?

He forced himself to get out of the car and walk toward the shop. He had to be prepared for whatever answer he got. Juliana was nothing if not unpredictable. And Charisma was very, very important to her.

He wondered if she would realize what he was doing and why. The whole, crazy scheme had come to him in a flash in the heat of the argument Saturday night and he still was not certain where it would all lead. He had been acting on instinct, trying to buy himself some time.

Would Juliana guess that he was using this bizarre deal to hold on to her for a while longer? And if she did, would she be furious or secretly glad?

Even if she did agree, he would have no way of knowing for certain just why she was doing so. She might be doing it because she was desperate to help her cousin and David Kirkwood. Or she might agree because he had made her aware of just how precarious Charisma's future was because of that foolish loan she had made to the Kirkwoods.

Or she might agree because she still cared a little for him and was willing to take the risk of being snared in financial bonds until they could work out the rest of their muddled relationship.

Then, again, she might simply hurl a cup of espresso in his face and tell him to get lost.

The lady or the tiger? Travis wondered as he pushed open the door. Life with Juliana was never dull.

"He's here, Juliana." Sandy Oakes, her multiple earrings clashing merrily, turned toward the door as Travis entered. Her hair was gelled into a slick 1950s ducktail and her eyes were bright with speculative interest. "Come and get him, boss."

Matt Linton looked up from where he was stacking espresso cups. "Yup. There he is. Poor devil. Look at him standing there, so naive and unsuspecting."

"Kinda breaks your heart, doesn't it?" Sandy observed. "I mean, the poor man doesn't even know what he's in for yet."

"If I were him, I'd run for it," Matt added with a grin.

Travis groaned silently, wishing Juliana would show a little more discretion at times. "You know, the plans for the expansion

of Charisma Espresso don't necessarily have to include you two,"
he muttered.

"Oooh," said Sandy. "I think I detect a threat."

"Juliana," Matt called more loudly. "Come and rescue us.
We're being threatened out here."

Travis lifted his eyes beseechingly toward the ceiling and set
his back teeth. An instant later Juliana came out of the back room,
wiping her hand on a towel. She was wearing a black jumpsuit
trimmed with fringe and a pair of black leather high-heeled boots.
Her hair was pulled back with two silver combs.

"What's going on out here?" she demanded, brows snapping
together. "Oh, it's you, Travis. It's about time you got here."

He shoved his hands into his back pockets. "I didn't realize
you'd be waiting so eagerly for my arrival."

"Of course I've been eager for you to get here," she informed
him waspishly. "We've got a ton of things to do before this evening, and I won't have time to do them all. You'll have to help
out." She ducked into her tiny, cluttered office and reemerged
with a piece of paper. "Here. This is what you have to pick up
from the grocery store. And on the back are some things I want
from the cheese shop three doors down. You might as well pick
those up, too. And while you're at it, get some champagne, will
you?"

Travis stared blankly at the list in his hand, a conviction growing within him that he had once again lost the upper hand. "Why
am I buying all this stuff, Juliana?"

"For the party we're having tonight, of course. Now run along.
I'm busy. Got a lot to do here. It's Monday morning, you know.
Melvin is late with my shipment of Colombian and I just got word
one of the coffee roasters has broken down. I'm swamped."

Travis refused to be budged. "Why are we having a party?"
he asked with forced patience.

"Don't worry, it's not a big deal. I've just invited David and
Elly over tonight to announce that you'll be going to work to save
Flame Valley Inn." She looked straight into his eyes and silently
defied him to argue.

Travis returned the challenging look, his fingers tightening on the paper in his hand. His gamble had paid off. "We have a deal, I take it?"

"We have a deal."

"You understand I can't give you any guarantees? I can't promise to save the resort. Things have gone too far for me to make any promises."

She smiled fleetingly. "If anyone can save it, you can."

"But if I can't, Juliana, I'll still expect to be paid."

"Stop carping. You'll get your fee."

Travis glanced around the interior of Charisma, aware of an almost light-headed sensation of relief. "I've always wanted to own part interest in an espresso bar."

"Since when?"

"Since Saturday night. See you later, *partner*."

CHAPTER FIVE

"THERE'S JUST one more thing about tonight," Juliana said, tossing a handful of chillies into the Asian-style noodles she was stir-frying. "I don't want anyone to know about our little, uh, arrangement."

The knife Travis had been using to slice mushrooms paused in midstroke. He glanced sideways at Juliana. "Why not?"

"Why not?" she echoed, exasperated. "Isn't it obvious? Because David and Elly will feel terrible if they think I'm paying your fee by making you a partner in Charisma. I don't want to put any more of a guilt trip on them than they're already under."

"Why should it bother them to know you're paying the fee? They didn't have any qualms about taking your money in the form of a loan."

"That was before things got so bad." Juliana concentrated on the noodles. "At the time it looked as if David really was going to be able to pull it off. Travis, have things really gone too far?"

"Probably. I told you, I set the whole thing up so that there wouldn't be any room for Kirkwood to maneuver. I won't know for certain until I get a good look at the books, but if I were you, I wouldn't hold my breath."

Juliana was undaunted. "It'll all work out. I know it will. Hand me those little tart shells, will you?"

"What kind of meal is this going to be, anyway? Just about everything here qualifies as an hors d'oeuvre in my book."

"Stop grumbling. Everyone knows the hors d'oeuvres are always the best part of a meal. I say why bother with the entrée? We'll just graze on the good stuff. When you've finished with the mushrooms, you can help me fill these shells with the cheese mixture."

"You like giving me orders, don't you?"

"It's just that you look cute in that apron. There's a glass platter in that cupboard to your right. Use it for the sliced vegetables. Hurry, David and Elly will be here any minute."

"How do I get myself into these situations with you?" Travis asked so softly Juliana barely heard him. "Every time I think I've got things back under control, I find out I'm barely keeping up with the new detour you're taking." He finished slicing mushrooms with sharp, fast strokes of the knife.

"About our partnership, Travis..."

"What about it?" His head came up warily.

"Well, I think we ought to establish right from the outset that you're more or less a silent partner. Know what I mean?" She smiled brilliantly. "I'll consult you, of course, before making major decisions. And heaven knows you're already involved in the planning process for Charisma's future. But in the final analysis, I'm the senior partner in Charisma. I just want to be sure we understand that little point."

"You can call yourself anything you like," Travis said easily, "just so long as you understand you can't make any major decisions without consulting me."

"Just what is your definition of a major decision?" Juliana retorted.

"We'll figure that out when we come across one. Where do you want this tray of vegetables?"

"On the end table near the sofa." Juliana glanced out the window and saw a familiar white Mercedes sliding into the space next to her coupé. "Good grief, they're here already. I'll bet David and Elly are dying of curiosity."

"Why? What did you tell them?"

"That you're going to save everyone's bacon, naturally." Juliana carried the tray of tiny cheese tarts into the living room.

"Don't make too many rash promises, Juliana. I've said I'll do what I can. I can't guarantee anything."

"I'm not worried, Travis. I have complete faith in you."

"You're too smart a businesswoman to have blind faith in any consultant."

"You're not the usual sort of consultant." Juliana swept toward the door, the skirts of her liquid silk hostess pajamas shimmering around her. "Open the champagne, Travis. David and Elly are going to be thrilled."

"I'll just bet they are."

David and Elly were not precisely thrilled. They regarded Travis with great caution as they walked into the living room and sat down. And they greeted Juliana's grand announcement initially with stunned surprise. The astonishment turned only gradually to careful, cautious concern, and all the questions soon developed a single focus.

"Why are you doing this?" David finally asked point-blank.

"Believe me, I've been asking myself the same question," Travis said dryly, helping himself to one of the mushrooms he'd sliced earlier.

"I mean, what's in it for you?" David persisted, brows drawn together in one of his rare, serious frowns. "Don't think we're not grateful, but I'd like to know what we're getting into here."

Juliana felt Travis's eyes switch to her face, obviously leaving the answer to that one up to her. She smiled at David. "Don't you see, David? He's doing it as a favor to me."

"A favor," Elly repeated, her eyes widening.

"A business favor," Juliana clarified. "Would anyone like another cheese tart?"

"But, Juliana," Elly persisted, "why would he do you any favors?"

"Yeah, why?" David echoed, but he looked thoughtful as he regarded Travis's unreadable expression.

"An interesting and timely question," Travis said. "Why would I want to do you any favors, Juliana?"

Juliana smiled fondly at him. "Why, to save Charisma's future, of course." She turned to David and Elly. "You have to understand something here. Travis had already committed himself to doing consulting work for Charisma before he realized the extent of my financial involvement with Flame Valley Inn. It set up a conflict of interest for him, you see. Once he discovered how much money Charisma stood to lose, he immediately insisted on trying to salvage the Flame Valley situation. He felt ethically bound to help Charisma. Travis is very big on business ethics, you know.''

''Is that right?'' David murmured. ''I believe I will have another cheese tart, Juliana. And another glass of champagne.''

''Certainly.'' Juliana reached for the tray of tarts. It was all going to work out just fine, she told herself as David plied Travis with further questions. Things were falling into place nicely. She ignored Elly's anxious glances.

Twenty minutes later, however, David cornered her in the kitchen where Juliana had gone to whip up another batch of stir-fried noodles.

''Just what the devil is going on?'' David demanded in low tones.

Juliana glanced up from the wok. ''What do you mean?''

''You know damn well what I mean. Juliana, I don't for one minute believe all that nonsense about Travis Sawyer suddenly being stricken with a severe case of business ethics. It's just you and me out here in the kitchen, kiddo, and we've been friends a long time. Now tell me the truth. Why is he galloping to Flame Valley's rescue? The real reason this time. What's in it for him?''

''David, really.'' Juliana switched off the electric wok and busied herself piling noodles onto a platter. ''Keep your voice down. Elly and Travis will hear you.''

''Are you the fee this time around, Juliana?''

David took a step closer, towering over her in the way Juliana used to find so exciting. She realized now she found it annoying.

''Don't be silly, David.''

''I'm serious, Juliana. What's going on between the two of you? Are you sleeping with him in exchange for his help? Is that the deal? Because if so, I won't let you do it and that's final. God knows I'll take all the help I can get up to a point. But I sure as hell won't let you sell yourself to Sawyer as payment for saving Flame Valley."

Juliana opened her mouth to order him out of her kitchen but before the words could be uttered, Travis interrupted from the doorway. His voice was cold and hard.

"Leave her alone, Kirkwood. Juliana doesn't need your protection. The deal she and I have made is a private one, and you don't have any need to know the details."

"He's right," Juliana said briskly. "The arrangement is strictly between Travis and myself. We're both satisfied with the details so you need not concern yourself. Here, take these extra napkins out to Elly. We'll need them for the next round of noodles."

"But, Juliana…"

"Go. Shoo. Get out of my kitchen. The noodles are getting cold. And stop worrying about me, David. You know perfectly well I can take care of myself. I always have."

"I know, but I'm not sure I like the setup here."

"You may not like it but you'll go along with it, won't you?" Travis asked softly. "Because it's the only chance you've got to save the resort."

David met his eyes for a few seconds and then, without another word, walked back into the living room with the napkins.

Travis turned back to Juliana. "You do realize that's how everyone's going to interpret this crazy deal we've made? Your folks, your Uncle Tony, David and Elly, they'll all come to the conclusion you're sleeping with me in exchange for my help."

"But you and I know the truth, don't we? This is a business arrangement. Nothing more."

"Oh, sure. Right. A business arrangement. Get real, Juliana."

"Look at it this way," Juliana said as she shoved a plate of noodles into his hands. "Since we know that the business side of this deal is just that, strictly business, we're free to continue working on our relationship without worrying about each other's motives." She started briskly for the door, heedless of the shock in Travis's eyes.

"Juliana. Damn it, come back here. What did you mean by that?"

Juliana ignored him, sailing into the living room with a warm smile for David and Elly. "Everyone ready for another round of noodles? Don't be shy. I've got plenty of hot sauce."

TRAVIS CLOSED IN on Juliana the instant the Kirkwoods' Mercedes pulled out of the lot.

"About our relationship," he began darkly.

Juliana had been feeling very confident earlier, but now that she was alone with Travis she wasn't quite so sure of herself. So she compensated by acting more sure of herself than ever. It was an old habit. When people assumed you could take care of yourself, you learned to do it. "What about it?" she asked as she began picking up napkins and plates.

Travis paced toward her very deliberately. "The last time I inquired into the subject, you had sworn off sleeping with me until I had made a commitment to marry you. As I recall, I was given one month to come to my senses. Then you said very specifically that all we had was a business arrangement. Now you're talking about a relationship. Are you changing the rules on me again, Juliana?"

"You want the truth? All right, I'll give you the truth. We're going to be seeing a lot of each other from now on, and I've been in love with you since the day I met you. To be perfectly blunt, I don't think I'll be able to resist you for much longer. Not if you put your mind to seducing me, that is." She picked up an empty tray and carried it into the kitchen.

"What the hell does that mean?" Travis stormed into the kitchen behind her and caught her in his arms as she set down her burden. "Tell me exactly what it means. No more cute games, Juliana."

"It means just what it sounds like. Are you going to put your mind to seducing me?" She twined her arms around his neck and brushed his hard mouth lightly with her own soft lips.

"Juliana." Travis breathed her name on a hoarse, urgent groan.

He caught her head between his hands and crushed her mouth hungrily beneath his own.

Juliana responded instinctively, willingly and with all the pent-up eagerness that she had been fighting to keep in check.

"Hold it," Travis ordered, although his arms were already tight around her waist. "I've got to figure out what's going on here. You say our business arrangement is separate. That is has nothing to do with this end of things. And you claim you still love me. So what is all this? You think that if you let me back into your bed I'll suddenly decide I have to offer marriage, after all?"

"Who knows? You might, you being such an ethical type and all."

He shook his head in slow wonder. "You never give up, do you?"

"No. But I don't want to talk about marriage right now."

"Good. Neither do I."

Travis kissed her hard and then took her hand firmly in his and started toward the bedroom. He turned out lights en route and by the time they reached the end of the hall they were deep in the never-never land of night and shadow.

"Travis?" She smiled up at him as he drew her to a halt near the bed. She trailed her fingertips along his shoulder, enjoying the strength she found there.

"I've been going out of my mind wondering when it would happen with you again." Travis caught her earlobe between his teeth as he began to unbutton the top of Juliana's silky hostess outfit.

"I should never have set that month deadline the first time around," Juliana confided, leaning into his vital warmth. "I should have known I'd never last that long."

"We agreed after that first night together that what we have between us is very special." Travis finished unbuttoning the yellow silk top and eased it off her shoulders.

Juliana felt the whisper softness of the fine material on her skin and shivered with anticipation. Travis looked down at her bare breasts and his crystal eyes glinted in the darkness. His palm closed gently over one budding nipple and Juliana inhaled deeply.

"You feel so good." Travis's mouth found the curve of her throat. "So right."

"So do you." She tugged at his tie and tossed it aside. Then she unbuttoned his shirt with fingers that trembled. As soon as she had freed him of the shirt, she locked her arms around his waist and leaned her head against his bare shoulder. The crisp mat of hair on his chest grazed her nipples. She wriggled against him experimentally, enjoying the teasing sensation.

Travis laughed softly, the sound husky and very sexy in the darkness. He slid his palms beneath the waistband of Juliana's silk pants and pushed them down over her hips. A moment later she stood nude in his arms.

"This is how it's supposed to be between us," Travis muttered as he picked her up and carried her to the bed. He settled her on the pillows and stood back to rid himself of the rest of his own clothing.

"I know." Juliana lay gazing up at him, glorying in the solid, hard shape of him. The strength in his shoulders and thighs appealed to all her senses and the boldness of his arousal pleased her on a deep, primitive level. But it was not simply the physical aspect of Travis that captivated her and made her so aware of him on a sensual plane, she realized. There were other men just as solidly masculine and far better looking.

"You look very serious all of a sudden," Travis observed as he came down beside her on the bed, a small foil packet in one hand. "What are you thinking?"

She looked up at him as he loomed over her. "I was just wondering what it is about you that makes you so sexy."

He grinned, teeth flashing in the darkness as he dealt with the contents of the packet. "You're trying to figure out why you couldn't resist me any longer?"

"Um-hm." She trailed her fingers through his hair and tangled one leg between his.

"Don't think about it too hard," Travis advised, leaning down to kiss the valley between her breasts. "Some questions don't have any clear answers. Just accept it and go with it."

"Whatever you say, partner." Juliana arched invitingly as his hand stroked down the length of her to her hip. When his fingers squeezed the curve of her thigh she sighed, feeling her own response deep within her body. He had such good, strong, knowing hands, she thought. The barest touch of his rough fingertips aroused her, and when he kissed her breast, she almost cried out. She could feel herself growing warm and damp already.

Turning slightly in his arms, Juliana snuggled more closely against Travis. She began to explore him intimately, rediscovering the secrets she had first learned during their one previous night together.

She could feel the sexual tension in him as her hand slipped over his body. The muscles of his back and shoulders were taut with the desire he held in check. Travis's obvious need elicited a fierce reaction within Juliana. She stirred restlessly against him. When his fingers slid between her thighs into the dampening heat of her she parted her legs and whispered his name softly. Her nails grazed his shoulders.

"The kind of woman who leaves her mark," Travis muttered, rolling her onto her back.

"What?"

"Never mind. Wrap your legs around me, sweetheart. Tight. Take me inside and hold me close."

Juliana gathered him to her, aware of his hard shaft pressing against her softness. She was aching for him, her body throbbing with need.

"Now," Juliana whispered, her eyes closed as she clung to him and tightened her legs around his lean hips. "Come to me now. I love you, Travis."

"I couldn't wait any longer if I tried."

Travis eased himself into her carefully, filling her completely, stretching her gently until she felt the spiraling tension begin to build to unbearable heights.

She lifted her hips and Travis responded by driving more deeply into her and then withdrawing with excruciating slowness. Juliana clung more fiercely, urging him closer. He stroked into her again and again withdrew.

"Travis," she hissed, clutching at him.

"I'm not going anywhere without you."

He surged into her again, more deeply than before and Juliana gasped as the delicious tension within her went out of control. She gave herself up to the release, Travis's name on her lips as she felt him plunge into her one last time. The muscles of his back went rigid beneath her palms and she was crushed into the bedding beneath his solid weight.

For a time there was nothing else of importance in the entire universe.

A long while later Travis stirred on top of Juliana and looked down at her, his gaze intent in the shadows. She smiled sleepily, her fingers sliding slickly through the traces of perspiration on his shoulders.

"Don't worry," she said, yawning delicately. "I'm not going to bring up the subject."

"What subject?"

"Marriage."

"You just brought it up," Travis pointed out, kissing the tip of her nose.

"Well, I'll change it to a more pressing issue."

"Such as?"

"Such as which of us gets up first in the morning to make the tea."

"I'll do it this time," Travis said.

"Such an accommodating man." Juliana yawned again and drifted off to sleep.

THREE DAYS LATER, at ten-thirty in the morning, Travis sat at his desk in the new Jewel Harbor offices of Sawyer Management Systems and tried to decide if he really needed to take a coffee break. Charisma Espresso was only a few blocks away. He could walk over, say hello to Juliana, grab some coffee to go and be back at the office within twenty minutes.

Or he could save fifteen minutes by helping himself to the office pot. Lord knew he needed every spare minute he could salvage to work on the Flame Valley Inn problem.

Travis eyed the stack of papers on his desk with a brooding eye. He and Fast Forward Properties had certainly done a very thorough job of setting the inn up for a takeover. The grim truth was that he was not at all certain he could save it now. A lot of creditors, including his own group of investors would have to be put on indefinite hold and a big infusion of cash would be required to get the inn back on its feet financially. It was a nightmare of a task.

Every time he thought of Juliana's blithe faith in his ability to pull the fat back out of the fire, he swore silently. Lately he found himself trying very hard not to think about what would happen if he failed.

The intercom on his desk murmured gently. "Mr. Sawyer, there's a Mrs. Kirkwood here to see you."

Travis gritted his teeth. The last thing he needed right now was a visit from Elly, but there wasn't much he could do about it. "Send her in, Mrs. Bannerman."

A few seconds later Elly came through the door, her fragile features accentuated by her short gamin haircut, her delicate figure set off by close-fitting white pants and a white silk blouse. The big blue eyes that had once seemed so clear and guileless to Travis were filled with an irritating apprehension. Had he ever really been in love with this woman, he wondered fleetingly. She was a sweet, pale azalea next to the vibrant orchid that was Juliana.

"Hello, Elly. Have a seat." Travis got reluctantly to his feet and waved her casually to a chair.

"Thank you." Elly sat down, never taking her eyes off him. She crossed her feet at the ankles and folded her hands in her lap. She looked very nervous but very determined. "I had to come here today, Travis. I had to talk to you."

"Fine. Talk." Travis sat down again and leaned back in his chair. He wished he'd made up his mind about going over to Charisma five minutes earlier. He would have missed this little heart-to-heart chat. It went to show that he who hesitated was definitely lost.

Elly took a deep breath. "You're sleeping with Juliana. You're having an affair with her."

Travis glanced out the window. He had a pleasant view of the harbor from here. He could even see The Treasure House restaurant down at the marina. "That's none of your business and you know it, Elly."

"It is if you're using her. She's my cousin, Travis. I won't have her hurt by you."

Travis looked at her. "Did you worry a lot about hurting Juliana when you lured Kirkwood away from her?"

"That's not fair," Elly cried. "I didn't lure him away. We fought our feelings for each other until...until..."

"Until Juliana finally noticed and let Kirkwood go?"

"Damn it, Travis. You don't know what you're talking about. Juliana didn't just let David go."

"Did she fight for him?" He waited tensely for the answer. He wanted to know how important Kirkwood had once been to Juliana.

Elly looked shocked at the question. "There was no fighting involved. They both realized they had made a mistake and they ended the engagement by mutual agreement. It was all very calm and civilized. Ask her. She'll tell you the truth. Travis, I don't want to talk about the past."

"Not even our own past?" he asked with mild interest.

"Especially not our own past." Her gaze slid away from his.

He nodded and tossed his pen down onto the desk. "You're right. It's a rather boring subject, isn't it?"

Elly leaned forward anxiously. "Travis, I must know if you're blackmailing Juliana into sleeping with you."

"Why?"

"Because if that's the price you've put on saving Flame Valley for us, it's too high. I won't let Juliana pay it."

"You think your cousin would let herself get blackmailed into sleeping with a man, regardless of the reason?"

Elly frowned, looking momentarily confused. ''Not under normal circumstances, but this is different.''

"How is it different?''

"She's very attracted to you. In fact, I think she's in love with you. I don't think it would be very difficult for her to convince herself that it was all right to sleep with you in exchange for your help. But she would be hurt when the end came, and I don't want her to pay that kind of price.''

Travis was suddenly impatient. "Don't worry about it, Elly.''

"She's my cousin. I can't help but worry. You've thrown everything into such chaos by coming back this way, Travis. You're a very dangerous man and I'm the only one who seems to fully comprehend that fact. David refuses to look below the surface to see what you're really up to, and Juliana is blinded by her emotions. My father and aunt and uncle are totally confused by the whole situation. They want desperately to believe the inn can be saved, and although they all love Juliana, they're used to letting her take care of herself.''

"So you've decided you're the only one left to sound the warning? Save your breath, Elly. Juliana won't listen to you.''

Elly got to her feet and walked nervously over to the window. She stood there, clutching her leather purse, her back toward Travis. "You're doing this to punish me, aren't you?'' she whispered.

Travis thought about that for perhaps twenty seconds. "No,'' he said.

"You didn't come back just because you felt you hadn't been paid for saving the inn five years ago. You came back because of what happened between us.''

Travis studied Elly's slender back and shook his head. Juliana had been right: this fragile, delicate, easily startled doe of a woman was not for him, had never been right for him. "I came back because I'd been cheated out of my fee, Elly. That's the only reason I came back.''

Elly swallowed a sob. "I'm sorry about what happened five years ago. I was sorry at the time. I didn't want to do it. I wanted to tell you the truth, about how I wanted to end the engagement, and I wanted to tell you just as soon as I realized we weren't right for each other. But Dad was sure you would walk out, and he said if you did, we would lose Flame Valley. He said things had gone too far and that you were the only one who could save it. He said I had to make you think I was going to marry you, and that you would get the partnership in the inn as a wedding present.''

"So you went along with the lie. I'll have to admit you were very convincing, Elly."

She swung around, an anguished expression in her damp eyes. "What was I supposed to do? I had to make a choice between my family and you."

"And your family won."

"Yes, damn you. There was no other option. But I won't have Juliana hurt because of what I had to do five years ago."

"You make a charming martyr, Elly. But you can relax. I am not hurting Juliana."

"You're using her. She's a stand-in for me. I know that's what it is. If you can't have one Grant woman, you'll take another, is that it? Your revenge wouldn't be complete unless you got one of us into bed."

Travis stared at her, real anger gathering in him for the first time. He stood up. "That's enough, Elly. You don't know what you're talking about. Just for the record, I will tell you that there is no way in hell Juliana could ever be a stand-in for you. Juliana is totally unique. She's not a stand-in for anybody. She could never be that. Now, I suggest you leave before you say another word."

"I haven't finished." Elly lifted her chin, defying him with all the boldness of a traumatized deer. "I want you to know I'm on to your tricks. I don't trust you one inch, regardless of what the others think."

"Is that right? Well, I'll certainly have to watch my step, won't I?"

Travis took a menacing step forward and Elly stifled a small shriek. "Don't touch me, you big brute." She leaped back, turned and ran for the door.

Travis watched with mild disgust as his former fiancée fled his evil clutches. Juliana would never have run like that, he reflected. She would have stood her ground.

Travis sat back down at his desk and picked up the stack of papers he'd been wading through a few minutes earlier. Elly's words flickered through his head.

I had to make a choice between my family and you.

Travis knew he'd been wrong when he had told Elly that Juliana was totally unique. She had one very important thing in common with Elly. She was fiercely loyal to her family.

Travis prayed he would never be in the same situation with Juliana that he'd been in five years ago with Elly—one where the lady was forced to choose between him and her family. He always seemed to lose in those situations.

That realization made him wonder again what would happen if he failed to save Flame Valley Inn.

The door burst open in the middle of that thought, and Juliana swept into the room bearing a paper sack with the Charisma logo emblazoned on the side.

"All right, what did you do to my cousin, you big brute?" She smiled sunnily as she set the sack down on the desk and removed an extra-large Styrofoam cup of coffee.

Travis studied her, a smile playing around the edge of his mouth. She looked very chic today in a full, pleated menswear style skirt, a tight fitting vest and a wide-sleeved shirt.

"Big brute?" Travis repeated, eyeing the cup of coffee with enthusiasm.

"I believe those were her very words." Juliana uncapped a second cup and sat down in the chair her cousin had just vacated. "The two of you had a little scene up here, I take it?"

"It's hard to have more than a small scene with Elly. She always takes off running just when things start getting interesting." Travis popped the lid on his cup and inhaled gratefully. "Just what I needed."

"I figured you'd be ready for your midmorning coffee break about now. Thought I'd save you the hike over to Charisma. Besides, I needed a break myself. Melvin and I are feuding again. So what did you and Elly argue about?"

"She thinks I'm blackmailing you into sleeping with me." Travis watched Juliana over the rim of the cup as he took a swallow of the rich, dark-roasted coffee.

"Her, too, huh?"

"I wouldn't be surprised if Sandy and Matt, your parents and Tony Grant suspected the same thing. Which would make the opinion practically unanimous."

"Too bad it's not true," Juliana remarked. "It's certainly an exciting thought."

Travis was irritated. "You weren't very excited the other night when I came up with the suggestion. As I recall you turned me down flat when I offered to take your fair body as my fee for saving Flame Valley."

"Well, of course I turned you down. I had to, for your sake."

"My sake?"

"Sure. If I'd agreed to let you blackmail me into sleeping with you, you would have worried yourself to a frazzle in no time."

Travis set down his cup cautiously. "About what?"

"About the real reason I was having an affair with you. Every time I kissed you or told you I loved you, a part of you would have wondered if I really meant it or if I was just saying it to keep you working like a dog on behalf of the resort. This way we keep business completely separate from our personal relationship."

Travis swore wryly. "Always one step ahead, aren't you?"

"I can't help it. It's my nature. I confess it was for your own good that I had to put my foot down on your thrilling blackmail attempt." Juliana got to her feet and came around to his side of the desk. Her eyes were filled with seductive, mischievous humor. "But never think for a moment that I didn't find the offer wonderfully exciting."

Travis grinned, set aside his cup and reached for her. He tumbled her down across his thighs, cradling her in his arms. "For your information, if you had accepted my blackmail offer, I wouldn't have worried about it all that much."

"No?" She kissed his throat.

"No. Next time you do something for my own good, consult with me first, okay?"

"Okay." She nuzzled his neck invitingly. "When's your next appointment?"

"I have no scheduled appointments this morning." Travis slid his hand up along her thigh, aware of the growing tautness in his lower body. Everything about this woman aroused him, he thought in wonder. He crushed a thick handful of red curls in his fist.

Juliana giggled. "Have you ever done it on the job, so to speak?"

"No." He grinned. "You?"

"Never."

"Sounds like we have some catching up to do."

He gently eased her up onto the desk so that she perched on the edge, facing him. Then he pushed the gray flannel skirt slowly up to her thighs. His fingers closed around her knees. Juliana had very nice knees, he thought. Beautifully rounded knees. Funny, he had never realized how attractive a woman's knees could be.

"Travis?" Her hand rested on his shoulders. Her topaz eyes gleamed.

"Yeah?"

"It wouldn't hurt once in a while if we sort of pretended you were blackmailing me into this, would it?"

He grinned wickedly and slowly spread her gorgeous knees apart. "I'm always willing to oblige a fantasy for you, sweetheart."

CHAPTER SIX

"JULIANA, this is a very serious situation. We are all gravely concerned about the implications. That's why we all decided to hold this family conference. We need to understand just what is going on."

"Sure, Mom. I understand. But everything's under control. Trust me." Juliana confronted the three serious faces around the table, sighed inwardly and then dug a spoon into her bowl of zesty black bean soup. Not a lot of trust in this little family group; just a lot of anxiety, she decided. The excellent California-style Mexican food provided here at the colorful shopping mall restaurant would have to serve as compensation for the doleful company she was obliged to endure.

When the invitation to lunch had come that morning, Juliana had tried to think of a polite excuse to refuse but there simply was no acceptable way to turn down her parents and Uncle Tony. Lunch this afternoon had been more or less a command performance.

"Tony and I have been over this whole thing a number of times," Roy Grant informed his daughter. He watched her closely through his bifocals, concern etched in the lines of his face. "We can't figure out what Sawyer is up to but there's no question but that it's got to be bad news for all of us."

"Damn right," Tony Grant chimed in, scowling at his plate, which was overflowing with a sour cream and chicken enchilada. "Sawyer is nothing but trouble. We all know that. He's after Flame Valley and he's going to take it one way or another. Spent five years setting us up. Can you believe it? *Five years.* Christ, the man holds a mean grudge, doesn't he?"

"We knew five years ago the situation could get dicey when

he found out Elly didn't want to marry him," Roy said. "Tried to pay him off then, but he wouldn't have any of it."

Juliana looked up. "As I understand it, the fee was supposed to have been a one-third interest in Flame Valley. Did you offer him that after Elly turned him down?"

"Hell, no," Tony exploded. "Couldn't go givin' away one-third of the place to someone outside of the family. For pity's sake, girl, where's your common sense? Flame Valley is a family thing. When the marriage was called off, that meant the deal was off, too. But Roy and I tried to compensate Sawyer. Wasn't like we just stiffed him completely."

"Uh-huh." Juliana helped herself to a handful of tortilla chips, dipping them into the salsa. "Did you actually offer him the cash equivalent of one-third of Flame Valley?"

Her mother's mouth tightened. "Of course not, dear. That would have meant giving him something in the neighborhood of close to a million dollars. We couldn't possibly have paid him or any other consultant that much in cash. But we did offer him a very reasonable consulting fee."

"The only thing wrong with the fee you offered was that it wasn't the fee that had been agreed to when he took the job."

Tony Grant turned red in the face. "It was just an understanding, not a signed contract, and it all hinged on his marrying Elly. That didn't work out, thank the good Lord. Whenever I think of how unhappy she would have been married to Sawyer, I get sick to my stomach. Hell, my stomach's upset right now."

Juliana rolled her eyes and munched chips. "I think that's the green chili sauce on your enchilada. You know it always upsets your stomach, Uncle Tony."

"Look, this is getting us nowhere," her father said brusquely. "Honey, we're not here to rehash the past. Right or wrong, what's done is done. It's the present we've got to worry about."

"But there's nothing to worry about, Dad." Juliana smiled soothingly. "I told you, it's all under control. Travis is working for me now. Because of his obligation to Charisma, he's agreed to try to salvage Flame Valley. He knows that if the resort goes under, I stand to lose a chunk of dough.''

"Darling, it makes no sense," Beth Grant said anxiously. "Why should Travis Sawyer do you any favors?"

"I told you why. Charisma is a client of Sawyer Management Systems. It's not a favor, it's a business arrangement."

"All those bloody investors in Fast Forward Properties are clients of his, too," Uncle Tony rumbled. "Bigger clients than Charisma, believe me. They'll come first and don't you forget it."

Juliana blushed. "All right, so maybe there's more to it than just Travis's sense of commitment to Charisma. Maybe he's doing it for me."

Her parents and Uncle Tony all stared at her, their mouths open. Beth Grant recovered first.

"For you? What do you mean, Juliana? What is going on here?"

"Well, if you must know, Mom, I'm hoping to marry the man one of these days. And I think he's kind of fond of me, too, although he's still shy about admitting it."

Her father looked appalled and then outraged. "Has that bastard led you down the garden path?"

"We're getting there," Juliana assured him.

"Damn it, girl, has he proposed to you?" Tony Grant blustered. "Is that what this is all about? Is he trying to make you a substitute for Elly in this blasted revenge business?"

"Well, no, Uncle Tony, he hasn't actually proposed yet, but I have great hopes."

Her mother leaned forward, topaz eyes deeply concerned. "Darling, surely you wouldn't be taken in by a proposal of marriage from that man? You're an old hand at dealing with proposals. Men propose to you all the time. They're never serious for long."

Juliana winced. "Thanks, Mom."

"Oh, dear, I didn't mean to hurt your feelings, but you know it's the truth. You've been collecting proposals since you were in college. Men are always asking you to marry them within about twenty-four hours of meeting you and then, about twenty-four hours after that, they change their minds.''

''And start looking for the nearest exit. Yeah, I know, Mom. A sad but true phenomenon. No doubt about it, I have a curious effect on men. I overpower them. But Travis is different. Nothing overpowers him.'' Juliana brightened. ''To tell you the truth, I consider it a good sign that he hasn't rushed into a proposal.''

''Why?'' Her father looked suspicious.

''Well, as Mom said, the others all do it within about twenty-four hours of meeting me. Travis is apparently giving the matter much thought, which means that when he does ask me, he'll be sure of what he's doing.'' Juliana smiled. ''But, then, Travis always knows what he's doing. He's always one step ahead.''

Uncle Tony pointed his fork at her from the other side of the table. ''You remember that, my girl. That man is always one step ahead of everyone. That's what makes him so dangerous.''

Juliana shook her head in exasperation. ''Just because he's fast and smart doesn't mean you can't trust him. I, for one, trust him completely. If anyone can save Flame Valley, he will.''

A sudden thrill of awareness caused Juliana to glance around. Travis was there behind her. She smiled in welcome as his large hand settled on her shoulder.

''Thanks for the vote of confidence, honey,'' Travis said.

''*Travis*. What are you doing here?''

''I called Charisma to see if you could get away for lunch. Sandy said you'd already been kidnapped and were being held for ransom here at the mall.'' Travis surveyed the glowering expressions of the other three people at the table. ''Thought I'd stop by and rescue you.''

''She don't need rescuing,'' Tony Grant muttered.

''Damn right,'' Roy Grant added grimly. ''My daughter can take care of herself.''

''She certainly can,'' Beth Grant said with maternal pride.

''Everybody needs rescuing once in a while,'' Travis said easily as he sat down next to Juliana and picked up a menu. ''I'm starving. Working on Flame Valley finances all morning is enough to give a man an appetite. Either that or make him slightly nauseous, depending on his point of view. Fortunately I've got a strong stomach. The resort's in a hell of a mess again, isn't it?''

Tony Grant blanched and then turned red. ''Pardon me,'' he muttered, pushing his chair back from the table. ''Got to get going if we're going to make it to San Diego this evening. Roy, you and Beth have a plane to catch.''

Beth rose to her feet and nodded at her husband. ''Yes, dear, we must run along.'' She frowned at Juliana. ''You will remember what we talked about?''

''Sure, Mom. Have a good trip back to San Francisco.''

With one last uncertain glance at Travis, Beth turned to follow her husband and brother-in-law out of the restaurant.

''Don't look now,'' Juliana said, ''but I think I just got stuck with the tab.''

''You can afford it. You've been making money hand over fist since the day you opened Charisma.''

''Does that mean I'm going to get to pay for your lunch, too?''

Travis closed the menu, looking thoughtful. ''It's customary for the client to pick up the consultant's expenses.''

''Oh.''

''Just how many marriage proposals have you collected since college, Juliana?''

Juliana blinked. ''Did a bit of eavesdropping, did you?''

''Couldn't help it. Everyone was so wrapped up in that little intimate family conversation, I hated to interrupt.''

''Forget my long and sordid history of collecting marriage proposals. None of them meant anything.''

''If you say so.''

TWO DAYS LATER Juliana again sat down to eat in a restaurant. This time she was alone with Travis.

''So how did the meeting with David go today?'' Juliana speared one of the pan-fried oysters on her plate and chewed with enthusiasm. The Treasure House always did this dish particularly well, she thought. When there was no immediate response from the other side of the table, her brows came together in a firm line. "Not good?"

"Let's just say that Kirkwood is not a happy camper at the moment." Travis ate his swordfish in a methodical fashion that did not indicate great enjoyment.

"You know, Travis, you've been in a rather difficult mood for the past couple of days," Juliana pointed out.

"I'm working eighteen hours a day trying to save that bloody resort, get my new office up and running, keep a lot of important clients happy and find some time to spend with you. What kind of mood do you expect me to be in?"

"Maybe going out to dinner tonight wasn't such a hot idea."

"It wasn't. I've got a pile of papers back at the office I should be going through even as we speak. But since eating out was my idea, I suppose I ought to keep my mouth shut."

"So how did the meeting with David go?"

"Like I said, he's not happy. I pointed out one possible way out of the mess and he didn't like it."

"What was that?"

"Find a buyer for Flame Valley. Maybe one of the big hotel chains. An outfit that will agree to pay off the resort's creditors and agree to let Kirkwood stay on as manager."

Juliana winced. "I can see why he didn't jump at that. The last thing he wants to do is sell the place. The whole point is to hang on to it." She paused, thinking of what her Uncle Roy had said at lunch two days earlier. "It's a family thing."

"He reminded me of that. Juliana, I have to tell you, there's a chance, a very real chance, that I won't be able to pull this off."

"You'll do it." She smiled at him with all the confidence she felt.

"Damn it, I wish you weren't so irrationally sure I can save the resort." Travis's impatience blazed in his eyes. "Oh, hell. Look, I don't really want to talk about Flame Valley tonight."

"All right. Want to talk about Charisma instead?" Juliana helped herself to the last oyster on her plate. "I've been thinking about adding a new line of mugs with the store logo on them.

Subliminal advertising, you see. Every time a customer uses one of them at home, he'd think of Charisma.''

"It's probably not a bad idea but right now I don't want to talk about it or anything else to do with Charisma.''

"Well, what do you want to talk about?'' she asked patiently as she forked up the remainder of her anchovy and garlic spiked salad.

"Us.''

"Us?'' She paused in midchew and eyed him intently. He definitely was in a strange mood tonight. "What about us?''

She watched Travis glance around the casually chic dining room. The place was filled with casually chic diners, casually chic ferns and a lot of waitpersons who could have modeled for magazine covers. Classic California restaurant style.

"Did you say Kirkwood brought you here the night he asked you to marry him?'' Travis asked.

"Yup. So did most of the others who have proposed since I arrived in Jewel Harbor.''

"How many would that be?''

She scowled at him. "Still after a number, hmm? Well, there really weren't that many. Two or three, at the most. I mean, you can hardly count the real estate agent who got me the lease for Charisma or the hunk who sold me my first espresso machine. They were very nice men, but extremely superficial. Salesmen types.''

"Uh-huh.''

"Look, Travis, I'm sorry about the fact that several men have asked me to marry them. I've explained before that none of them were serious for long.''

Travis smiled wryly. "You terrorized them all, didn't you?'' He reached for his wallet. "Come on, let's get out of here.''

"Where are we going?''

"For a walk.''

"At this time of night?''

"This isn't downtown L.A. It's Jewel Harbor, remember? I want to talk to you and I don't want to do it in here.'' Travis caught the waiter's eye and the young man came hurrying over to present the check.

Five minutes later Juliana allowed herself to be led outside the restaurant and down to the marina. For a while Travis strolled beside her in silence. It was a lovely evening, filled with soft breezes and the scent of the sea. Beneath Juliana's feet water slapped the wooden slats of the docks. The boats bobbed in their slips, and here and there cabin lights indicated owners who lived on board.

Travis took a seemingly aimless path that led them to the farthest row of slips. He paused finally and stood in brooding silence, staring out over the water.

Juliana tolerated the silence for a moment or two before her curiosity overcame her. "Why did you bring me out here, Travis?"

"To ask you to marry me." He didn't look at her. He seemed mesmerized by the dark horizon.

Juliana couldn't believe her ears. *"What?"*

"You said I had a month to come to my senses. I don't need a month. I've known for quite a while that I want to marry you. It was just that everything was so damned complicated. It still is, for that matter. Nothing has changed. But I'm tired of waiting for the right time. At the rate things are going with the resort, there may not be a right time."

"Travis, turn around and look at me. Are you serious? You want to marry me?"

He turned his head slowly, a faint smile curving his mouth. "I'm serious. I haven't had time to buy a ring, but I'm very serious."

"You're not going to change your mind within twenty-four hours like the others, are you?" In spite of her confidence in him, old habits died hard, Juliana discovered. She was instinctively cautious when it came to receiving marriage proposals.

"Juliana, I guarantee I'm not going to change my mind about wanting to marry you. Trust me."

She smiled tremulously. "I do."

"Do I get an answer tonight or are you going to make me suffer awhile?"

"Oh, Travis, how can you even ask such a silly question? Of course I'll marry you. I practically asked you first, remember?"

"I remember."

Elation seized Juliana as she studied his face in the soft light. She couldn't recall a happier moment in her whole life.

"I'm sorry about the anchovy and garlic on the salad," she said as she hurtled toward him, her face raised for his kiss.

"Juliana, no, wait…"

It was too late. Normally there would have been no problem. Travis was getting used to catching Juliana's full weight against his body. But tonight the dock under his feet was bobbing precariously and he was caught off balance when she went flying into his arms.

At the last possible instant Juliana realized that disaster loomed. She clutched at Travis, her eyes widening in startled dismay as she felt him stagger back a step. She tried to catch her own balance but one of her two-inch heels got caught between the dock slats.

Travis groaned in resignation as they both went over the edge of the walkway, landing with a splash in the waters of the marina.

Juliana surfaced a few seconds later, spitting salt water out of her mouth. Her hair had been instantly transformed into a wet, tangled mop. She could feel the weight of her clothing dragging at her.

"Travis? Where are you?" She turned quickly, searching for him.

"Right here," he said from behind her, splashing softly as he made his way back toward the dock.

Juliana whipped around in time to see him plant both hands on the edge of the dock and haul himself out of the water. Juliana smiled up at him, vastly relieved. "Thank goodness. Are you all right?"

"I'll survive." Sitting on the edge of the dock he reached down to grab her hand. "I should have known that the simple task of asking you to marry me would turn into an adventure in Wonderland. By rights I ought to charge you hazardous duty pay.''

"Just add it on to your usual fee, Mr. Sawyer.''

HIS USUAL FEE. Much later that night as he lay awake in bed beside Juliana, Travis reflected that for his usual fee, he usually produced results. This time he was not at all certain he could satisfy the client.

And he wondered if an engagement ring would be strong enough to hold Juliana if he failed to save Flame Valley Inn.

He couldn't seem to escape the premonition of disaster that hovered over him these days. In an effort to fight it off he turned on his side and gathered Juliana more tightly into his arms. She came to him willingly, fitting herself instinctively against him. After a while Travis was able to find sleep.

JULIANA LOUNGED BACK in her squeaking desk chair, her booted feet propped on the edge of her desk and cheerfully chewed out her supplier who was late on a delivery.

"No, Melvin, I do not want a double shipment of the regular Sumatra. I want the aged stuff. I can tell the difference, so don't try to con me. I've got standards to uphold, remember?''

"You don't even like coffee,'' the man on the other side of the line complained good-naturedly.

"That doesn't mean I don't know how to taste it. By the way, how are you doing getting me another batch of those good Guatemalan beans? I'm using them in my new house blend.''

"I'm trying, Juliana, I'm trying. The two estates I usually buy from have cut back shipments for a while. Weather problems. How are you doing with the decaffeinated blends?''

"Going like hotcakes. Although why anyone would want to drink decaffeinated coffee defeats me. Seems sort of pointless. I mean, why drink the stuff at all if you're not going for the caffeine jolt? Say, Melvin?''

"Yeah?''

"You know anything about buying tea?''

"Sure. Tea is a staple sideline in my business. Why? You interested in adding a line of tea there at the shop?"

"I'm thinking about it. Actually, I was thinking about opening a whole shop devoted to tea."

"Forget it. There aren't enough tea drinkers around here to keep you in business. Try adding tea there at Charisma as a sideline before you go off the deep end."

"I'll discuss it with my new business partner."

"Partner? You've got a partner now? That's a surprise. I thought you liked owning Charisma lock, stock and barrel."

"The new partner is my fiancé," Juliana confided, feeling smug. She studied the toe of her lizard skin boots. The exotic footwear went nicely with the yoked and pleated pastel jeans and the snappy little bolero jacket she had on today.

There was silence on the other end of the line. "I don't know, Juliana. I'm not so sure it's a good idea to mix business and marriage. Just look at me. I've been through three wives. Gave them all a piece of my business. Every time I got a divorce I got wiped out financially and had to start over again."

"You should have paid as much attention to your wives as you do to your coffee-importing business," Juliana chided. She glanced out the door of her office and spotted a familiar dark-haired woman entering the shop. "Look, I've got to run. See what you can do about the aged Sumatra, okay? And the Guatemalan stuff. As a favor to me, Melvin."

"Juliana, if I do you any more favors I'll probably go out of business."

"Just be sure you leave me a list of other coffee importers I can go to if you go under."

"You're a hard-hearted woman, Juliana Grant."

"I'm a businesswoman, Melvin. Just trying to make a living and keep the customer satisfied. Talk to you later."

Juliana slid her feet off the desk and recradled the phone as she stood up. She hurried out of the office and hailed the woman who had just come into the shop.

"Angelina. Just the person I want to see."

Angelina Cavanaugh smiled from the other side of the counter. Her aristocratic Spanish ancestry was evident in her fine dark eyes and the sleek brown hair she wore in a classic chignon. "Good morning, Juliana. How are you today?"

"Great."

Sandy grinned. "Be careful, Angelina. She's finally cornered her man. She's brought him to his knees and she's still wallowing in her victory."

Angelina laughed in delight as Sandy handed her a small cup of intense, dark espresso. "Is that true, Juliana? You got a proposal out of your business consultant?"

Matt leaned over the counter conspiratorially. "It wasn't easy. Sawyer told me this morning just how it happened. She tripped the poor guy, got him off balance and threw him into the marina. He said that by the time he surfaced, he knew he was finished. He decided to surrender before she tried something more drastic."

"That," proclaimed Juliana, "is a gross distortion of events."

"Hey," said Matt, "I got the story from the victim, himself."

"Never mind him, Angelina. Come over here and sit down. I want to talk to you about the engagement party and wedding plans. Have you got room for me on your client list?"

Angelina's bright red lips curved in a smile. "Angelina's Perfect Weddings always has room for one more client, not that we aren't quite busy, what with repeat clients."

"This wedding will be a one-time event," Juliana declared.

"That's what they all say until the divorce. Have you set a date?"

Juliana frowned. "Not for the wedding. Travis is very busy right now with, uh, other matters. But I don't see any reason why I can't go ahead and schedule the engagement party on my own. Travis won't mind."

"Are you thinking of a major event?"

"Are you kidding?" Juliana chuckled in anticipation. "I'm pulling out all the stops. I want Travis to have the wedding of his dreams, and that includes the perfect engagement party."

"I see," Angelina drawled. "And have you checked with Travis to find out just exactly what his dreams entail?"

Juliana waved that aside. "I told you, he's very busy these days. I'll take care of the wedding and engagement party details for him."

Matt, eavesdropping unabashedly, nearly choked. "Poor Travis. And he thought getting dunked in the marina was the end of his problems."

"Ignore him, Angelina. How do you like the espresso?"

"It's wonderful. Full-bodied and distinctive flavor. Very rich and strong."

"Yeah, it'll put hair on your chest, all right," Juliana agreed. "Have another cup while I start making some notes on the engagement party. Sandy," she called across the room, "fix me a cup of tea, will you, please? I hid a tin of English Breakfast behind the counter this morning."

TRAVIS, his sleeves rolled up to the elbows, his tie loosened and his shirt rumpled, regarded the man who sat across the overflowing desk.

"There just aren't a lot of options, Kirkwood. You've been teetering on the edge of bankruptcy for months and you know it. I'm telling you, the best I can do is try to find a buyer for the inn."

"No, damn it." David leaped to his feet and paced to the window. His expression was haggard. "I told you selling out is not an option. I can't sell the inn. Just call off your wolves and buy me some breathing space."

"Breathing space isn't going to do you any good." Travis flicked a pile of papers that all spelled impending disaster. "I might be able to stall my investors but that still leaves the banks you've been dealing with. It also leaves you needing cash. A lot of it. Even if I can get my group to hold off for a few months, which is unlikely, there's no way in hell I can ask them to pour more money into your operation."

"Fast Forward is your company. You told me yourself, you make the investment decisions."

"I do. But I've got obligations to my backers. I've made certain commitments that have to be met."

David looked back over his shoulder, his eyes intent. "I can't sell the inn, Sawyer. Even if you can dig up a buyer at this late date, I just can't sell out."

Travis studied him in silence for a minute. "Because of Elly?" he finally asked quietly.

David turned back to the view of the harbor. A deep sigh escaped his chest. "Yes. Because of Elly. I've made a lot of commitments, too, Sawyer. Told her I was going to make the resort the biggest and best on the coast. Told her I'd keep it in the family, just like her Daddy wanted. Told her she'd always be proud of it. I don't think she'll ever forgive me if I lose it."

"What will Elly do if you can't keep your promises?"

"I don't know."

"You think she'll leave you? Is that what you're afraid of?"

"Shut up, Sawyer. You worry about saving the inn. I'll worry about my marriage, okay?"

"Whatever you say. But you'd better get it through your head that I may not be able to save the inn."

David hesitated and then said under his breath. "And I may not be able to save my marriage."

There was another moment of silence. "It looks like we'd better get back to work," Travis said eventually.

Fifteen minutes later he looked up again. "Did I tell you I'm engaged to Juliana?"

David reluctantly dragged his gaze away from an accounts journal he had been studying. "What's that?"

"I said, I've asked Juliana to marry me."

David smiled slowly. "Are you sure that's the way it happened? You asked her? She didn't ask you?"

"As I recall, she told me I had a month to ask her properly. I did so last night and she rewarded me by pushing me into the water at the marina."

"Very romantic. I hope you know what you're getting into."

"So do I." Travis smiled to himself as he remembered Juliana sending them both into the harbor the previous night.

"You're doing this for Juliana, aren't you?" David asked. "Not because you're her business consultant, but because you want her to marry you and you know that if you destroy the inn, you'll lose her."

Travis shrugged and went back to his papers.

"Be a little weird if this turns out to be an instant replay of five years ago. Maybe Juliana is leading you on, getting you to save the inn and planning to dump you once Flame Valley is in the clear."

"That's enough, Kirkwood."

"You know, it's obvious to me that you would have been all wrong for Elly and she would have been wrong for you," David said conversationally.

Travis put down his pencil and folded his elbows on the desk. "Yeah?"

"Yeah." David waited, his eyes full of challenge.

"I'll tell you something, Kirkwood. You're right. Elly and I would have been all wrong for each other. And I'll tell you something else."

"What's that?"

"You and Juliana would have been a damned bad mismatch, too." Travis picked up his pencil and then reached out for the phone.

"Who are you calling?"

"An eccentric old venture capitalist I know. Tough as nails. Got money coming out his ears and no one to spend it on. Thrives on a challenge. Sometimes he'll go for something off the wall that no one else will touch."

"I told you, I don't want to sell the inn," David said angrily.

"I'm not going to try to sell this to him," Travis explained. "I'm going to see if I can talk him into paying off your biggest creditors and pour some cash into the resort."

David's expression lightened. "Think he'll go for it?"

"No, but it can't hurt to ask. We're running out of options."

Travis concentrated on the phone. "This is Travis Sawyer," he said when a pleasant voice came on the line. "Tell Sam Bickerstaff I'd like to talk to him for a few minutes, please.... Yeah, I'll wait."

ELLY FLEW through the door of Charisma Espresso shortly after lunch. She plowed through the standing-room-only crowd of coffee aficionados, searching the place until she spotted Juliana.

Juliana saw her cousin approaching and knew immediately she had heard about the engagement. Elly looked stricken.

"*Juliana*. Juliana, I just heard. Oh, my God, how could you do it? You don't know what you're doing."

"I always know what I'm doing, Elly, you know that. Everybody knows that. Now calm down. Here, I'll have Sandy make you a nice latte. You like her lattes. You can drink it in my office."

Five minutes later with Elly cradling the cup of steamed milk and coffee in her hands, the two women shut the door of Juliana's office and sat down.

"All right," Elly said tensely. "Tell me first of all if it's true. Are you engaged to Travis?"

"It's true," Juliana said cheerfully. "How did you hear about it? I was going to call you this evening. In fact, what are you doing here in Jewel Harbor? Surely you didn't feel compelled to race all the way into town just because you got the word about my engagement."

"David has an appointment with Travis today. I came with him into town. I just saw him at lunch a few minutes ago and he told me Travis is claiming he's engaged to you. Juliana, how did that happen?"

"Well, it wasn't easy, I can tell you that. Travis has been so busy what with all this business with the resort. But last night..."

"I knew it, he coerced you into sleeping with him but that wasn't enough to satisfy his ego, was it? Oh, no. He had to go all the way and trick you into an engagement." Elly shook her head sadly. "He really is trying to duplicate the past except that this time around he's using you instead of me."

Juliana smiled a little grimly. "You know me well enough to realize I wouldn't have gotten engaged to a man unless I was in love with him. Look how much practice I've had gracefully declining marriage proposals. Now stop carrying on about how I'm being suckered in a revenge plot and let's get on to a more interesting subject."

"Like what?"

"My wedding." Juliana scrabbled around on her desk, uncovering two hefty tomes she had picked up at the Jewel Harbor Library.

Elly blanched at the sight of the books on wedding etiquette. "You can't. Juliana, please. Think about this. Don't rush into anything. You mustn't set yourself up like this. He's only using you. He has no intention of marrying you."

"I talked to Angelina Cavanaugh this morning. Remember her? She has that wedding business in town. She gave me a booklet to read and recommended these books. The first step is the engagement party. I was thinking of something spiffy at The Treasure House. They have a special room they rent out for catered events."

"Juliana, this is insane. Listen to me, he won't go through with it. He just wants revenge and he'll get it by leading you on and then dumping you when he finally takes over Flame Valley."

Juliana opened one of the etiquette guides. "He's working to save the inn, remember?"

"I don't believe it," Elly whispered. "I know David believes him, but I don't. It's all a game with Travis. A game of vengeance. Neither of you know him. Ask your folks or my father. They know Travis for what he is. They know how dangerous he can be. They heard him vow revenge five years ago."

"People change," Juliana said easily.

"God. I feel like Cassandra calling out a warning that no one will heed."

Juliana nodded in commiseration. "Always a frustrating role."

"It's not funny," Elly flared. "This is serious. Very serious. Right now Travis is feeding David all sorts of nonsense about getting another investor involved in the inn. Somebody named Bickerstaff. That's all we need. Another creditor. Oh, Juliana, what are we going to do? It's such a mess.''

"Travis will straighten things out. Now about my engagement party. I think I want a buffet affair with lots of yummy goodies rather than a sit-down dinner. And it would be fun to have a band, don't you think? I wonder if Travis knows how to dance.''

"I can't stand it. Nobody will listen to me.'' Elly put aside her cup of latte, covered her eyes with her fingers and wept. Juliana sighed and reached for a tissue. She handed the tissue to her cousin as she got to her feet.

"Here, Elly. Dry your eyes. I'll be right back.''

"Where are you going?'' Elly asked, lifting her tear-stained face.

"To get you a cup of tea. When the chips are down, a good cup of tea is infinitely better for the nerves than a cup of coffee.''

Juliana walked back into the office a few minutes later, tea in hand and found that Elly had, indeed, managed to stop the flow of tears.

"Thank you,'' Elly mumbled as she took the tea.

"Feel better?''

Elly nodded, sipping daintily at the brew. "I'm sorry to be so emotional but I'm frightened, Juliana.''

"I can see that. But you're worrying yourself sick over nothing. Everything's going to be all right. Travis is going to save the inn and give you and David a second chance with it. You'll see.''

"But what if he doesn't? Even if he's not deliberately plotting against us, he might not be able to save it. David hinted at that much today. Juliana, I'm scared about what will happen if we lose Flame Valley.''

Juliana drummed her nails on the desk. "It would be unfortunate, but it would not be the end of the world, Elly.''

"It might be the end of my marriage.''

"Oh, come on now.''

"I mean it, Juliana. David's been acting tense lately. Not like his usual self at all.''

"He's worried about the inn. We all are."

"It's more than that." Elly looked up from the steaming tea. "If we lose the Flame Valley, I might lose David."

Juliana sat very still. "That's ridiculous. Why do you say that?"

"He wanted the resort very badly back in the beginning. You know that, Juliana." Elly's voice was a mere thread of sound.

"I know he's been interested in it right from the start. He's thoroughly enjoyed running the place and planning for its future," Juliana agreed carefully. "But..."

"Sometimes I think that he married me to get Flame Valley...."

"Elly. How can you say such a thing? It's not true. It's absolutely not possible. I was there when you two met, and I was there when you realized you were in love, remember? In fact, I realized the two of you were in love before either one of you admitted it to each other."

"We tried so hard to hide our feelings, didn't we? Even from ourselves," Elly recalled wistfully. "We didn't want to hurt you, Juliana."

"I'm well aware of that. Now pay attention. David cares very deeply about you. One of the reasons he cares so much about Flame Valley is because he knows how important it is to you. It's the legacy your father wants you to have, and David feels obliged to hold on to it for you at all costs."

"I tell myself that over and over again, but lately I've begun to wonder. And now I realize that a part of me has always wondered. Ever since..."

"Ever since what, Elly?"

"You have to remember that I just narrowly escaped being married once before because of the inn. To Travis Sawyer. I guess I'm sensitive on the subject."

Juliana narrowed her eyes and studied her cousin. "It's no wonder women occasionally question the motives of the male of the species," she observed. "We've all been burned a few times. But women are born to take risks. You know what they say—no guts, no glory."

Elly smiled mistily. "Juliana, you're incredible."

Juliana smiled and picked up another piece of paper she'd been studying earlier. "Now, about the engagement party menu. What do you think about having those little rounds of marinated goat cheese wrapped in grape leaves?"

"Nobody actually likes goat cheese, Juliana. They just eat it because it's trendy."

"Being trendy is an excellent reason for including goat cheese. Besides, believe it or not, I like it."

Elly's brows rose. "And it is your party, isn't it?"

"Right."

CHAPTER SEVEN

THAT EVENING Travis turned the key in the lock of Juliana's front door and was amazed at the quiet sense of pleasure he experienced in the small, mundane act. Another day was over and he felt as if he were home. It was true he had not yet officially moved in with Juliana, but he was spending so many nights here, he might as well do so. He could smell something savory in the oven, and he knew his redheaded lady would be waiting on the other side of the door with a glass of wine in her hand.

What more could a man ask, he wondered as he stepped into the white-tiled hall and set down his heavy briefcase. If only he didn't have to worry about how long he would be able to claim these small, vital treasures.

"I'm home." Travis listened carefully to the words as he said them. Not quite the whole truth and they might never be the whole truth, but he liked the sound of them anyway.

"Be right there," Juliana called from the kitchen.

Travis walked through the living room, picking up the evening paper that was lying on the coffee table. He scanned the headlines and then glanced up as Juliana appeared in the kitchen doorway. He smiled slowly.

She was holding a glass of wine in one hand and a spatula in the other. Her hair was caught up in a high shower of curls and she was wearing a Charisma Espresso apron over her pastel jeans. He saw that she had removed the lizard-skin boots she had put on that morning and replaced them with a pair of fluffy pink slippers. The slippers had bunny faces in front and a pouf of a bunny tale at the ankles. Juliana had once carefully explained to him that the silly looking slippers had something called "a charming wittiness.'' Whatever it was, they still looked like dead rabbits to Travis.

''You seem exhausted,'' Juliana announced. She came forward, and because she wasn't wearing heels, had to go up on her toes to give him a kiss as she put the wineglass in his hand.

Travis felt her tongue tease his bottom lip and he groaned as his body reacted immediately. ''I am exhausted. But I know my duty and I'm sure that, with the right stimulus, I can manage to get in a quickie with you before dinner.''

''Absolutely not,'' Juliana said with mock horror. ''Married people save it until after dinner.''

''We're not married yet,'' he complained, following her into the warm, fragrant kitchen.

''We have to start practicing. Besides, I don't dare leave this walnut and blue-cheese sauce just now, and the corn bread would certainly burn if I surrendered to your lecherous ways.''

''I take it back. Maybe I am too exhausted. What a day.'' Travis, newspaper still in hand, sat down at the cozy little breakfast table and took a sip of wine.

''Another meeting with David, right?''

''If you can call it that. I have to tell you, Juliana, I can see now why Flame Valley is on the brink of collapse. Even I didn't realize how easy it was going to be to take over the inn. Kirkwood is pigheaded stubborn in some areas. No wonder he's in trouble.''

''He's stubborn in areas that have to do with Elly, and the resort has a lot to do with Elly.''

''Yeah, I'm beginning to see the problem. Any man who lets his business decisions be dictated by his need to please a woman is setting himself up for a—'' Travis broke off abruptly as he realized what he was saying.

Juliana batted her eyelashes outrageously. ''Yes, dear? What was that about basing one's business decisions on the need to please a woman?''

Travis felt a rueful smile tug at his lips. ''All right, so the poor jerk and I have something in common besides the fact that we both proposed to you.''

"You'd better not have too much in common. I don't want to catch you running off with a petite blonde."

"Not a chance. I'm only interested in redheads these days. Tall redheads who know how to cook." Travis paused, eyeing her thoughtfully as he remembered Kirkwood's fear of losing his wife as well as the inn. "Did it hurt a lot?"

"Did what hurt a lot?" Juliana asked, concentrating on the sauce.

"When Kirkwood left you for Elly?"

"Well, it wasn't the high point of my emotional life, I'll say that much. But by the time it happened, I was more or less prepared for it. I'd seen it coming before either of them did. Whenever they were in the same room together there was a certain electrical charge in the air. They both just sort of hummed with it. I envied the force of the attraction but I knew from the beginning I couldn't duplicate it. Not with David, at any rate."

"So you just let him go and wished them well?"

"That's me. Gracious, even in defeat," she agreed brightly.

"Is that so? Funny, the word *gracious* never came to mind the night you threw guacamole dip all over me." Travis smiled at the memory.

"That was different," she retorted.

"Was it?"

"Darn right. I could see early on I'd made a mistake thinking David was the right man for me. But I learn from my mistakes, and this time around I was sure I had picked the right man. It really annoyed me when I discovered you hadn't had the same blinding realization."

"Oh, I'd had it. Sort of," Travis mused, thinking about it. "But there was the business with Flame Valley and a big chunk of the past in the way. Blinding realizations sometimes take a while to clarify themselves. Juliana?"

"Umm?" She frowned over the cheese sauce and stirred ferociously.

"If things turned sour again between us, would you fight for me a little harder than you fought for Kirkwood? I don't think I want you being gracious in defeat in my case."

She didn't look up from the thickening sauce. As she stirred frantically with one hand, she tossed a huge handful of pasta into a pan of boiling water with the other. "If I ever catch you hanging out with petite blondes, I'll nail your hide to the office door. There. How's that for feminine machismo?"

"Very reassuring," Travis murmured and wished the situation with Flame Valley Inn was as simple and straightforward as dealing with a petite blonde would have been.

"Did you and David make any progress today?" Juliana asked, changing the subject as she scooped the pot of cheese sauce off the burner.

"Not much. He's in worse shape than I thought and that's saying something. I played a long shot and called a guy named Bickerstaff. Offered him the wonderful opportunity of paying off the inn's creditors and pouring a ton of cash into the place. In exchange, I promised to guide the restructuring of Flame Valley and personally guarantee to get the present owner back on his feet."

Juliana smiled, looked very pleased. "Good idea. I knew you were the resourceful type. Did this Bickerstaff go for it?"

"He said he'd consider it and get back to me."

"What does that mean?"

"Knowing Bickerstaff, it means he'll consider it and get back to me."

"Oh." Juliana chewed on her lower lip as she emptied the cheese sauce into a bowl. "It sounds like a good idea to me. And you can be very convincing. I'll bet he goes for it."

Travis shook his head, sighing to himself over Juliana's irrepressible faith in his business acumen. "Don't hold your breath. I'm not. Bickerstaff likes a calculated risk, but he didn't get where he is by playing real long shots."

"We'll see." Juliana opened the oven door and a tantalizing aroma wafted through the kitchen. She bent over to get the pan of golden corn bread out of the oven. "Ready to eat?"

Travis took another swallow of wine and studied the sight of Juliana's pastel jeans pulled taut over the full curve of her derriere.

"Starved," he said. "Let me know if you want me to do anything."

"No, not tonight. You've been working too hard lately as it is." She straightened with the pan of steaming corn bread in hand.

"You know, Juliana, I have to tell you that you really have a terrific gluteus maximus. World class, in fact."

"Why, thank you. That only goes to show you can find something nice to say about anyone if you try hard enough. To be honest, I think yours is rather cute, too." She busied herself getting dinner on the table. "Did I tell you I had a nice chat with the lady who's going to help me plan our engagement party and wedding?"

The wine slopped precariously in Travis's glass, and his stomach, which had been relaxing nicely, tightened abruptly. "No, you didn't tell me. Isn't that moving a little fast? You just agreed to marry me last night."

"No point waiting, is there?"

"Uh, no. I guess not." He felt dazed. What would happen if she actually married him before he found out if he could save the inn? Travis wondered.

"We'll need to start putting together a guest list. Start jotting down names as you think of them, okay?"

Travis reflected briefly, trying to catch up with her. "I don't have any names to jot down."

"Don't be silly. Of course you do."

"Can't think of anyone to invite. Well, maybe the staff here at the new office. That's about it."

"Just your staff?" Juliana gave him a severe glance as she sat down across from him and began slicing corn bread. "What about your parents, for heaven's sake?"

He shrugged, his mind on the corn bread as he watched her transfer a chunk to his plate. He hadn't had homemade corn bread in years. "I don't see any point in you going out of your way to invite my folks. They didn't bother to come to my last wedding."

Juliana's hand froze over the corn bread. Her gaze collided with his, her topaz eyes full of demanding questions. "You've been married before?" she got out in a throaty whisper.

"It was a long time ago." Travis massaged the back of his neck, aware he hadn't handled the announcement very well. He certainly hadn't meant to drop it on her like this. He wasn't thinking clearly tonight. Too tired, probably. Lord, he was exhausted. "Back in my early twenties. It was a mistake. Didn't last long."

"What happened? Who was she? Where is she now? Are there any kids? Exactly how long were you married? And why didn't your parents come to the wedding?"

Travis wondered why he hadn't kept his mouth shut. He really didn't feel like going into all this tonight. But it was too late now. "Jeannie and I were married less than a year. She was a secretary at the firm where I got my first job. There was a slight misunderstanding on both our parts. I thought she wanted to build a successful future with me. She thought I could make her forget her first husband."

"What happened?"

Travis took a big bite of corn bread. "She went back to her first husband. I left the firm to go out on my own. Turned out we both made the right decision."

"Kids?"

"No kids. There's nothing more to the story than that, Juliana. It was over a long time ago."

"Why didn't your parents come to the wedding? Did you elope?"

"No."

"Didn't your folks approve of your intended bride?"

"They never even met her. Approval wasn't the problem. Neither Mom nor Dad showed up at the wedding because each knew I had invited the other."

Juliana frowned. "I don't get it."

Travis helped himself to more corn bread. "They divorced when I was fourteen. It was a very bitter separation and neither one has been able to say a civil word to or about the other since the legal proceedings were final. Not that they had too much to say to each other before the divorce, either. When I invited them to my wedding, each wanted to know if the other had been invited.''

"Oh, dear." Juliana's eyes filled with sympathy.

"When I said yes, my mother made it clear she would not attend unless I promised to disinvite my father. And my father made the same stipulation. I refused to be put in the middle like that and they both got even by not attending the wedding.''

"Oh, Travis, that's terrible. They put you in a terrible position. Of course you couldn't not invite one or the other. Didn't they realize that? Didn't they realize how that would make you feel?''

"I don't think my feelings came into the matter," Travis said dryly. "They were both too wrapped up in their own emotions. Always were. I hated the weekends I spent with Dad because he always told me what a lousy mother I had and when I got back to Mom she always grilled me on what my father was doing and who he was dating.''

Juliana grimaced. "How awful."

"Not that uncommon in this day and age, and we both know it. Frankly, it was easier on everyone not to have either of my parents show up at my first wedding, and I think I can safely promise the same thing this time around. Don't bother inviting my side of the family, honey.''

"Do you have any brothers or sisters?"

"A couple of stepbrothers and two stepsisters. I don't know them very well. Mom and Dad both remarried soon after the divorce and started new families. But I left for college three and a half years after they split up, so I didn't spend much time with my new baby brothers and sisters. The only time I was invited to get involved in their lives was when each of my parents asked me to make a contribution toward their college funds.''

Juliana wrinkled her nose. "Which you did, I bet."

"Sure. Why not? I can afford it and they all know it. I'm still picking up the tab on three of them. The oldest graduated last year and got a job at a company where I know a few people.''

"And everyone just lets you do it? Lets you finance your step-brothers' and sisters' educations and lets you help find them all jobs? Yet they can't be bothered to come to your weddings?"

"I believe picking up the college costs is seen as my contri-bution to the family. Everybody definitely agrees I'm the one in a position to handle it financially. And what the hell, they're right. Look, don't go wasting a lot of sympathy on this, okay? It's not worth it. Are you going to let that cheese sauce congeal or are you going to serve it over the pasta?"

Juliana gasped and leaped to her feet. "Good grief, the pasta. I forgot about it. It's going to be soggy mush. I can't stand over-cooked pasta. It's no good if it isn't *al dente*."

"The cheese sauce isn't too bad over the corn bread," Travis said, running an experiment on his plate.

"Travis," Juliana said from the sink where she was dumping the pasta into a colander, "I want you to give me the addresses of your parents. I really think we should invite them, regardless of what they did the last time you got married. After all, that was a long time ago. They've probably mellowed by now."

"I doubt it, but do what you want."

"Do you ever see your parents?"

"Once in a while. I call them on their birthdays and they call me on mine, and I've managed a few short visits over the years. Which is sufficient for all concerned."

"Why do you say that?"

Travis helped himself to more corn bread and conducted an-other experiment with the cheese sauce. "After they remarried, my folks concentrated most of their attention on their new fami-lies. They both wanted to make fresh starts, I think."

Juliana's eyes widened as realization struck. "But you were a reminder of the past, weren't you? You were the living evidence of their failure. They probably felt guilty about the way they'd torn your world apart and made you witness their battles for so many years. It's easier not to have to face people who make you feel guilty."

"I think it was definitely a relief to all concerned when I left for college. The interesting thing,'' Travis said thoughtfully as he poured more cheese sauce over the corn bread, ''was that they turned out to be fairly good parents the second time around, at least as far as I can tell. My stepbrothers and stepsisters seem happy and well adjusted. And my parents' second marriages seem to have worked out.''

''Ouch. Darn it.'' Juliana turned on the cold water faucet and held a finger in the spray.

Travis glanced at her with concern. ''What happened? Burn yourself?''

''Just a little. It's all right,'' Juliana said quickly. ''I'll be over there in a minute. I think we lucked out. The pasta isn't too squishy after all.''

''AFTER THEY REMARRIED, they concentrated most of their attention on their new families.''

Travis's laconic explanation of why he wasn't very close to his parents echoed through Juliana's mind that night as she sat in bed waiting for him to emerge from the bathroom. It was clear to her that after the divorce and remarriage of his parents, Travis had been left out in the cold. He had not become a real part of either of the new families.

A few years later, his first marriage had ended in divorce when his wife had gone back to her first husband.

Five years ago his engagement had ended when his fiancée had used him to help her family and then called off the engagement.

All things considered, Juliana decided, Travis had not had a particularly good experience with family life. He'd always been the one left out. He was never the one chosen when choices had to be made—never a real member of a family. But people were quite willing to use him when it suited their purposes.

The bathroom door opened and Travis strolled out with a towel around his hips. He yawned and Juliana decided he was enormously sexy, even when he was yawning. He looked like a big, sleek wild animal that had somehow wandered into her very civilized white-on-white bedroom.

Travis saw her looking at him. His eyes glinted. "Still think I'm too short?"

"There are compensations," Juliana declared loftily. She put down the book she had been reading. "I called Melvin today."

"The guy who supplies your coffee?"

"Right. I asked him if he could supply the shop with tea, too. He said yes."

"Uh-huh." Travis did not look overly interested in the conversation. He rubbed the back of his neck as he walked toward the bed.

Juliana plunged ahead with enthusiasm. "I've been thinking about getting into tea in a big way. Travis, have you ever noticed that there are zillions of espresso shops and coffee houses opening all along the coast clear to the state of Washington, but no tea shops?"

"There's a reason for that," Travis explained as he slung the towel over a chair. "The money's in coffee, not tea. Nobody drinks tea."

"That's not true. I drink tea. Lots of people drink tea." Juliana was momentarily sidetracked by the sight of Travis's nude body. "And I'll bet there are thousands of people just like me."

"Closet tea drinkers? I doubt it." He pulled back the covers and slid into bed beside her.

"We aren't closet tea drinkers, we just tend not to drink a lot of tea in public because it's so hard to get it properly made in restaurants. Wimpy tea bags plopped into lukewarm water don't cut it for a real tea enthusiast. Most tea drinkers drink coffee when they're out rather than pay for bad tea."

"What's your point?" Travis plumped up his pillows and leaned back against them. He reached for a stack of papers he'd left on the nightstand.

"My point is that if tea drinkers knew they could get properly made tea at a certain place, they would go there and order it. Tons of it. They'd buy it in bulk to take home with them. They would experiment with different teas of the world and enjoy them the way coffee drinkers enjoy coffee."

Travis scanned the figures in front of him, frowning intently. "You want to add a tea option at Charisma? No problem. Go ahead and do it."

"Travis, you don't understand. I don't want to just put in a line of tea at Charisma. I'm going for the whole enchilada. I've been thinking about this for several months now and I've decided to open a shop devoted entirely to tea. The first in a chain."

"No, you're not." Travis didn't even bother to look up from his paperwork.

"Now, Travis, I'm serious about this. The tea shops would be a first around here."

"And a last because everyone around here drinks coffee. You'd lose your shirt, and right now, Juliana, you cannot afford to lose a single dime. Believe me, I'm in a position to know."

"We'd push for the upscale crowd, the same way we do at Charisma. We'd make tea drinking trendy. We'd serve power teas to business people and their clients, and we'd package a whole line of tea under our own label."

Travis grunted and finally raised his eyes from his paperwork as the enthusiastic determination in her voice finally sank in. He glanced at her nightstand. "You've been reading that book again, haven't you?"

Juliana looked at him innocently. "What book?"

"That book about the Boston tea heiress whose ancestor was a witch. Leaves of something-or-other by Linda What's-her-face. I saw it on your nightstand earlier."

"*Leaves of Fortune* by Linda Barlow," Juliana corrected automatically. "It's a great story and it's given me all sorts of ideas, Travis."

"It's given you delusions of grandeur. You are not going to make your fortune in tea, Juliana. Fancy coffee is where the future is and you're perfectly positioned with Charisma to take advantage of it. As your consultant and partner I'm not about to let you fritter away your money and energy chasing an unrealistic business goal."

"I've been giving this a lot of thought," Juliana persisted. She broke off as Travis began rubbing the back of his neck again. "What's wrong?"

"Nothing. I'm just a little stiff and sore from sitting hunched over four years' worth of Kirkwood's income tax forms all day." Travis eased himself into a slightly different position on the pillows.

Juliana pushed back the covers. "Turn over on your stomach and I'll rub your back for you."

He hesitated and then shrugged. "It's a deal."

Travis rolled onto his stomach, sighing heavily as Juliana straddled his thighs. The long skirts of her frothy French nightgown flowed around his lean hips.

The muscles of his back were sleek, strong and well defined, she thought as she leaned forward to begin working on his shoulders. Very sexy, very masculine. She could feel the rough hair on his legs against her soft inner thighs. She adjusted her position, settling herself more firmly.

"No fair wriggling." Travis's voice was muffled in the pillow.

"Sorry." Juliana applied herself to the massage, easing the tension in Travis's shoulders and neck with smooth, deep movements.

"Lord, that feels good. If you'd told me you could give a massage like this I probably would have asked you to marry me the first day I met you."

"I wanted you to admire my brain, not my brawn. Now, about my tea shop idea. I've been going over a lot of different aspects of the project lately and I've come up with a basic plan. When you've got some free time I'll lay it out for you. It's going to work, Travis. I know it is."

Travis said nothing. Encouraged by the lack of a negative response, Juliana kept talking as she massaged. Slowly the hard muscles beneath her palms relaxed. As she stroked the strong contours of Travis's back she began to think of other things beside the future of her tea shops. She grew increasingly aware of the hardness of Travis's buttocks beneath her much softer shape and wondered just how tired he really was. Perhaps the massage would prove invigorating as well as relaxing. In the meantime, she kept talking about tea.

Fifteen minutes later when she finally came to a momentary halt in the middle of her monologue, Juliana realized that Travis had fallen asleep somewhere along the line. She groaned.

She was ruefully aware that while her efforts had apparently thoroughly relaxed Travis, they had had the opposite effect on her. Smiling wryly, Juliana dismounted from her sleeping stallion and crawled over to her side of the bed.

"Don't think that you can escape every discussion of my tea shop plans this easily," she whispered as she turned out the light.

Travis did not respond.

Two DAYS LATER Sandy poked her head into Juliana's office. "Don't forget the coffee tasting at noon," she said. Then she frowned at the array of crumpled papers on the floor. "Hey, what's going on in here? You writing out a resignation or something? Going to turn Charisma over to me and Matt? I knew you'd see the light one of these days. We've already made plans to put in an ice-cream parlor out front."

Juliana didn't look up from where she was busily penning still another version of the letter she had been trying to write all morning. "The problem with owning your own business is that it's tough to resign. Forget the ice-cream empire. As it happens, I'm writing to Travis's parents."

"Introducing yourself?"

"Yes and inviting them to the wedding."

Sandy looked at all the aborted efforts. "What's so hard about writing a simple note telling them Travis is making a brilliant marriage to you?"

"I want to get just the right tone. They didn't come to Travis's first wedding and he doesn't think they'll come to this one. They're divorced and remarried, and apparently there was a lot of bitterness between them after they split. One won't be found dead in the same room with the other, not even at their son's wedding."

"Hmm. A messy situation, socially speaking."

Juliana sighed and leaned back in her chair. She tapped the tip of the pen on the desk. "Such childish behavior for adults. It's incredible. It's disgusting."

"It's also fairly common these days. Not much you can do about it."

"Travis's folks have been divorced for years and have raised second families. It's time they remembered their first-born son."

Sandy shrugged. "They'll probably remember him fast enough if and when he gives them a grandchild. It's been my observation that the older people get, the more interested they are in their descendants."

Juliana stared at her. "You know something, Sandy, you have just made a brilliant observation."

"I've been telling you since the day you hired me that I'm brilliant." Sandy folded her arms and leaned against the doorjamb. "How are you going to get Travis's parents to come to the wedding?"

"Well, I have been working on a pleasant, conciliatory approach." Juliana waved a hand at all the crumpled notes on the floor. "Something along the lines of what a really terrific daughter-in-law I'll be and how I want to get to know my husband's parents, et cetera, et cetera. But after talking to you, I think I'll try a different tactic."

"What's that?"

"Threats."

Sandy raised an eyebrow. "What sort of threats?"

"I don't know yet. I'll have to think about it." Juliana got to her feet. "Everything all set for the coffee tasting?"

"Yes. You wanted to do a comparison of Indonesian, Hawaiian and Mexican coffee today, right?"

Juliana wrinkled her nose. "Right."

Sandy laughed. "Your enthusiasm is overwhelming. You should be looking forward to going out front in a few minutes. This series of comparative tastings you've been running the past month has really increased sales. The shop is already crowded."

"The problem with tasting days is that I have to actually drink the stuff.'' Juliana groaned. ''The sacrifices I make for my business.''

The phone rang just as Juliana was about to follow Sandy out of the office. She reached over and grabbed the receiver, hoping Travis would be on the other end of the line.

''Oh, hello, Melvin.''

''You sound disappointed. And after all I've done for you.''

Juliana chuckled. ''You caught me on the way to my lunch-hour coffee tasting.''

''I won't keep you. Just wanted to let you know I've got that aged Sumatra for you. I'll deliver it this afternoon.''

''Great. I've got 'em standing in line for it. Customers seem to go for the word *aged*.''

''Makes 'em think of fine wine, I guess,'' Melvin said absently. ''Although there's no comparison between aged coffee and aged wine. Most aged coffee is kind of flat tasting. This Sumatra's not bad, though. Nice, heavy body. Should blend well. How are the plans for the tea shops going?''

''I'm still discussing the concept with my partner.''

''Which, translated, means you still haven't sold him on the idea? I'm surprised at you, Juliana. What is it with this fiancé of yours? He must have a will of iron if you haven't managed to whip him into shape by now. Can't imagine any man holding out this long in an argument with you.''

''We're not arguing about it, we're discussing the possibilities,'' Juliana snapped, irritated. ''You make me sound like a shrew, Melvin. One of those tough, hard-edged, aggressive businesswomen men always dislike.''

''Hey, don't put words in my mouth,'' Melvin said hastily. ''I only meant that you're a very forceful lady and when you go after something, you usually get it, that's all. I'm just surprised this guy you're engaged to hasn't thrown in the towel and acknowledged the brilliance of your tea shop concept yet, that's all.''

''Goodbye, Melvin,'' Juliana muttered. ''Make sure that Sumatra gets here by three o'clock, or I'll find myself another supplier.'' She tossed the receiver into the cradle and stood glowering at Sandy.

"Something wrong?'' Sandy asked politely.

"Tell me the truth. Do you find me forceful? Even a tad aggressive, perhaps? The sort of female who usually gets what she wants, no matter how many hapless males get in her way?''

Sandy grinned. "Definitely. And I want you to know I admire you tremendously. I consider you my mentor. When I grow up I want to be just like you.''

Juliana smiled brilliantly. "Good. Glad I'm not losing my touch. For a while there I worried that being engaged might have softened my brain a bit. Let's go drink some coffee.''

CHAPTER EIGHT

TRAVIS WAS PORING over the papers he had spread out on the kitchen table when he heard the refrigerator door open and close in a stealthy fashion.

Out of the corner of his eye he watched Juliana pry the lid off the container she had just taken out of the freezer compartment. She had been working quietly at the kitchen counter for several minutes now, her back to him so that he could not see precisely what she was doing. All he knew was that it had something to do with a banana.

"I give up," he said, tossing down his pencil. "What are you doing over there?"

"Fixing you a little something special. I think it's about time you took a break. You've been working there since we finished dinner." She did not turn around but it was obvious she was very busy.

Travis exhaled heavily. "I think it's about time I took a break, too."

"Any word from Bickerstaff today?"

"No."

"Does that mean yes or no?"

"It means," said Travis, "that he's still considering it."

"Good. I'm sure he'll go for it."

Travis shook his head, awed, as usual, by her boundless faith in him. He could guess what would happen when that faith was shattered. Juliana was a businesswoman. She would expect him to live up to his end of the deal they had made, and if he didn't...

"How are the engagement party plans going?"

"Great." Juliana opened a cupboard and removed a package of

nuts. "Everything's all set for the fourteenth at The Treasure House. Be there or be square."

Travis groaned. "Why The Treasure House?"

"For sentimental reasons, of course. That's where you proposed."

"Not precisely. Unlike every other male who proposed to you in the restaurant, I showed some creativity. I took you down to the docks, remember?"

"Details, details. You're just irritable on the subject because you fell in the water that night." She reached for a jar of chocolate sauce.

"I did not fall in the water, I was thrown in. What are you making?"

"I told you, it's a surprise. Just be patient. I talked to Melvin again today."

"Yeah?" Travis mentally girded his loins for battle. He knew what was coming next.

"He wanted to know how the plans for the tea shops were going. I explained you and I were still discussing the concept but that things are moving forward rapidly."

"The hell they are," Travis said mildly. "They haven't moved forward one inch and you know it. You are not opening a tea shop, Juliana, and that's final."

"You're just feeling a bit negative because you've got so many other things on your mind," she assured him. "We'll get down to details after this business with the resort is settled."

"We will never get down to details because there are no details to get down to. There will be no tea shops. I would be worse than a fool, I would be criminally negligent in my responsibilities if I allowed you to go ahead with your bizarre plan."

"You've said, yourself, I'm a very good businesswoman, Travis."

"You are. Very savvy and very realistic. A natural entrepreneur. Except when you get emotionally involved with something the way you did when you loaned money to Kirkwood and the way you're doing lately with the idea of a tea shop. When it comes to things like that, you let your personal feelings and emotions take over. That's a bad way to do business and we both know it.'' Just look at the situation he was in because of personal feelings and emotions, Travis thought as he glanced bleakly at the paperwork in front of him.

"I really think there's a wonderful potential for the tea shops," Juliana said resolutely, opening a jar of maraschino cherries.

"There is no potential for the tea shops."

"I can make them work."

"Nobody could make them work. You can add a line of tea at Charisma but that's the end of the tea business for you."

"I appreciate your consulting expertise," Juliana said, an edge on her words. She opened a drawer with a jerk and snatched a spoon out of the silverware tray. "I assure you I will bear your comments on the subject in mind as I make my decision."

"You can't make any decisions of this magnitude without me," Travis reminded her quietly. "I'm not just your business consultant, I'm your partner. Remember?"

"I remember. Believe me, I remember." Juliana turned toward him, her culinary masterpiece held in both hands. Her eyes sparkled militantly. "But you're going to have to realize that I got where I am with Charisma all on my own. I know what I'm doing."

"Most of the time. But everyone's got a blind spot. Tea happens to be yours. Along with Flame Valley, of course."

"My, you are in a grouchy mood tonight. Maybe this will perk you up."

Travis's attention wavered from the argument as he studied the most spectacular banana split he'd ever seen. Three giant scoops of ice cream resided between halves of a plump banana in a large glass bowl. All three scoops and the banana were lavishly glazed with chocolate topping, nuts, whipped cream and three cherries. Travis's mouth watered.

"Maybe," he agreed.

"How does it look?" Juliana asked expectantly. She nudged

aside some papers and put the concoction down on the table in front of him.

"I haven't seen anything like this since I was eight years old and the one I ordered then wasn't nearly this big." Travis picked up the spoon and wondered where to begin.

"I decided you needed some quick energy." Juliana reached across the table and dipped the edge of her own spoon into one of his scoops of ice cream. She popped the bite into her mouth. "Now, about the tea shops."

The lady was as tenacious as a terrier, Travis thought, not without a sense of grudging admiration. "I've told you before, forget the tea shops. You're fated to get rich as a coffee merchant." He carefully chose his first mouthful of ice cream and nuts.

"I want to try the tea shops, Travis."

"Look. When I've got some time, I'll sit down with you and show you just why you won't make any money with tea shops, okay? Right now I've got my hands full trying to save Kirkwood's rear."

"Damn it." Juliana jumped to her feet, eyes suddenly ablaze. "Talk about a blind spot. You won't even listen to me."

Travis scooped up another bite of ice cream. "I've listened to you. Your idea is lousy. As your partner, I'm not going to agree to allow you to go ahead with the plans. That's all there is to it."

"Well, I am going through with my plans and that's final," she hissed, her hands on her hips.

"You're not going to do a thing without my approval."

"You can't start giving me orders, Travis. As far as I'm concerned you haven't earned your fee yet. You haven't saved Flame Valley and until you do, you're not a real partner in Charisma."

"Yes, I am. We already agreed that the partnership was my fee and I would collect my fee regardless of how successful my efforts were with Flame Valley."

Juliana folded her arms under her breasts and stood defiantly, feet braced slightly apart, in the middle of the kitchen. "Charisma is mine. I created it and I made it what it is today. Even if you're a partner in it, you're the junior partner. Don't ever forget that,

Travis. I make the decisions about the future of my business and that's the end of it. Don't think that just because you're going to marry me you can start telling me what to do.''

Travis sighed. He had known this showdown was coming. He just wished it hadn't arrived tonight. He had too many other things on his mind. ''And don't think that just because you got me to propose to you that you can lead me around like a bull with a ring through its nose,'' he said evenly.

''Why, you mule-headed, stubborn, hard-nosed son of a... You do remind me of a bull. A very thick-headed one.'' Juliana turned on her heel and stalked out of the kitchen.

A moment later the bedroom door slammed shut.

A fine example of high dudgeon, Travis decided as he reluctantly went back to work. He wished he'd gotten in a few more bites of the ice cream before Juliana had exploded. He hadn't even started on the banana. A slow grin edged his mouth. Juliana was the kind of woman who would keep a man young or wear him out. Either way, he would never be bored.

JULIANA REAPPEARED an hour later. Travis's eyes narrowed as he slowly became aware of her presence behind him. He turned his head and saw her lounging with sultry insouciance in the kitchen doorway. She was wearing what he privately considered her sexiest nightie, the black see-through one with the small lace flowers strategically placed over the relevant portions of her anatomy. Her mass of red hair frothed around her shoulders. Her feet were bare and her eyes were luminous.

''I've decided to forgive you,'' she said, her voice husky.

Travis felt desire seize his insides. ''This must be my lucky day.''

''I shouldn't have tried to discuss the tea shop idea with you tonight. You're much too involved with Flame Valley right now to be bothered with other business decisions.''

Travis decided this was not the time to tell her that his opinion on the tea shops was not likely to alter regardless of how busy he was. ''You're sure you're not just trying to use sex to get me to see the brilliance of your plan?''

She smiled with glowing innocence. "I would never stoop to that sort of tacky behavior."

"Too bad. I've always wondered what it would be like to be the victim of that sort of behavior."

Juliana held out her hand invitingly. "We could always pretend."

"Yeah. We could. We're pretty good at creating fantasies together." Travis got to his feet and went toward her. She was fantastic, he thought. He'd never before met anyone quite like her, and he knew deep inside he never would again. *He must not lose her*. He would cling to this fantasy with all his strength.

"Travis?" She was still looking at him with smoky sensuality, but there was a trace of concern in her gaze as she studied his face. "Is something wrong?"

"No," he muttered as he came to a halt directly in front of her. "Nothing's wrong."

But there was and he knew it. Every day that passed without a response from Bickerstaff or any of his other contacts meant losing one more piece of the small chunk of whatever hope he had of saving the inn. But he couldn't think about that tonight, Travis decided, not with Juliana standing here, inviting him to make love to her.

He kissed her, startling her a little with his sudden urgency. She hesitated a split second and then responded, as she always did, with everything that was in her. There was nothing like being wanted by this woman, Travis reflected, his hunger for her soaring.

"Do you feel yourself changing your mind about the tea shops yet?" Juliana whispered teasingly against his throat.

"No, but I definitely feel lucky." He was taut and heavy with his desire. He began nibbling on her ear. "Is this the way you're going to forgive me every time we argue?"

"Probably. I'm not the type to hold a grudge." She unbuttoned his shirt slowly until it hung open to reveal his chest. Then she ran her fingers through the crisp hair. Her eyes were soft with a woman's sweet need as her nails lightly circled his flat nipples.

"No," he acknowledged softly, "you won't hold grudges, will you? That's not your way. You'll yell at me for a while, slam a few doors and then put on a sexy nightgown and seduce me. I won't stand a chance."

"Putty in my hands," she agreed, pressing her breasts against him. "Does the thought make you nervous?" She unzipped his pants and unbuckled his belt.

"I'll take my chances." His hand slid down over her soft, curving belly. He found the small lace flower that barely concealed the triangle of red curls at the apex of her thighs. His palm closed over the flower and a glorious sense of satisfaction roared through him when Juliana moaned and melted against him.

He caressed her intimately through the filmy material of the gown until he felt her growing hot and damp. Her fingers slipped inside his pants and he groaned as she touched him. When he could take the subtle torture no longer, he picked Juliana up and carried her into the bedroom and put her down onto the bed.

A moment later, his own clothes in a heap on the floor, Travis slid into bed, gathered Juliana into his arms and rolled onto his back. She sat astride him taking him deep within her warmth. Her legs pressed demandingly against his thighs.

Travis reached up to cup her breasts, coaxing the nipples into tight, sensitive buds. When he grazed the delicate peaks with his palms Juliana caught her breath and stiffened. Travis could feel her tightening around him and it was all he could do to muster some remnants of self-control.

Juliana began to breathe more quickly and her head tipped back. Her hair flowed in a silken wave around her shoulders. Travis waited until he couldn't stand it any longer and then he moved, easing Juliana down onto her back. When she reached for him, pulling him close once more, he slid all the way into her heat and surrendered to the fabulous oblivion.

A LONG TIME LATER Travis felt Juliana stir in the shadows beside him.

"Are you awake?" she asked softly.

"Umm." He had been unable to sleep, wondering if he should

put in another call to Bickerstaff's office in the morning. But he didn't want to look too anxious, he told himself. Bickerstaff would get skittish.

"I shouldn't have lost my temper tonight just because you don't agree with me about opening a tea shop. The thing is, Charisma's always been mine. I've always made the decisions, all the decisions, about its future."

"I know." He let his hand drift over her curving thigh.

"I guess it's like having raised a kid all by yourself and then marrying and having to let someone else have a say in the kid's future."

Travis said nothing. As usual, he felt himself edging away from any topic that was even remotely concerned with children. One of these days he would have to deal with the subject, he told himself. But he intended to put it off as long as possible.

"Travis?"

"Yeah?"

"I know you mean well and I know you think you know what's best for Charisma but..."

"But you don't like having me tell you what's best for Charisma when it conflicts with what you want, right?"

"Right."

"Don't take it personally, Juliana. Don't let emotion enter into your decision-making process. Charisma is business. Keep it that way."

"Sometimes the two get mixed up, don't they?"

Travis thought about his current situation. Revenge, business and desire were irrevocably entwined into a knot he was not at all certain he could unravel.

"Yes," he said quietly. "Sometimes they get mixed up."

JULIANA WAITED another two days before she introduced a subject that had not yet been discussed and which she had hoped Travis would bring up first. So far he had not done so and she was, as usual, too impatient to wait for things to happen in their own time.

She decided to do it very casually. Craftily she waited until she had coaxed him away from his desk for a walk on the beach. She led up to her topic slowly.

"You don't mind living in my condo until we decide where we're going to live permanently?" she asked.

"Your condo's fine." Travis's hand tightened around hers as he paced barefoot beside her on the damp, packed sand at the water's edge. As far as I'm concerned, we can live there permanently."

"It's a little small."

"Plenty of space for two people." He sounded unconcerned. "I'm just about moved in now as it is and everything's working out fine."

That much was true. Juliana still found it something of a novelty to open the closet and discover a row of conservatively tailored men's white shirts hanging inside, but she was adjusting. She had complained briefly about Travis using up all the hot water during his morning showers but he had resolved the issue by making her share the shower with him. So far none of the problems of living together had been anything more than a minor challenge.

Obviously commenting on the small size of the condo was not going to open up the area of discussion that was foremost on her mind today. She would have to find another approach. *Subtle,* she told herself. *Keep it subtle.*

"Everything is all set for the engagement party," she reported. "Seven o'clock this Friday night. Just about everyone who was invited is coming. Even my parents are coming down from San Francisco. I've had several talks with the chef at The Treasure House, and the food is going to be fabulous."

"Fine."

The neutral tone of his voice disturbed her. Lately it seemed to Juliana she had been hearing that tone more and more from Travis. She sought for a way to ease the conversation from engagement party plans to the more important subject and gave up. So much for being subtle. She couldn't wait any longer to bring up the one undiscussed subject that remained. She would have to take the bull by the horns.

"So," Juliana said boldly, "what would you say if I told you I was pregnant?"

It didn't take long for her to sense she had made a mistake.

Travis came to an abrupt halt and spun halfway around to face her, his face rigid with anger. "You're *what?*"

It dawned on Juliana that she had obviously thrown the poor man into shock. "I was just wondering how you would feel if it turned out I was..."

"You're not pregnant," he cut in swiftly. "You can't be pregnant. We've been taking precautions. There haven't been any accidents."

"I know, but..."

"Are you telling me you are pregnant?" he asked through set teeth.

"No, no, it's okay, Travis. You're right. I'm not pregnant. It was just a hypothetical question."

"A hypothetical question? Are you nuts? You don't throw hypothetical questions like that around. What the hell got into you?"

"All right, so I didn't phrase it very well."

"No, you did not."

He stood looking at her with an expression that rocked her as nothing else had done since the moment she had watched him confront her cousin Elly that night on the terrace. Juliana pulled herself together quickly.

"I'm sorry, Travis," she said quietly. "I didn't mean to alarm you. I just thought it was time we talked about children. It's something we haven't discussed yet."

His unreadable gaze searched her face and then shifted to the ocean horizon over her left shoulder. "No, we haven't talked about children, have we? I somehow got the impression you weren't particularly interested in having kids. Ever since I've known you, you've seemed wrapped up with your plans for Charisma. You never said anything about wanting to have babies."

"I hadn't thought about babies very much before I met you," she admitted, realizing for the first time the truth of that statement. "There was never a time or a man that made me think about having kids. But now there's you and we're getting married and neither one of us is exactly young and, well..." The sentence trailed off.

"And you've decided you want children." Travis closed his eyes wearily and then opened them again. His crystal gaze was more unreadable than ever.

Juliana drew a deep breath. "Are you trying to tell me you don't?"

He began to massage the back of his neck. "This is a hell of a time to bring up the subject."

"What better time?" She studied him anxiously. "If you don't want children you should tell me now, Travis."

"Kids complicate things."

"Living is a complicated business. What sort of complications are you worried about?"

"Damn it, Juliana, you know what the complications are. Don't act naive. If things don't work out between us, we don't want to hurt anyone else, do we?"

She sucked in her breath. "You're already looking ahead to a divorce?"

"No, of course not. It's just that these days people have to be realistic. Half of all marriages fail, and there are probably a lot of others that would collapse if given a slight push."

"So what are you suggesting? That people stop having babies?" she snapped.

"I'm suggesting they give the matter a lot of thought before they go ahead with something as irrevocable as the decision to have a child," he muttered, resuming his pace.

Juliana hurried to catch up with him. "I agree with you, Travis. Babies should be planned and wanted. No question about it. But if two people are sure of their commitment to each other and if they both want children, then they shouldn't be afraid to go ahead and have them."

"Do we have to discuss this now, Juliana?"

Her palms were damp, Juliana realized vaguely. A sick feeling slashed through her. For the first time since she had met Travis she questioned her own judgment. Had she chosen the wrong man, after all?

"No," she said. "We don't have to discuss this now."

"Good." He glanced at his watch. "Because I've got to get back to the office. Bickerstaff still hasn't called and there are one or two other people I want to contact this afternoon."

"Sure. I understand. I'd better get back to Charisma, too. Lots to do today. I want to talk to my staff about trying a darker roast on some new beans I bought." She tried a bright smile on for size and thought it stayed put fairly well.

Travis slanted her a brief glance, nodded and turned back up the beach to where Juliana had parked her car. Little was said on the drive back into town.

Juliana dropped Travis off at his office and drove very slowly back to her apartment. She would think about trying a darker roast on the new coffee beans some other time.

She parked the red coupé in front of her apartment and went inside. The first thing she did was put a kettle of water on the stove. The second thing she did was not answer the phone when it rang two minutes later.

When the tea was ready she carried it over to the kitchen table and sat down. She was still sitting there, staring out the window, when she saw Elly's car pull into the parking space beside the coupé.

The phone had been easy to ignore but there was no point ignoring the knock on the front door. Juliana knew there was no way she could pretend she wasn't inside.

"There you are," Elly said as Juliana opened the door. "I stopped at Charisma but your staff said you hadn't returned, and when you didn't answer the phone I thought I'd just stop by on my way back to Flame Valley. What's wrong?"

"Nothing's wrong. Why do you ask?"

"Don't give me that. You never come home in the middle of the day." Elly stepped past her and went straight into the kitchen. "And you're having a cup of tea all by yourself. What's going on around here?"

"Elly, please, I'm just a little tired. I'm not feeling very sociable."

Elly peered at her. "Something's wrong, isn't it? Don't bother trying to lie, Juliana. We've known each other too long."

"I've had a rough day." Juliana sat down at the table and picked up her teacup.

"So have I. That's one of the reasons I wanted to talk to you today. I'm getting very nervous about David and what's going to happen if Travis doesn't pull off the deal with Bickerstaff."

Juliana nodded without much interest. "I know you're worried, Elly."

"But," Elly continued quietly as she sat down across from her cousin, "at the moment I am a lot more worried about you. You're not acting like yourself, Juliana."

"How can you tell? You just walked in the door."

"I can tell. You're normally as vivid as a neon sign. Right now you look as if someone has just unplugged you."

In spite of her morose mood, Juliana managed a flicker of a smile. "Not bad, Elly. A good analogy."

"It's Travis, isn't it? Tell me."

"There's not much to tell. I'm just wondering if I'm making a mistake. That's all."

Elly's brows rose. "I don't believe it. After all my ranting and raving failed to deter you, after the lectures from your parents and my father went unheeded, *now* you're suddenly wondering if you've made a mistake? That's a shock. All right, let's have it. What went wrong today?"

"I asked Travis how he'd feel if I got pregnant. He was furious."

"Are you?" Elly asked sharply.

"Pregnant? No. It was just a hypothetical question. I wanted to find a subtle way to introduce the subject of babies."

"Men aren't big on hypothetical questions," Elly observed with unexpected insight. "Or subtlety, either. You probably gave the guy the shock of his life. There he was, not thinking about anything except trying to salvage Flame Valley and you hit him up with something like that.''

"He didn't calm down when I explained I just wanted to discuss the possibility of having children.'' Juliana met her cousin's eyes. "I don't think he wants kids, Elly. I think he wants to hedge his bets.''

"What do you mean?''

"I get the feeling a part of him doesn't really expect our marriage to work. I think that deep down he doesn't want to have any loose ends around if things collapse. Probably because, as a kid, he was a loose end, himself.''

"I think I'm beginning to see the problem. But, frankly, I'm surprised you're letting it get you down. You usually rise to a challenge the way a fish rises to bait. I've always envied your talent for self-confidence. Nothing really shakes it, not even when you lose once in a while. You just reorganize and bounce back. You're always so strong, Juliana. Everybody in the family says that, you know. We all see you as the strong one.''

"I don't feel strong now. If you must know the truth, I feel scared. I was so sure of him, Elly. So sure he was the right one for me. I knew it the day he walked through the front door of Charisma. I practically jumped on him then and there and told him he was going to marry me. I knew I'd been waiting for him all my life. It was all I could do to control myself until the night he…we…the night we went to bed together for the first time.''

Elly studied the table for a moment. "You were still sure of him even after he and I had staged that scene out on the terrace at Flame Valley, weren't you? You were mad at him, but still certain he was the right man for you.''

Juliana nodded. "It's true. I was very annoyed with him that night. Furious that he'd tricked me about his past relationship with my family and even more upset to discover he'd once wanted to marry you. I mean, it's obvious you and he are all wrong for each other.''

"Obvious.''

"But I figure everyone's entitled to a mistake or two. Heck, I've made a few small ones, myself."

"Very understanding of you."

"And he soon saw the error of his ways," Juliana continued. "Didn't he turn right around and agree to try to save the inn and didn't he ask me to marry him?"

"True. That's just what he did."

"But this thing about the babies has shaken me, Elly. This is a different matter entirely."

"Not everyone wants to have children, Juliana. You've never shown much interest in them yourself until today."

"But I've always known that when the right man came along I would want to have them. There was never any question in my mind."

"It takes two to make an important decision like that."

"I know." Juliana sighed. "If it were a simple matter of Travis not wanting to be a father, I might be able to understand. But there's more to it than that. He talked about not wanting to see kids hurt in a divorce. He talked as though one went into a marriage planning for the worst possible case."

Elly sat back in her chair, frowning. "Whereas you, with your boundless certainty and enthusiasm are going into it prepared to give it your all."

Juliana looked up, feeling raw and very vulnerable. "Exactly. Elly, I can't marry a man who isn't as committed to making the marriage work as I am. I won't marry a man who feels he has to hedge his bets just in case things don't work out."

"Be reasonable. What do you expect from Travis? He's a businessman, Juliana. And I've told you from the very beginning there's a cold-blooded streak in him. He's not an emotional creature like you. If you ask me, it's perfectly in character for Travis to hedge his bets. Be grateful he's got enough integrity not to want to leave you holding the baby, so to speak."

Cold-blooded? Travis? Never. But it was true he was a businessman and he could be incredibly stubborn. Juliana reminded herself of how difficult he became every time she brought up the subject of the tea shops. Perhaps he was looking at marriage the same way he would look at a potential business investment.

The thought was enough to make her nauseous.

"Juliana? Would you like another cup of tea?" Elly got quickly to her feet. "Here, I'll make it for you."

At any other time the notion of Elly reversing roles with her and becoming the reassuring, bracing one would have made Juliana laugh. But when Elly put the fresh cup of tea down in front of her, she could only feel wanly grateful.

"Thank you," Juliana murmured.

Elly sighed. "I suppose I should be encouraging you to have these second thoughts. After all, I'm the one who's been warning you not to marry the man. But for some insane reason I can't bear to have you think you've made such a horrendous mistake. It's just not normal for you to be acting like this. You've got to get a grip on yourself, Juliana. Depression doesn't look good on you."

"I know." Juliana sipped her tea. It was too weak but that didn't seem to matter today. Nothing really mattered today except that she was staring at the possibility of having been totally wrong in her estimation of Travis Sawyer. He was afraid to have kids because he was afraid the marriage would end. Which meant that he was not really committed to making it work.

"Juliana? Feeling any better?"

"No."

"Oh, Juliana, I'm so sorry."

Juliana stared unseeingly out the kitchen window. "What am I going to do, Elly?"

"I suppose you may have to consider calling off the wedding, if you're feeling this uncertain of the future."

Juliana gripped the teacup. "Heaven help me, Elly. I don't think I have the courage to do that."

CHAPTER NINE

"JULIANA? I'm sorry, but it looks like I'm not going to be able to get away from here in time for dinner tonight."

"That's two nights in a row, Travis. Is something happening with Flame Valley?"

"I'm not sure yet. Maybe."

"You don't sound encouraged."

Probably because I'm not, Travis thought. "I don't want anyone to get his hopes up. Look, I'd better get back to it. I don't know how long I'll be." He waited, praying she would tell him that it didn't matter how late he was, she would be expecting him when he was finished at the office.

"You'll probably be exhausted when you're done for the evening."

"Yeah. Probably." Travis's fingers tightened on the phone as he prepared himself for what he sensed was coming next. Juliana was going to say the same thing she had said last night when he'd called her to tell her he'd be late. *"You'll probably want to go straight home to your place and fall into bed."*

"Don't bother stopping by here. I know you're tired. You'll want to go straight home to your own apartment and collapse into bed," Juliana said with far too much calm understanding for Travis's taste.

"Yeah. I was just thinking that might be best. I'll see you tomorrow, honey."

"Fine."

"Everything on line for the party Friday night?"

There was a slight pause before Juliana spoke. "Yes. Everything's fine."

Travis could feel her sliding away. He gripped the phone harder, frantically searching for a way to keep her on the other end for just a bit longer. "Did you find a dress yet?"

"No. Elly insists I give it one more try tomorrow. She's going with me. I told her not to worry about it. If I don't find something new, I can always dig something out of my closet."

Travis closed his eyes in bleak despair as he heard the lack of enthusiasm in her voice. He knew that under normal circumstances Juliana would never have said such a thing. She would have been searching California from one end to the other for a new gown to wear to her engagement party.

"Good luck shopping," Travis finally said, knowing he was the one whose luck was running out faster than water through a sieve. "I'll try to stop by Charisma tomorrow for a cup of coffee."

"All right. See you tomorrow." Juliana hesitated. "Good night, Travis."

"Good night."

Travis slowly hung up the phone and watched as night enveloped Jewel Harbor on the other side of the floor-to-ceiling windows. The darkness looked cool and comforting—velvety soft. A place to hide. Inside his office everything was fluorescent bright and there was no place to hide from the failure he saw looming on the horizon.

That failure had been crouching there all along, of course. He had caught glimpses of it right from the start when he had first agreed to try to save the inn. But Juliana's indestructible faith in him had somehow obscured reality for a while. Even as her breezy confidence in him had irritated him, it had buoyed him.

Hell, for a while there, he had almost believed he could pull it off.

But Juliana hadn't expressed any of the familiar, serene assurance in his abilities for the past two days. There had been no bright, bracing lectures on how everything was going to work out.

There had also been no call from Bickerstaff.

But Travis knew the cold feeling in his gut tonight didn't come from facing the harsh business reality; it came from having to face the fact that Juliana was distancing herself from him before disaster even hit.

She had been growing cool and remote since that day they had walked on the beach, when she had asked him what he would do if she told him she was pregnant.

Since then, Travis reflected, she had stopped trying to pin him down to a wedding date. There had been no talk of the tea shops. And now Juliana seemed to have lost interest in shopping for a new dress for the engagement party. The signs couldn't get more ominous than that.

His bright, vibrant, enthusiastic Juliana was slipping out of his grasp even though nothing had happened to Flame Valley yet.

Travis reran the conversation on the beach in his mind for what had to be the hundredth time, trying to figure out what had happened to make Juliana grow cold.

His first thought this morning was that he had made a terrible mistake. Perhaps she had gotten pregnant accidentally and had tried to tell him, and his anger and refusal to believe her had hurt her deeply.

But that couldn't be it. He remembered he'd asked her point-blank if she was pregnant and she had denied it. She wouldn't have lied to him about a thing like that.

His second thought was that sometime during the past couple of days she had finally realized that the chances for saving the inn and the money she had in it, weren't good after all. Deep down, under all that flash and optimism, Juliana was still a realistic businesswoman. Maybe she was finally getting realistic about Flame Valley and its future.

And the bottom line was that if he couldn't rescue the inn, Travis knew he would automatically revert to the role of the bad guy. He had recognized that from the start. He was faced with only two options. He would be either the problem or the solution. There was no middle ground. If he didn't save Flame Valley, he would become the one who destroyed it.

Travis had tried to force himself to face that prospect from the beginning but somehow he had let himself believe some of the glowing press Juliana had insisted on giving him.

When he was with Juliana it was difficult not to get caught up in her enthusiasms, Travis reflected. But he had never had to deal with a Juliana who had lost her effervescent assurance.

It was beginning to look as if she had lost her faith in him.

Travis reminded himself that he had known from the start that if the chips were down, Juliana would side with her family. She would blame him for destroying Flame Valley and probably her cousin's marriage in the bargain.

The raw truth was that she would be right.

When it was all over, Travis knew he would be the outsider again. It was a role he had played often enough in the past and he recognized it immediately.

When choices had to be made, he got left out.

He tried to tell himself that maybe it was better this way. His relationship with Juliana had been on borrowed time from the start. Maybe it would be easier if she began to withdraw from him now.

But the idea of losing her before the final roll of the dice was more than Travis could endure. He would face the end when there was absolutely, positively no hope left of saving Flame Valley. Until then he was determined to grab what he could of Juliana's fire.

He loosened his tie and went back to work searching for the loophole that he knew didn't exist. It was ironic that he was going to walk away from this mess with the resort. After five years of being obsessed with the damned place, he now discovered he never wanted to see it again.

But one way or another, he decided, he would see that Juliana got her money back. It might take a while, but he would find a way to see she got paid off. He knew that wouldn't buy her back but it was the least he could do for her.

She had given him a great deal during the past few weeks and Travis prided himself on always paying his debts.

"GOOD GRIEF, Juliana, you can't be serious about that outfit." Elly stared in shock as her cousin paraded forth from the dressing room.

"What's wrong with it?" Juliana glanced down the length of the demure winter-white crepe two-piece suit she was wearing. The long sleeves, high neckline and modest below-the-knee skirt were totally inoffensive as far as she could tell.

"What's wrong with it?" Elly's delicate brows snapped together in a severe frown. "Are you out of your mind? That dress is not you at all. It's got no spark, no sizzle, no color. It's plain, plain, plain. It might look fine on the sweet angelic type or a traditional preppy type, but it's definitely not you."

Juliana felt a momentary flash of annoyance. "Well, you suggest something, then. I'm getting tired of trying things on."

"You never get tired of shopping and trying on new clothes."

"I'm tired of it today, okay?"

"All right, calm down. You're not yourself today, Juliana. Just settle down and listen to me. Go back into the dressing room and try that green and gold number, the one with the V-back cut to the waist."

Juliana heaved a sigh as her irritation died and was replaced by the now familiar sensation of disinterest. She trooped back into the changing room and reached for the racy green evening dress Elly had selected earlier.

As she smoothed the slender skirt down over her hips a part of her realized that the green and gold gown was done in the sort of dashing style that normally appealed to her. The deep V-back was at once elegant and daring. It ended in an outrageous bow at the small of her back. The snug outline of the skirt emphasized the curve of her hips and her long legs. For a moment or two Juliana almost got enthusiastic as she considered how a pair of rhinestone shoes she had recently spotted in a shop window would look with the dress.

But apathy set in again as she recalled exactly why she was buying the gown.

"Much better," Elly decreed as Juliana emerged from the

dressing room. "In fact, perfect." She glanced at the hovering saleswoman. "She'll take it."

Juliana started to protest and then shrugged, not feeling up to arguing.

Twenty minutes later Elly led her out into the parking lot of the huge shopping center. The green dress was in a bag under Juliana's arm. A pair of rhinestone studded heels were in another sack.

"I've never seen you like this before, Juliana. You just aren't yourself today." Elly slid into the front seat of the Mercedes and turned the key in the ignition. "Things are really going bad in a hurry between you and Travis, aren't they?"

"How would I know? I haven't seen Travis in nearly three days. He's spent the last two nights at his old apartment."

"But he hasn't told you to cancel the engagement party, has he? He's a very assertive individual," Elly pointed out as she pulled away from the parking slot. "If he wanted to call off the party, he would do it. You, I presume, haven't changed your mind?"

Juliana stared out the window. "No. I've been telling myself things are terribly wrong and I should call it all off while I still can but I just can't get up the nerve to do it. I love him, Elly. What am I going to do if it turns out he doesn't love me enough?"

"I don't know." Elly eased the Mercedes onto the freeway, her expression sober. "I spend a lot of time asking myself the same question lately."

Juliana was instantly contrite. "You're still worrying about what David will do if you lose the inn, aren't you?"

"David and I haven't been communicating very well lately, to put it mildly. Not much better than you and Travis, as a matter of fact. He spends all his time either locked in his office or closeted with Travis. When he comes to bed at night, he falls asleep before I get out of the bathroom. The next morning he's gone before I get out of bed. I can't tell what he's thinking, but I know he's depressed and worried. I'm scared, Juliana."

"Join the club."

TRAVIS WAS SURPRISED at how hard he had to work to psych himself up to stop at Charisma Espresso on Friday. The fact that he had to work at the task at all alarmed him. He was accustomed to facing problems head-on but the problem of Juliana seemed to be unique.

It was noon, he reminded himself as he got out of his car. Only a few more hours to go until the engagement party. And no word yet from Bickerstaff. Time was running out on him fast. The closer Travis got to the bitter end, the more he perversely tried to believe Bickerstaff would call at the last minute and say he wanted in on the deal.

Talk about the irrational hope of the doomed.

Charisma was filled with people who were standing around with small cups and little notepads in their hands. Belatedly Travis remembered that this was one of the coffee-tasting days Juliana had inaugurated last month. Through the glass doors he could hear her behind the counter giving her lecture on coffee while Matt and Sandy poured sample cups.

Travis pushed open the door and stood quietly, listening to the windup of Juliana's talk.

"Always keep in mind that most of the coffee in your cup is water so you must pay attention to water quality. There's no point brewing a pot of coffee using water that doesn't taste fresh and good. Now, let's run through the three blends we tasted today. The first was the dark roasted Colombian. Remember that when you drink dark roasted coffees, you're tasting mostly the effect of the roasting process, not the specific characteristics of the beans used. The coffees taste stronger, but the caffeine level is actually about the same, sometimes even less than in lighter roasts."

Juliana looked a little wan today, Travis thought, frowning. As if she weren't feeling up to par. He wondered if she was coming down with a cold.

"The second cup we tasted was the Kona blend. The coffee grown in the Kona district of Hawaii is the only coffee grown in the United States. Production levels are small but the coffee, at its best, can be outstanding. Medium acidity, smooth, clear flavor.''

She not only looked a little wan today, Travis decided; she looked a little preoccupied. Usually when she played to a crowd of customers, she was like a good actress onstage, full of presence and definitely *on*. Today she seemed to be just going through the motions. She was a professional, however, and she conducted the coffee tasting with all the panache of a wine-tasting event.

''The third sample was a blend using chiefly Tanzanian arabica beans from the slopes of Mount Kilimanjaro. Tanzanian coffee is known for its excellent balance. I hope you noted the intense flavor and full body.'' Juliana smiled at her customers. ''And that wraps it up for today, folks. I hope to see you all next week when we'll be trying out several coffees brewed by a variety of methods. We'll also be discussing some more coffee history.''

Travis watched Juliana smile one last time at her audience, a pleasant enough smile, but it lacked that extra measure of brilliance he was accustomed to seeing in it. Then she spotted him at the back of the room, and for just an instant he thought her smile bounced up to its usual dazzling wattage. He wasn't certain because the effect didn't last long. The smile slipped right back into the pleasant, polite level and stayed there as she came around from behind the counter.

''Hello, Travis. Taking a lunch break?''

''I want to talk to you.''

Something that might have been fear flashed in her eyes but it disappeared instantly. ''All right. I'm finished with the tasting. Let's go outside and sit at one of the courtyard tables.''

He followed her as she wove her way through the milling crowd of people ordering freshly ground coffee at the counter. A minute later they emerged into the relative calm of the courtyard.

''Well? What is it, Travis? Having second thoughts about tonight?'' Juliana asked with typical bluntness as they sat down.

''No. But I thought you might be having a few.'' Travis faced her across the table, willing the truth from her. He felt as if he were standing on the edge of a cliff.

"It's not as if we're getting married tonight," Juliana pointed out coolly. "It's just an engagement party. Nothing permanent. No reason to panic."

"Right. Are you sure you're not panicking?"

"I'm a little nervous, but I'm not panicked," she retorted with a burst of anger.

Travis nodded. "All right, calm down. I was just asking."

"Why?"

"Because you've been behaving a little strangely for the past few days," he said quietly. "Since that day we took a walk on the beach, in fact."

"Oh. Maybe it's nerves."

He waited but when there was no further explanation forthcoming, he tried again. "Juliana, did I say something to upset you that day? If you're hurt because I came down on you like a ton of bricks when you implied you might be pregnant, I'm sorry. It was just that I was so sure you couldn't be pregnant, I was stunned to hear that you might be and I..." He let the sentence wind down into nothing. "I overreacted, I guess."

"Don't worry about it. I didn't bring up the subject in a diplomatic fashion, did I?"

"Someday we'll talk about kids," Travis promised.

"Will we?"

He nodded, hastening to change the subject. "Is there anything else that's worrying you?"

She looked straight at him. "No."

"I thought maybe you were concerned about the situation with Flame Valley."

"No."

Of course she wouldn't come right out and tell him she was wavering in her faith in him, not after all the buildup she had given him for the past few weeks. She would keep her growing uncertainties to herself.

"It's not looking good, Juliana," Travis felt obliged to say one last time.

"You've already told me that several times," she said impatiently.

Travis felt his temper fray. He got to his feet abruptly. "Yeah, I have, haven't I? Maybe it's finally sinking in. See you tonight, Juliana. Shall I pick you up?"

"No. I'll drive myself. I want to go to the restaurant a couple of hours early to make certain everything's in order." She jumped to her feet. "Travis, I didn't mean to snap at you. It's just that I'm a little tense."

"Yeah. Me, too."

He stalked out of the sidewalk café into the sunlight. When he reached the Buick he glanced back and saw that she was still staring after him. He thought he saw pain in her eyes and he almost went back to her. But even as he hesitated, uncertain of what to do or how to handle her, she turned and walked back into Charisma without a backward glance. He saw her dab at her eyes with a napkin she had picked up off the table and his stomach twisted.

Travis looked down into the yawning chasm below the edge of the cliff and wondered how it was going to feel when he went over.

HE FOUND OUT exactly how it was going to feel when he hung up the phone after the final conversation with Bickerstaff. It felt rather as he'd expected it to feel—as if the ground had just dropped out from under his feet. There was nothing to hang on to, nothing he could use to save himself.

It was over.

Travis wondered at the unnatural sense of calm he was feeling. He rubbed the back of his neck and glanced at the clock. A few minutes past seven. The engagement party was already underway and he was late. He wondered if Juliana would guess the reason why.

Feeling more weary than he could ever remember feeling in his life, he got to his feet, went around the desk and retrieved his jacket. No point going back to the apartment to dress for the occasion. He wouldn't be staying long at his engagement party.

"IF THIS IS ANY indication of the future, Juliana, you'd better be prepared to find yourself standing alone at the altar."

"Not a good sign, friend, when the future groom is late to his own engagement party."

"I can't believe it, Juliana. How could you plan everything right down to the shrimp dip and then forget to make sure your fiancé got here on time? Not like you, pal. The prospect of marriage must have addled your brain."

Juliana managed a smile as she endured another round of good-natured teasing. It had been like this since shortly after seven when guests had begun arriving and discovered that Travis was not yet there. Most were treating it as a joke, fully expecting Travis to walk through the door at any moment.

The only ones who showed any real evidence of concern were Elly and the other members of Juliana's family. The Grants, as a group, looked decidedly grim.

"Do you think you should call his office? Or his apartment? Something may have happened, Juliana." Elly spoke from right behind her cousin.

"He'll be here when he's ready," Juliana said, wondering at the odd sense of resignation she was feeling. She felt almost anesthetized, she realized. It was something of a relief after all the painful anxiety and uncertainty she'd been experiencing most of the week.

She took another look around the room and saw that everything was running smoothly, if one overlooked the minor fact that the future groom was not present.

The large room The Treasure House rented out for special occasions was festively decorated with silver balloons, colorful streamers and a wealth of exotic hothouse flowers.

The centerpiece was a magnificent buffet table that stretched almost the entire length of the room. It was laden with a staggering array of delicacies that included everything from garlic toast to shrimp brochettes. In a moment of nostalgia, Juliana had even ordered a bowl of guacamole and had stipulated it be set in a place of honor in the middle of the table.

The room was filled with laughing, talking people decked out in typical California style, which meant that every conceivable variety of fashionable attire from silver jeans to elegant kimonos were represented.

David and Elly had arrived at six, volunteering last-minute services. It was the first time Juliana had seen David since the night she had invited him and Elly to dinner to tell them Travis was going to save the resort. One glance at his handsome face had warned her Elly was right; he did look worried. He tried to hide it behind his familiar genial smile, but Juliana knew David was deeply concerned. Elly was struggling just as hard to maintain a cheerful front.

Her parents and Uncle Tony were putting on a good front chatting with other guests but every so often one of them glanced toward the front door and scowled darkly.

Thank heavens she had decided to invite Travis's parents only to the wedding, not to the engagement party, Juliana thought.

She sighed to herself as she studied the crowd. How had she let things get this far? She ought to have called the whole thing off days ago, right after that fateful walk on the beach. She glanced at the clock for the fiftieth time. Seven-thirty. She wondered if Travis would bother to show at all.

Juliana was seriously considering the possibility of disappearing out the back door of the restaurant when she heard a murmur of awareness go through the crowded room. She swung around instantly, knowing Travis must have arrived. As she looked toward the door, her spirits lifted briefly. Hope died hard, she was discovering.

A roar of approval went up as Travis walked into the room. There was another round of teasing comments and congratulations and much laughter.

Travis ignored it all. He walked straight toward Juliana without glancing at anyone else in the room. He was wearing his familiar working uniform, a white shirt with the sleeves rolled up, a conservatively striped tie and dark trousers. He had his jacket hooked over his shoulder.

Juliana took one look at his grim, implacable face and knew that everything was lost.

She stood very still in the middle of the room as Travis paced toward her. She realized her hands were trembling. She folded them together in front of her. The crowd began to realize that something was wrong. The teasing became more muted and gradually disappeared. People stepped out of Travis's way and a hush descended.

Travis walked the last few steps in a charged silence. He seemed unaware of anyone else in the room except Juliana. His eyes never left her face as he came to a halt in front of her.

"I just got off the phone with Bickerstaff," Travis said in a terrifying cold, quiet voice. "It's all over. He doesn't want to get involved with Flame Valley. Too big a risk, he said. And he's right."

Juliana's mouth went dry. "Travis?"

"Sorry it went down to the wire like this. For a while it was close. You even had me thinking there was a chance, and I, of all people, should have known better. Bickerstaff was the last shot and he's out of it now."

"What are you trying to say?" Juliana demanded tightly.

"That I can't save Flame Valley from the wolf—can't save it from myself. Looks like I'll have my revenge, whether I want it or not. I just came here tonight to let you know that you don't have to call off our engagement. I'll do it for you and save you the trouble."

Travis turned on his heel and walked swiftly back out of the room.

Juliana stared after him, feeling as if she had just been kicked in the stomach. The layer of anesthetizing numbness that had been protecting her for the past few days began to crack. Underneath it lay a world of hurt.

Travis was walking out of her life.

"Juliana?" Elly came toward her quickly, keeping her voice low. "What's wrong? What did Travis say to you?"

"That Flame Valley's last chance just went down the tubes so he's calling off the engagement. Saving me the trouble of doing it myself, he said.''

"Oh, my God.'' Elly closed her eyes. "What will David do?'' Then the rest of Juliana's words hit her. Elly's eyes flew open. "Travis is calling off the engagement? Now? Tonight? Just like that? In front of all these people?''

"You've got to hand it to the man, once in a while he displays a real flair for the dramatic.''

"Juliana, I'm so sorry. So very sorry. I didn't think it would end like this. I really didn't. Do you know, during the last couple of weeks I'd decided he really did love you, that he wasn't using you for revenge. I'd actually decided we'd all been wrong about him and you'd been right.''

"He never once told me he loved me, you know,'' Juliana said wistfully. "I thought he was working up to it, though. I really did.''

"What are you going to do, Juliana? All these people. All this food. The music. What will you tell everyone?''

The last of the numb feeling fractured and disintegrated. The pain was there, just as she had known it would be. But so were a lot of other emotions, including anger.

"How dare he do this to me?'' Juliana said through her teeth. "Who the hell does he think he is? He's engaged to me, by heaven. And if he thinks he can walk out on me like this, he's got another think coming.''

She started through the crowd toward the door.

"Juliana,'' Elly hissed. "Where are you going? What shall I tell the guests?''

"Tell them to enjoy the food. It's paid for.''

Juliana dashed through the startled crowd of guests and out the front door of the restaurant. She came to a brief halt on the sidewalk, scanning the parking lot for the familiar tan-colored Buick.

She heard the engine before she spotted the car. Travis was just pulling away from the curb.

"Come back here, you bastard...I said come back here.'' Juliana hiked up her skirt and ran at top speed across the restaurant driveway, no easy feat in her glittering high heels.

She cut through two rows of parked cars and reached the Buick just as Travis paused to glance over his shoulder to check the traffic behind him.

He did not see her when she threw herself on the hood of the Buick but he certainly heard the resulting thud. His head came around very quickly, and he stared at the woman in green sprawled across the engine compartment as if he had just seen a ghost.

"Juliana!"

"You're engaged to me, you bastard," she yelled back through the windshield. "You can't walk out on me like this. I deserve an explanation and I'm warning you right now, whatever that explanation is, it won't be good enough. Because we aren't just engaged, we're partners, remember? You might be able to end an engagement like this, but you can't end a business relationship so easily."

Travis switched off the engine and opened the car door. "I don't believe this," he muttered as he got out. "On the other hand, maybe I do. Get down from there, Juliana."

She ignored the order and stood up on the tan-colored hood, balancing a little precariously. She paid no attention to the marks her heels were leaving in the paint. She folded her arms and gazed down at him with fire in her eyes. "I'm not going anywhere until I choose to do so. I want an explanation for the way you're trying to end our engagement. You owe me that much, Travis Sawyer."

He looked up at her, the lines of his face harshly etched in the glare of the parking lot lights. "I gave you your explanation, Juliana."

"What? That business about not being able to save Flame Valley? That's no explanation, that's an excuse."

"Didn't you hear me? I can't salvage the damned inn for your precious cousin and your ex-fiancé and the rest of your family. Flame Valley is going to go under and there's nothing I can do to save it."

"Stop talking about that stupid resort. I don't care about it right now. Our engagement party is a hell of a lot more important."

"Is that right?" he demanded roughly. "Are you really trying to tell me you want to go through with marriage to the man who's going to be single-handedly responsible for destroying Flame Valley?"

"Yes!" she yelled back.

CHAPTER TEN

THE ONLY THING that made it possible for Travis to hang on to his self-control was the sure and certain knowledge that if he lost it now, he would never be able to regain it. He looked up at the magnificent creature standing on the hood of his car and felt the blood pounding through his veins. Her hair was a wild, crazy shade of orange in the glare of the parking lot lights. Her shoes sparkled garishly as if they'd been coated with some sort of cheap glitter dust, and the huge satin bow at the back of her green dress had come undone.

Travis knew he had never in his life wanted a woman as badly as he wanted this one.

"Juliana, listen to me. I'm the Big Bad Wolf in this story, remember? That resort has been in the Grant family for over twenty years. I'm going to tear apart everything your father and his brother built. I'm going to ruin your cousin and Kirkwood. And you're going to lose a big chunk of your savings in the process. This is bottom-line time. You have to choose sides whether you like it or not and *I'm on the wrong side*."

"So you decided you'd make the choice for me? Forget it, Travis. I make my own decision."

His hand clenched into a fist. "You're going to hate my guts when you watch Elly and Kirkwood lose the resort."

"I could never hate you, although I might get madder than hell at you from time to time."

"Juliana, sometimes you have to make choices. You can't be on your family's side and my side, too, not in this. Don't you understand? You'll have to choose. I've already told you, I'm on the wrong side."

"I don't care which side you're on. That's the side I'm on and that's final. You can't get rid of me by telling me I have to choose between family and you. That's not how it is. Besides, I've already made my choices. I made them the day I met you. I chose you, Travis.''

Travis took a step forward, coming up against the hard metal of the Buick's fender. He could have reached out and touched Juliana but he didn't dare. Not yet.

"Are you trying to tell me that you still want to get engaged to me? That you want to marry me? Even though I can't stop what's going to happen to Flame Valley?" he demanded. He could hear the rasp in his voice. His mouth was dry.

"Travis, for a reasonably intelligent man, you are sometimes awfully slow to catch on. Yes, that's what I'm trying to tell you. For crying out loud, I didn't fall in love with you because I thought you could save Flame Valley. I fell in love with you weeks before I knew anything about your connection to the inn.''

"But after you found out about my connection to the inn things changed, didn't they?''

"I got mad but I didn't stop loving you. I've never stopped loving you. Besides, you offered to try to fix the damage. That was good enough for me. You made all the amends you needed to make.''

"I didn't do a very good job of fixing things, did I?''

Her smile glowed. "That doesn't matter," she said, her voice suddenly husky. "You tried. If anyone could have saved Flame Valley, it would have been you.''

Travis swore. "Trying isn't always good enough, Juliana.''

"Yes it is. Most of the time, at any rate. And certainly this time it is.''

"What makes it good enough this time?''

"Because you did it for me." She threw her arms open wide, and her smile was even more dazzling than usual. "And you did your best. You worked night and day to try to save the inn.''

"But I didn't pull it off. Don't you understand?''

"You're the one who doesn't understand. You don't understand what your efforts meant to me. Nobody has ever even tried to do something on that scale for me before. They all think I can take care of myself. But you went to the wall for me, Travis. For *me*, not for Elly or David or my parents or Uncle Tony. You did it for me. It was for me, wasn't it?''

"Hell, yes, it was for you. If you hadn't been involved everything would have been a damned sight simpler, that's for sure. I'd have taken over Flame Valley without a second's hesitation and I would never have looked back.''

"That's true. And you would have had every right. But you didn't do it because of me. Nobody does stuff like that for me, because I'm the strong one. Do you know how wonderful it is to have someone step in and try to save me?''

Travis was at a loss for words for a few seconds. All he could think about during that brief moment of charged silence was that until now no one had ever chosen him when a choice had to be made.

"Are you sure you want me?'' was all he could manage to get out. "Your parents, Elly and David, Tony, they're all going to blame me for not being able to pull the fat out of the fire.''

"They can blame anyone they want. We both know you did everything that could be done,'' she retorted vehemently.

"You're overlooking the fact that the fat was in the fire in the first place because of me,'' Travis felt obliged to point out.

"That doesn't matter. You had your reasons for doing what you did.''

"Revenge is a good reason?''

"Well, certainly it's a good reason. You had a right to get even for what happened five years ago. One can hardly hold that against you.''

"Your logic is incredible. But who am I to argue with it?''

Her smile was brighter than the parking lot lights. "Does this mean you're going to come back inside The Treasure House and celebrate your engagement to me in front of all those people?''

He touched the toe of one of her glittering high-heeled shoes. "Yes, ma'am, that's exactly what it means.''

"Then what are we waiting for?'' She held out her arms.

Travis felt the joyous laughter well up from somewhere deep in his gut. For a soul-shattering instant he knew the meaning of pure happiness. He reached out and scooped his lady off the hood of the car, paying no attention to the small paint scars left by her heels.

"You know something, Juliana? You make one hell of a hood ornament."

She laughed up at him as he set her on her feet. With great care he retied the huge satin bow at the small of her back. When he was finished he traced the elegantly bare line of her spine with his finger. She was warm and silky and so magnificently feminine that he ached for her. But there were a lot of people waiting inside The Treasure House, he reminded himself.

He reparked the car. Juliana reached for his hand as they started back across the parking lot but Travis forestalled her. He'd never felt more swashbuckling in his life. So he picked her up and carried her into the restaurant.

A cheer went up as Travis strode into the crowded room with Juliana in his arms. The band immediately struck up a waltz. Travis set Juliana on her feet and took her into his arms. He whirled her out onto the empty dance floor before she had quite realized what was happening.

"I didn't know you could waltz," Juliana murmured as the applause rose around them.

"Neither did I. But I think that tonight I could do just about anything." *Except save Flame Valley from myself.*

Out of the corner of his eye Travis caught glimpses of Elly and David and the Grants watching with anxious concern. By now they must have realized that their precious resort was history, he thought, but no one made a move to stop Juliana from dancing with him.

Then a sense of exultant satisfaction swept through him. Of course no one was going to try to come between him and Juliana. No one in his or her right mind got in Juliana's way when she wanted something, and she was making it very clear tonight that she wanted him.

Juliana had made her choice.

SEVERAL HOURS LATER Juliana was still humming a waltz to herself as Travis took her key and opened the front door of her condominium. He looked at her, amusement and something far more intense gleaming in his crystal eyes.

"Enjoy your engagement party?" he asked as he followed her into the hall.

"Had a lovely time. It was a perfect engagement party. The engagement party to end all engagement parties." She did one or two twirls on the carpet, enjoying the way her rhinestone shoes glittered beneath the green skirt of her gown. "What about you?"

Travis folded his arms and leaned one shoulder against the wall. He watched her dance around the living room. "It was a hell of a party, all in all."

"I thought so." She came to a halt in the center of the room and studied her long-nailed fingers. A diamond ring sparkled in the lamplight. "You even remembered the ring."

"I bought it right after I asked you to marry me. I've been carrying it around ever since."

"And you brought it to the party with you tonight even though you were only planning to stay long enough to say the engagement was over." Juliana smiled, feeling deliciously smug.

"I'd put it in my pocket earlier before I went to the office to call Bickerstaff one last time," Travis explained.

"Maybe it was your good-luck charm."

Travis's smile came and went. "If it was, it didn't do me much good when it came to dealing with Bickerstaff."

"Forget Bickerstaff. The business with the inn is over." Juliana walked toward him. "Now that we've settled the little matter of our engagement, I think it's time we ironed out a few small details of our relationship."

Travis's brows rose. "Such as?"

She looped her arms around his neck and looked straight into his eyes. "I love you, Travis. Do you love me?"

Travis unfolded his arms and put his hands around her waist. His eyes were startlingly serious now. "I love you."

"Is this a forever kind of love or the kind that lasts until the divorce?"

He pulled her hips tightly against his thighs and kissed her hard on the mouth. "It's the forever kind."

She relaxed, believing him. "You've never said, you know. I got a little nervous there for a while."

"That day on the beach. The day we talked about babies. That's when you started getting nervous, didn't you? I could feel you retreating from me, pulling back emotionally. I thought you were finally beginning to realize I might not be able to save the resort."

"I got scared, all right, but not because of Flame Valley. It occurred to me for the first time since I had met you that I might be making a mistake. You didn't seem ready to make a complete commitment. You were afraid to talk about anything as permanent as a baby. That's what made me so nervous."

He lifted his hands from her waist to spear his fingers through her thick hair. "I'll be honest, honey. The thought of having kids makes me uneasy."

"Perfectly understandable, given your background. That I can handle. We can work on your fears together. But I was worried that maybe you weren't sure of your commitment to me. And that terrified me."

"There was never any doubt in my mind about my feelings for you. But tonight when I talked to Bickerstaff and realized Flame Valley was going under, I didn't want to hear you tell me the engagement was off. So I decided to tell you first. I should have known you wouldn't let me get away that easily."

Juliana brushed her mouth against his. "Yes. You should have known. How could you do it, Travis? Would you really have walked away from me tonight and never looked back?"

"I figured I didn't have a prayer of marrying you, at least not anytime soon, but I sure as hell didn't intend to walk out of your life."

"Because you knew I'd come after you?"

His smile was slow and tantalizingly wicked. "No, not because I knew you were going to throw yourself on the hood of my car.

I knew I'd be seeing you again because I'm your partner in Charisma, remember? We have a deal, you and I. I am supposed to collect my fee regardless of whether or not I saved the inn. There's nothing like business to make sure two people see a lot of each other.''

She laughed up at him, delighted. ''Very clever.''

''A man has to be clever to stay one step ahead of you.''

''Who says you're one step ahead of me?'' she purred, liking the way her new ring flashed when she stroked her fingers along his shoulders.

''Right now I don't care which one of us is ahead of the other. I just want to get together. It's time we really celebrated our engagement.''

His mouth closed once more over hers, and Juliana felt herself being lifted up into his arms for a second time that night.

''I'm a little big to be carried around like this,'' she murmured against his mouth.

''You're just the right size for me,'' he said as he carried her into the kitchen.

''Funny, I was just thinking the same thing. What are we doing in here? The bedroom is the other direction.''

''Open the refrigerator,'' he ordered.

She did so and saw the bottle of chilled champagne inside. ''Ah-hah. This beats crackers in bed anytime.''

''Don't forget the glasses.''

Juliana plucked two glasses off the counter and cradled them, along with the champagne, as Travis carried her down the hall to the bedroom. Inside the white-on-white room he set Juliana lightly onto the bed. She pulled her legs up under her green skirt, and the rhinestone shoes glittered in the shadows. Travis watched her as he stripped off his clothing. Then he reached out and took the bottle of champagne and the glasses out of her hands and put them on the nightstand.

''Definitely the world's most stunning hood ornament,'' he muttered as he came down beside her on the bed.

''You don't think I was a bit gaudy? For a Buick, I mean?''

"Juliana, my sweet, you're always in the best of taste."

He kissed her shoulder and simultaneously found the bare skin of her back. Juliana trembled as his rough fingertips traveled down the length of her spine to her waist. Then he slowly undid the satin bow.

She stretched languorously, her pulse throbbing with anticipation as Travis slowly lowered the bodice of the green gown. "Your hands feel so good," she whispered.

"You're the one who feels good. Soft and silky and sleek." He leaned down to kiss the slope of her breasts as he bared them.

A moment later the dress was on the floor along with the rhinestone heels and Juliana's filmy underwear. Her breath was coming more quickly now in soft little gasps as her senses reeled with the gathering excitement.

"You always go wild in my arms," Travis said, sounding thoroughly pleased and deeply awed. "You make me crazy with the way you want me. You know that, sweetheart? No one's ever wanted me the way you do."

"I've never wanted anyone this way before," she confessed, clinging to him as he slid his hand down toward her moist heat.

"We agreed the first time that what we have is special. We were right." He parted her gently and found her sensual secrets.

Juliana clutched his arms and arched herself against him. *"Travis."*

He raised his head to look down at her. "I'll never get tired of watching you when you're with me like this." He stroked his fingers into her and withdrew them with calculated slowness.

"Oh, Travis, I can't seem to wait, I want..." Juliana felt the small convulsive contractions seize her with little warning. She cried out.

"No need to wait," Travis assured her, pulling her hips close to his thighs again. "There's more where that came from and we've got all the time in the world tonight. Go wild again for me, sweetheart."

"Not without you." She reached for him, sliding one of her legs between his, searching out the heavy, waiting length of him.

When she touched him intimately, cupping him and caressing him, Travis sucked in his breath. After that there were no words, only soft sounds of growing need and spiraling desire.

Juliana was lost in the wonderland of passion when she felt Travis open her legs with his strong hands. Her nails sank into his shoulders as he thrust boldly into her, and the delicious shock set off another ripple of release that seemed to travel throughout her whole body.

She heard him mutter her name as he surged into her again and again, felt his body tighten under her hands and then there was only the marvelous sense of free-fall that always followed the peak of their lovemaking. Juliana welcomed it, losing herself in her lover's arms even as he lost himself in hers.

The rhinestone shoes lying on the white carpet glittered in the shadows, the small stones sparkling as if they were diamonds.

"JULIANA?" Travis said her name softly in the darkness a long time later. He was sitting naked on the side of the bed, pouring champagne into the two glasses they had brought from the kitchen.

"Ummm?" She was feeling deliciously relaxed and content. She studied his broad shoulders and strong back with a loving eye. He really was just the right size, she told herself happily.

"If you did happen to get pregnant, hypothetically speaking, I'd be the happiest man alive."

"IT'S JUST TOO BAD you couldn't appreciate the expressions on everyone's face last night when you went racing out the door chasing Travis and then returned ten minutes later in his arms. It was an absolutely priceless scene. A scene of legendary proportions, as far as the management of The Treasure House is concerned." Elly sipped at her coffee latte and shook her head in wonderment.

"Sometimes a woman has to go after what she wants." Juliana savored the rich color of the Keemun tea in her cup and then automatically glanced around Charisma's pleasantly crowded serving area with an appraising eye.

Saturday mornings had typically been light until three months ago when she had put in a full range of newspapers and breakfast pastries. Customers had surged into the shop ever since on Saturdays to take their morning coffee and a croissant while reading something exotic and foreign like the *New York Times*.

"Your parents and my father were a bit stunned, I'll have to admit," Elly continued. "Especially after I told them that Travis was not going to save Flame Valley after all. You know what your father said?"

"What?"

"He told Dad to wait and see. 'It wasn't over until the fat lady sings,' I believe were his exact words."

"I hope the rest of you aren't holding any false expectations," Juliana said gently. "Travis said there really was nothing more he could do except find a buyer for the resort. That way, at least, we won't all lose our money. But you and David aren't going to own and operate Flame Valley, and the inn will definitely go into new hands."

"I know. David and I had a long talk last night about our future," Elly said. "We settled a lot of things we probably should have settled much sooner."

Juliana frowned. "Well? How did it go? Are you still worried about him leaving now that the resort is dead in the water?"

Elly smiled sweetly, her eyes clear. "Oh, no. He never was thinking of leaving me. The poor man was scared I might leave him. That's why he was so uptight these past few weeks. Can you believe it?"

"Yup. I always knew the two of you were meant for each other." Juliana sat back. "So what are you going to do?"

"Well, one possibility, if Travis finds us a buyer, is to take the money and try the resort business again, this time on a much smaller scale. Maybe a little bed-and-breakfast place on the coast. Another possibility, according to David, is to see if Fast Forward Properties can negotiate us a contract with the new owner, whoever it is, to run Flame Valley. Under Travis's guidance, of course. We don't want to make the same mistakes we made last time."

"Would that bother you, Elly? To stay on at the resort after it goes to a new owner?"

"I think I could handle it and so can David. I'm not sure Dad or your parents will like it. It will probably gall them to see family members reduced to being just the managers of Flame Valley."

"On the other hand," Juliana pointed out, "Uncle Tony and my folks aren't the ones who have to make the decision are they? It's you and David who have to decide what to do with your future."

"That's exactly what David and I told each other last night. I feel amazingly relaxed about the whole thing now that it's over. It's as if because of this mess David and I have finally stepped out from under Dad's shadow. Whatever happens now, our marriage will be the stronger for it."

"Uncle Tony always means well," Juliana said, "just like my parents always mean well."

"True. And we know they love us. That's the most important thing. But there's no denying they can be a little overbearing at times."

"Look at it this way, as irritating as the situation can be, it's better than winding up with parents who couldn't care less about what you do with your life."

"Who's got parents like that?" Elly asked in amazement.

"Travis."

Elly looked at her. "Oh. That's right. I suppose you have plans to fix the problem?"

Juliana smiled with cheerful confidence. "Let's just say I've got plans to give Travis's parents one more chance to dance at this wedding."

"And if they don't show up?"

"They'll show up."

"How can you be so sure?"

"Because thanks to a talk with Sandy I decided no more Ms Nice Guy. I'm going to blackmail Travis's folks into showing up and behaving themselves."

Elly's eyes widened. "You're going to blackmail them? I

should have guessed. You don't lack the nerve, Juliana. You always go after what you want, no holds barred.''

"It's one of my best features," Juliana agreed. "Just ask Travis. Say, I was planning to start the big hunt for my wedding gown this afternoon after Charisma closes for the day. Want to come with me? I guarantee this is going to be one special dress.''

"Now I know for certain you're back to normal,'' Elly said.

"STRANGE HOW SOME of the things you fear most in life aren't the ones you have to worry about after all, isn't it?'' David took a long swallow of his beer and looked out over the harbor.

"Life's funny that way sometimes." Travis was sitting next to David at one of the outdoor tables of the Golden Keel, a trendy pub near the marina. Both men had repaired to the bar by mutual agreement to discuss the future of Flame Valley. But so far all they'd talked about was their relationships with the women in their lives. "I take it you and Elly have come to an understanding.''

"She was worried I'd leave if we lost the inn. I think some part of her had never been completely certain I hadn't married her because of Flame Valley.''

"Juliana was always sure the two of you were in love right from the start.''

David chuckled. "Juliana is always sure of everything.''

"Yeah.'' Travis grinned fleetingly. "And sometimes she's right.''

"I've got to hand it to you, Sawyer. I don't know of any other man who could handle Juliana Grant.''

"If any other man ever tries, I'll break his neck,'' Travis said calmly.

"That's assuming Juliana doesn't do it first.''

"True. So what now, Kirkwood? You want me to try to find a buyer and see if I can get you a contract to manage the inn?''

David lounged back in his chair. "I've got a proposition for Fast Forward Properties.''

"What's that?''

"How about letting me and Elly run the place after you take

possession of the property? Hell, nobody knows the resort as well as we do.''

Travis studied the condensation on his beer glass. ''It wouldn't be the same as owning it,'' he warned. ''I'll have a responsibility to my investors. It would be my job to make sure the resort got back on its feet. I'd be on you all the time. Looking over your shoulder. Watching every move. I'm good at what I do, Kirkwood, but the fact is, I'm hell to work for.''

''I think I could deal with it.'' David looked unperturbed. ''Who knows? I might learn something about financial management from you.''

''I'll think about it. Run it past my investors.''

''Fair enough,'' David agreed. ''So when's the wedding?''

''Juliana's got it scheduled for the end of the month.''

''The end of the month? Why so soon? You're engaged and you're practically living together. Why is Juliana rushing the wedding?''

''It was my idea,'' Travis said. ''I'm not taking any chances. When I sew up a business deal, I sew it up tight. No loopholes.''

David grinned. ''I know. You sewed up the deal on Flame Valley so tight even you couldn't find a way out. Juliana doesn't stand a chance.''

''That's the whole idea.''

CHAPTER ELEVEN

"HE'S GOING to stand her up at the altar, I just know he is." Beth Grant, looking every inch the mother of the bride in mauve lace and silk, paced back and forth in the small church anteroom.

"Uncle Roy and Dad will get a shotgun if Travis tries to duck out now," Elly declared with a small smile. She was fussing with the satin train of Juliana's gown.

"Relax, both of you. Travis isn't going to stand me up." Juliana scrutinized her image in the mirror. The sweetheart neckline had been the right choice, after all. She'd had a few second thoughts yesterday when she'd tried the gown on one last time. But today it looked perfect. The wedding dress was everything a wedding dress was supposed to be, spectacular, frothy and extravagant. She'd spent a fortune on it and didn't regret one dime.

"I'm not so sure Travis wouldn't walk out at the last minute," her mother said. "It would be the ultimate revenge on the Grant family, wouldn't it? First Flame Valley falls into his clutches and then he leaves you at the altar. Where is that man?"

"He'll get here on time if he knows what's good for him," Elly murmured, giving the train another small twitch. "He knows that if he doesn't show there'd be no telling what Juliana would do. He's still complaining about the scratches her heels left on the hood of his car."

"I'm not worried about Travis getting here," Juliana said, feeling perfectly calm as she bent closer to the mirror to check her lipstick. She wondered if she should have opted for a more vivid shade. The coral looked a tad pale. Then again, brides weren't supposed to go to the altar looking as if they'd just walked out of a makeup ad, she reminded herself. Angelina Cavanaugh had made that very clear to her a week ago. *Tone it down, Juliana.*

Brides are supposed to look sweet and demure, not like an empress claiming her empire.''

"You don't look concerned about anything except your makeup," Beth sighed, watching Juliana....

"Well, to tell you the truth, I am a little concerned about one thing. I was wondering if Travis's parents had arrived. Any sign of them?"

"I'll check with the usher," Elly said, heading for the door. She disappeared out into the hall, obviously glad to have something useful to do.

Beth came toward Juliana with a misty, maternal gleam in her eyes. She hugged her daughter briefly. "You look beautiful, dear. I'm so proud of you."

"Thanks, Mom."

"I will personally throttle that man if he doesn't show up."

"He'll show up." Juliana spoke with complete confidence. Nevertheless, she was touched by her mother's unusual protective instincts. "The thing about Travis is that you can always count on him."

Beth shook her head wonderingly. "I cannot understand how you are always so certain of him. As far as I can tell he's done absolutely nothing to warrant your total confidence in him. He didn't even save Flame Valley."

"He did everything that could be done. At least with him in charge of Fast Forward Properties the transfer to new ownership will be as smooth as possible. And David says he and Elly are going to get the contract to run it."

"I suppose that's better than nothing. Maybe someday we'll find a way to get the resort back into Grant hands. Your father still thinks there's every possibility this will all work out in the end. Even your Uncle Tony seems amazingly optimistic. But I still don't see how you could have had such faith in Sawyer right from the start."

"You don't really know him. I do."

"What makes you think you're such an authority on Travis Sawyer?"

"We have a lot in common," Juliana said simply, adjusting a straying curl beneath her veil. "We trust each other and we love each other. It's all really very simple."

"I wish I could be sure of that. I hope you know what you're doing, Juliana."

"I always know what I'm doing, you know that, Mom. Would you hand me my flowers, please? It's almost time."

Beth looked more anxious than ever as she handed the bouquet of exotic flame-colored orchids to her daughter. "You can hardly walk down the aisle in front of all those people if Travis isn't waiting at the other end. I won't allow it. The humiliation would be unbearable for the entire family."

"He'll be there."

Beth eyed her daughter's serene expression and smiled reluctantly. "Your complete faith in him is getting contagious."

"You'd better go take your seat, Mom. Dad and Uncle Tony will be getting nervous."

Beth looked at her. "You're absolutely certain Travis will show up today?"

"Absolutely certain."

The door burst open and Elly stuck her head around the corner. She was excited and amused. "They're here, all right. The usher says he just seated the groom's parents. All four of them. And a bunch of stepbrothers and stepsisters."

Juliana nodded, content. "Good. Another example of winning by intimidation. Mom, run along now. It's time."

Elly bit her lip. "Uh, Travis's folks are here, but Travis isn't here yet, Juliana."

"He'll be here."

Beth cast her daughter one last worried look. "You're sure?"

"Yes, Mom, I'm sure."

"You do look lovely today, dear." Beth smiled tremulously and went out of the room.

Elly gave Juliana a hard stare. "*Are* you sure?"

"Of course I'm sure. Would I be standing here in this dress if

I thought I'd get stood up at the altar? Travis would never do that to me.''

"Well, there was that little incident at the engagement party," Elly reminded her delicately.

"Travis showed, didn't he? He didn't stand me up. He just didn't plan to hang around very long after he got there, that's all."

"That's a very charitable view of the situation. If you hadn't run after him and thrown yourself on the hood of his car, I don't know what would have happened that night."

"A woman has to go after what she wants."

"And you really want Travis Sawyer, don't you?" Elly said with soft understanding.

A knock on the door interrupted Juliana's reply. "We're ready, Miss Grant," said a muffled voice on the other side.

Juliana nodded with satisfaction and pulled the waist-length veil down over her face. "Right on time. Get your flowers, Elly."

Juliana opened the door and walked confidently down the hall to the point where she would make her entrance with her father. She peeked down the aisle toward the altar and was not at all surprised to see Travis standing there, waiting for her. He looked incredible in formal clothes, she thought fondly. She'd have to find a way to get him dressed up more often.

"He just drove up two minutes ago," Roy Grant muttered, shaking his head as he took his daughter's arm. "Tony and I were just about to go after him. Thought for sure you'd been stood up."

Everyone was feeling protective of her today, Juliana thought happily. It must have had something to do with her role as a bride. Parental instincts coming out, no doubt.

"There was no need to worry, Dad. Travis said he'd be here."

The music swelled. Juliana smiled her most brilliant smile and started down the aisle on her father's arm.

Travis never took his eyes off her as she came toward him. Her gaze met his through the veil. When she reached the altar he accepted her hand as Roy Grant released her.

"Sorry I'm a little late," Travis murmured very softly. "Got held up at the office. Bickerstaff changed his mind."

"He *what*?" Juliana hastily lifted the gossamer veil so she could get a better look at Travis's laughing eyes.

"You heard me. Flame Valley is technically again in Grant hands as of about fifteen minutes ago. Got a hell of a load of debt hanging over it, but David and Elly are the official owners."

Juliana threw her arms around him, laughing with surprise and delight. "I knew you'd pull it off, Travis. There's nobody like you in the whole world."

A ripple of astonishment went through the crowd as Juliana hugged Travis. The minister coughed to get everyone's attention. "I believe we're ready to begin," he said with a touch of severity.

Juliana released Travis, grinning. "First you have to make an announcement," she informed the man of the cloth.

The minister's brows rose in amused curiosity. "What sort of announcement would that be?"

"Just say that Bickerstaff changed his mind."

The minister looked out over the crowded church. "Bickerstaff," he intoned solemnly, "has changed his mind."

Juliana thought she heard a small gasp from Elly and then the bride's side of the church broke out in wild applause. Anxious not to offend, the rest of the guests quickly followed suit.

When the applause finally faded the minister looked sternly at an unrepentant Juliana. "Now may we begin the wedding service?"

"You bet," Juliana said.

"Hang on a second," Travis said and reached out to lower the veil back down over Juliana's dazzling smile. When he was finished arranging the filmy stuff he nodded, satisfied with the old-fashioned, demure effect. "A man's got a right to insist on a little tradition once in a while."

"I'M THINKING of buying an interest in this restaurant," Travis muttered some time later as he stood, champagne glass in hand, surveying the throng of guests at the reception. "At the rate we're using this place, we might as well own a share of it. One of these days you're going to have to arrange a party at one of the other restaurants in town. Just for variety.''

"Now don't grumble, Travis. The Treasure House always does a wonderful job with wedding receptions.''

"Uh-huh.'' He sipped his champagne. "At least I'm finally putting an end to your hobby of collecting proposals here.''

She batted her lashes at him. "Yours was the only proposal that counted.''

"Damn right.''

Juliana beamed. "Do you realize this is the first moment I've had you to myself since the wedding? I thought I'd never get you away from David and Uncle Tony and Dad.''

"They wanted all the details about the Bickerstaff deal.''

"I'll bet they did. Why did Bickerstaff change his mind?''

"It's complicated and I don't really feel like going into it now, but to sum it up, I called in an old favor from a banker friend of mine. When he found out Bickerstaff was interested in the resort, he agreed to restructure some of Flame Valley's debt. That, in turn, tipped the scales as far as Bickerstaff was concerned. He decided to go ahead with the deal.''

Juliana whistled faintly in appreciation. "Sounds tricky. What about your investors?''

"They'll be paid off the same way they would have been in a buy-out. It's complicated, but I think it's going to work. Assuming Kirkwood cooperates.''

"He will.''

"Yeah, I think he will.'' Travis glanced over Juliana's shoulder and his eyes hardened faintly. "Here comes Mom and her second husband.''

"I like your mother. And your father. We all had a nice chat earlier.'' Juliana turned to smile at the attractive, champagne-blond woman who was approaching with a slightly portly, well-dressed man in tow.

"Hello, Mrs. Riley. Mr. Riley. Enjoying yourselves, I hope?''

Linda Riley returned the smile and so did her husband. "Very much, dear." She looked at her eldest son. "You've chosen a very lovely bride, Travis."

"She chose me," Travis said, not bothering to conceal his satisfaction. "Glad you and George and the kids could get here today," he added a little gruffly.

"Wouldn't have missed it for the world," Mrs. Riley said dryly as she slanted an amused glance at Juliana. "We never see enough of you, Travis. You really ought to come visit more often. The kids are always curious about their mysterious big brother, you know. They admire you. I believe Jeremy wants to talk to you about going into land development."

"Is that so?" Travis looked wary but interested.

Mrs. Riley's smile deepened with understanding as she turned back to Juliana. "Thank you very much for inviting all of us, Juliana. You know, sometimes families drift apart without really meaning to. People lose perspective in the heat of selfish emotion. Pride becomes far more important than it should. But that doesn't mean any of us want it that way or that we can't see the light eventually."

"I know, Mrs. Riley," Juliana said, returning her mother-in-law's smile. "As I told Travis, people change. Weddings are great opportunities for getting families together, aren't they?"

"Better than funerals," Travis remarked.

Juliana wrinkled her nose at him and then helped herself to a canapé from the buffet table while he talked to his mother and stepfather. She was quite pleased with the way things had turned out, she decided. Everyone had been well behaved at the church and seemed to be acting like adults here at the reception.

Travis's father, a tall, distinguished-looking man who had introduced himself earlier, was at the other end of the room with his second wife. Both were in deep conversation with Roy and Tony Grant.

Travis's stepbrothers and sisters, ranging in age from the late teens to early twenties, were a lively, talkative crew who appeared to regard the brother they shared with some awe and fascination.

"So how did you do it?" Travis asked as his mother and step-father drifted off to join another group.

"Do what?"

"Don't play the innocent with me. I know you too well. How did you get both my mother and my father to attend the wedding?"

"Travis, I think you should make allowances for the fact that reasonable people are quite capable of change over a period of time. It's been years since they refused to attend your first wedding. They were probably still very bitter toward each other back then. Now they've had a chance to mellow and mature. Intelligent people grow up sooner or later."

Travis picked up a cucumber and salmon canapé and popped it into his mouth. He considered Juliana's words carefully and then dismissed them. "I'm not buying it. What you say about their maturing may be true but I don't see you just sending out invitations and hoping for the best. You wouldn't take any chances. You wanted them here, so what did you do to make certain they showed up today?"

"Blackmailed them."

Travis grinned. "With what?"

"I made it very clear that neither your mother nor your father would be invited to see their first grandchild if they didn't have enough courtesy to attend the wedding."

"I should have guessed." He put down his champagne glass. "Care to dance, Mrs. Sawyer?"

"I would love to dance, Mr. Sawyer."

Juliana went into his arms, the heavy skirts of her wedding gown whirling around her low-heeled satin slippers.

"I see you decided not to wear high heels today," Travis observed as he looked down slightly to meet her eyes.

"I figured a bride should be able to look up to her husband on her wedding day," Juliana explained demurely. "Tradition, you know."

Travis laughed and the sound of his uninhibited masculine pleasure turned the head of everyone in the room. "Are you sure you didn't wear the low heels because you wanted to be prepared to run after me in case I didn't show up at the church?''

She looked up at him with all her love in her eyes. "I knew you'd show. I never doubted it for a moment.''

Travis's gaze grew suddenly, fiercely intent. "You were right. Nothing on earth could have kept me from being at that church today.''

"I love you, Travis.''

He smiled. "I know. I've never been loved by anyone the way you love me. Just for the record, I love you, too.''

"I know,'' she said, pleased. "Hey, you want to sneak out of here early and start on our honeymoon?''

"That depends. What, exactly, are you planning to do on our honeymoon? Toss me in the marina? Chase me through parking lots? Dump guacamole over my head?''

"Gracious, no. I was thinking we could spend the time going over the plans for my chain of Charisma tea shops.''

"You never give up, do you?''

"Never.''

"I've got a better idea,'' Travis said. "What do you say we go someplace private and talk about babies?''

"While it's true I never give up,'' Juliana responded smoothly, "I can be temporarily distracted. I would love to go someplace private and talk about babies.''

"It's a deal,'' Travis said.

He came to a halt in the middle of the dance floor, took Juliana's hand in his and led her toward the door—and their future.

MIDSUMMER MADNESS
Christine Rimmer

For my sister, B. J. Jordan,
who always believed in me,
And for my brother, Paul Smith,
who held out a hand when I needed one

CHAPTER ONE

"CODY, um, I'll take over...if you want...."

Cody McIntyre didn't hear the hesitant proposition, partly because it was spoken so softly, and partly because he was glaring at the phone he'd just slammed back into its cradle. His mind was occupied with dark, murderous thoughts—thoughts that concerned the immediate and permanent elimination from the world of the "expert" from Hollywood who was supposed to have shown up in Emerald Gap the day before, and who had just called to say he wasn't going to be showing up at all.

"Cody...."

This time he heard something. "Hmm?" he asked absently, glancing at the only other person in the room, his bookkeeper, Juliet Huddleston, whom he'd known all his life. Juliet sat at the spare desk in the corner, with his midmonth payroll spread out in front of her. "You say something, Julie?"

Maybe he really should sue the bastard, Cody was thinking, though lawsuits were generally not his style. Men like Cody considered a handshake a bond—and simply cut off dealings with people who didn't.

Juliet sat on an armless swivel chair. Now she spun in the chair, until she faced him straight on. "I said, I'll do it."

Cody hadn't the faintest idea what she was talking about, but he figured it must be important. She was looking directly at him, her hazel eyes unwavering. For shy Julie Huddleston, a dead-on look like the one she was giving him was such a rarity as to be kind of spooky.

"You all right, Julie?"

"I'm fine." She straightened her narrow shoulders and tugged on the jacket of the gray business suit she was wearing. "And I want to do it." She looked downright resolute.

"Er, do what?"

She cleared her throat. "I want to take over that director's job. I want to run the town pageant this year."

Cody stared at her, his surprise at what she'd just proposed so complete that he more or less forgot how to talk for a moment. Then his voice returned. "Midsummer Madness?" He muttered the name of the annual ten-day festival in frank disbelief. "*You* want to run Midsummer Madness this year?"

Juliet picked up his amazement at her suggestion, and blinked. She suddenly looked more like herself. Her eyes got that soft, anxious look. But she didn't give in. She confirmed, "Yes," the affirmative weakened only by the little gasp she took between the *y* and the *e*.

Cody stole a moment to comb his hair back with his fingers. He liked Julie, always had. In fact, ever since they were kids, he'd always made it a point to keep one eye out for her. The last thing he wanted to do was disappoint her; she was such a gentle soul.

But the Juliet Huddlestons of the world were not festival directors, not by a long shot. Once again, he silently cursed the delinquent professional he'd hired, this time for making it necessary for him to hurt poor Julie's feelings.

Cody regretfully shook his head. "That's sweet of you, Julie. But we've got to face facts. Running a pageant isn't really up your alley."

Cody watched the hopeful light fade from her eyes and felt like a rat for putting it out. Her shoulders fell, and she slowly turned back to the open check register and the stack of time cards on the desk.

Cody started around his own desk, to get closer to her and ease her hurt feelings a little. But he was stopped by the knock on the door.

"It's open," he called.

The door was flung back, and the room was filled with the sounds from the busy kitchen outside. Cody's office was behind

McIntyre's, the bar and grill he owned and operated himself. He also owned and managed the hardware store down the street, and the family ranch a few miles out of town. Cody was a busy man. Too busy, he thought again, to run the damn summer pageant himself this year. But that was exactly what he was going to be doing.

Each of the merchants in town took a turn, and this year was his. He'd thought it a stroke of brilliance to convince them to bring in an expert. So much for brilliance. So much for damn experts....

"Here you are, you devil. The bartender said I could find you back here." The shapely brunette in the doorway to the kitchen wore painted-on jeans and a little-girl pout. "Remember me?"

Cody's mama had raised him right. He tried to be tactful, in spite of the fact that he couldn't recollect ever seeing this woman before in his life. "Pardon me, but I don't recall where we met before, ma'am." Over the woman's shoulder, he could see the day pot washer, Elroy, paused in midscrub and leering suggestively. "Why don't you just come on in and close that door?" Cody suggested.

The woman made a big production of shutting the door. She glanced once in Juliet's direction, and then shrugged, apparently deciding to pretend Julie wasn't there. Next, the woman leaned against the closed door and sighed, a move which displayed her generous breasts to distinct advantage. "I kept hoping you'd call."

"Excuse me, but who are you?"

"God, you are one gorgeous hunk of man."

"Ma'am. Won't you tell me your name?"

"Lorena. I wrote it on that matchbook that I gave to the waitress with the red hair. Last Saturday, it was. You sang that Garth Brooks song. I was at that itty-bitty table, way in the back corner. I had a date. But I whispered to that waitress to explain to you that I was a totally free woman, ready, willing, and able to get to know a terrifically incredible guy like yourself—"

"So then we've never met before, ma'am?"

At the small desk in the corner, Juliet couldn't help but hear all this. She stifled a small, sympathetic smile and almost forgot her own problems as she tried to block out the sound of poor Cody dealing with another avid admirer.

"Well, we haven't met formally, of course," the brunette allowed. "But come on, admit it, you saw me back there. Don't try to hide it from me. You felt it, too, when our eyes collided. Bam. Like a jolt. A bolt out of the blue."

"Well, ma'am. I can't precisely say that what you're describing happened for me...."

Juliet shook her head. Poor Cody. The women just wouldn't leave him alone. He had a talent with a harmonica and a guitar. He also had a slow, sexy singing voice and sometimes even wrote his own songs. When the mood struck, on occasional weekends, he'd sing a few numbers in the bar out front. That drove the ladies wild.

Also, besides being a talented musician and singer, Cody McIntyre just happened to be drop-dead gorgeous—in a very manly sort of way.

"Honey—" the brunette put a hand on her hip and sighed again "—I can *make* it happen for you. You just give me a chance...." She looked at Cody as if she longed to gobble him alive.

Objectively, Juliet could understand the brunette's desire. Most women felt the same way when they looked at Cody. He could have been the prince in a grown-up woman's fairy tale.

His shining gray-green eyes, with whites so white they dazzled, looked out from under straight brows. His nose was perfectly symmetrical, with nostrils that flared just enough to show sensitivity, but not enough to make a woman doubt his ability to take charge. His mouth was a sculpture, firm yet responsive, with the engaging tendency to curl with humor on the right side. His chin was strong, but not too square. His hair was brown with golden highlights. His ears did not stick out. And most important for a handsome man, he really didn't seem to care a bit about how he looked.

And on top of all that, he was a genuinely good person.

As the brunette went on leaning against the door and sighing with great enthusiasm, Juliet filled out another check and tried to mind her own business.

She didn't entirely succeed. From thoughts of how poor Cody couldn't keep the women at bay, she found herself deciding that there was a certain similarity between herself and him.

Strange. She herself was the invisible woman, so plain and bland that everyone—men especially—saw right through her. And Cody McIntyre was a living, breathing masculine dream. Yet he lived alone as she did, having failed so far to find the right woman among all the ladies who threw themselves at his feet. Sometimes lately, Juliet found herself feeling more sorry for him than for herself.

Correction, Juliet thought, shaking a mental finger at herself. I do *not* feel sorry for myself. Not anymore. I've taken the reins of my life in my own two hands now. And I'm making the next thirty years more exciting than the past thirty were, or I will die trying.

Such was Juliet Titania Huddleston's birthday resolution. She'd made the vow just four months before, on the day she hit the big three-oh. She'd told no one, partly because no one asked, and partly because this was her own private project, her business alone.

Juliet had already taken some specific steps to make her resolution a reality. And she intended to keep taking steps, until she had reached her goal.

Juliet straightened in her chair at just the idea of her vow. At that moment, the shapely brunette sashayed across the room to Cody's desk, trailing an insistent cloud of musky perfume.

"So what do you say, darlin'?" the woman breathed. "How 'bout you, me, a bottle of wine and a big, fat full moon?"

Cody kindly demurred, and then ushered the woman back toward the door. With a gentle skill born of extensive experience, he had the woman out the door and on her way before she even realized she'd been turned down.

Juliet was busily filling out the final check when a shadow fell across the paper.

"Julie?"

She looked up into Cody's beautiful and sympathetic eyes—and made one of those wimpy little questioning sounds she'd been making all her life.

Inside, Juliet groaned at her own ingrained meekness. But then she gamely reminded herself that no one got assertive overnight. Little by little, she'd eliminate everything wimpy from her life, but she wasn't going to be too hard on herself if she backslid now and then.

"Are you going to be all right?" Cody was asking.

Juliet knew what he was talking about. He wanted to be sure she had accepted the fact that directing Midsummer Madness was not a job for her.

Juliet considered. She had to admit that he was probably right. The truth was, she'd never directed anything in her life. And telling other people what to do was something for which she'd yet to show the slightest aptitude. Some people are born to lead; they shine in the limelight. And some are born to sit in the background, tallying receipts. Juliet knew quite well into which category she fell. She opened her mouth to tell him she understood why he didn't want to give her a chance.

But something inside her choked the words off before they took form. There was her birthday vow to remember. If she hungered for more out of life than she'd had so far, she simply had to get out there and take what she wanted.

She decided she just wasn't willing to give up on this yet. "I...I can do it, Cody. Let me try."

Cody's expression turned pained. He ambled away and hitched a leg up on the corner of his desk. He looked down at the rawhide boot on his dangling foot. "Now, Julie," he said, still studying his boot. "I'd say you haven't really given this notion much thought."

"I h-have, too. Give me a chance."

He looked up from his boot and into her eyes. His face spoke of great patience, and even greater conviction that she was asking to take on more than someone like her could ever hope to handle.

Juliet looked right back at him and found herself experiencing a truly alien emotion for someone as terminally timid as she'd always been.

The emotion was annoyance. He didn't have to be so utterly certain that her running the pageant would be a disaster. Maybe leadership wasn't her strong suit, but she did have some of the necessary qualities, after all. She'd earned a four-year degree and managed her own bookkeeping business, so she possessed the requisite organizational skills. And she'd been involved with the pageant, in minor capacities, almost every year of her life. She knew what needed to be done.

"Julie," Cody said then, still in that infinitely understanding tone. "Be realistic. You'd have to oversee the entire opening-day parade, not to mention plan the Gold Rush Ball and direct the Midsummer Madness Revue. How are you going to manage all that, when most of the time I have to ask twice just to hear what you said?"

Juliet felt her shoulders start to slump again. He was right. She couldn't do it. Not a timid mouse like her. Not in a million years....

Hey, wait a minute here, that new woman deep inside herself argued. Who took that weekend assertiveness training retreat last month and came out of it with a new awareness of how to know what she wants and take steps to get it? Who's been going to Toastmasters International in secret since April, driving all the way to Auburn every Friday night in order to conquer her fear of public speaking? Who's stood up there and spoken before the group three times in the past two months, achieving a higher score each time?

Me, Juliet, that's who.

"I can speak up," she said aloud, "if I force myself. I've been working on that."

Cody, for his part, was studying her, puzzled why shy Julie would even consider taking on such a task, let alone insist on it. Then it came to him how to settle this problem once and for all.

He lowered his dangling foot to the floor and stood up. "All right, then," he said, seeming to give in to her.

She blinked. "You agree? You'll let me handle it?"

"It's not my decision."

"What do you mean?"

"I mean—" he shrugged "—that you can talk to the merchants' association at seven tonight." The words were offhand, though he knew they'd have a crushing effect. Julie would never get up in front of a group of people and give a speech. Now she would have no choice but to back down.

Cody began a casual circuit of his desk, not looking at her anymore. There was dead silence from Juliet's corner of the room. He was positive she'd be wearing that stricken look she got when anyone even suggested she do something that might draw attention to herself. He'd always hated to see that look on her face, because he knew it meant she was suffering agonies of shyness.

However, a little suffering now was preferable to her getting too carried away with this crazy idea that she could take over Midsummer Madness for that damned delinquent expert from Hollywood.

Cody continued in an offhand tone. "You can impress them all with what a great idea it would be to hire you. I mean, you might as well start forcing yourself to speak up right away, don't you think?"

Cody reached his leather chair and plunked himself down in it. He allowed a benign smile, confident that he'd handled this little predicament just right. Faced with the prospect of getting up in front of all those people, shy Julie would run the other way quicker than a cat with its tail on fire.

He looked directly at her again, steeling himself for the agony he'd see on her face, and for the defeated expression that would come next. It took him several seconds to absorb what he actually saw.

Her chin was set, her lips pressed together. She looked—by

God, she looked determined. When she spoke, Cody couldn't believe his ears.

"All right," she said. "I'll speak to the merchants' association at seven tonight."

"AND, AS FOR THE Midsummer Madness Revue," Juliet announced in a calm, clear voice, "well, I just think we can have a lot of fun with it this year. We'll have music by the Barbershop Boys and the school choirs, as always. And I also think maybe I could line up a few of our local favorites to give us a number or two. There'll be poems by Flat-nosed Jake." Juliet winked at Jake, a bearded, scruffy character in the front row, whose nose appeared to have collided with something unyielding at some point in his life. "Jake, as most of you know, is poet emeritus of our fair city. And we'll include a skit detailing the settlement of Emerald Gap by a group of prospectors back in 1852. Also, Melda Cooks has written a reenactment of the hanging of Maria Elena Roderica Perez Smith, who, as you might recall, was a local laundress lynched here after she stabbed a man to death in a brawl in the spring of 1856...."

At the back of Emerald Gap Auditorium, where the bright spill of light that shone on Juliet's pale hair did not reach, Cody sat in one of the creaky old theater seats and wondered what the hell was going on.

What had happened to shy Julie Huddleston?

This afternoon, no sooner had she knocked his boots off by saying she'd speak before the merchants' association, than she'd demanded all the planning materials he'd been saving to give to the pro from Hollywood. With the big folder tucked safely under her arm, she'd taken right off for her own small office two blocks away.

She must have gotten right on the phone, because all the people she was claiming were going to help her out were sitting down front now, nodding and smiling and looking like they were willing to follow her off the nearest cliff if she asked them to.

And why the hell not? Her start had been a little rocky—that much was true. She'd had that freaky spooked rabbit look for just a minute there when she got behind that podium and realized all those faces were staring at her. But she'd recovered—boy, had she. She'd recovered just fine.

Up on the stage, Juliet continued. "And, since this is gold country after all, I think the ball on Saturday, the third, should be a genuinely gala event. This year we'll really put some effort into making it a true costume affair, talk as many locals as possible into dressing in the period...."

Back in the darkness, Cody shook his head. On the one hand, he was experiencing a massive feeling of relief because it looked like the association was going to hire Julie to do the job. Cody was going to be let off the hook for it.

On the other hand, though, he felt a kind of creeping disquiet. He looked at Julie up there in the light, and he wondered if he knew her at all.

Which was crazy. He'd known her practically all his life. They were the same age and had gone through school together.

Cody smiled to himself, remembering Julie on the first day of kindergarten. The teacher, Miss Oakleaf, had called the roll. And Julie had been too scared to say her name. She'd stared down at her lap, her white skin flushing painful red, her little hands shaking.

In his memory, Julie had always been like that—afraid of her own shadow, keeping to herself, quivering visibly at any notice paid to her. He'd been a little surprised that she got through state college, wondered how she'd survived the crowds. But she'd done it, and she'd returned to Emerald Gap to set up her own business, with herself as her only employee. He'd hired her right off, and so had half of the other merchants and small businessmen in town. She was doing well, but always in that quiet, retiring way that she had. At least until recently.

Cody made a low sound in his throat, as it occurred to him that for the past few weeks Julie had been driving around in a red sports car. He'd seen the red car, on a morning when he'd gone out to do the chores, parked in front of the guesthouse at his ranch. Her little brown economy car had been nowhere in sight.

And that was another thing. Three months ago, he'd decided to rent out the guesthouse. Julie had taken it. It had never crossed his mind to question why she would suddenly decide to move out of the big house in town that her parents had left to her when they retired, and into a two-bedroom cottage fifteen miles from most of her clients; he'd simply been glad to get someone dependable so easily. But now he wondered....

Not that he was likely, the way things were, to find out much. They lived less than three hundred yards from each other, yet it might as well be three hundred miles; they each maintained strict privacy.

Up on the stage, Julie laughed. It was a shy little laugh, but a charming one. Her pale hair, which was straight and hung to her shoulders, had a smooth, curried sheen in the flood of light from above.

Cody shifted in the seat, trying to accommodate his long legs more comfortably without doing what he longed to do—swing his boots up on the row in front of him. Andrea Oakleaf, still very much a schoolteacher, was down in the second row. If she turned and saw him with his boots up, he'd be hearing about it in no uncertain terms.

Juliet made a mild joke. A ripple of laughter passed through the hall.

She was definitely changing, Cody thought. His efficient yet touchingly bashful bookkeeper wasn't so bashful anymore. What could have made her decide to step out of the shadows after all these years?

Maybe, he thought, he should ask her out to dinner sometime and find out. After all, they were friends, weren't they? There couldn't be any harm in spending an evening or two enjoying each other's company. They could laugh over old times together and really get to know each other—

Cody straightened up and cut off the rambling thought.

What the hell was going on here? He'd been wondering what was happening with Julie. Maybe a better question would be, what was happening with *him?* Why the big interest in a woman who'd been around since they were both in diapers?

Cody decided not to think about that. It was no big deal. He'd put thoughts of Julie—and thoughts about why he was thinking so much about Julie—right out of his mind.

That decided, he focused on the stage again—and saw Julie.

All at once, unable to sit still, he swung his boots up on the back of the chair in front of him, recalled Miss Oakleaf, and swung them back down again. They hit the old pine strip floor a mite too firmly, and Andrea Oakleaf turned briefly around to shoot one of her famous squinty-eyed looks toward the darkness where he sat. After that, Cody kept his feet on the floor and his mind, more or less, in control.

Up on the stage, Juliet finished her speech. She left the podium to the accompaniment of approving applause. She sat, feeling as if she floated there, on a folding chair to the left of the podium, while questions were asked of her. She had answers to all of them.

It was incredible.

Melda Cooks asked how Juliet would handle casting the play she'd written. Juliet remembered past years, when they'd had try-outs, and no one had shown up. Or when they'd cast by asking around, and some people had felt left out.

So Juliet said she'd combine the two methods: a day of tryouts, and then any uncast roles would be filled by appealing to the community consciousness of people who might fit the parts. Juliet raised her eyebrows just a fraction when she said "community consciousness," and everyone chuckled a little. They all knew what she meant; they'd end up begging a few softhearted souls to get involved.

Babe Allen pointedly remarked that Juliet could hardly expect to be paid what they'd agreed to pay the expert from Hollywood. Juliet, prepared for that one, smiled sweetly and answered that she was willing to do the work as a community service—provided the merchants donated the full fee they would have paid to the new community park down at the foot of Commercial Street.

It was so…marvelously simple. And *fun.* She just used her head, and then explained what she'd figured out, and it made sense. People listened. Amazing. Wonderful.

After they took the vote and elected her, Juliet approached the podium again to murmur a brief thank-you and to ask her committee heads—whom she'd lined up just this afternoon—to confer with her briefly in the lobby after the meeting was over. Then she gathered up her materials and left the stage through the wings, floating out the stage door, and then circling around to wait for the others in the quiet lobby out front.

Within a half hour, all her people were assembled. Jake, who was not only a poet but also worked part-time on the *Emerald Gap Bulletin,* agreed to get right on the posters and newspaper notice for the revue tryouts, which would be held on Monday evening. Reva Reid, parade committee chairman, would make the rounds tomorrow to firm up the list of all the floats and themes. The frog jump and Race Day chairpeople respectively agreed that they'd have each event fully planned by Tuesday evening, when the pageant committee would meet once again. Andrea Oakleaf volunteered to check with the Pine Grove Park Commission about the permit for the big closing-day picnic. And Burt Pandley promised to find, by next Friday, at least twelve more participants for the Crafts and Industry Fair, which was slated to run upstairs in the town hall the whole ten days of the festival.

It was after nine when Juliet finally left the lobby of the old auditorium. Outside, the night was balmy and moonless, the air very still. She stood for a moment beyond the big entry doors, between a pair of Victorian gas street lamps, and shivered just a little with excitement and triumph. She drew a deep breath and thought she could smell the pines and firs that cloaked the surrounding foothills.

How beautiful Broad Street looked, clothed in night, with its brick-fronted buildings, and the old-fashioned gas lamps all along the street. On the corner diagonally across from her, she could see the lights in the window of Cody's restaurant.

Now where, she wondered suddenly, had Cody disappeared to? He'd been waiting for her in the front row when she first entered the auditorium tonight. He'd wished her luck and then taken the podium for a moment to explain about the loss of the professional from Hollywood. He'd introduced her and left the stage.

And then she'd forgotten all about him in the excitement—and terror—of getting up and making herself heard.

Juliet grinned. Well, she'd see him soon enough. Between the work she did for him and the fact that she lived on his ranch, they ran into each other almost daily.

It was going to be fun, she decided, to tease him about not believing in her. He'd be a little embarrassed, she knew, and he'd smile that beautiful right-sided smile....

Juliet shivered a little, though the windless, warm night didn't justify goose bumps. Odd, that she should think about teasing Cody. She wasn't a teasing type of person, really.

Or she hadn't been. But now, with what she'd accomplished tonight, Juliet was beginning to think that she could be just about any kind of person she wanted to be.

And if she wanted to tease a friend a little, why shouldn't she? There was nothing wrong with that....

"Great job, Juliet."

Juliet jumped, like someone caught thinking naughty thoughts. "Oh." She gave a guilty giggle. "You surprised me, Jake."

Flat-nosed Jake's squashed face wrinkled with amusement. "*You* surprised all of *us,* gal. Damn good show."

"Well, thank you."

"Thank *you,*" Jake said. "We can use a real leader around here for once."

"I'll do my best."

Nodding, Jake turned and strolled off down the street toward the ancient green pickup he'd been driving for as long as Juliet could remember.

Juliet stood for a moment more, savoring Jake's praise, staring at a street she'd known all her life, but which tonight seemed the most beautiful place on earth. And then she turned and headed for McIntyre's, because she'd parked her car just a few feet beyond the restaurant's doors.

When she reached her car, Juliet paused once again, as she had outside the auditorium. She gazed fatuously at the automobile. It was a night to feel good about herself, and the car just added to the wonderfulness of it all.

Low, long, and sleek, it was the color of a scarlet flame. The salesman had told her it had eight cylinders, which he had implied was plenty, and which she suspected was probably immoral these days. She certainly felt immoral whenever she bought gas, which was often. It was not a practical car, nor was it precisely new— it had had one owner before her, who'd put quite a few miles on it, actually. But the salesman had assured her that the car was in tip-top condition. And she hadn't bought it for practical reasons, anyway.

She'd seen it and wanted it, and now it was hers. For Juliet, the car was a symbol, a material representation of the way she was creating a whole new life for herself. So she looked at it awhile, on this special night-of-all-nights, and thought it was the most beautiful thing she'd ever laid eyes on in her life.

Still floating on air from her triumph with the merchants' association, Juliet shrugged out of the gray jacket that went with her suit. She tossed the jacket and her pageant materials in back and slid beneath the wheel. The car was so low and streamlined that Juliet almost felt as if she were lying down when she settled into the driver's seat. It was a glorious feeling.

Stretching out, sighing a little, she rolled down the window and unbuttoned the top two buttons of her white cotton blouse. The warm night air came in the window and kissed her throat.

Sensuous, Juliet thought. Downright sensuous, just sitting here.

And then she giggled. Sensuous. What a thought. Especially for plain-Jane Juliet Huddleston, who was getting real close to being considered a spinster by everyone in town.

The warm air played on blushing skin now, as Juliet rather

primly reminded herself that everyone had sexy thoughts now and then, even thirty-year-old virgins who probably ought to know better.

But then, why *should* she know better? A woman who could do what she'd done tonight was no doubt perfectly capable of removing all her clothes and having an intimate experience with a man.

Eventually.

...Given that he was the *right* man, of course.

As she sat up enough to stick the key in the ignition, Juliet considered what the right man might be like.

He'd be good and kind and funny. A steady man, who, like herself, would never waver in his devotion. An attractive man— but not too attractive. Juliet was a realist, after all. She wanted, when the time came, a man to last a lifetime. And really good-looking men—men like Cody, for instance—were forever being tempted by one woman after another.

Juliet turned the key that she'd stuck in the ignition, and then forgot all about her mental shopping list for the ideal man. Because something strange happened when she turned the key, something totally unexpected: nothing. The car didn't start.

Juliet checked to see that she was in neutral. She was. She shifted it out and then back into neutral again, just to be sure. Then she turned the key again.

And again, it didn't start.

So she popped the hood latch and went to look at the engine. Which told her exactly zero. Juliet knew nothing about cars, except how to drive them and where to put the gas.

She did notice, however, that it didn't look quite so spanking clean under the hood as it had when she'd bought the car three weeks ago. There appeared to be oil leaking out in some places. She thought that strange.

"Got a problem?"

Juliet sighed in relief at the sound of the familiar voice. Cody. As always, when Juliet had a problem, Cody just naturally seemed to appear to help her out.

She removed her head from beneath the hood and shyly smiled at him. "Hi." Her voice did that funny wimpy thing, between the *h* and the *i,* that little hitching sound, but she didn't let it bother her. She went on, more strongly. "My car won't start."

For a minute, he just stood there and looked at her. It was odd. She wondered if she had engine oil on her nose or something. She was just about to ask what was wrong, when he added, as if he thought he should explain, "Saw you from the window." He gestured in the general direction of his restaurant.

She said, "Oh," and thought about how she'd leaned back in the seat and unbuttoned her blouse and imagined taking off her clothes for a man. Had he watched her through all that? She felt her face flushing.

Which was ridiculous. Even if Cody *had* been watching her the whole time—which she was sure he hadn't—what was wrong with leaning back in the seat and loosening her collar? Nothing. What she had been thinking was her own business. He could know nothing of that.

They kept on looking at each other. She wondered about something she'd never wondered about before: What was Cody thinking?

She opened her mouth, planning to ask him what was on his mind and be done with it, when he seemed to shake himself. He blinked and said, "Want me to have a look?"

She almost asked, "At what?" but then remembered. Her car. He would look at her car.

"Yes. Great. Thanks."

He stuck his head beneath the hood and fiddled with a few of the wires. He took a few caps off of various doohickies in there.

"Battery's not dry," he muttered. "Nothing seems to have come unhooked." He leaned out toward her where she stood on the sidewalk. "Get in and try it again."

She did as he'd asked. And once more, nothing happened. He fiddled some more under the hood, she tried starting it once more, but still nothing happened.

After the third try, he said, "Was it giving you trouble before this?"

"No, none at all."

"Just now, did it turn over at all the first time you tried it?"

She shook her head.

"You got nothing, not even a groaning sound?"

"Not a thing."

"Then it's probably not your battery. Maybe it's just a loose connection, or possibly your starter. Hell, it could be a hundred things." He took a handkerchief from a pocket and wiped his hands on it. "Tell you what, I'm heading back to the ranch now, anyway. Why don't you ride home with me? You can call the garage in the morning."

Juliet, worried about her beloved car, shook her head. "Do you think it's anything serious?"

"That it won't start…? Probably not. But these gaskets look shot, and the seals don't seem to be holding."

"What does that mean?"

He gave her a look with way too much patience in it to be reassuring. Then he asked, "Where'd you buy this car, Julie?"

"Don's Hot Deals, outside of Auburn."

"How much did you pay for it?"

She told him.

He looked pained. "I've always thought of you as practical, before this."

"I know." She giggled, forgetting altogether that she was not a giggling kind of person. She added, downright pertly, "There are a lot of things about me that aren't the way they used to be."

"I noticed."

He looked at her some more, and she looked back. It was kind of fun, Juliet thought, these long pauses where they just looked at each other. At least, it was fun for her. Looking at Cody McIntyre was a purely pleasurable pastime.

"How much do you owe on it?" he asked eventually.

"The car?"

"Yeah."

"Not a cent. I paid cash."

"Hell, Julie."

Juliet smiled and shrugged. "I wanted it. So I bought it."

"You still have that little brown car?"

"Nope. I never want to see a brown car again."

Cody shook his head. "Come on. Let's not stand here all night. Get your things and let's go home."

Juliet got her jacket and the big manila folder and followed Cody to his shiny black pickup in the lot behind McIntyre's.

They were quiet as Cody pulled out of the lot and headed for the edge of town. But once they'd left the lights of Emerald Gap behind and begun the twenty-minute ride to the McIntyre ranch, Cody had a suggestion. "You can use my spare pickup, if you want, until you get that car fixed."

She looked over at him, smiling. "You're so good to me, Cody. You always have been. Don't think I haven't noticed."

He looked a little embarrassed at that, and spent a few moments paying great attention to the road. Then he said gruffly, "I've got to be honest, Julie. I think you bought yourself a world of headaches with that car."

Juliet sighed. "I love it, anyway. I'll get it fixed, that's all." She was a little worried about the car. But tonight, even the possibility that she'd spent several thousand dollars on a bona fide lemon didn't daunt her. Nothing could faze her tonight.

Because she, Juliet Huddleston, who'd spent her whole life in the background taking orders rather than giving them, was going to run Midsummer Madness this year! The prospect was terrifying, but exhilarating, as well.

She rolled down the window and let the warm wind blow back her hair. Then she turned to Cody, ready to tease him a little as she'd imagined doing a while before.

"You didn't stick around to congratulate me."

He chuckled. "After the meeting, you were occupied in the lobby. I figured I'd see you soon enough, and you could give me a hard time about my lack of faith in you."

"Why, Cody McIntyre. When in our lives have I ever given you a hard time?"

He threw her a glance. "When have you ever led a festival? Or owned a red car? Or rented your big house in town, to move out in the sticks?"

"It is not the sticks," she reproved him. "It is the McIntyre ranch, where I have longed to live ever since first grade when your mom gave that pool party the last day of school. And now I *do* live there."

He didn't laugh this time, but there was humor in his voice when he said, "I get it. Living in my guesthouse is the fulfillment of a lifelong dream."

"Not exactly. Not quite so permanent as a dream. More temporary. Like a fantasy."

He grunted. "As your landlord, I'm bound to ask, exactly how *temporary* do you mean?"

"Oh, Cody. Don't worry. I'll give a month's notice before I leave. And it won't be for a year or two, at least. What I mean is, it's just something I always wanted to do, not something that lasts a lifetime. That's all."

He was quiet for a time, digesting this. Then he said, "So what gives, Julie?"

His serious tone surprised her. She answered in her old way, with that little frightened catch. "Wh-what do you mean?"

"You're different. You've changed. I didn't really notice it until today, when you suddenly insisted I let you take on the pageant. But it's been happening for a while, a few months at least. I can see that now, looking back on things."

She turned in her seat to face him. He gave her a quick, encouraging smile. Then he looked back at the road, which was climbing now, up into the pines, as they grew nearer the ranch. "I'd really like to know, Julie," he said, this time not glancing over.

"Y-you would?"

He nodded.

She realized she wanted to tell him. Maybe it was that he'd

actually asked; no one had asked before. Or maybe her confidence was finally high enough, that after tonight, she wouldn't need to keep her resolution secret anymore.

But she supposed it didn't really matter why. What mattered was he'd asked.

As he drove the twisting road to the ranch, she told him everything. About her vow that her next thirty years were going to amount to more than the past thirty had—and about all the steps she'd taken to make that vow come true.

He listened and nodded, and laughed a little when she told about that first time up in front of the group at Toastmasters International, when she'd been so nervous that she'd gestured wildly, knocking over her water glass into her shoes, which then made embarrassing squishing sounds every time she shifted her weight through the rest of her speech.

The miles flew by. She was just telling him how terrified she'd been for those first seconds up on the stage this evening, when the front entrance to the ranch came into sight. It was a high stone wall broken by two widely spaced stone pillars, with an iron *M* on a rocker in a cast-iron arch across the top.

Beyond the arch, Juliet saw the sloping lawn of the house grounds and a blue corner of the big pool. Kemo, Cody's dog, stood between the pillars, wagging his tail in a hopeful manner. Juliet waved at the mutt and caught a brief glimpse of the rambling two-story house before they sped past and turned into the small drive that led to the guesthouse next door.

Juliet finished her tale as he pulled up before the little house she rented from him.

"So that's that," she told him. "I'm making myself a whole new kind of life, from now on."

He gave her his beautiful right-sided smile. "And then what happens?"

"When?"

"After Midsummer Madness is over. After you've proved beyond a doubt that you're the most assertive woman around."

"Well," she confessed, "I haven't thought that far ahead yet."

She scooped up her jacket and her manila folder and leaned on the door latch. It gave, and she jumped down. "But I'll let you know, as soon as I figure it out. If you're still interested, that is."

She turned and practically skipped up the stone walk to the small porch of the guesthouse before she realized that in her excitement over all she'd accomplished, she'd forgotten to thank Cody for the lift home.

Conveniently, he hadn't driven away yet but was still sitting there staring after her, with his engine idling. She rushed back to the driver's side and leaned in the window.

"Thanks, Cody. Thanks a bunch." She kissed his cheek—it was warm and a little rough, very pleasant to the lips, actually. And then she whirled and danced back up the walk.

Cody sat and watched her go, bewildered at the change in her. Why, damned if her blouse hadn't been open two buttons down. He'd got himself the sweetest glimpse of that little shadow between her small, high breasts when she leaned in the window and put her soft lips on his cheek.

He couldn't figure it. What in the hell was innocent Julie Huddleston doing showing cleavage, making a man think about her in a whole new way?

He had half a mind to call her back and tell her to button up. But she was already bouncing up the steps of the guesthouse, turning once to wave, and disappearing inside.

Cody sat there a few minutes more, deciding that telling her to button up would have been presumptuous anyway. He was glad he hadn't done it. It would have sounded nothing short of crude— and besides, then she would have known that Cody McIntyre, who had always looked *out* for her, had just now been looking *down* her blouse.

CHAPTER THREE

JULIET'S ONLY PROBLEM that night was getting to sleep. She was just too keyed up to simply close her eyes and drift off. So she lay with the window open and only a sheet for a cover, staring up at the ceiling and enjoying daydreams of her success.

She planned a little, thinking it would be fun to try to get a real professional auctioneer this year to raffle off the baked goods at the big picnic on closing day. And this year, for the frog jump, she was going to see that there were separate categories for out-of-county frogs. Recently, some tourists had been buying some real long jumpers from Sacramento pet stores and running them against the more short-hocked local frogs. It just wasn't fair.

Smiling into the darkness, Juliet rolled over and tried to settle down. But ideas kept coming. She thought of a better way to arrange the booth spaces for the Crafts and Industry Fair even as she started planning her own costume for the Gold Rush Ball. Maybe she'd go as Maria Elena Roderica Perez Smith, the doomed laundress from local history. Or as one-eyed Charlie Parkhurst, who'd lived her life pretending to be a man. Or maybe Madame Moustache, the lusty bighearted saloon owner of Nevada City fame....

Juliet rolled over again and looked at the clock; it was past midnight. She really ought to get some sleep. Tomorrow was Friday, a regular workday. She had to finish off the payrolls for Duane's Coffee Shop and Babe Allen's Gift and Card Emporium, not to mention get a good start on that unit cost analysis for McMulch's Lumberyard.

From outside, she heard the crow of a rooster who was up way past his bedtime. Juliet grinned. She knew the rooster. The ranch, which was mostly timberland, didn't support too many animals.

Cody kept three horses, Kemo the dog and a cow called Emeline. There were a few chickens pecking around the stables, and one big mean black rooster that Cody swore was destined to be thrown in the pot one day soon. Cody called him Black Bart, and he was the only one ornery enough to stay up making noise all night.

Black Bart crowed again. And as the sound of his crowing faded off into the night, Juliet heard, drifting in the open window, the sweet, high sound of a harmonica.

It was Cody. Playing that silver mouth organ of his in the way that only he knew how, the notes sliding all over the scale, from so high and sweet your heart ached, to those low, sexy notes that vibrated down inside a person in the most stimulating way. Lord, Juliet thought, that boy could make music. No wonder his songs drove the ladies wild.

For a while she just lay there, as she had many a night since she took the guesthouse, her senses gratified and her spirit soothed by the impromptu concert that drifted through the window on the night air.

And then it occurred to her that getting Cody to perform in the Midsummer Madness Revue would be a coup of sorts. Every year they asked him, and every year he very courteously declined. Cody would provide goods and capital to the festival, but he always claimed he was too busy to commit himself to getting up on the stage every single night.

Juliet closed her eyes and hummed along a little, until her own lack of musical talent made her fall silent, so that she could better enjoy the magic spell that Cody could weave with just a song.

Yes, she thought, as he began a new tune, she would definitely ask him. As she'd learned in assertiveness training, nothing was ever lost by asking. If the answer was no, you were in no worse a position than before you asked; if you got a yes, you were one ahead. Besides, maybe Cody would agree to perform if Juliet was the one asking. Maybe he'd do it for the sake of their lifelong friendship—if she caught him in the right mood.

As the second tune ended on a high note, the thought came to her: Why not just go ask him now?

She nodded at the ceiling. Yes, that would be a good approach. To ask him right now, spontaneously, in the middle of the night when neither of them seemed to be able to sleep.

Juliet pushed back the sheet and rose from her bed. She pulled on her light robe over her pajamas and decided not to even worry about her feet. She could use the little iron gate in the stone fence between the two houses. That way, there were only smooth paving stones and soft grass between his house and hers.

She went out the back door and down the few steps to the stone walk that led to the gate. The stones, as she padded from one to the next, were still warm from a summer day's worth of sun.

Overhead there was no moon, but the stars were very bright. The gold grasses of the open pasture on her right, which was separated from her house by a wooden fence, seemed to reflect the starlight, so Juliet had no trouble seeing the way. She flew past the hay barn and small stables, which loomed just on the other side of the fence. Cody began another song as she pulled open the gate to the main grounds and slipped through.

Beyond the gate was another world. Six acres of sloping, manicured grass were bisected by a gravel drive that ended in a roomy garage. On the near side of the drive lay the swimming pool, lit now and casting its eerie light up toward the night sky. On the far side of the drive, up a walk lined with rose bushes, was the house, a two-story white clapboard structure with green roof and trim.

Originally, as Cody's mother had once explained to Juliet, the guesthouse had been the main house. The ranch had been smaller then, more of a homestead than anything else. Cody's great-grandmother had run the place, while his great-grandfather owned and operated the Rush Creek Digs mine. They'd closed the mine in Cody's grandfather's time; Cody's grandfather had bought more land, then built his family a bigger, more comfortable place to live. Cody's father, retired and living in Arizona for the past few years, had opened the hardware store in town and added the Olympic-size pool at the house. When he retired, Cody's dad had signed both the ranch and hardware store over to his only son. Now Cody took care of it all, as well as the bar and grill that was his contribution to the family holdings.

The huge yard of the main house was surrounded on three sides by a stone wall. The north side, except for the garage, was divided from the pasture by a wooden fence. It was a stunning effect, Juliet had always thought: the pampered, lush grounds, cut off from the road and the outbuildings by the high wall—but opened right up to the wild, wide field on the north side. There, the tall grasses rolled away for a half mile or so until they hit the woodlands of the surrounding hills.

Once inside the gate and sheltered by the spreading shadow of a big fruitless mulberry tree there, Juliet hesitated, partly in hushed appreciation of the starlit yard, and partly to gauge the source of the music that curled through the still night.

The melody came, as she had suspected, from the wide front porch that faced her across the drive. She could see Cody there, now that she looked for him. Since the porch light was off, he sat in shadow, lounging against one of the two pillars that flanked the front steps. He faced the main gate and had his back to the garage. He was shirtless—she could see the sheen of bare skin—and barefoot, too, just as she was. His naked feet were on the second step. Not far away from him, near the porch railing, she could make out the sprawled black shape of the dog, Kemo. The dog's head was raised and pointed in her direction.

Cody, staring off toward the front gate, seemed lost in his music. If he had looked, he could have seen her, even in the shadow of the mulberry, for her robe was the palest shade of blue and drew what little light there was within the darkness. But he didn't look.

Kemo, still peering in Juliet's direction, whined. Cody stopped playing to murmur a soft order to the animal. The dog laid his sleek black head on his paws once more.

Juliet stood for a while, listening to the song, suspended in the moment and glad to be there. All of her senses seemed heightened. There was the music, the faint gleam of Cody's skin across the yard, the cool caress of moist grass at her feet. The grass had a sweet, full earthy smell that mingled deliciously with the dusty scent of the drier, wilder grass on the other side of the fence.

Cody paused for a breath. From somewhere on the green lawn, a frog croaked; it was a rough, humorous sound, after the beguiling beauty of the song. Juliet smiled. Cody played on.

It occurred to her that, were she to circle the pool and cross the drive up by the garage, she could approach from the side steps and keep from disturbing Cody for a few minutes more. It seemed appropriate, somehow, for her to come up on him quietly. It was in keeping with the enchanted mood of moonless darkness and haunting song.

The thick grass tickled her feet as she crept, still smiling to herself, beneath the trees that grew close to the stone wall. By the time she reached the wooden fence, it had become a sort of game to her. She shot across the open space, picked her way over the pebbles of the drive in front of the garage and then flew across the unprotected space on the other side. Then she had one of the pair of huge old chestnut trees that grew in front of the house for cover as she approached the side of the porch.

When she put her dew-damp foot on the bottom step, Cody began yet another song, one of his own that Juliet had heard once or twice over the years. It was a love song, about a poor boy who loved a rich girl whose family kept them apart. Now, of course, he only played the melody. But Juliet recalled the general flow of the lyrics, and felt sad for the penniless lover, whose dream girl could never be his.

Juliet mounted the steps and then, still unchallenged, began to approach the man who sat on the front steps with his back to her, playing one of those songs that broke women's hearts.

The wooden boards of the porch were with her; they gave out nary a squeak. The dog, too, seemed to be on her side. Though he raised his head and watched her, he made no sound.

Juliet tiptoed to the Mission-style easy chair, one of a pair that flanked the double front door. And then, lost in the music, she hovered there, staring at the marvelously sculpted musculature of Cody's bare back, until the sad song came to an end.

There was a silence, one that slowly filled up with the sounds of the night. An owl hooted somewhere behind the house. The crickets spun out whirring songs of their own. A mourning dove cried. Out in the field, a quail loosed its piping call, just as Kemo's snaky black tail began beating the porch boards, and the dog opened his mouth to pant in a welcoming way.

Cody said, "Julie."

He said it softly, in a different way than anyone had ever said her name before. He turned his head, slowly, and smiled at her.

Juliet smiled back, with no shyness or hesitation. It seemed that her triumph at the meeting earlier had boosted her confidence, while the magic safety of the darkness made her bold.

"You saw me," she accused in a teasing manner, as Kemo rose and went to her to be scratched behind the ear.

Cody nodded. "When you came through the gate."

"The music was so beautiful. I didn't want to break the mood. So I sneaked up on you, hoping that you wouldn't stop." The dog, satisfactorily scratched, went to the end of the porch nearest the front gate. There, he walked in a circle, at last lying down again, all curled into himself.

Juliet came to sit next to Cody, first adjusting her robe where it met on her lap, then wrapping her hands around her knees. "I've enjoyed it each time you played, ever since I moved in."

"You never came over before. How come?"

She glanced off toward the rippling lights of the pool. "I don't know. I guess I was just never the kind of woman to run across a lawn barefoot in the middle of the night."

"But now you are?"

Juliet chuckled, considering the question, considering her own lightness of spirit, her boldness, her sense of glowing self-confidence. Tonight, she felt disconnected from her usual self. It was as if her usual self were some other woman, a woman for whom she felt a little sorry. A woman frightened of life, of its sights, scents and sounds, of its sweet and sensual beauty that tonight seemed created for her alone.

"Well?"

"What?" She looked at him.

"I asked if now you were the kind of woman who—"

"I remember. And I don't know. Tonight is different. I feel different. But we'll see."

He smiled again, that slow warm smile that lifted the right side of his mouth a fraction more than the left. Juliet thought, as he did that, that it was fully understandable why the women went wild for him.

Lord, he was one beautiful hunk of man. Much too much man for someone like Juliet—she knew that. But absolutely splendid nonetheless.

"Believe it or not," she went on, in an effort to distract herself from the surplus of masculine splendor before her—from the hard, broad chest, the corded neck, the gleaming eyes and the right-sided smile, "I did come over here with a specific purpose in mind."

"And that was?"

"To ask you a favor."

He was watching her mouth. "A favor?" He repeated the word right after her, as if he'd caught it from her lips and then playfully tossed it back her way.

"Yes," she confirmed, surprised at the steadiness of her own voice. Inside, she was drowning in the most wonderful yearning sort of feeling, an utterly delicious feeling, one she was sure she should restrain, but one to which she wanted to give free rein.

"Well?"

She recollected her supposed purposed. "It's about the revue."

"The Midsummer Madness Revue?"

"Yes."

"What about it?"

"Well, I was thinking…"

"Yeah?"

"I was *hoping,* actually…."

"You were thinking and hoping what?"

She went ahead and said it right out at last. "I would really appreciate it if you would agree to sing a song or two in the revue this year.''

He said nothing for a moment. Then he murmured her name in a regretful tone, and she knew that next he'd be telling her how busy he was.

In a gesture that seemed perfectly natural, she put a finger on his lips. ''Shh. Don't answer now. Just think about it. Okay?''

''I don't think so,'' he told her. His lips were firm, his breath warm on her skin. It was a lovely sensation, touching his mouth, feeling the movement beneath her fingers each time he spoke.

Juliet shook herself, remembering that, no matter how good his lips felt, they were getting dangerously close to saying ''no'' to her request. She shushed him again. ''Didn't I ask you not to answer now?''

He smiled, which she felt as a brushing softness on the pads of her fingers. ''All right. I'll think about it.''

''Good.'' She gave a satisfied little nod, and then realized she couldn't go on touching his lips forever, no matter how good it felt. She pulled her hand away and faced the pool again. He didn't move. She could feel his eyes on her.

A little silence happened, one that had a peculiar edge to it. A precipitous edge, Juliet thought.

She turned to him. ''I, um, suppose I should go back to my house now.''

''Why?'' He seemed to be looking at her mouth. And then her neck, and the little V that was formed where her pajamas buttoned up and the facings of her robe met.

''Well, I…I did what I came out here to do. I asked you to be in the revue.''

''That's all you came out here for? To ask me to be in the revue?''

She nodded.

He didn't seem to believe that. ''You sure?''

When she'd touched his mouth to hush him, she'd scooted right up next to him. And then, even when she'd looked off at the pool, she hadn't actually moved away. So now she was seeing him at very close range.

It was an enthralling experience. So near, his male beauty was absolutely mesmerizing. She stared at him, forgetting to even try to talk, marveling at the perfection of his firm mouth, his symmetrical nose, his shiny brown hair.

Goodness—the realization caused her to hitch in a quick breath—why, she wanted to kiss him! Her lips were practically twitching with the longing to be pressed to his.

He looked back at her, and it was as if he *knew* her forbidden wish, because the impossible happened. He shifted forward just a fraction and her wish came true.

They were kissing.

It couldn't be happening—but it was.

And it felt wonderful. He made a lovely, rough sound in his throat, and his hard, naked arms went around her. She heard the harmonica clatter on the porch boards as he pulled her up against him.

Ah, how utterly delightful. Juliet didn't want to pull away. So she didn't.

His hands rubbed her back in slow, sweet circles, and his lips played with hers for a while, teasing and nibbling, kind of getting to know her mouth.

And then his tongue got involved, slipping out to press at the little seam between her lips. Juliet gasped at first, since she'd never in her life been familiar with another person's tongue. But then she felt herself go easy and soft in his arms, because being familiar with Cody's tongue felt just fine. Just terrific, after all.

Since his tongue seemed to hint at the possibility that she might allow her lips to part, she did it, with a little sigh.

He whispered "Julie," and then his tongue slipped in. She smiled in welcome, liking it immensely, and even shyly touching the gentle intruder with her own tongue. The deepened kiss continued.

And then he pulled away. She gave a cry. But the loss of such joy was only temporary. He only wanted, she learned soon enough, to do a little rearranging of their bodies before he kissed her some more.

He turned her and guided her down, across his lap, cradling her on one arm, so he could sip from her mouth some more.

Juliet raised her lips eagerly to him, and stroked his shoulders, deeply pleasured by the taut feel of his skin, and the hard bulge of the muscles beneath.

"Oh, Cody." She sighed against his mouth. "Oh, Cody, how wonderful.... No one ever told me..."

He chuckled at that, a husky chuckle that seemed to ignite all her senses the more. She went on stroking his sleek shoulders, and then sliding her fingers up to toy in the silky hair at his nape.

Meanwhile, he was not idle. Besides the long, drugging kiss that never seemed to end, his free hand caressed her, in long strokes at first. From the slim curve of her hip, to the cove of her waist, it moved up to slide along her rib cage, then back down again.

Somehow, the belt of her robe was gone, the robe fully parted. Cody's exploring hand drifted over her hip, bringing the hem of her pajama top along, until he was rubbing the bare skin of her waist beneath the top.

Oh, it was heaven. How on earth could she have lived for thirty whole years and known next to nothing of this heady bliss? It was better than anything. Better than ice cream on a sweltering day, better than hot cocoa of a cold winter's night. Better than— Oh, Lord, yes, it was true—better than driving her red car, or running Midsummer Madness for the first time in her life!

This *was* Midsummer Madness. Incredible. Divine.

Cody's warm, big hand slid up her waist—and, light as a breath, skimmed the nipple of her left breast.

"Oh, my goodness!" Juliet gasped.

His hand repeated the action. Juliet gasped again. And then—

He pulled away.

Juliet, who realized her eyes were dreamily closed, opened them. She looked into Cody's eyes, which were heavy-lidded and full of sensual promise. "I said, 'oh, my goodness,'" she pointed out. "I didn't say stop."

Juliet found she didn't regret her bold words when, for a moment, it looked as if he might resume where he'd left off—lower his mouth to where she could get at it, and start doing those lovely things with his hand again.

But the moment stretched out too long, and she had to admit that his expression had rearranged itself; he was now looking more stern than aroused.

Gently he guided her to a sitting position once more and handed her the belt to her robe, which had somehow ended up wrapped around his neck.

He said, "I shouldn't have done that."

Juliet, attempting to take things in stride, decided to be grateful for what she got. "I know," she replied, "but I surely do thank you anyway, Cody McIntyre."

Cody frowned at that. "Don't thank me," he said, rather harshly, she thought.

"But I—"

He cut her off. "Let it go." Then he relented a little. "I went too far. I'm sorry."

"You did?" She thought about that. "I don't know. Isn't... what you did natural? I didn't ask you to stop."

"Damn it, Julie. You're a virgin."

Juliet's face flamed at the blunt way he said that. She turned away.

"Well, aren't you?" he demanded.

She couldn't bring herself to look at him, but she managed to nod.

He swore again. "That's what I mean. You don't know what the hell you're doing. And damn it, neither do I. I don't take advantage of virgins."

Juliet wished she could crawl under the porch. Her ears were on fire from hearing Cody talk so bluntly about her lack of experience. She almost lurched to her feet and ran across the lawn for home. But then she decided that one of the reasons she was still a virgin at thirty was a distinct lack of nerve. She'd never really get to experience life if she always backed down. So she forced herself to stay put and dared to speak. "Well, um, then," she began somewhat wiltingly. She drew in a bracing breath and went on with more gumption, "If you don't take advantage of virgins, then why did you kiss me?"

He granted her another long look. Then he muttered with feeling, "Hell, Julie...."

She stared right back at him. "'Hell, Julie,' is not an answer."

"Damn it...."

"Neither is 'damn it.'"

"Look, I didn't mean it to go so far—I didn't mean it to go *anywhere*."

Juliet felt a sad little sinking feeling in her heart when he said that, but she went ahead with her next question anyway. "Well, what did you mean, then?"

"I don't know," he said, finger-combing his hair and shifting on the step. "I couldn't sleep. I came out here to play myself a lullaby. And then you came, trying to sneak up on me. It was like a game, and I started playing. I wanted to kiss you, so I did kiss you. And it went further than it should have."

Juliet, absorbed in her own confusions, didn't fully realize what a rough time Cody was having. He was both frustrated in his desire, *and* disgusted at himself for toying with an innocent. Partly in an effort to get his bearings—and also in an attempt to hide the evidence that his lust still wasn't exactly under control—Cody slid even farther away from her on the step until he was practically wrapped around the big post that supported the porch roof.

Juliet noted his withdrawal, and thought regretfully of the delicious caress of his hand on her breast—a caress she was becoming more and more certain she would never experience again. She forced herself to take a long, hard look at the situation—and to recall that a man like Cody McIntyre was not a man for her.

She said, a little sadly but very firmly, "You're right." She solemnly nodded. "We went too far."

Cody listened with only half his attention; he was still pondering the prospect of trying to stand up without embarrassing himself.

Juliet rebelted her robe and tied it with a no-nonsense tug. "We'll just have to forget this ever happened, okay?" She rearranged the robe to cover her knees. "A gorgeous man like you is nothing but trouble for a plain woman like me."

Forgetting the problem with his jeans, Cody whipped his head around to face her again, ready to inform her that looks do not make the man—and to add, for her information, that he didn't find her plain at all. Lately.

But she prattled on before he could get a word in. "You've been good to me over the years. You always stood up for me when Billy Butley used to pick on me back in school, and you were my first client when I opened my service. I'll always like you. A lot. But I don't want to get mixed up with you. I'd only get my heart broken, and that's a simple fact."

"Now wait a minute—"

"No. You wait. Cody, the women are always after you. And one of these days, one of them would be sure to tempt you right away from me."

Cody stared at her. He had half a mind to point out to her just how wrong she was. He could use his father as an example. From the time he met Cody's mother, Wayne McIntyre had never so much as *looked* at another woman. Cody's grandfather, Yancy, had been the same way. Cody came from a long line of truehearted men. No other woman could tempt him away from the woman he'd chosen for his own....

But then again, telling her that might give her the wrong idea. After all, he'd only just kissed her for the first time a few minutes ago. And though he'd like to do a hell of a lot more than kiss her, he had no intention of getting into anything permanent—not on such short notice, anyway.

Besides, as he'd been doing his damndest to explain to her, only a jerk would seek a casual affair with an innocent like Juliet. Cody always did his best not to behave like a jerk.

But then, *was* this casual? It didn't exactly feel casual. Something *had* happened to him. Her innocence, coupled with this bewitching new frankness, had him spinning. He didn't know which way was up.

She was so different than the women he'd known—women who understood completely what they were getting into when they made love with a man. However, it was true that the past few years, he'd been spending more and more nights alone. The experienced ladies who always seemed to seek him out just didn't do much for him anymore—though he hadn't given a lot of thought to what he might be looking for instead.

Could Julie be it?

The question bounced around his brain like an echo in a mine shaft. It was a damn dangerous question, and one he wasn't prepared to answer tonight. It would be insane to try to.

That's why he had to do something—very soon. Because if he sat there any longer looking at her in her pajamas and thin robe and remembering the feel of her mouth under his, he damn well might just go ahead and decide that Julie Huddleston—who'd been here all along—was the woman he'd been waiting thirty years to find.

He'd end up acting like a man who'd gone over the edge completely. He'd be begging her on bended knee to give him one chance—or promising that he'd never so much as look at another woman for the rest of their lives!

Cody stood up, wincing a little when his jeans bound that part of him that refused to take orders from his brain. "Whatever you want," he croaked. "It's fine with me."

Juliet swallowed, looking up at him, wishing she could grab his leg and trip him…so that he fell into her waiting arms. Lord, he was beautiful.

But not the man for her.

"I'm glad you understand," she said.

He bent to scoop up the harmonica and then turned for the door.

"Um, Cody?"

"What?" He half turned back to her.

"Just forget what I asked you, about being in the revue, okay? We're around each other a lot anyway. Might as well not make it worse."

"Sure. Fine," he said. "Kemo." The dog lifted his head and thumped his tail. "Come on." Kemo rose and followed his master inside.

Juliet felt bereft when the door closed and left her on the front porch alone. Cody had been so curt and abrupt. He'd never behaved that way toward her.

But, then, he'd never kissed her and touched her breast before, either.

Juliet stood up and pulled her robe closer about her. Then she began the short stroll back to her own little house.

When she climbed into bed again and settled under the sheet, she told herself that it would all work out fine in the end. She and Cody had been friends for too long for one foolish indiscretion to make all that much difference in how they behaved toward each other.

She'd stay away from him for a few days, and then things would settle back into their normal routine. In a week or two, everything would be just as it had always been between them. She was sure of it.

CHAPTER FOUR

WANTED

Singers. Actors. Dancers. Performers of all types and persuasions. Get involved. Help the community. Try out this year for the MIDSUMMER MADNESS REVUE. Town Auditorium, 401 Broad Street. Monday, July 15, 7–10 p.m. For more information call 555-3462.

CODY TRIED TO ignore the notice as he walked past it. It was posted in the window of his restaurant, right beside the copy of the open menu. It had been there for four days—since Friday, when Flatnosed Jake had strolled in with a stack of the things and asked to be allowed to put one up where it would be seen by everyone.

Cody had told him to go ahead and stick it in the front window. It hadn't even occurred to Cody that, over the next few days, he might find it bothersome, to see it out of the corner of his eye every time he went in the front door.

In previous years, the revue had never been anything more than something he enjoyed as a member of the audience—and tactfully avoided as a potential performer. But for some reason, this year, he couldn't get the thing out of his mind. He blamed this preoccupation on the damn notice, which he had to walk by umpteen times a day. The fact that Julie was directing the revue, and had ended up asking him *not* to get involved, had nothing to do with his irritation. Julie's request that he stay out of it fell right in with his own intentions. He didn't want to get involved—never had, never would. If it wasn't for that notice, he wouldn't even have to *think* about getting involved.

In fact, thinking about it, he realized he could choose *not* to think about it. And that was exactly what he intended to do.

Having decided never again to notice the notice, Cody strode grimly into the cool, dim interior of McIntyre's. To his left, the long mahogany bar gleamed. Around the divider that sectioned off the main restaurant, he caught a glimpse of one of the tables, set for four. The polished wooden surface of the table looked comfortable and inviting. The glassware sparkled in the recessed overhead light. At the reservation podium, his night hostess was greeting a party of six and turning to lead them to their seats.

Cody made for the bar. He sat at the end, where there were some vacant stools, and signaled to one of the bartenders for a draft beer. The bartender, as per instructions, served Cody only when all the customers were content.

When the beer was set before him, Cody asked, "Where's Archie?" There were two bartenders behind the counter; one of them at this hour on Monday night should have been Archie Kent.

"I traded shifts with him, just for tonight," the substitute, Bob Meeker, quickly explained.

"Everything okay with him? Is he sick?" Cody asked.

"Oh yeah, he's fine. He wants to check out the revue—see if he can get involved."

"What for?"

"You know Archie. A big ham."

"A big ham with a *job,*" Cody trenchantly pointed out.

Bob Meeker shrugged. "He's on days now, remember? That is, except for Monday nights. He figured he could work it out, if he got a part. He's pretty excited about it, if you want to know the truth—ever since the bookkeeper got a hold of him."

"What bookkeeper?"

"You know. *Your* bookkeeper. Ms. Huddleston."

"Julie." Cody muttered the name with bleak resignation. Then, suspiciously, "What do you mean '*got a hold* of him'?"

"You know, since she worked on him to try out."

"Was she in here?"

"Yes."

Something tightened inside of Cody. He felt disappointed and hurt. He'd hardly seen Julie since last Thursday night when he'd gone out on the porch to relax himself with music and ended up with her in his arms. She'd been avoiding him since then—he knew it. It was understandable that she'd want a little distance between them after what had happened. So her avoiding him probably shouldn't bother him. But it did.

"When was she in here?"

"Saturday. During the break after lunch."

"When I wasn't." Cody muttered the words more to himself than to Bob.

"Er, right. She passed out flyers, said she was making the rounds of all the businesses on Broad and over on Commercial, too. She said she was reminding everyone about the revue and that they were welcome to come out for it." Bob Meeker gave a musing chuckle. "Took us all by surprise at first, her speaking up like that, strolling up to each of us, smiling a big how-do-you-do and then launching into her little pitch. She didn't hardly seem like the same scared little mouse who's been creeping around here, scared of her own shadow, for as long as any of us can remember."

Cody growled, "What do you mean, 'creeping'? Julie never creeped—er, crept."

Bob Meeker, who wanted to keep his job, agreed, "Whatever you say, Cody."

"Tell me what happened between her and Archie." The command came out a little harsher than Cody might have intended.

Bob Meeker looked at him sideways. "You okay, boss?"

"I'm fine. Tell me."

"Nothing happened. She could see he was interested, so she talked to him a little longer than she did the rest of us."

"How much longer?"

"Look, Cody, it really wasn't a big deal."

"Fine. Just tell me."

"I don't know." Bob polished the bar. "A few minutes, maybe. She said how glad they'd be if he could take a part in one of the little plays they're doing, or something like that."

Cody pictured Archie in his mind—sandy-colored hair and a ready smile, good-looking and personable. Women liked Archie. He was charming and boyish. Maybe too charming—not for a bartender, of course, but too charming by a long shot for Julie.

Someone like Archie Kent wouldn't be right for Julie at all. Julie was innocent, damn it. She had to be careful of charming men who would not take her seriously. Hell, if Cody was willing to put his own desires aside and protect her from *himself,* he couldn't go letting someone like Archie Kent take advantage of her, now could he?

Bob Meeker, who knew a chance to escape when he saw one, had moved to the center of the bar and begun studiously washing glasses, shoving them on the scrubber-covered posts in the frothy dishwater, scooping them through the rinse and setting them to drain. Still, he had enough curiosity in him to inquire as Cody made for the door, "Where you going, boss?"

He got no answer. Cody was already gone.

"Unhand me this very instant, *señor!* I am a married woman. My husband will not like what you do!"

"Gimme a kiss...."

"No!"

"Yes!"

"Oh! I warn you, *señor!*"

"Stop fighting me, sweet thing...."

"No, no, I will not have my honor besmirched...I warn you...."

"Ha-ha. You little wildcat.... Argh, ah! My God, you've stabbed me, you scurrilous wench!"

"Okay, that was wonderful. You can stop now," Juliet said.

The couple up on the stage lowered the looseleaf notebooks they were reading from and looked expectantly down at Juliet in the front row.

"Give us just a minute," Juliet told the two, then she went back several rows to confer with Melda Cooks, the author of the piece, which was entitled, *The Mysterious and Suspicious Events Surrounding the Cruel and Untimely Death by Hanging of Maria Elena Roderica Perez Smith.*

"What do you think?" Juliet kept her voice low.

"They're splendid." Melda peered over the top edge of her thick spectacles. "I was enthralled."

"So we have our laundress and the man she stabbed."

"As far as I'm concerned, we do."

Juliet was pleased. She'd especially encouraged Archie Kent, the man up on the stage, to come to tryouts. And the woman, Yolanda Hughes, was just perfect for the part of Maria Elena, who killed a man and hung for it rather than lose her honor. It was said that Maria Elena had possessed "shining black eyes and a lush mane of hair to match." Yolanda, who owned and operated a hairdressing salon, fit the bill physically and had some acting talent as well.

Juliet went back to the couple on the stage, thanked them and told them to be sure to leave phone numbers with Andrea Oakleaf, who was acting as her assistant tonight. Then she turned to the small group of people in the first rows who still hadn't had a chance to get up on the stage and read something.

"Now," she told them, "how about if you three—" she gestured at two men and a woman who were sitting together "—open up to page 22, which is a scene from the Living History Play...." She went on to tell them which parts to read and was just waiting for them to move onto the stage, when the big double doors at the head of the center aisle were pulled back. She glanced up.

It was Cody, whom she'd not only been avoiding, but whom she'd been trying her best not to think about, since Thursday night. At the sight of him, her pulse was suddenly racing, and her cheeks felt pink.

She could think of no reason why the sight of a man she'd known all her life should suddenly send her senses into overload. But somehow, in the past few days, he had suddenly become even better looking than before—which surely wasn't possible. Was it? She stared at him in his dark slacks and Western shirt and tooled boots that he wore evenings at his restaurant and wondered: had his chest always been so broad and deep, his hips so marvelously lean and hard?

Yolanda Hughes, who was gathering up her huge purse from a

seat near where Juliet stood, murmured dreamily, "God, what a hunk...." Then, realizing that Juliet had heard, she gave a husky laugh. "I can't help it, the man is pure eye candy."

Juliet felt her irritation rise—and for the purest of motives, she told herself. All these years, women had been fighting being made into objects, and here was a woman doing the same thing to a man. "He's much more than that," she shot back, only aware after the words were out how self-righteous—and self-incriminating—they would sound.

Yolanda, swinging her bag over her shoulder, muttered, "Some girls have all the luck..." as she sauntered toward the side door.

In the meantime, Andrea Oakleaf saw an opportunity to improve the revue—and took it. She jumped out of her seat and marched up to Cody, a triumphant gleam in her gunmetal-gray eyes. "Cody McIntyre!" She gave a nod, and the tight bun on the back of her head bounced briskly. "How heartening. It's about time you decided to donate your talents to the revue."

Cody, who'd entered looking extremely purposeful, suddenly hesitated and backed up a step. "Now, Miss Oakleaf, let's not go jumping to conclusions. I didn't come here with trying out in mind."

Juliet jumped in to help him out. "Yes, Andrea. Cody's much too busy—"

"Pshaw," said Miss Oakleaf, who knew way too much about most folks in Emerald Gap, since she'd once been just about everyone's kindergarten teacher. "He's a spoiled only child who thinks it will kill him to make a commitment of his time for a few hours a night a few days in the summer."

"Aw, come on Miss Oakleaf." Cody sounded a little hurt. "Is that fair?"

Andrea thought about that. "Well, all right. Perhaps the word *spoiled* is too strong. But it's still about time you gave us a song or two in the revue."

"That's the truth, and you know it, Cody." Flat-nosed Jake spoke up from over near the stage.

"Yeah, get involved, Cody!" one of the auditioners said.

Someone else chimed in, "Sing us a song. We need you!"

"Come on, Cody!"

"Where's your community spirit?"

Cody looked as trapped as he probably felt. Juliet stared at him, wondering what could have brought him here. Before, he'd always had the sense to be nowhere in sight when revue auditions were in progress. He was shaking his head, making sorry-but-I-really-can't noises, when Archie Kent, who had disappeared toward the rest rooms for a moment and just now returned, piped up with "Yeah, boss. Help us out a little, will you?"

Cody stopped looking sheepish so suddenly it was almost comical and turned a hard glare on Archie. "*You're* the one I'm looking for."

Archie's easy smile fled. "Hey, what's the matter? Didn't Bob show up? He promised to fill in for me...."

"Bob showed up," Cody answered stiffly.

Archie was now looking somewhat bewildered. "Then what's the problem?"

"The problem is..." Cody's voice trailed off. It was as if he himself didn't know what the problem was.

"Yeah?" Archie prompted.

"The problem is....you don't have time for this, that's what. You know how busy we get during the festival."

"But, Cody. I'm on *days*." Poor Archie now looked utterly confused.

And Juliet didn't blame him. Cody had always been generous with his people when it came to the festival. All the merchants in town were, because the festival brought in droves of tourists; tourists were the major industry of Emerald Gap. In fact, many businesses counted on bringing in up to twenty percent of their yearly income during the ten days of Midsummer Madness. For Cody to keep any one of his employees from the revue—especially when there was no serious scheduling conflict—made no sense at all.

Juliet's own bafflement was clear in her voice when she asked, "Cody, what has come over you?" She reached for poor Archie's arm and patted it reassuringly. "*I* talked Archie into trying out. I was sure you wouldn't mind. You never have before."

Cody didn't look her in the face. He seemed to be glaring at her hand, where it lay on Archie's arm. "Well, this time is different," he growled.

"But how?" She gave Archie's arm one more pat and then dropped her hand.

At last Cody looked into her eyes. She felt a hot little shiver, something quick and alive, arrowing down into the center of her, and spreading outward, like the ripples in a pond.

"It's different," Cody said, scowling. "And I want a few words alone with you, Juliet, to explain just how."

Juliet. He'd called her Juliet. Not in all the memory of their friendship had he called her by her full name, or addressed her in such a stiff, cold manner.

Juliet's heart sank. He'd been curt and gruff with her on Thursday night, but she'd understood that, given what had happened. She'd been sure in a few days everything would be fine between them again. However, looking at him now, she could see things were not fine. What in the world could she have done to have made him so angry with her?

It hurt in the worst way, to have him look at her with such disdain—and in front of all these people, too. The auditorium seemed suddenly very quiet. Juliet realized that she and Cody were the focus of everyone's attention. They were all watching, wondering what would happen next.

At that moment, all of her former shyness chose to flood back in on her. The ultimate nightmare of her timorous self was happening. Everyone was looking at her, speculating about what was actually going on here between plain Juliet Huddleston and gorgeous Cody McIntyre, every woman's dream.

Juliet longed to just open her mouth and tell Cody that to talk alone would be fine. But for the moment, she was paralyzed with timidity. She managed, somehow, to glance at Jake, who had come nearer during the last exchange and now stood by her right shoulder. Since Thursday night, she'd talked with Jake several times, discussing the flyers, and the newspaper notice, and how he and Andrea would help her run the tryouts. Now, after spending all of her life thinking of Flat-nosed Jake as that old eccentric who lived in the log house way out in the woods, she also had started to think of him as her friend. She telegraphed him a pleading look.

Jake seemed to hear her wordless call for help. He grinned and broke the awful silence. "Good idea, Cody. You two wrangle it out later. Now, we got these auditions to finish up."

"Yes, everyone's waiting," Andrea Oakleaf concurred. Then she added with a crafty smile, "You just agree to sing us two songs, young man, and you may be excused."

Cody, who had been staring way too hard at Juliet, managed to drag his gaze away to try to stand up to his kindergarten teacher. "Now, wait a minute—"

"No, *you* wait, Cody McIntyre," Miss Oakleaf snapped back. "You finagled your way out of directing the whole festival this year, and our Juliet here is doing your job for you. The least you can do in return is perform in the revue. I want a commitment, young man."

"But—"

"A commitment."

Cody finger-combed his hair. "Hell."

"Two songs."

There was another of those hanging silences. Then Cody finally gave in. "All right. I'll do it."

There was actually a smattering of applause. "Good going, boss!" Archie cheered.

Cody gave his employee a look that had him waving goodbye and out of there within seconds. Then Cody turned his eyes on Juliet. "Is your car fixed yet?"

She somehow found her voice. "Uh, no. They, um, told me tomorrow for sure." She was still using his spare pickup truck.

"Fine. You can drive me home, and we'll talk then. I'll be at the restaurant, as soon as you're through here."

"O-okay," she stammered.

He curtly nodded and turned for the big doors at the top of the aisle. Juliet watched him go, thinking that this thing with Cody simply was not turning out as she'd thought it would.

Staying out of his way for a few days, until things got back to normal between them, didn't seem to have done one bit of good. Not when he could march in here and, with no more than a look, make her insides turn to molten lava. Not when he now seemed angrier with her than he had been when he left her on the porch the other night. Not when he was suddenly behaving completely unlike himself, demanding that poor Archie not take part in the revue.

"Juliet?" Andrea asked. "Shall we resume where we left off?"

Juliet valiantly put her worries about Cody away until the proper time to deal with them. After all, she did have a job to do, one that she'd been handling quite well until Cody marched through those big double doors.

She smiled and nodded at Andrea, sensing the return of her confidence. "All right, everybody," she said, her calm assurance belying the turmoil within. "Let's get back to work."

Cody was waiting in his office when Juliet looked for him at ten-fifteen.

"I'll leave the new pickup here. You can bring me back in the morning." He said it curtly; it was a mandate, as if she were his chauffeur rather than a friend who was giving him a ride in order that they might have time to talk. He stood up and began straightening a few papers on his desk, not even bothering to look up at her.

For a moment Juliet felt her shoulders slumping, as misery tried to creep up on her again. Cody had been her friend and champion for so long—and now he was treating her with such cold disregard. It hurt. Very much.

But then she realized that she honestly could think of nothing she'd done to make Cody behave this way. His nasty attitude had caught her off guard in the auditorium; she'd reacted to such hostility in her old way, going all numb and speechless. But she didn't have to keep acting like that. She *refused* to keep acting like that.

Juliet lifted her chin and said perkily, "Well, yes, Cody, I'd *love* to drive you into town tomorrow. It would be no problem for me at all. And, though you didn't bother to ask, we have just had an extremely successful audition, thank you. We have seven musical acts, two poets and every last part in each skit has been cast—not to mention Lalo Severin's performing poodle act and Raleigh McDuff's singing cat. Isn't that wonderful?''

Cody made a low growling sound in his throat, which Juliet decided to take as congratulations.

''Why, thank you. We are all extremely pleased. And everyone is especially thrilled that you will be taking part this year.''

He did look up then, from under his brows. ''Everyone's thrilled but you, right?''

He looked almost hurt. Lord, she had no idea of what to make of him lately. ''Oh, Cody....''

He was insistent. ''Right?''

She dropped the pretense of perkiness to answer frankly. ''I had thought it would be better—it's true—if we weren't around each other so much. But that's not how it's turning out. So we'll just have to make the best of it, I suppose.''

''Sure. We'll make the best of it.'' The words were heavy with sarcasm.

''Cody.'' She stared at him, bewildered, across the barrier of his desk. ''What *is* the matter with you?''

''We'll talk about it,'' he said, coming around the desk toward her. ''On the way home.''

They went out to the old pickup that he'd lent her. She drove. They were barely out of McIntyre's parking lot, when all of a sudden he demanded, ''Where did you get that dress?''

She glanced over at him. It was dark enough that she couldn't read anything in his face, but his tone had been nothing short of accusatory.

''At a department store, where else?'' Her tone was bright, but with a slight brittle edge. She realized she was finally beginning to feel exasperated with him; it was a rare emotion for her, but one that was probably inevitable given the changes in her and the way he was acting. ''Why? Is there something wrong with it?''

"It's red," he said, as if wearing red were some kind of capital offense.

She gave him another glance, wondering if perhaps there were something seriously wrong with him that was ruining his attitude and that he hadn't told her about yet—perhaps he had contracted a terminal disease, or had lost everything gambling in Tahoe and would soon be on the street. But, really, neither tragedy looked likely. He was the picture of health. And since she was his book-keeper, she would probably already be aware of it if he had some sort of problem with gambling.

Maybe there *was* something wrong with the dress. She looked down at it briefly, but could see nothing that could cause him to scowl in such extreme disapproval. It had a scoop neck, no sleeves, a fitted drop waist and a full skirt. Perhaps it showed her figure more than the clothes she used to wear did, but it was hardly risqué.

"I like red," she said, quite reasonably.

"You never used to wear red," he grumbled. "Or high heels, either." He cast a disparaging frown at the floorboards where her feet were.

That did it. They had just reached the two-lane highway that led to the ranch. Juliet spotted a place where the shoulder of the road looked wide enough and pulled off there.

"What the hell is this?" he demanded.

She ignored him until she'd safely parked the pickup beneath a big fir tree and turned off the engine and lights.

"Cody," she said then, letting her own hurt feelings show. "You are acting like someone I don't even know. I explained all about the changes I'm trying to make in my life. Why are you behaving as if I've done something *criminal?* I just don't understand it."

A logging truck rumbled by, close enough that its tail wind caused the pickup to rock just a little. "This is damn dangerous," Cody said.

"Then answer my question, and we'll leave."

"What question?"

"Why are you angry with me?"

"I'm not angry. Did I say I was angry?"

"No. You didn't have to. You haven't said a civil word to me since you came stomping into the auditorium and demanded that poor Archie withdraw from participation in the revue."

"'*Poor Archie,*'" he echoed, in a distinctly snarly tone. "There's nothing poor about Archie. I pay him union wages, and he makes damn good tips."

"I wasn't referring to the fatness of his wallet, Cody, and you know that, too. I mean poor as in pitiful. I felt sorry for him, the way you jumped on him."

"I didn't jump on him—exactly."

"You did so."

"And besides, he's not pitiful, believe me. All the women love him. Why do you think he wants to work days? Because he's always got a date at night, that's why."

"So what's wrong with that? Maybe he likes to have fun."

"Does he ever. Stay away from him."

"What?"

"He's not the guy for you. Don't get mixed up with him."

"But, Cody—"

"No buts. I'm dead serious."

"Cody—"

"He's all wrong for you."

Juliet squinted at Cody, across the darkness of the cab. "Well, I know that," she said.

He was quiet for a moment. Then he said "Uh...you do?"

She nodded, and then briskly explained, "What I'm after, in the long run, is a full life—one that includes meaningful work, good friends and good times. Eventually I plan to marry a nice man. Someone steady and true, with a good sense of humor and an ability to take life in stride. We'll have a family—two girls and a boy."

"You will?"

She nodded. Since Thursday, she'd been giving the matter some serious thought, especially at night, when she was trying not to think about Cody. "Archie—though I do like him a lot—isn't the man for me at all."

"He isn't?"

"No."

"Why not?"

"Well…"

"Because he's not steady and true?"

"Isn't he? I never thought about that."

"But you said the man in your life would have to be—"

"Steady and true. Yes I said that."

"So…?"

"So, I never got to the point of wondering that about Archie Kent."

"Why not?"

"Because it just…doesn't *happen* when I look at Archie."

"It?"

"Yes."

"What is *it?*"

What happens when I look at you, she thought, and blushed, then felt grateful for the darkness. She gestured rather awkwardly and hit her hand on the steering wheel. "Ouch," she said, instead of answering his question.

"Julie, you're making no sense at all," he said.

She held her bumped hand and observed, "Well, at least you're calling me Julie again."

He said nothing for a moment. And then he actually smiled. She saw the whiteness of his teeth in the dark. "Okay. I was a jerk."

"You were."

"I've made it a point all my life *not* to be a jerk."

"Up until recently, you've been a great success."

"I thought you were interested in Archie Kent. I was…" He looked away, out the windshield, as if the fir tree were suddenly of great interest to him.

"You were what?" The question came out sounding frankly hopeful, which she hadn't intended at all.

He looked at her again, and then leaned toward her a little, so that his face came into sharper focus within the shadowed cab. She was imminently aware of him, of his big, lean body, so close. Of the warmth that emanated from him, and of the sudden, intense longing she had that he might lean closer still.

"Worried," he said, his voice paradoxically husky. "I was worried about you." His beautiful mouth formed the words.

"Worried. Why?" Her own voice sounded mildly dazed.

"I didn't want you to get hurt."

"Well, that's my problem, whether I get hurt."

"I know, but..." He didn't finish.

She didn't care that his voice trailed off into a sigh. She was busy remembering....

Everything. About last Thursday night. As if it were happening right now, in fragments of glorious sensation....

The feel of his lips covering hers, the sweet fire that bloomed and rose as the kiss went on and on. The exquisite brush of his hand on her breast, and the way her nipple had pebbled up, becoming achingly sensitive, begging for more.

Now, just recalling it, she felt her nipples hardening again, though he wasn't even stroking them, though he wasn't touching her at all. She longed to lean forward, offer him her mouth and pray that he would take it.

But she didn't. She reminded herself that, in spite of the way *it* happened whenever Cody McIntyre looked her way lately, he was no more the man for her than Archie Kent was. With a hunk like Cody, *it* wouldn't last forever. She'd lose him eventually to some more desirable woman. And she'd end up with a broken heart.

No, she knew she would be better off to wait for the right man. Someone less beautiful than Cody, someone less *everything* than Cody. But someone she could count on. She would seek a balance—steady and true, first and foremost. And with at least a smidgen of *it* to make life worthwhile.

The thought made her suddenly sad. To end up settling for a smidgen, when with Cody she could probably experience a hugeness, an immensity of *it*....

Cody murmured her name then, softly. And she realized she'd leaned toward him as he was leaning toward her. A wonderful, voluptuous feeling came over her—a melting sort of feeling. How delicious it would be to just dissolve right into Cody's arms.

But that would only be asking for trouble. She caught herself, with a little shudder, and withdrew to a safer distance against the door.

A funny expression crossed his face, one that almost looked like regret or hurt—that she'd backed away? But then she told herself it was just wishful thinking. She couldn't see very well in the darkness anyway.

They were both quiet for a moment. Another big truck went by, rocking the cab.

She remembered what they'd been talking about before *it* intervened. "Well, if you think Archie's wrong for me, that's okay. I think so, too. And so does Archie, more than likely. There's really nothing between us."

He gave a low laugh. "Okay. I'm convinced."

"So can he be in the revue?"

"Why not?"

"Great. Now take back the mean remarks you made about my dress, and we can go home."

"I don't know," he replied, and she was glad for the humor in his tone. "That dress is...downright red. And what would your mother say if she saw you in it?"

Juliet thought of her mother; it helped to settle her down a little, soothed her dangerous desire to keep on flirting when what she should be doing was starting the engine and getting them home—to their separate houses.

She admitted, "My mother brought me up to be reserved and old-fashioned, it's true. But lately she's changed...."

Since he'd met her mother more than once over the years, Cody made a small disbelieving sound, though he didn't actually comment. They looked at each other for a moment, and the subject of Juliet's mother became the last thing on either of their minds.

Finally Cody said in a hesitant voice that touched and vibrated something in Juliet's heart, "Julie...I haven't liked this. The way you've been keeping away from me. I thought..."

"Yes?" There it was, that high, hopeful note again, in her own voice.

"I thought, when you shocked the hell out of us all and got up in front of the association last week, that it was kind of sad. The way we've known each other all our lives, the way we call each other friends, live a few hundred yards apart—and yet we don't *really* know each other."

Juliet considered that. "Yes. I see what you mean. I've always been so shy. And you looked out for me, took care of me, more than anything else."

"Yeah, I guess," he said, and then struggled for a moment to arrange his thoughts. "But, at least in the past you never actually *avoided* me. Hell, what I'm trying to say is, even if we never were real close, I did consider us friends, longtime friends. And since Thursday, I feel like—" he dragged in a breath "—I feel like I've lost a friend."

"Oh, Cody. I'm sorry."

"Look," he went on, "if you don't think I'm the right kind of guy for you, that's okay. I can deal with that. But, damn it, Julie. I *miss* you. Can't you be my friend again?"

"Oh, Cody...." She didn't know what to say. There was a lump in her throat that she had to swallow before she could even begin to explain. "I just thought it would be better, for a while," she managed to say at last, "to stay away from each other."

He said nothing for a moment, then looked out his side window. "Right. I figured that."

And she knew she could no longer continue to reject such a friend as he was. As he'd always been. Eventually, she was sure, this new and frightening attraction she felt for him would pass. And then it would be a pure pleasure to be friends again.

But for the sake of the hundred and one ways he'd always been there for her over the years, she wasn't going to deny their friendship now.

"All right." She smiled. "Avoiding you doesn't seem to have done much good anyway. I'm through with that. As of now."

He looked at her then. "Thanks, Julie," he said. Her silly heart seemed to turn over in response to the flash of his teeth in the darkness.

She drew a deep breath and ordered her heart to stop racing like that. It would all work out fine, she told herself. This crazy attraction was just a passing thing. Not surprising at all, when she considered all the changes she'd been going through of late. She'd set a goal of becoming more assertive, and going after her goal had set in motion some other changes. She was...awakening as a woman. And Cody had helped her along in that awakening—with those incredible kisses the other night.

But this was real life, not *Sleeping Beauty*. Cody might look like a handsome prince, but that was as far as the fairy tale went in this case. A kiss, these days, rarely signified the start of a lifetime's commitment. And just because what they'd done had thrilled her to her toes didn't mean she was in love with him or anything.

No, it had been a...physical reaction, that was all. And she would always be grateful to Cody for doing such a marvelous job of showing her what all the hoopla was about when it came to this mysterious and remarkable thing that went on between men and women.

Cody reached across the cab to briefly squeeze her hand. "I'm glad we talked," he said.

"Me, too." Her voice cracked a little, because his touch, quick and light as it was, created a chain reaction. From the point of contact, an electrical jolt shot right down into the center of her, where it struck a spark that heated everything up and began a minor internal meltdown.

Juliet started the pickup and concentrated on getting back out on the road and home to the ranch.

Soon enough, she told herself soothingly, as she waited for the meltdown to pass and her body to settle down, this won't happen every time he comes near me. Soon enough, everything will be like it was before.

She had no idea that Cody, smiling contentedly on his side of the cab, saw things in a slightly different light. He really was grateful that they were no longer going to be staying out of each other's way. And it *had* been bothering him that they'd been friends for so long and yet always maintained a certain distance with each other.

To Cody, right now seemed the perfect time for them to become much better friends than they had ever been before.

CHAPTER FIVE

JULIET had just rolled over and banged on her alarm to make it be quiet, when the knock came at the kitchen door.

"Uugh," she muttered, and tried to make the world go away by covering her head with her pillow. But the knock came again.

She sat up. "All right! Just a minute."

She was just belting her light robe over her sleep-wrinkled pajamas when she threw back the door.

"Morning." Cody grinned at her. He wore old jeans and a plaid shirt and his most ancient pair of rawhide boots. To Juliet, he looked even better than he had the night before when he'd burst through the double doors of the auditorium and demanded that Archie Kent back out of the revue. Yes, she thought sleepily, covering a yawn with the back of her hand. It really was true. He kept getting better looking every time she saw him.

She peered at him, still half asleep, wondering vaguely if she looked as rumpled and groggy as she felt, telling herself it shouldn't bother her if she did.

She heard panting and a thumping sound and managed to stop staring at Cody's incredible face long enough to glance down at his dog. Kemo sat beside Cody, looking up at her, his mouth open and his tongue lolling cheerfully to one side.

Cody gestured vaguely at the barn and stables beyond the fence. "I was just doing the morning chores."

Juliet nodded. "Oh. Right. The chores."

"Yeah. And I thought—"

"Hmm?"

"Well, I thought I'd just drop by and invite you over to the house for breakfast."

"Breakfast."

"Yeah. You know. Eggs. Bacon. Toast. Coffee."

"You want me to come over for breakfast."

He started combing his hair with his fingers. "Well, yeah." He looked down at his dog, who made a little whine that actually sounded like encouragement, and then he looked back at her. "How about it?"

She didn't answer for a moment. She was thinking that not avoiding him was one thing, having breakfast with him another. "Well, Cody..." she began, wondering how to tell him no without hurting him.

His face fell. "No?" he asked flatly. "You won't come?"

"Cody, I—"

He put up a hand. "Never mind. It was only a thought." He turned away, and she felt totally heartless, in spite of the emotional danger he represented, to reject him this way.

"Wait."

He turned back. "Yeah?"

"Give me twenty minutes to get myself together."

His face lit up. "Great." He slapped his thigh in a signal to the dog, and left without another word.

Juliet stared after him for a moment, slightly stupefied that he had asked her over for breakfast—and that she had accepted. Then it came to her that in twenty minutes she had to be showered, dressed and ready to eat. So she closed the door and flew toward the bathroom, shedding her robe and pajamas as she went.

Cody, who had changed into a newer pair of jeans and a fresh shirt, had the food almost ready when Juliet knocked on the door. He led her to the kitchen and gestured toward a chair in the breakfast nook, which looked out on the open field where two of his horses were grazing. He poured her coffee and asked how she liked her eggs, and then he fried them and set the meal before her, slipping into a chair across from her after that.

Juliet drank some coffee, picked up her fork, ate half an egg and then asked the question she'd been pondering all the time she showered and dressed. "Cody, what is this all about?"

He stopped in the middle of munching a slice of bacon. "What?" He looked extremely innocent.

"This. You having me over for breakfast all of a sudden."

He shrugged. "I don't know. It seemed like a nice idea. So I invited you."

"But we never do things like this together."

"Like what?" he challenged, then went on without waiting for her answer. "We have lunch together now and then."

"Business lunches."

"Food's food," he said.

"Wrong." She munched a little bacon herself and then she accused, "And you know it, too. A business lunch is a far cry from cooking for someone in your own kitchen."

"You mean you appreciate my efforts?" he asked, missing the point entirely.

"Well, of course I do—"

She didn't get to qualify her statement by explaining that perhaps sharing breakfast was a little more than what they should be doing together right now, because he grinned widely—presumably in appreciation of *her* appreciation—and her heart distracted her, going all rambunctious for a moment. He looked her over, and beneath her conservative suit, her whole body tingled.

"Hey," he said. "I like that suit."

Juliet, who still hadn't explained that they couldn't be spending *too* much time together, after all, glanced down at the outfit in question and wondered what he saw to like about it. She'd bought it several months ago, before she'd made her birthday vow. The cut was undistinguished, and the color was called "wheat." "Wheat" sounded nice when the clerk at the department store described it. "Just your color, my dear. A lovely, subtle wheat...." But when Juliet got the suit home, she realized the truth; "wheat" was just another name for brown—a sort of watered-down brown, actually.

Juliet finished contemplating the bland suit and looked up at Cody once more. "I hate this suit," she said, with perhaps more malice than was called for. "But I'm still practical enough that

I'm not willing to get rid of it. I don't know what you can possibly see in it.''

He pondered for a moment, then said thoughtfully, ''I don't know. Maybe it kind of…reassures me that you're still a little bit the Julie I used to know.''

He reached across then, so swiftly that she had no opportunity to move back, and snared her hand where it lay on the edge of the table. His touch was warm and enveloping. All coherent thought fled her mind. Slowly he pulled her nearer, across the barrier of the table between them.

''*Are* you still the same Julie?'' he asked, in a hushed, breath-held kind of tone.

''I…um, certainly, to a certain extent, yes.…''

He smiled, then, because her voice itself had proved she told the truth. It had broken on a gasp between the *y* and *e* of *yes,* just the way it used to before.

''Good,'' he said, and released her.

Her hand felt hot. Her wrist, where he'd held it, tingled deliciously. She stared at him, unable to utter a word.

He lifted his coffee cup and gestured with it. ''Eat your food before it gets cold.'' He returned to his own meal with gusto.

Juliet continued to stare at him a bit longer, waiting for the tingling that had spread from her hand to her whole body to subside. At last, when she felt she was more or less back to normal again, she realized she was starved and eagerly dug back into the meal.

She looked up just as she was polishing off her second piece of toast to find him watching her. She cast about for a way to explain how things like this breakfast shouldn't happen again for a while.

But before she found the words, he wiped his mouth with his napkin and asked, ''So tell me about your mother.''

Her mouth was open—she'd been just about to speak. She closed it and gave him a baffled frown. ''My mother?''

''Last night,'' he elaborated, ''you said she's changed.''

Juliet raised her cup to her lips and realized there was nothing in there. So she stood up, went to the coffeepot, and returned to fill their cups. Unfortunately, she hadn't thought about how close she'd have to stand to him to give him more coffee until she was already at his side. She poured, poignantly aware of the solid warmth of him, the silky rust-colored hairs on the back of his hands and the gleam in his eyes.

"Julie?" He was grinning up at her.

"Um, yes?" She realized his cup was full and brought the pot upright just in time.

"I asked you about your mother."

"My mother."

"If she'd changed."

Juliet cleared her throat. "Right. My mother. She has. Changed."

He looked doubtful. "Since when?"

She ordered her legs to carry her away from him, back to the counter to return the pot to the warming plate. As soon as she gained a little distance from him, she found it was easier to think about the question he'd just asked. "She's changed since she and Dad sold the antique store."

"Changed how?"

Juliet stayed there at the counter for a moment, leaning back against it. Putting aside the nagging voice of her wiser self that urged she tell Cody she wouldn't be having breakfast with him again soon, she considered his question. "My mother's...relaxed her standards a little, I'd say. She isn't as prudish and proper as she used to be. Until they sold the store, it kind of defined them. They'd owned it for so long, since way before I was born...."

Thinking of the antique store, Juliet found herself caught up in memories of it. As a child, she'd spent long hours in the musty old brick building that had been an assay office during the gold rush. Her memories of those years seemed mostly to consist of her parents urging her to "hush"—and to be careful of this or that priceless heirloom. Her parents had been older, in their early forties when she was born. They were a quiet, retiring pair, set in their ways.

She went on, musingly, "Yes, they defined themselves by that store. And then, when they finally sold it, they began to look at the world in a different way."

"What way?"

"I don't know, more open-mindedly, I suppose...." Juliet stared out the window beyond the table, but she wasn't really seeing the big, wide field. She was seeing herself as a solitary little girl, an only child who quivered at the prospect of trying to make a friend, whose aging parents had interests way beyond her childish comprehension.

"Julie? You all right?" Cody's voice was edged with concern.

"Yes, yes. Just thinking."

"About what?"

She shifted her glance from the open field to Cody's face. "My father used to call me 'Little Mouse.' Did you know that?" Cody shook his head. She went on, "He meant it affectionately, but eventually I kind of began to feel like one. Like a little mouse hiding in the dusty junk left over from other people's lives...." Totally without her permission, a single tear trickled down her cheek. Juliet's voice faded off.

"Julie...." His tone was soft.

She swiped the tear away. "Don't worry. Just indulging in a little self-pity. But I'm through now." Her voice became brisk as she continued, "I think the difference in my mother is partly due to Hawaii." After they sold the antique store, her parents had bought a condominium on the island of Maui and they'd retired there.

"I guess," he conceded wryly, "that Hawaii might have a certain effect, even on your mother."

"You never did like my mother," she remarked a little sourly, coming back to the table and reclaiming her chair.

"No," he contended. "*She* never did like *me*."

"That's not true." Juliet regretted how unconvincing she sounded.

"Oh, isn't it? Then what about that time I brought you home

after Billy Butley tore your dress and pushed you into Nugget Creek? She immediately assumed I was the one who did it."

"I straightened her out."

"Not until after she told me never to come near you again."

"She took that back."

"Only because she couldn't do otherwise."

"Oh, Cody. She could just never understand why someone like you would look out for a mouse like me. She was suspicious."

"Of what?"

"Well, that you were...up to no good."

"How?"

Juliet felt her face coloring and hesitated before answering.

Cody figured it out for himself before she spoke. He choked on his coffee as awareness dawned. "She thought I was out to *seduce* you?"

Juliet nodded. "It's silly, I know." She hastened to add, "But she doesn't feel that way anymore."

He gave her a disbelieving frown. "You're just saying that."

"No. On my honor, it's true. After all, there were all those years where you dated so...widely. And people do talk, after all. When she found out you had so many girlfriends, she decided there wasn't much likelihood you'd be needing to take advantage of *me*. And now, since Hawaii, well, she and my dad both have loosened up a lot. As a matter of fact," Juliet went on as proof positive of the change in her mother, "when she called last week, she mentioned that she's bought a bikini."

"Emma Huddleston. In a bikini?" Cody sounded frankly incredulous.

"People *can* change."

Cody said gruffly, "Tell me something I don't already know."

He was looking at her in a very focused, intense way. Outside, she heard the roar of a lawn mower starting up. The loud sound made her jump, as she thought of what he'd done a few minutes before, taking her hand, pulling her closer, making her long to get closer still.

This was all playing with fire, and she knew it. It had not been wise to come into his house and share breakfast with him. Certainly, they'd been friends forever and a day—but distant friends, with strictly proscribed limits on their relationship. It made no sense at all to go expanding the boundaries of their friendship right now, when she quivered clear down to her toes every time he so much as smiled at her. But somehow, every time she tried to tell him how she felt about all this, he either melted her with a look, or changed the subject before she even had a chance to begin.

She decided grimly that talking to him about this wasn't going to work. It was action that was called for. Breakfast was over, and she would see that a situation like this didn't arise again until this...*crush* she had on Cody was no more than a sweet, distant memory.

She stood up. "You know, it's probably time we got going. I should be over at McMulch's Lumberyard by nine." She added, unnecessarily, "I'm doing a unit cost analysis for them."

"Oh, yeah. Sure." He stood up, too, and started carrying things to the sink. She helped him.

All was in order in no time. They went out together, got in the old pickup that she'd parked in the front drive and started for town, waving at the old caretaker, Bud Southey, who was out on the riding mower cutting the six acres of grass when they left.

Juliet was careful to keep the talk away from anything personal as they drove. They agreed she could just leave the old pickup in the lot behind McIntyre's if her car was through at the shop. She told him that since he wasn't in any of the skits, he probably wouldn't be called on to rehearse for the revue until the last few days before opening, when they put the whole thing together.

When she left him at Emerald Gap Hardware, she thanked him for the breakfast.

"My pleasure," he said. "Anytime."

She smiled and nodded and tried not to pay any heed to the way her heart fluttered inside her chest, and her skin got too warm and her breath hitched and caught.

He left, turning once to wave before going in the hardware

store's back door, and when he was gone she grimly muttered, "'Anytime,' hah. Not anytime soon...."

Cody, though, had meant exactly what he had said. Breakfast with Julie *had* been a pure pleasure. And he intended to make sure the pleasure was repeated soon.

Whistling, he entered the narrow, cramped storeroom behind the hardware store that his father had built. There was nobody there yet. The store didn't open until ten.

He busied himself making the coffee that he provided for his employees, and when it was through dripping, he poured himself a cup. Then he went out to the floor safe beneath the register in the store itself, and took the money and receipts to the back again to tally up. The take, he discovered, hadn't been bad for a Monday.

He felt pleased, much more than the few extra bucks he was looking at warranted.

Still whistling, he put the money in a leather bag and waited for Elma Lou Bealer, who would open up. When she arrived, he exchanged a few pleasantries, unlocked the register and took the leather bag the half block to the back entrance of McIntyre's.

Inside the restaurant, which was also deserted, since it didn't open until eleven, he repeated the process of counting the money earned the day before.

He had to count twice, because Julie's image kept superimposing itself over the faces of Washington, Lincoln and Jackson. When he was done, he put the restaurant's money into the leather bag with the cash from the store and glanced up at the big clock on the office wall; it was nearly ten.

He went out to his truck and drove to the bank, where he didn't even have to wait in line for the merchant's window. By ten-fifteen, the money was safely deposited. He went back to the restaurant to go over the meat order with the head chef.

From noon to a little before two, he stayed at the restaurant, playing host, overseeing things. After that, he stopped in at the hardware store to discuss housewares and garden stock with a local salesman.

Before he knew it, it was dinnertime. He wondered if Julie had eaten yet. She probably would be working tonight on the festival, either at the auditorium or down at the town hall. It was very important that she take time to eat.

He went back to the restaurant and ordered two meals of halibut steak with new potatoes and string beans and carrots almondine. Lots of protein and fresh vegetables. Very important for a woman working overtime. When the prep man packed it up for him, he had him add a nice bottle of wine.

Just before six, he parked his pickup in front of the refurbished Victorian building where Julie rented office space. Then he carried the big basket of food inside.

He was in luck. She was there, her office door open. He could hear the printer of her computer, making quick, low hissing sounds as it printed something. She was sitting at her desk.

He set the basket down and knocked on the door frame. "Julie?"

She looked up from the spread sheets she was studying. He had the feeling that he kept having lately whenever he looked into her eyes—like the floor had dropped out from under him for a moment. She blinked. "Cody?"

He said, "Julie," and then stood there for a few minutes grinning like an idiot. Then he remembered the basket. He bent, hoisted it and held it out, offering it proudly. "I thought you might be hungry, so I had Roger grill us a couple of halibut steaks."

She stared for a moment. Then she said, "Oh, Cody," as if he'd done something he shouldn't have.

"What?" He felt like a fool all of a sudden, standing there with a big picnic basket, when a minute before it had seemed like a completely logical thing to do—to bring dinner for her.

Her printer finished printing. The graceful old building seemed very quiet.

"Come in," she said. "Close the door."

He brought the basket beyond the threshold and turned to shut out the hallway. Then he sat in one of the two wing chairs across from her desk and looked down at the gray slacks that he'd changed in to in his office before coming over here.

"Cody, I can't handle this," she said. Her soft voice broke once, in the middle of *can't,* the way it used to do all the time, before she started becoming someone he couldn't stop thinking about.

He decided to try to lighten the mood. "Can't handle what? You hate halibut?"

She didn't even crack a smile. "I agreed to stop avoiding you, not to spend every spare moment with you."

That hurt. "You don't like to spend time with me?"

"I do like it, Cody. I like it too much."

"So what's wrong with that?"

"A lot."

"Why?"

"Oh, Cody...."

"*Oh, Cody,* tells me nothing."

"Oh, Cody...."

He waited.

Finally she managed, "I explained it, last Thursday night. Eventually, I'd be the one to get hurt, if you and I...got involved."

"Who says we're getting involved?" She chose not even to answer that and just gave him a frustrated frown. So he went on. "And, if we did, who says you'd get hurt? Maybe *I'd* get hurt. Hell, maybe *neither* of us would get hurt. Did you ever think of that?"

"Oh, Cody. Be realistic. Look at you. Look at me. It's obvious who'd end up with the broken heart when it was over."

Something inside him snapped then. He stood up in a quick, angry motion. She shrank back in her swivel chair. "That's the dumbest damn notion I've ever heard," he growled. "I *have* looked at you, and you look just fine."

And she did, too, with her fair hair around her shoulders, and her hazel eyes wide. There were two warm spots of color high on her cheeks. And she'd taken off the jacket of that nice suit she said she hated and gone and unbuttoned the top buttons of her blouse again.

She looked…like a woman who ought to be kissed. And Cody was damn willing to take on the job. He came around the desk. She watched him come, her eyes widening even more. When the desk no longer separated them, he stood looking down at her.

"Cody.…"

He decided not to say a damn thing. She'd only start arguing with him again, and she talked too much anyway, lately. He bent down to her, putting his arms on her chair arms, bringing his face level with hers.

Her wide eyes relaxed a little, then, as she lowered her eyelids to look at his mouth. "Cody.…"

Since she seemed so interested in his mouth, he moved it a little closer, so that he could feel her warm, sweet breath as it sighed in and out.

"Oh, Cody.…"

He wrapped his hands around her arms and straightened up very slowly, pulling her with him. Then he gathered her close and took her mouth with his own.

CHAPTER SIX

FOR JULIET, the meltdown began.

Cody's lips played over hers and his arms held her tight and all she could think of was that she hoped he would never stop. He nudged her lips apart with gentle urgings, and his tongue darted in and...oh, down in her abdomen, there was a slow-spreading heat that made her feel all liquid and yearning for more.

His hands strayed up and down, touching and stroking the entire of her back from the gentle flare of her hips, up over the curve of her waist, and out to her shoulders. Pulling her nearer, he caressed her neck and then held her head still, one firm hand along each cheek, so his mouth could torment her even more thoroughly than it had done up till now.

She groaned, an utterly abandoned sound, and her head fell back. He cradled her head then, with one hand, while he combed her hair in long, sweet strokes with the fingers of the other hand, lifting his mouth from hers enough to whisper low, seductive things that made her blush at the same time as she longed to hear more.

And then, once again, he was kissing her, slanting his lips one way and then the other, trailing little love bites down her neck, and then kissing her collarbone, which tingled deliciously at such sensuous attention.

His hand slid up and under the silk of her white blouse, pushing it aside as he touched her bare skin. The tiny white buttons of the blouse, moored loosely, slipped free of their holes and the blouse gaped a little, exposing her plain white slip.

"Oh my goodness," she murmured, just as she had last Thursday night. And she felt the blouse glide down over one shoulder.

Cody's warm, big hand slid beneath the strap of her plain slip, guiding it gently over the swell of her shoulder, until it fell down her arm, pulling one side of the slip with it, and exposing one cup of the lacy push-up bra she'd bought on a shopping spree in Sacramento a few weeks before.

He pulled away a little, and looked down at the soft swell of her breast nestled in the lace of the new bra. ''Pretty.'' He sighed, and his hand drifted lower, until he cupped the small mound.

Juliet looked down, too, experiencing a most wondrous, languorous feeling. She watched as his thumb teased her nipple through the lace and felt the nipple grow hard and protruding. Then he slipped his thumb under the lace, and he guided the lace beneath the swell of her breast, so the nipple was revealed.

''Oh, Cody....'' She moaned aloud, and her head dropped back. He caught her on his free arm.

Then he lowered his mouth and kissed her exposed breast, first with little brushing, breathy kisses. Then, his lips finding the hard nipple, he licked it and blew on it and at last took it inside his mouth.

Oh, it felt lovely when he kissed her that way. Juliet's senses whirled madly as he suckled on her breast. Nothing half so wonderful had ever happened to her in her entire thirty years. And when he pushed down the slip on the other side, and got the bra out of the way there, too, she thought perhaps she had tumbled out of the real world into some alternate universe—a realm of the senses, where pleasure thrilled and consumed and nothing mattered but the delicious torment of Cody's lips on her burning skin.

And then, out in the hall, she heard the rumble of the janitor's cleaning cart. And she realized where she was.

''Oh, my Lord....'' she murmured.

Cody must have sensed the sudden unwelcome tension in her body, because he stopped doing those incredible things to her bare breasts and lifted his head enough that their eyes could meet. His gaze was hot, heavy-lidded with desire.

He said, very low, ''You want me to stop?''

For a brief eternity, she had no words to answer him. Since the moment he pulled her slowly from her swivel chair, it hadn't occurred to her that there was any possibility of stopping this marvelous, frightening thing that was happening between them. It all seemed...inevitable. Like the sun setting at night, only to rise again with the dawn.

While she dazedly contemplated his question, he made the decision for her.

"This isn't the place," he muttered. And began putting her clothing to rights, the gentleness of his hands belying the grim set of his jaw.

After staring at him dumbly for a few seconds more, she bestirred herself and helped him. It took no time at all, and her breasts were once again properly covered with bra, slip and blouse.

But Juliet herself felt completely naked. As the seconds passed, she found it more and more difficult to look at Cody, who now seemed a silent and forbidding presence—first right in front of her, and then, as he quietly moved away, on the other side of her desk.

When she made herself sit down and forced herself to look at him, she realized he was unpacking the basket of food he had brought.

He caught her eye, and she thought she detected a spark of anger in his look. If there was, she couldn't really blame him, as there were so many inconsistencies in her behavior lately. She kept saying things like they couldn't spend so much time together—and then melting in his arms the moment he touched her.

"It's getting cold," he said of the food. "No sense wasting it."

She didn't know what to do right then, so she let him feed her for the second time that day, watching numbly as he cleared the papers off of her desk, laid place mats and set out the covered plates. He even poured wine.

She ate without really tasting, though she was obscurely aware that the food was excellent. She hadn't much appetite after what had just happened, but she knew her body needed fuel to get through the evening meeting with her committee chairpeople that lay ahead.

Once, in the course of the silent meal, the janitor rapped on the door. Juliet called to him that they would be finished soon, and he moved on down the hall.

When they were both done and Cody was repacking the basket, Juliet thanked him for the dinner. The words sounded awkward and falsely social, dropping from her lips into the cavernous silence that now yawned between them. The intimacy of his touch had been too shattering this time. It had made even the stunningly erotic kiss of last Thursday seem like child's play by comparison. Now, thanking him for the dinner was little more than meaningless noisemaking—a polite sound to cover the demolished state of her nerves.

"You're welcome." He gave the empty pleasantry right back as he lifted the basket and strode to the door.

Just before he pulled the door open, she found some small reserve of courage that she'd feared had deserted her. "Cody."

He stopped without turning. "Yeah."

"In spite of the way I acted when you kissed me, I meant what I said. I don't want to get involved with you in a…romantic way."

"Why did I know you would say that?" He spoke with resigned irony.

"Do I have to start avoiding you again?"

He didn't answer for a moment. Then his sculpted shoulders lifted in an eloquent shrug. "Hell, no." He turned to face her. "Don't worry. I'm no genius, but I think I got your message this time. If you're still willing to tell me no after what happened a little while ago, then I'm willing to believe you really mean it. Don't bother to avoid me, Julie. Because I'll be avoiding you." He turned away again and pulled open the door. The janitor was once more approaching in the hall. "Come on in," Cody said, stepping beyond the threshold. "We're finished in here."

Cody was a man who meant what he said. For over a week Juliet caught no more than passing glimpses of him—on the street, or early in the morning, when he went out to feed the animals. Twice, late at night, when the demons of forbidden desire were at their most devilish, he gifted her with impromptu concerts from the porch of the main house.

No one would ever know how difficult it was for her to stay in her bed at those times. She, who'd always been too timid to even dislike anyone, almost hated Cody McIntyre when he played those beautiful songs on the harmonica, and she pictured his mouth making the music happen, and remembered what his mouth had done to her.

She tossed and turned. But somehow, by grimly reminding herself that she wanted more from the first man she made love with than unparalleled ecstasy and an eventual broken heart, she managed to stay where she was.

Her car—which the man at the garage had sworn, with a bit of a smirk, was as good as new—offered some solace. She found great comfort in putting on something red and driving the mountain roads a little faster than she should have, feeling the powerful engine purring at her command. She'd roll all the windows down and open the sunroof when she drove like that, letting the wind play with her hair. And she'd only slow down when it became impossible not to imagine Cody's hands, playing with her hair—and every other part of her, for that matter.

And, thank heaven, there was the festival to take up so much of her spare time that there weren't many opportunities for dreaming about a man she couldn't have anyway.

Midsummer Madness was shaping up marvelously. For the revue, the little play about Maria Elena, starring Yolanda and Archie, was nothing short of grand melodrama, and even the poodle act looked like fun. Reva Reid, chairperson of the Opening Day Parade committee, had signed up a record of thirty-five different floats. And Burt Pandley had already filled the town hall with more crafts and industry booths than they'd had any previous year.

Flat-nosed Jake, who was always full of surprises, had a friend on the staff of the *Sacramento Bee*. The friend had come to visit, and it looked as if there was going to be a cover story about the festival in the *Bee*'s Sunday supplement on the twenty-first, the Sunday before the festival began. Everyone was thrilled. Even

Babe Allen, who'd groused about having to pay a director's fee when Juliet wasn't a true professional, had changed her tune; twice she'd mentioned ways they could expand further on a good thing *next* year—when, of course, Juliet would be handling things once more, wouldn't she?

If it weren't for this craving for Cody that wouldn't go away, Juliet's life would have been just about as perfect as she ever might have imagined in her wildest fantasies of prospective assertiveness. But the craving to have Cody's arms around her was always there, underlying everything, even her triumph as festival director.

Sometimes, she'd try to think of her burning desire as a good thing, a sort of learning experience of the senses. She'd tell herself that what she was going through was a long-overdue sensual awakening—and then she'd want to scream because the man she longed for to help her wake up all the way would only cause her heartache in the end.

Sunday, the twenty-first, arrived. And with it came the front-page article about the festival in the Encore section of the *Sacramento Bee*. The cover of the supplement featured a full-page color photograph of the brick-fronted Gap Auditorium, hung from end-to-end with a huge banner announcing Midsummer Madness. The Victorian gaslights on the sidewalk, hinting nostalgically of another era, framed the shot.

Juliet, who got up at five and stationed herself outside the supermarket to wait for the papers to be delivered, bought ten copies.

In the article, Juliet was mentioned four times—and quoted twice. The writer described her as "this year's festival director, a local bookkeeper with a calm, no-nonsense air and a knack for getting the job done." Juliet was so thrilled that she clipped a copy of the article and sent it to her parents on Maui. Her mother called to congratulate her a few days later, saying that she and Juliet's father were impressed and excited with their daughter's success.

"Oh, Juliet, I knew it," her mother said just before she hung up. "I knew that you were changing, getting outside yourself, making the most of your life. And I'm so terribly grateful. The truth is that your father and I were rather... preoccupied parents, not to mention somewhat stuffy and judgmental—no, no, don't be sweet and say it's not true. We'd gotten in a rut as a childless couple, and we never really adapted to the changes that happened when you came along. We...kept you down, in a way. Wanted you quiet and untroublesome, above everything else. You gave us exactly what we asked for—a shy mouse.... Remember, that's what your father used to call you?''

''Yes,'' Juliet said softly. ''I remember.''

''But lately I've noticed several signs that you're becoming more outgoing. And when we received this clipping, well, I knew for sure that I'd been right. I think it's perfectly splendid of you. I truly do.''

Juliet, feeling extremely emotional, managed to murmur a thank-you.

''Don't thank me. Thank yourself. You've done it all, I know.''

They talked for a few minutes more, her mother enthusing about the breathtaking beauty of Maui and the spectacular black-sand beaches she and Juliet's father had visited on the big island recently.

At last Emma said, ''And now I must go. Your father's waiting for me—our morning swim, you know.''

Juliet pictured her seventy-two-year-old mother in her new bikini, and smiled as she said goodbye.

She sat for a while in bed after she hung up the phone, basking in her mother's approving words. She *had* come a long way since the day she'd turned thirty, and she resolved to keep in mind, whenever the vagaries of life got her down, all the strides she'd made.

Her resolve was tested that very evening, at the first of two dress rehearsals before the opening of the Midsummer Madness Revue, which was slated to kick off the festivities that Friday night.

Because everyone in the revue was working on a volunteer basis, Juliet had kept the time each act had to rehearse at a minimum by never scheduling a complete run-through until the last two rehearsals before opening night. This was time-saving overall, but made for a pair of grueling evenings when it finally came down to the wire. Not only did the set changes and act shifts have to be added in, but the lights and sound had to be used in sequence for the first time, too.

By two hours into the Wednesday night run-through—and less than halfway through the first act—tempers were generally on simmer up to boil. One of Lalo Severin's poodles had chased Raleigh McDuff's singing cat around the stage, finally treeing it on the act curtain. The cat then had to be coaxed down with a can of sardines, and the poodle was taken to where Andrea Oakleaf could administer first aid to the several long scratches on its nose. Yolanda Hughes, who had begun to show signs of artistic temperament, was in a rage over her costume, which she claimed bound her about the bust. Archie Kent was late. And two of the four Barbershop Boys had sore throats.

Juliet was beginning to feel the tension herself, trying to direct Yolanda through her death scene, while the bit players who were supposed to be the crazed members of a bloodthirsty mob kept wandering offstage and returning with cans of soda pop or boxes of cheese crackers.

"Adiós, amigos…. Adiós amigas," Yolanda gallantly intoned— and then started fiddling with the front of her dress, muttering invectives against its faulty design.

Somehow, Yolanda stopped fidgeting long enough to be effectively hung. But then the doleful music, meant to signify the passing of a blameless soul, did not come on. And the single spot which was supposed to narrow down onto her slowly swinging figure, somehow ended up on Bobby Dumphy, down left, drinking a cola and munching a candy bar.

Juliet felt so discouraged, she wanted to cry.

"Could I make a suggestion?" The voice came, rich and low, into her ear.

Cody. Juliet stiffened. She'd seen him come in and sit in the back to wait for his turn to perform. But then she'd firmly blocked him from her mind.

She turned her head. Even in the dim light that bled from the misplaced spotlight on stage, he looked wonderful.

"What?" she asked flatly.

"Hey, Juliet, what now?" someone demanded from up on the stage; the mob was becoming restless.

"Help Yolanda down, bring up the lights and everybody take five," Juliet instructed.

The lights came on, greeted by a halfhearted cheer from the disbanding mob. Archie, who'd finally arrived, helped the hangman to lower the swinging Yolanda.

Juliet shifted in her seat to face the object of her strictly forbidden fantasies. "What's your suggestion?"

He answered with calm assurance. "Send everybody home but the technical people. Then run it through—twice, if possible—with just the lights and sound and set changes. Have a few volunteers stick around to stand in the right places for light changes. Then, tomorrow, when you've got the technical side down pat, you can add the performers, and it should go reasonably well."

Juliet considered his suggestion—and had to admit it made better sense than trying to do everything at once. The performers, at least, already had a good idea of where they were supposed to be and how to get there. If she could just bring the lights and sound up to par, they might be all right.

"Good idea," she said after a moment. "Thanks."

"No problem," he said, and then went back up the aisle without another word. Juliet stared after him for a moment, thinking that even now, when she'd told him to stay away from her, he still came to her aid when she needed help. She knew sadness and longing then, which she couldn't afford to examine. So she forced herself to face front again, before he disappeared through the double doors.

"All right, everyone!" she announced. "If I could have your attention for a moment...."

Cody's plan worked well, all things considered. The lights and sound ran like clockwork the next night, and the performers did much better at holding up their end. The poodle once more growled at the singing cat, and Yolanda, who'd altered her costume herself, still was not pleased. But Archie Kent was on time, and all four Barbershop Boys were ready to sing "Sweet Adeline" in harmony.

Cody, who treated Juliet with distant politeness, sang a rollicking tune about a cowboy and a splay-shanked mule in the first act. His other number, in the second act, was a new one, a ballad. Juliet was called backstage just as it started it, so she didn't hear the song itself. But he was playing the final chords on his twelve-string when she returned. After the last note faded, there was silence, and then even Bobby Dumphy stopped eating long enough to applaud.

That final rehearsal ended near 1:00 a.m., but everyone left in high spirits. The revue wasn't perfect by a long shot—but nobody said it was supposed to be. It was silly and fun and full of color and music. That should be enough, as far as they were all concerned.

The next day, Juliet didn't even bother to try to put in a day's work at her office. She conferred with the Methodist Women about the next morning's pancake breakfast, and briefly viewed each of the thirty-five floats—most of which were actually finished—that were scheduled for tomorrow afternoon's parade. She went over, once again, the float order with Reva, and then toured the upstairs of the town hall, where the Crafts and Industry Fair was—more or less—ready to go.

At four, she went back to the ranch and took a long tepid bath and lay down in her undies for forty-five minutes, getting up only after she had fallen asleep and dreamed, disconcertingly, of Cody asking her sadly why she had turned her back on him. She woke with a start, to find two wet tears had run down the sides of her face and into her hair.

She sat up and brushed them away and went to put on her new red dress. When she was ready, she stood before the mirror in her room.

A summer-weight knit, the dress hugged her slim curves to below the waist, where it flared out abruptly. Beneath the flare of the skirt, which fell to midcalf, she wore a red crinoline-edged half-slip. Of course, no one would be seeing the slip, but she did love the naughty way it whispered with each step she took.

Juliet winked at herself in the mirror. She put the leftover sadness from her dream behind her. She was ready for the opening night of the Midsummer Madness Revue.

When the curtain went up, the old Gap Auditorium was *standing room only.* Juliet gave up her own seat to the elderly woman from Ukiah who claimed she'd never missed a first night of the revue in thirty years—but next year, the woman suggested, maybe they'd better arrange to take reservations so the people who really cared could be sure to be accommodated....

Juliet posted herself up near one of the side doors as the house lights went down. Listening to the rustle of excitement in the audience, she couldn't help anticipating the thousand and one things that might go wrong.

But nothing did, excluding a few missed light cues and late entrances, of course. From the first notes of "Sweet Adeline," by the Barbershop Boys, to the closing "Star Spangled Banner," performed by the Gap High Madrigals, it was an evening of pure magic.

All the animals did what their trainers told them to do. Yolanda didn't fool with her bodice once; Juliet even thought she heard one or two sniffles from the audience when the doleful music began at her untimely death. Flat-nosed Jake brought the house down with dramatic renditions of his poems, "Yukon Joe and the Woman He Wronged," and "Show Her Mercy, Not Scorn, She Is Tattered and Torn."

And Cody, wearing a black shirt with mother-of-pearl buttons, black jeans and black boots, had everyone stomping their feet and clapping their hands when he sang the song about the mule. Juliet clapped and stomped with the best of them, singing along at the chorus and applauding wildly at the end.

Since she hadn't heard it in rehearsal, she was not prepared for his second song, which came at the end of the show, right before the patriotic closing number. He wore the same shirt and jeans and sat on a stool in a single spotlight. And he sang about a man who wanted a woman who refused to let herself want him back.

The song was stunningly sensual and yet so sweetly tender at the same time. The audience fell silent—all crackling of programs and crossing of legs ceased. Juliet, who knew she shouldn't, closed her eyes, and let her body relax against the wall at her back.

She allowed herself the forbidden illusion that Cody sang that song for her. And she relived the two wondrous times she'd been in his arms—first, lying across his lap on the front porch of his house, and later, in her office, when he slowly uncovered her breasts, and then made love to them with his mouth.

As the song ended, there was silence. In the hushed moment, Juliet sighed, lost in her fantasy of Cody's lips on her skin.

Then thunderous applause crashed in on her. She snapped upright, darting guilty glances to either side. But no one seemed concerned that she'd just been swooning against the side wall, lost again in taboo moments that she'd sworn to forget. Everyone was riveted to the stage, clapping madly for Cody and his beautiful, seductive song. Juliet, feeling lost and disoriented, pulled herself together and joined in the applause.

Then came "The Star Spangled Banner," and after that, ten minutes' worth of curtain calls. At last, Babe Allen got up and said a few words about the big parade tomorrow and the pancake breakfast—and all the coming attractions over the next ten days.

Juliet went backstage briefly to congratulate everyone on doing a marvelous job, and to fill her own role as director and remind them not to get cocky, since they had nine more performances to go. Her voice broke once while she spoke, because she foolishly made eye contact with Cody, who was staring at her with an unreadable expression on his face, and had a leg hitched up on one of the makeup counters.

When she was through speaking, Cody stood up and invited everyone to McIntyre's for drinks on the house. Juliet stared at him, so achingly handsome in his fancy-buttoned shirt. And she wanted to go—just for a little while.

And why shouldn't she go, after all? The revue was a triumph. She had a right to celebrate.

So she left the auditorium with Jake and Andrea, chattering excitedly with them about the revue and the festival, as they walked the half block to McIntyre's in the romantic light of the gas lamps with a full moon overhead.

The long bar area was packed when they arrived. Every stool was taken, and all the high tables and the high seats round about were full. Juliet jostled her way in with the rest of them, laughing and waving to everyone she knew.

Heady praise filled the close air. "Great job, Juliet!" "Hey, Juliet, way to go!" "We knew you could do it, girl, and we weren't wrong!"

When she got up to the bar, there was a drink—a strawberry daiquiri—plunked right down in front of her, which Cody must have told the bartender she liked. She felt her face warming, wondering if he'd seen her come in, glancing quickly around to find out where he was. But he was nowhere in sight.

She took a long, cool sip. The icy concoction was the best she'd ever had.

Several more people told her how wonderful she was, she received more than one pat on the back and then soon enough another star of the evening appeared at the door, and the crowd turned their approving salutations that way.

Juliet, feeling the beginnings of a happy, hazy glow, leaned back against the bar and tapped her high-heeled shoe to the music from the jukebox in the corner, and decided that tonight made the agony of teaching herself to step forward worthwhile.

She drank the last of the daiquiri, and another appeared at her elbow. When she offered to pay, the bartender waved her money away. She thanked him, took a satisfying sip of the drink and then, weaving through the press of bodies, made her way to the jukebox to scan the selections it offered.

"Choose a few on me, Juliet...." Someone dropped several

quarters into her hand. She took her time, sipping her drink, punching up mostly country-western songs about outlaws and hopeless love.

"Having fun?"

The hazy euphoria of the whole evening suddenly seemed to be concentrated in the gray-green eyes of the man who leaned against the side of the jukebox and smiled at her with a sweet kind of fondness, the way he used to before everything changed between them.

She didn't answer. She really felt no pressure to say anything right then. She just indulged in the pleasure of looking at him, and confessing silently that, beyond wanting him, she'd missed him—so very much.

"Are you having fun?" he asked again, his voice gently teasing as it used to be in the old days, when he'd try to lighten her spirits after some little thing would send her into an agony of embarrassment or fright.

She nodded. Down inside her, something shifted.

She understood, at that moment, that some things just had to be allowed to happen. And, though she might suffer in the end, a woman who tried to deny the urgings of her heart would have only lived half a life when it all came down to dust.

She said in a whisper, with no more thought of holding back the truth, "I've missed you."

It was his turn to say nothing. He looked deep in her eyes. At last he answered, "Me, too."

All around them, the party went on. People jostled and joked, loud and excited. But to Juliet, right then, there was no sound but the hard beating of her heart, the quickened rush of her own breath in and out and, far away, the music she'd chosen on the jukebox.

He said what she knew he would say. "Come home with me tonight."

She put her hand on the side of his face, thrilling at the smooth warmth of his freshly shaved skin. He covered her hand with his in an enveloping caress. And then he kissed her palm, his breath like a tender brand on her skin. "I want you, Julie," he said. "I'm tired of trying to pretend I don't."

Her heart took wing.

So what if it couldn't last? So what if it would probably end badly—with her losing a lover, a friend and a client, too? She was thirty years old and had never known the feel of a naked man's body warm and close in the night. The first time ought to be with someone she adored, during the Midsummer Madness Festival, when she was living out her lifelong dream of being the strong, assertive woman she'd always felt was trapped inside her, begging to be set free.

Cody was looking at her, waiting for her answer.

She gave it. "I'm tired of pretending, too, Cody. Yes, I'll go home with you."

CHAPTER SEVEN

SHE LEFT HER red car in the restaurant's parking lot, and they went home in his pickup, the magical full moon ahead of them all the way, playing hide-and-seek with them through the branches of the trees as they climbed toward the ranch. When they drove through the front gate, the big silvery ball hung suspended, ripe and glorious, heavy on the rim of the far mountains over the north field.

Kemo was waiting, tail wagging and tongue lolling, by the front step. He wriggled over, whining with happiness. Cody scratched him behind the ear and smoothed his sleek black coat before he came around to Juliet's side and flung back the pickup door.

"Come here, woman!" he commanded, and then scooped her up against his chest. Beneath her skirt the red crinoline hem of her slip ballooned up and then settled in a crimson froth over his arm. Juliet laughed and hugged him close.

He bore her up the porch steps and shifted her weight to fiddle with the lock on the big double door. At last the lock turned. He kicked the door open. Then he carried her, both of them laughing, over the threshold, across the foyer to the staircase and up the stairs.

His room was the master bedroom and faced north on the open field. It had a huge bay window, like the one that formed the breakfast nook below, only here there was a curving seat where a person could sit and simply enjoy the view.

Once in the room, the laughter they'd been sharing faded.

Cody set her down before the window and then wrapped his arms around her from behind. For a while they just stood there, with only the silver moon outside for light.

The moment, a suspended place between anticipation and fulfillment, spun out. A thin cloud drifted across the face of the moon, darkening the world in night shadow, and then gently floated by, so that the moon gave full light once more.

"Is this…still what you want?" Cody softly asked in her ear.

She turned in his arms and looked into his face. "Yes."

"Scared?"

"Definitely."

"We'll go slow."

"Good."

She twined her arms around his neck as he lowered his lips to hers. The kiss became a series of kisses, a languorous sensual exploration. His lips brushed her mouth—back and forth, up and down—and then moved on to sweetly caress her chin and her cheeks and the tip of her nose.

He lifted his head after a time and said in a husky voice, "I forgot my manners. Can I get you a drink?"

Juliet, still sweetly hazy from her two daiquiris, shook her head and then lifted her mouth again for more slow, delicious kisses.

Cody willingly obliged her and for a while there were soft sighs and small chuckles in the moonlit bay window overlooking the north field. But soon enough, his hands grew bold. He touched her breasts.

She sighed at that, and arched for him, so that he could caress her to their mutual delight through the fabric of her dress. Then, after a while, he guided her, in slow steps, toward the wide bed, where they both fell back, giggling once again.

When the laughter faded, he rose up on an elbow to look down in her eyes. "Hey, I like this dress," he said.

She gave him a playful, disbelieving frown. "It's not the old me at all."

"I think," he said, tracing a heart on her bare shoulder where he'd just pushed the dress aside, "that I'm beginning to appreciate the *new* you."

"Is that so?"

"Yeah, it's so." His voice was husky now. His hand wandered, down over the sweet rise of her breast and the scooped-out slimness of her belly to the place where the skirt began to flare. He took hold of the skirt there, at her hip, and very slowly began to raise it.

"Juliet Titania Huddleston," he murmured, as the red crinoline-edged slip was revealed, "what have we here?"

She didn't answer, didn't even move, as the skirt was lifted and the red petticoat displayed. When all of it was showing, he gently smoothed its tousled folds, and then kissed her once more. It was a very thorough kiss that ignited her nerve endings and started the familiar meltdown in her abdomen.

"Oh, Cody," she managed to say, shivering a little with excitement—and apprehension—of what was to come.

He whispered something erotic and yet reassuring, as his hand strayed beneath the hem of her skirt until he'd found the elastic waist of the slip. He slid his finger under there—her belly quivered, he whispered "Shh, it's okay"—and then, with slow stroking motions, he stretched the elastic and glided the slip over her hips.

"Lift up, Julie...." He nibbled her ear.

She moaned and raised her hips enough so that he could whisk away the naughty slip. He dropped it then, somewhere on the floor. She certainly didn't notice where, because he was touching her again, his finger slipping beneath the back straps of her high heels, each in turn, sliding them off and away just as he had done with the red slip.

She wore no stockings. He ran a caressing finger up the length of one bare, smooth leg, setting off little heated shivers all along her skin until he reached the place, high on her thigh, where he'd lifted her skirt to get to the red slip.

He boldly went higher, beneath the yards of crimson fabric, till he touched the fragile scrap of cloth that covered the womanly center of her. Never had anyone touched her there before. She gasped and stiffened in awareness. He made more soothing, quieting sounds, and then once again his hand was stroking, petting her through the silky cloth so she forgot everything but the pleasure he gave.

Her body, seeming to know what to do in spite of her inexperience, lifted in invitation beneath his ardent touch. His mouth covered hers again, in an unending kiss, as he rubbed and stroked her and she moved, unashamed, beneath his hand.

Under the flimsy veil of her panties, she grew very wet. She knew he must feel that. For a moment, she froze, embarrassed that he should know such a thing about her body's response to him. But he whispered huskily against her mouth that it was okay, it was just right. Relaxing, allowing herself the freedom once more to revel in this wonder, she began to move again.

He murmured more encouragements, stroking her more swiftly while she writhed and moaned and kissed him with a building sense of urgency that made her clutch his shoulders, inchoately, yearning for a fulfillment that she didn't quite know how to achieve.

But Cody seemed to know. In a smooth, unhurried movement, his hand drifted up her belly. She moaned, not wanting him to stop.

His lips moved over her cheek, to toy with her ear. "It's okay, Julie. Just let yourself go...."

Then his hand was at the elastic of her panties, sliding beneath, moving lower. Juliet gasped, because she knew what he was doing now, just as his hand found her, opened her and began doing what it had done before, only without the thin barrier of cloth. He was caressing the heart of her, in slow, deep, knowing strokes.

It was the most shocking, starkly beautiful thing that had ever happened to her. She gave up all thought of what he must think. She gave up everything to this magic world of the senses, which seemed, behind her closed eyes, to shimmer, like her body, with heat and wonder and building comprehension of the fulfillment to come. Never in her lonely, virginal life, had she known anything half so marvelous as this.

And it kept building, tightening. He went on touching her, his hand moving, it seemed, in instant response to her body's signals as the beautiful sensations coiled tighter and more heated still, second by second, into an erotic infinity that seemed as if it might never, ever end.

And then something happened. Something incredible. From the place he touched her, there was a sudden, unbelievable explosion of sensation. The heart of her bloomed, opening, pulsing, sending ripples of intense feeling outward in an overwhelming release that seared her every nerve and made her throw back her head and cry out loud, a wondrous agony that seemed unending, turned her inside out and left her, at last, limp with satisfaction on the bed.

For the longest time, as the waves of pleasure pulsed and slowly receded, she didn't think. She drifted, boneless, relaxed and content in a way that she had never been before.

Ultimately, though, she began to come back to herself. She gradually became aware that her head was buried against the spread, turned away from him, and that he lay, still fully clothed, against her other side.

As reality reclaimed her, a sudden, distressing thought surfaced. Had she been ridiculous?

She felt her skin flushing as she remembered the way she had writhed and moaned and carried on quite shamelessly, even crying out loud there at the end. She had read in novels that making love could bring great pleasure, but she had never considered what it must look like, to a man, for a woman to thrash and cry out and go a little crazy with the way it felt.

She found, all at once, that she couldn't bear to turn her head to look at him—or even to open her eyes, which were still closed as they'd been since that final ecstasy claimed her.

The silence stretched out. She felt more a fool with each second that passed. She decided, since she wasn't even facing him, that she should at least drum up the nerve to open her eyes. She did, and saw, by the dim light of the moon and stars outside, the fat shape of the pillows at the head of the bed.

One of Cody's arms was beneath her neck, cradling her against his body. And his free hand was still down there, still touching her, still making her body pulse just a little, making her long— oh, this was crazy—to start all over again.

Just as she thought the forbidden thought that she wouldn't mind starting over, his hand moved, leaving the secret heart of her and sliding out from under the rucked-up tangle of her skirt. She quivered a little at the loss of his touch, thinking that her fear must be correct; he must be embarrassed at the way she had behaved, and wondered how he could tactfully get rid of her. She was sure that next he would sit up and pull away from her.

But instead, he touched her face, his fingers scented of her own passion. "Julie? What is it? Are you okay?" His voice, surprisingly, didn't have that distant tone she had expected. With the gentle pressure of his hand, he turned her face to his. "Julie?"

His eyes, in the darkness, shone with what looked like tenderness and concern. She blinked, thinking she saw wrong. But when she opened her eyes again, his expression was the same.

"Is something wrong? Tell me."

She tried to pull away.

He held her steady. "Tell me."

She sighed and relaxed a little. "Oh, Cody...."

"Come on," he coaxed. "Say it."

Bolstered by the appeal in his eyes and reassured by his touch, she managed to tell him. "I guess...I went a little crazy, huh?"

He looked at her for a moment, as what she said sank in. Then he chuckled. "Yeah. Yeah, you sure did."

"I...made a fool of myself. I know it." She moved to sit up.

He gently pulled her down and canted up on an elbow to lean over her. "Not so fast, there." His eyes were full of understanding. "I said you went crazy. I didn't say anything about your making a fool of yourself."

"But I—"

"You were beautiful. Sexy. Incredible."

"Oh, Cody...."

"I was so turned on, I couldn't think straight." He pushed his hips against her a little more tightly. "As a matter of fact, I still am...."

"What?"

"Turned on."

She felt what he meant as he pressed close against her. "Oh." She dared a small smile. "You were? You are?"

"You bet."

"Then you still want to, um…"

"More than anything." He kissed her nose.

She realized she believed him. Relief and happiness flooded her; her whole body went lax. She wrapped her arms around him and kissed him, full on the mouth, with all the warmth and excitement she herself was feeling right then.

When the kiss was done she thought of something else that needed to be considered, and pulled back to ask, "Cody?"

"Yeah?" He rolled away enough that he no longer pinned her to the bed, and she took the opportunity to sit up and gather her feet under her dress.

"Well, um…" She found it difficult to go on. He looked at her, waiting. She hesitated for a moment more, not knowing exactly how to broach the subject, but then she sucked in a breath and plunged in. "I didn't bring anything. For contraception."

"Don't worry." In a lithe movement, he sat up and left the bed, crossing to a dresser where he opened a drawer and pulled out a small pouch that she realized must contain a condom.

She blushed, glad that the issue was settled. "Good."

Then neither of them did anything for a moment. They just looked at each other, and they were both smiling. At that moment it occurred to Juliet that the shattering completion he'd already brought her to had made what was to come seem less frightening.

She held out a hand to him. He came back to the bed and took it, giving it a warm, companionable squeeze. Then he let go, set the small pouch on the bedstand and sat down. The bed gave slightly beneath his weight. He pulled off his black boots, one at a time.

Juliet, still seated Indian-style behind him, watched the simple actions with joy and a kind of awe. At last, after years of watching and wondering from the sidelines, she would discover the secrets of the ultimate mystery between men and women. And she'd learn them with Cody, the most beautiful man in the entire world.

Cody slipped off his socks. And then she saw his arms move as he unsnapped his shirt. The marvelous symmetry of his back came into view as the shirt was removed and tossed over a chair. Then he stood, and he unbuttoned his jeans and took them off, too. And finally he got rid of his briefs, sliding them off casually, without fanfare, the action as natural as dropping to the bed and pulling off his boots had been.

She had never seen a completely naked man except in pictures. His body, she thought, was like a sculpture, almost too perfect and beautiful to be real flesh and blood. He was still aroused.

She moistened her lips a little in nervousness, wondering if he would fit inside her. And then she told herself not to be silly, of course he would fit. He was a man and she was a woman, and they were made to fit.

He came to her, taking the few steps back to the bed, and reached for her hand. She gave it, without hesitating, and he pulled her up to her knees on the edge of the bed. Then he found the hem of her dress and he tugged it up, over her head. She raised her arms and felt it glide along her skin, beyond her lifted finger-tips and away. Her fine, straight hair flowed with it, and then drifted back down to settle lightly around her shoulders.

He looked at her, in the red lacy bra and matching panties. So tenderly, he said, "Aw, Julie. Naughty girl."

She told him pertly, "Red's my color now."

He said, "It suits you, now," and reached for her. She held out her arms, and twined them around his neck. Their bodies met, there at the edge of the bed.

His thighs felt strong and hard against the supple smoothness of hers, and the crisp hair on his chest rubbed the soft swells of her breasts above her bra. He bent his head and kissed her, and Juliet lifted her mouth to him, eager for the taste of his lips.

The kiss was long and audaciously carnal. Juliet gloried in it, her hands avidly stroking his back and the strong cords of muscle at his neck, then toying in the silky hair at his nape. She brazenly rubbed her whole body against him, pleasured not only at the feel of him, but at his response to her, which was clear in the low sounds he made in his throat, the hungry way his lips took hers and the jutting evidence of his excitement that pushed against her at the place where their thighs joined.

After a time, he began kissing her throat, which she obligingly arched for him. His lips trailed down to her breasts. He kissed each one through its shield of lace, and then he unhooked the front clasp and slipped the bra off and away.

He began kissing her breasts, as he had done that afternoon in her office, teasing them at first with light nibbles and licks, and then more thoroughly, sucking and cupping them with his hands. Juliet, lost in that marvelous realm of the senses he so expertly created, fell back on the bed; Cody followed her down.

His mouth worked magic at her breast, while his hand trailed down her quivering belly to disappear once again beneath the elastic waistband of her panties. She moaned and bucked in excitement as he began, again, to bring her to readiness, pausing only long enough to slide the wisp of silk off and out of the way.

Now they were both totally nude. His hand continued to stroke and arouse her, and Juliet felt the build to climax begin once again. Though a part of her longed to just ride the crest of the wave of pleasure he created to its own fulfillment, she grabbed his wrist and stilled his hand.

He froze and opened his eyes to look at her.

"If you keep going, I'll finish without you," she managed on a gasping breath.

"That's okay."

"No," she told him. "I want...everything, Cody. I want you. Please?"

Shyly, both curious and hesitant at the same time, she reached for him, encircled his hardness. He gasped, and his hand retreated from the heart of her just a little, so that it only rested on her soft mound. She smiled, and stroked him experimentally, and he groaned and lifted his hips. Juliet thought it absolutely marvelous, to see him gasp and move in response to her touch, just as she had moved when he touched her.

"If you keep that up," he warned in a low growl, "*I'll* be the one finishing without *you*."

She kissed him then and pulled away to find the small pouch on the nightstand. Blushing a little, she asked to be allowed to help put it on. He obliged her, showing her what to do, groaning again when she slipped it over him, and guided it in place.

Then, when it was on, his hand found her again, and he stroked her some more, making sure she was as ready as she could be, given this was her first time.

At last, he moved above her and gently nudged her thighs apart. He positioned himself and, very gently, lowered his weight until she began to feel the pressure of him, pushing to breach the barrier her body held out against his male invasion.

She made a small sound of discomfort. He swore that after this time, it would never hurt again. And his voice was so tender and full of concern that she knew he would have trouble at the prospect that he would have to hurt her now.

So, bold as the woman she was becoming, and so swiftly he didn't know what she planned, she wrapped her legs around him and thrust herself against him, breaking the barrier herself.

It hurt. A burning, scraping kind of pain. And Cody cried out her name as he filled her, sounding like it hurt him, too.

And then he stayed very still, stretching her to the limit, so that she could absorb and adjust to his presence there. In the stillness her own breath came in hard little pants. And she concentrated on it, commanding it to slow, telling her body to relax, the worst was over.

And, incredibly, her body believed her. She felt her inner muscles slackening their frantic hold on him. The pain receded, and she began to realize how complete and good it felt, to be with him in this most intimate of ways, to be connected, to be filled.

It felt...why, it felt...exciting. And yet satisfying, too, to have his big body covering hers, and him deep within her. It felt as if...as if she was becoming aroused again. She moaned.

And he seemed to sense, as if the male in him knew this, that her moan was no longer one of discomfort, but of building excitement. Slowly he lifted his hips. Juliet moaned again. And he came down to fill her once more.

"You're okay?" he breathed against her cheek.

"Yes." She clutched his back and lifted her body to meet his next thrust. "Yes, Cody, yes...."

He said, "I'll try to be careful...." His voice was strained with his effort to hold back, to go slow for her sake.

She felt the urgency, the tension in him, as he tried to wait for her, to give her time to reach the end with him. But it was no use, not this first time, and she knew it. To have him inside her, she had found, was a delicious thing. And that was enough to discover for right now.

So she boldly pushed her hips against him, urging him to lose himself the way she had earlier. He moaned, muttered roughly, "Don't...."

And then he surrendered to his own need, moving hard and fast within her, and at last thrusting a final, deep lunge. She clung to him, holding him fast inside, as his completion came.

When it was over, she cradled him close, feeling his heartbeat slow, and his breath come less frantically into his chest. She stroked his back, marveling at the hollows and hard muscles there.

At last he stirred, lifting up on his arms and gazing down into her flushed face. "I meant to wait for you."

"It was beautiful, just the way it was."

He smiled then, that right-sided smile that, lately, seemed to steal her breath. And she pulled him back down, so she could feel him all along the length of her.

She whispered fiercely in his ear, "Oh, Cody. Thank you. I was beginning to think I'd never know...about the things that can happen between a man and a woman."

He lifted up enough to give her a rueful smile. "This isn't going to be like the last time you thanked me, is it? When the next thing you said was to stay away from you?"

Juliet pulled him back down. "No way.... Stay as close to me as you want to. The closer the better." She hugged him tight.

Cody hugged her in return. For a while, they just held each other. Then he lifted up and kissed her sweetly on each cheek, taking a languorous time to comb her hair with gentle fingers into a fan around her face. Then, reluctantly, he pulled away and got up to visit the bathroom.

When he was gone, Juliet lay there unashamed, nude upon the bed. From outside, faintly, came the crow of a rooster. Juliet smiled at the dim ceiling overhead. Black Bart. At it again.

Some moments, she thought, as she lay there waiting for Cody to return, were too beautiful to bear. Like this moment, right now, in Cody's moonlit bedroom, sprawled across the rumpled spread which, she knew, now bore evidence that she was no longer a virgin. It was a moment of pure happiness.

Outside, Black Bart crowed again. Juliet rolled her head to look out the window. She couldn't see the moon. Sometime while she and Cody made love, it must have gone down. The stars now held sway, a million pinpoints of light poked in the ebony fabric of the sky.

It was at that precise moment, as she gazed at the star-scattered sky, that the truth hit her. It came at her with all the flattening force of a runaway train, so fast and overwhelming that she had no time to throw up her usual defenses.

She, Juliet Huddleston, who should have known better, had gone and fallen in love with Cody McIntyre!

It was like drowning, in a way, to finally admit it, this truth she'd been running from for over two weeks now. Like water, it flowed over her, and she was buoyed by it, at the same time as she felt it closing over her head, taking her air.

I love Cody McIntyre....

Stunned, Juliet lay there. How had it happened?

The answer came: she'd let it happen. By indulging in her fantasies about him, by surrendering to her own desire and coming here to his bed tonight.

Oh, it was not a bright thing to have done. It did not fit in with her plans for herself in the least.

But, nonetheless, it was true. She loved Cody.

The door to the adjoining bath squeaked. Startled, Juliet sat up with a gasp. She looked across the room at Cody, who stood silhouetted in the light he'd turned on behind him.

He must have seen some of her stunned confusion in her face. "Julie? You all right?"

She forced her mouth to smile. "Yes, Cody. I'm fine." He switched off the light and came to her, across the smooth wooden floor.

She kept smiling as he approached. In her mind, her own voice whispered, *I love you. I love you, Cody*.

But she did not say the words out loud. She just couldn't tell him. Not now. Perhaps not ever.

She had to be realistic. Cody was not the man for her—not in the long run. He was way out of her league. Oh, she'd learned to assert herself a little, and she was wearing brighter clothes. But deep inside, the shy mouse still quivered. And Cody was and always would be Gap High's star quarterback, a compassionate hunk who made every woman weak in the knees with just a glance. If he ever found the right woman for him, she'd be his equal, someone as gorgeous and outgoing as Cody himself.

And if Juliet had a smidgen of sense left, she would do her best not to even let herself imagine what it might be like to spend the rest of her days at his side. Because it would never happen, not in real life. This beauty and magic was all a big fantasy. Midsummer Madness, that was all.

Cody knelt before her on the bed. "Julie?" His tender fingers smoothed a strand of hair behind her ear. "What is it? Tell me."

"It's nothing." She gave the lie sweetly. "Really." She swayed toward him, lifting her mouth. He kissed her, and she sighed against him, pulling him close. A wave of sadness washed over her—and then flowed away.

Her love was her secret. She'd learn to accept that. And she'd make the most of every moment they had. This was Midsummer Madness. Brief, crazy and sweet. Her time to know ecstasy, and her time to shine in the light.

CHAPTER EIGHT

IT TOOK CODY a few days before he began to suspect that Juliet was shutting him out.

At first, nothing could bother him. He was as content as a cat in a creamery. He even got himself involved up to his eyeballs in Midsummer Madness—and then discovered that he didn't mind a bit. In fact, he was so conspicuously available that Andrea Oakleaf, with a gleam in her gunmetal-gray eyes, declared that she greatly admired his sudden awakening to civic responsibility.

Thus, he was tied into an apron at the Methodist Women's Pancake Breakfast. He performed the humble task of dishwasher because Yardley Forbes, brought down by an excess of celebration the night before, didn't show up.

At the parade, when they were one judge short, he was prevailed upon to fill in, and marked his choices on the ballots for most clever, most original, most beautiful, most just about everything else a man could possibly imagine. There were over thirty floats, and Cody was reasonably sure there were at least that many categories. Not surprisingly, just about every entrant walked away with ''best of'' something or other.

At the frog jump on Sunday, somehow he ended up down on his knees at the finish line, trying to fairly determine which little croaker crossed the line first. That night, after the revue, when he and Julie were at last alone, he complained that refereeing the finish line for racing frogs was not a dignified assignment for a man.

She laughed, kissed him and told him that it took a real man to get down in the dirt at frog level, the way he had, and still look commanding and authoritative when he stood up. When he frowned at her doubtfully, she kissed him again and thanked him quite sweetly, and he realized that he'd probably get down in the dirt again the moment she asked him.

He was enchanted. And with Julie Huddleston, of all people. It was as if all these years he'd been looking at her through some hazy obstruction, like one of the lace curtains that used to hang in the bay window of his parents' bedroom before it became his room and he had it made over to suit himself.

Somehow, over the past few weeks, the lace curtain that had obscured her had been slowly pulled aside and he saw her clearly, slim and lovely, wearing a red dress and smiling that sweet, innocent smile that could turn naughty and tempting the minute they were alone.

It astounded him, took his breath away, the way she could be when they were alone. Hers was a mesmerizing combination of innocence, frank curiosity and natural sensuality that got him so turned on, he often found it difficult to hold out long enough to see that she found her full pleasure every time they made love.

More than once, it ended like the first time, with him hitting the peak before she got there. But she never minded. She'd stroke his back and hold him and get him going all over again. And the second time, he'd make sure he drove her wild before surrendering to his own satisfaction.

Never before had it been like this for him with a woman. Never so fun. Never so exciting. Never so tender. And never so comfortable.

If he had been a man prone to self-analysis, he might have decided that his looks had always, in the ways that mattered, kept people at a distance. Women, especially, behaved toward him as if he wasn't a real human being with the same needs and desires as all people had. Too many women had treated him as if he were a *thing,* designed for their pleasure, to swoon and ooh and ah over. A sex object, not a man.

That had been fine while he was very young, when his wants had been simpler—a few drinks, a few laughs and, later, a purely physical release. But as the years passed, it had simply not been enough. He'd retreated from encounters that didn't satisfy him any longer.

And maybe, he began to suspect, he'd retreated from his friends and community, as well. He'd become, as Andrea Oakleaf had so astringently pointed out, unwilling to commit himself on any level—from accepting a date with yet another woman who would swoon over him and not treat him as an equal, to getting up on stage every evening and doing his bit for his town in the Midsummer Madness Revue.

But now, at last, with Julie, all that seemed to have changed. He wanted to spend every night with her, just like it was now, making love until both of them were grinning with satisfaction. And then they would drift off to sleep together, with her cradled in the crook of his arm, her hair laid across his shoulder like strands of the finest pale gold silk. With her beside him, he didn't mind at all committing himself to do whatever had to be done when it came to the festival.

They'd been friends forever, in that distant way, and both of them had known that he had done most of the giving in the past; he had taken care of her and looked out for her over the years. But now, from the night she gave her innocence to him, everything seemed, to Cody, to have turned around the other way. Now she gave. Of her laughter and her warmth and her gentleness that he hadn't known he needed till it was there in her touch and in her hazel eyes.

As the days of Midsummer Madness came and went, he longed to tell her all of this, to share in words all the ways his life was better since they had become more than friends. But therein lay the only cloud on this current chain of sun-bright days.

As the days passed, he began to notice that every time he tried to talk to her about what was happening between them, she deftly changed the subject. She would just *have* to ask his opinion about some minor detail concerning the festival, or she'd suddenly remember some important thing she just couldn't put off doing for another moment.

For the first few days, Cody accepted with good grace her skittishness when it came to talking about the two of them. Truth to tell, he himself had little experience in talking about the future with a woman. But by midweek, it had begun to nag at him.

After all, he just wanted to talk about it; he himself wasn't sure what it all meant yet. But she wouldn't talk about it. No matter how innocent-seeming her tactics she wouldn't even let him broach the subject without suddenly shutting him out.

He decided to try a little harder to get through to her. He thought maybe if he could get her away from everything for a while, somewhere where there were no distractions, that he might get her to open up about her feelings when it came to the two of them.

So on Wednesday, in spite of his work and her work and all the demands of the festival, he convinced her to play hooky from everything until noon, under the pretext of giving her her first riding lesson.

He tacked up Lucky, a twelve-year-old sorrel gelding and the gentlest of his three horses, for her, going through the whole process very slowly, from bridle to saddle cinch, demonstrating it all so that next time she could try it herself. Then he explained that Lucky liked it best if she mounted from the left and got down on the right.

He held the reins while she stuck her left foot in the stirrup. She then made a reasonably good show of swinging her right foot over and seating herself.

To start, he led Lucky around the paddock a few times, allowing horse and rider to get used to things. Finally he let Julie hold the reins herself and she cautiously ambled around the enclosed space while he reminded her to keep Lucky's head down. After a while, she made it up to a fairly credible canter, though he saw a lot of daylight between her cute little bottom and the saddle. He suggested, more than once, that she get into Lucky's rhythm, or she was going to be sorry later.

At last, he mounted his own favorite, Blaze, and, with Kemo bouncing alongside, they left the paddock, crossed the north field and entered the trees at the west corner. This was the beginning of what in his family had always been known as the Sunset Trail.

The Sunset Trail was good for a beginner because it meandered lazily up the side of Sunset Mountain, never getting too narrow or too steep. Most of the way, Sunset Creek bubbled along below the trail, tumbling cheerfully over the rocks and providing shaded views of clear water, white-barked birch trees and lichen-covered boulders.

Cody, sure of Lucky's tractableness but playing it safe anyway, rode ahead, keeping it to a walk. Kemo raced up and down the hillside, barking occasionally at invisible lizards and such, but staying clear of the horses' hooves.

The ride was uneventful and pleasant, just as Cody had intended. Squirrels scolded the rambunctious dog from the trees, jays squawked and the morning sun fell in glittering, shifting patterns through the lacework of the pine branches overhead.

Soon enough, they reached the spot he had sought, where the trail dipped down to the side of the creek. There, the creek widened out to a pool, and the space the pool made between the trees gave a few patches of toasty sun for basking in.

He dismounted and helped Julie down. Kemo, who was still bouncing distractingly around, was granted a stern glance. The dog whined and dropped to the ground to lie panting happily in the sun.

Cody had brought a blanket, which he spread at the base of a boulder. There, he and Julie sat down, their backs against the big rock. Once comfortable, they shared a few moments of companionable silence while the horses drank from the creek and nibbled the short grass nearby.

Eventually, Julie sighed. "This is heaven, Cody. My fantasy-come-true."

He remembered that night she'd spoken before the association, when he gave her a ride home because that outrageous car of hers wouldn't start. She'd said that living at his ranch was "not quite so permanent as a dream. More temporary. Like a fantasy." He decided that it was time, now that he'd gotten them off to themselves, to pursue the subject that had been on his mind so much lately.

He asked, "So is that what this is to you, a fantasy?"

She turned those wide hazel eyes on him. "What do you mean, Cody?"

"You and me. Are we just a fantasy?"

She tipped her head, as if the idea demanded great thought. But when she spoke, it was not to answer. "You sound disapproving."

"I just want to know."

"What?" She looked innocent.

He tried again. "You and me. Are we just a fantasy?"

She smiled. "Oh, Cody. What makes you ask that?"

"Look. Just answer me."

She leaned toward him. "Yes, we're a fantasy. A fantasy come true."

"What exactly does that mean?"

"Oh, Cody...." She kissed his neck, her soft lips brushing his skin.

"Julie...." The point of the discussion began to elude him.

She whispered, "We're the most wonderful thing that's ever happened to me."

The scent of her surrounded him. It was clean and fresh like soap and water, but with just a hint of a citrusy something that added a provocative tartness.

"Julie...."

He had thought that this would be a perfect spot for talking. But now, with the soft caress of her lips on his skin, it occurred to him that more than talking could easily go on here. They would not be disturbed. Without fearing interruption, he might take off the cropped red knit shirt she was wearing and kiss her breasts. He might caress her in the sunlight, freely, to their mutual delight.

He valiantly tried to forge on. "I want to talk about where this is going, that's all."

She nibbled his ear. "Fine. If you want to."

"Julie, I'm serious...."

She trailed a finger down the front of his white T-shirt and did what, just yesterday, he had told her aroused him no end: she cupped his manhood through his jeans. "I'm listening."

But by then whether or not she was listening didn't matter in the least. Cody's good sense had lost out to his senses. He buried his hands in her hair and pulled her face up to his. His lips covered hers, and she eagerly murmured, "Oh, Cody, oh yes...."

He wasted no time in making his imaginings real. He lifted the hem of her little shirt and tugged it over her head, tossing it away to where it caught on a willow branch. Next, he took her bra away. And then, his eyes heavy with building desire, he looked at her, in the sunlight, at her small, high breasts and her shell-pink nipples that were already standing up, eager for his touch. He took one in his mouth, glorying in her moan of pleasure, and guided her down on the blanket, working at the buttons of her jeans as he suckled her. She helped him, moaning, eager as he was, somehow managing to toe off her boots and shimmy out of her jeans and shuck her panties in mere minutes, while he went on kissing her breasts.

It was crazy, what she did to him, what none of the series of skilled lovers he'd known before had ever done. She made him forget everything, except her sweet face and hazel eyes. She made him forget his own intentions to get a little clarity between them.

Lord, he was starved for her, as if they hadn't made love mere hours ago. She wriggled and moaned and brushed him with her soft hand through the rough cloth of his jeans. He touched her, and she was ready.

He couldn't wait. Didn't want to wait. And if her hungry moans and thrusting hips meant anything, neither did she.

He ripped down his zipper, and got his pants out of the way and slid on one of the condoms that, lately, he had sense enough to carry everywhere they went. Then he rose over her. She opened for him, her face flushed, her eyes closed. He looked down at her, astounded that he could ever have thought her plain.

"Julie..." It was a rough, raspy sound, something that felt torn from the deepest part of him, that part that only she had touched— at last, after a long string of lonely years.

She reached for him, her slim arms pulling him down. He entered her, sliding in easily, encountering no resistance, only heat and eagerness and a long sigh of welcome. She moved beneath him, urging him to lose himself.

And he thought again, in an unformed, clouded way, of the aim he'd had in coming here, and the way she had averted it. Somewhere, in the heart of his desire and excitement, a tiny kernel of anger formed.

It was hardly conscious; he really didn't even acknowledge the feeling. But he was hurt, because he had begun to fear that she thought of him as all the others had: as an object, a handsome face whose heart didn't matter, someone to spin fantasies around, but not someone with whom the future needed to be discussed.

The unrecognized anger strengthened him, so that the maelstrom of pleasure didn't suck him down. He held out against her sweet urging, long enough to bring her to a shattering release, her head flung back, soft neck straining, to watch her lose herself completely, twisting and moaning beneath him, calling out his name.

At last, when she went limp and satisfied, he came down full length upon her. She clutched him, melting against him, murmuring little wordless things, her breath warm against his ear. The moment was unbearably sweet, and his own desire mounted again within it, stimulated beyond holding back now, by the totality of her surrender.

He began to move. She sighed in pleasure, replete but still so willing, and moved in rhythm with him. The rhythm mounted, took on a life of its own, and Cody, at the center of it, surrendered to it utterly. The rapturous pressure built, until it could no longer be contained, and then it claimed him, splintering outward in a hot burst of pulsing sensation. He thrust deeply into her; she rose to meet him. And he called out, flinging his head back, crying his completion to the sun-dazzled sky.

After a time when there was only her soft body beneath his and her gently stroking hands, he lifted up, kissed the tip of her nose and then rolled away to dispose of the condom and straighten his clothes. It was quickly done, and left him time to turn and watch her as she reclaimed her tossed-away top and bra, put them on and then wriggled into her jeans and pulled on her boots.

She glanced at him now and then as she dressed herself, sending him a grin or a sweet, conspiratorial wink. At first, he simply enjoyed watching her, feeling close and companionable after the overwhelming wonder of the intimacy they had just shared.

But then he remembered his original purpose in riding out here. He frowned, wondering if he really wanted to try to get through to her again. She was now sitting beside him, fully dressed, working the tangles from her pale, fine hair with a little pocket comb she'd carried in her jeans.

Maybe he should just let it be, he thought. The ride to get here had been a pleasure, their lovemaking beautiful. Why spoil the morning with talk about a subject she seemed not to want him to broach?

In the silence of his indecision, one of the horses whickered softly and nipped the other one. Cody asked, "Julie?"

She glanced at him, her comb paused in midstroke, "Hmm?"

He boldly tried again, "I still want to talk."

"About what?"

"About you and me, about this whole thing between us...."

Suddenly she was pocketing her comb and glancing at her watch. "Oh my goodness, it's past eleven. I have to meet Babe Allen for lunch at twelve-thirty. Can you believe it? She's thinking of donating six Hummel figurines from the Gift Emporium for the raffle tomorrow evening."

Cody stared at her. "What's a Hummel?"

She stood up. "You know. Those china figurines. They're collector's items."

He looked up at her, irritation tightening his stomach. He'd mentioned the two of them, and suddenly she couldn't sit still a second longer. "So?" His voice was somewhat curt. "You have to have lunch with Babe to get her figurines for the raffle?"

"More or less." She glanced away modestly. "Babe wants to talk about next year, and whether I'll be directing things again."

She began motioning him to get up, so she could shake out the blanket. "I just didn't realize how late it was getting."

"Julie, wait." He seized her arm when she knelt to grab the blanket's hem.

"Don't." She jerked away, rocking back on her heels—and then immediately looked ashamed. "I'm sorry. I really am. I just didn't know how late it was getting.... Now, can you please get up?"

For a long minute, he stared at her. Finally he said, "You can't get away from this forever. Sometime we have to talk about you and me."

Suddenly she looked like she might cry. "I know."

He felt like a rat, bringing tears to her eyes like that, but this was important, so he forged on. "Then when?"

She was still kneeling, though she'd forgotten all about shaking out the blanket. She seemed, all at once, to realize that he wasn't going to get up until she gave him an answer. So she stood, a somewhat frantic move, and hurried to the edge of the creek. She looked down, perhaps at her own blurred reflection in the slowed waters of the little pool.

Then, abruptly, she turned to him. "Are you... Do you like this? I mean, are you enjoying what's happening between you and me?" Her voice was soft, hesitant, reminiscent of the old Julie, who was so little in evidence of late.

"Hell, yes."

"Then what...what's wrong?"

He felt more like a rat by the second. "I didn't say anything was wrong, exactly."

"Then why can't we just...enjoy this?"

"We are. I am. That isn't the point. I want to talk, that's all."

She looked at him, her expression desperate and unhappy. Finally she pleaded, "Can't we just wait? Please?"

"Until when?"

She sighed. "Until the festival's over. Can't we just have a wonderful time until then?"

"Live out your fantasy, you mean?" His voice had a bitter edge.

She looked away. "Yes. I suppose."

He was quiet, considering, thinking grimly that the only reason she could be putting him off was because she saw no future for them. He was her fantasy-come-true and nothing more. Soon enough, she'd be ready for reality again—and he'd be out the door.

He forced himself to weigh her proposal, trying to be philosophical instead of giving in to his hurt and his anger that she would use him this way. Once he considered it, he realized that he fully intended to do just as she asked. He wanted the next few days, too. And maybe, when they finally talked, it wouldn't turn out as bad as he feared.

He agreed to her terms with a casual shrug that belied the sudden heaviness of his heart. "All right. Until the festival's over. Sunday night, after the last performance of the revue. Then we'll talk about you and me."

All of a sudden, she was smiling, holding out her hand. "Good. Now, come on. I really do have to get back."

He stood up, feeling an answering smile tug on his own lips as Kemo also rose and stretched and whined eagerly to be on the way. Her slender hand closed around his. She pulled him close and wrapped her arms around him, lifting her mouth.

She kissed him—a sweet, playful kiss. And then she was spinning away from him, grabbing up the blanket, shaking it out. He watched her, thinking ruefully that it was hard to stay mad at her when she was so damned adorable, so full of laughter and vitality, her pink skin still glowing from their lovemaking, her hazel eyes alight.

Hell, maybe she *was* using him. But it was almost worth it to see her this way—timid Julie Huddleston, taking on the world at last.

He resolved to do it her way, to enjoy the waning days of Midsummer Madness at her side, and not to think of what would happen when the festival drew to a close, when she would finally have to reveal to him the secrets she would not share now.

"Help me fold this thing," she begged sweetly.

He went to her, smiling, his resolve lightening his mood. Right then, he honestly thought everything would be fine until Sunday night.

In his own way, Cody McIntyre was as innocent as Juliet when it came to the ways of the heart.

CHAPTER NINE

BABE WAS WAITING patiently in the sandwich shop, sipping an iced tea, when Juliet slid into the seat across from her.

"I'm sorry, Babe." Juliet glanced at the time, which she'd been doing, harriedly, through the entire drive from the ranch.

Babe waved her hand. "It's okay. I had a cool drink to keep me company."

"Cody took me riding." Juliet delicately shifted in her seat. "My first time. I think tomorrow I'll be feeling what a good time I had."

Babe grinned. "You and Cody are quite an item." Juliet felt her face pinkening, hated that it was happening, and knew that it was pinkening all the more. "A lot of women in this town are green with envy, I'll tell you."

Juliet, who didn't want to think about how much other women wanted Cody, grabbed for the menu. "Well," she asked over-brightly, "have you already ordered?"

Babe, who was there with the firm intention of getting Juliet's commitment to run Midsummer Madness next year, knew when a subject would gain her no points. "No, I waited for you." She also whipped open her menu and studied it with great interest. "The waitress said the pastrami is fresh, but she recommends the grilled turkey and Swiss...."

Juliet relaxed as she realized Babe would not pursue the subject of herself and Cody any further. The waitress came and took their order.

The meal was a success in the eyes of both women. Not only was the grilled turkey and Swiss as good as the waitress had promised, but Juliet got her figurines for the raffle the following evening. Babe, for her part, extracted from Juliet a commitment that she'd handle the festival next year. Babe also insisted on picking up the check.

When she left the restaurant, Juliet felt so good that she wanted to share it all with Cody. Babe had even sworn she could get the association to raise Juliet's fee. The money, next year, would go toward the new seats that were needed in the Gap Auditorium.

Deciding that she just had to tell Cody all about it right now, Juliet strolled the few blocks to McIntyre's. She was sure that he'd still be there, finishing up after the lunch rush.

She pushed back the door and strode into the cool dimness, blinded for the briefest moment as her eyes adjusted after the bright sunlight outside. When the long bar came into focus, the first thing she saw was Cody—and a beautiful woman.

He stood with his back to the door. The woman, a tall redhead in a silky blouse and slim skirt, was bending close to him, lifting an unlit cigarette to her lips.

Cody picked up a pack of bar matches and gave her a light. Then he murmured something brief and immediately moved away. The woman caught his arm. Cody looked down at her red-nailed hand, and then very deliberately back into her face. She let go.

Juliet understood that the scene she was witnessing happened several times a week. Cody was an incredibly handsome man, and his business brought him into contact with available women every day. He was bound to get offers. She herself had seen him get offers all the time over the years.

But this time, the sight of him smoothly turning down another lovely woman twisted inside her like the turning of a sharp knife. She wanted to whirl and run.

But he'd already seen her. "Julie!" His voice was full of pleasure at the sight of her. Even Juliet, in the agony of her insecurity, could hear that.

Behind him, the beautiful redhead gave Juliet a long, cold glance. The woman was probably wondering what a man like Cody could see in someone like Juliet Huddleston.

Cody strode across the oak floor, his eyes alight. Juliet, accepting a chaste hug and a quick, welcoming kiss, asked, "Who is that?"

Cody followed the direction of her gaze, saw the redhead, and shrugged. "I think she said her name was Laura. New in town. An agent for Bruckner's Real Estate."

"She's...very pretty."

"Yeah," Cody agreed with another shrug that said the subject of the redhead wasn't one that had much interest for him. He put his arm around her shoulders, "Come on, let's go to the office." He led her out of the bar, asking before they'd even made it through the kitchen, "So how'd it go with Babe? I know you're dying to tell me." He grinned his right-sided grin.

As she gazed up at him, Juliet forgot all about the beautiful woman with the fiery hair. There was nothing else in the world but her love for him, so strong right then that she had to press her lips together to keep from blurting out, *I love you, Cody,* while they were walking through the kitchen, with cooks and pot washers all over the place.

It had been that way this morning, when he kept trying to get her to talk about the two of them. She'd suspected what he wanted to tell her—that she shouldn't get too attached to him, because what they had couldn't last forever. She'd longed to throw herself at him, passionately declare her never-ending love and beg him not to leave her. But she hadn't, because she didn't want to lose him any sooner than it was going to happen anyway.

So instead of speaking honestly, she'd shamelessly seduced him. And then later, when he tried to talk again, she'd pretended to be in a big hurry to meet with Babe. In the end, he'd agreed to wait until Sunday night to have their discussion about the future.

And she was grateful. She was determined to keep her mouth shut about her hopeless love and enjoy the few days they had left.

"Julie?" He was looking into her eyes, his expression concerned. "What is it? Suddenly you look a million miles away."

"I'm sorry. Just thinking."

"About what?"

"Oh, everything...." She gestured vaguely as he followed her into his office and closed the door.

"About Babe, you mean?"

"Yes. Yes, about Babe. She's donating the figurines, and that's not all...."

The few precious remaining days of Midsummer Madness passed much too quickly. It seemed to Juliet that she merely blinked, and it was already Saturday, the next-to-last day of the festival. That night there would be no revue—because there was the Gold Rush Ball instead.

Juliet's entire day was spent at the Oddfellows Hall over on North Pine Street, supervising the decorating crew and helping the musicians—a six-piece band, including washboard and fiddle, all friends of Flat-nosed Jake's—to set up. Cody was in and out all day, lending a hand wherever he could. He urged Juliet to come over to the restaurant for a quick dinner at five-thirty, but she simply couldn't spare the time. At six, she rushed home, grabbed a sandwich, showered and got into her costume.

At seven, she was looking herself over in the full-length mirror on the back of her bedroom door. She wore a navy blue mid-nineteenth century soldier's uniform, complete with shiny brass buttons, black boots and a billed hat. She saluted her reflection, deciding she presented a fair representation of Lotta Crabtree in one of her most beloved impersonations, The Drummer Boy. She'd even managed to borrow a drum and drumsticks from the elementary school.

The costume, which she'd decided on after long deliberation, had not been easy to come by. On Thursday morning, she'd ended up making a special trip to a shop in Sacramento to find it. And she was paying quite a bit for it—mostly because she'd had such time restraints that she'd been forced to get it early and wouldn't be returning it until Monday, when the festival was over.

When the festival was over....

The drummer boy in the mirror looked back at her through sad hazel eyes.

Juliet shook herself and turned away from her own mournful

reflection. Her magical week had been everything she could have dreamed of—and it wasn't over yet.

She drove back to town in her red car, with the windows down and the radio up high to keep her spirits from sagging. Actually, having the radio on loud served another purpose. It kept the engine's irritating knocking noise from bothering her. She reminded herself—again—that she'd have to get that looked into, just as soon as the festival was over.

As soon as the festival was over....

The thought, again, made her sad. She cranked the radio up another notch and stoutheartedly sang along.

Before going to the hall, she stopped in at her own office. From her safe, she collected the cashboxes that would be used that night, as well as the rolls of tickets that Jake had had printed a week ago and given her to hold until the ball. At seven-thirty, she reached the Oddfellows Hall. She was in luck and didn't have to park in back because someone pulled out just as she drove up. She got one of the six spaces right on the street in front of the hall.

Leaving her drum and sticks in the car to collect later, Juliet scooped up the rolls of tickets and the two cashboxes and made for the double front door.

Inside, the brick building was comfortably cool, as well as rather grand by Emerald Gap standards. The lobby area was graced by a crystal chandelier donated in the twenties by Evan McMulch, patriarch of the McMulch family. The McMulches had once owned the now-closed Royale mine and they still ran McMulch's Lumberyard, for which Juliet kept the books.

The walls of the lobby, serendipitously for the Gold Rush Ball, boasted a series of murals depicting the discovery and mining of gold in Emerald Gap. The murals had been painted twenty years ago by Rutger Dunlap, a sometime artist and local troublemaker whom one of the Oddfellows had mysteriously turned loose with his paints in the lobby. Rutger had painted the murals and then disappeared from Emerald Gap, later to become a famous artist in Europe—which made Burly Jones, the Oddfellow who'd allowed

Rutger to paint the murals, feel quite smug. Since then, anyone who did something incomprehensible that later turned out to be clever or noteworthy was said in Emerald Gap to have "pulled a Burly."

Juliet was standing before the murals, thinking of all this to keep from thinking how close the end of Midsummer Madness was, when Andrea found her.

"Oh, there you are, Juliet. And with the tickets and cashboxes, at last." Andrea, with the no-nonsense briskness born of years of telling small children what to do, whisked away the tickets and boxes and turned to call to Reva Reid, who had just slipped through the second set of oak doors that led into the main part of the hall. "Reva. Here, Reva. Would you take care of these?"

Reva, dressed in a formal gown that looked as if it owed more to the thirties than to the gold rush, murmured, "Of course." She relieved Andrea of the metal boxes and ticket rolls, then disappeared once again inside the main hall.

Andrea took Juliet by the hand. "Now, wait a moment here." She stood back from Juliet, her head tipped to the side. "Let me see. I have it. General Grant?"

Juliet groaned, wondering if Grant could have had something to do with the gold rush that she herself had forgotten. "Lotta Crabtree. The Drummer Boy," she corrected. "I left my drum in the car for now."

Andrea, who herself seemed to be dressed as a pioneer woman of some sort, complete with poke bonnet and muslin apron, shook her head. "That simply goes to prove that even kindergarten teachers don't know everything. Now, come along. I must show you all that's been accomplished since you went home to change."

With a rustle of her long gathered skirt, Andrea swooped toward the second set of double doors and, one at a time, swung them back and anchored them open with a pair of doorstops. Juliet moved to the open doorway to look. Reva Reid, setting up the parallel ticket tables right beyond the entrance, glanced up and winked. Juliet smiled back and then stood staring, appropriately awed.

Overhead, obscuring the beamed ceiling, gold foil dangled in loops and whorls, glistening in the little spotlights that had been cleverly concealed in every nook, cranny and corner. In the center of all the looped and coiling foil hung a huge nugget made of papier mâché, itself covered with foil so that it sparkled as it slowly turned in the light.

Across the hall from the entrance, the stage where the band would play had been done up to look like a mountain glen, with imitation boulders and plastic bushes and small fresh-cut trees on wooden stands. Down the center of the stage, skirting the piano and the microphone stand, ran a stream made of wrinkled aluminum foil, which gleamed quite convincingly in the light from above. The stream "trickled" off the stage a little left of center, ending rather abruptly when it hit the dance floor.

On one side of the stage stood a mountain of borrowed stereo equipment. Burt Pandley would be putting that to use whenever the band took a break. Burt was highly qualified for the job of choosing recorded dance music, as he'd been a D.J. in Auburn at one time.

The bar, courtesy of McIntyre's, was tucked up on the other side of the stage. Behind it, Archie Kent, wearing a white shirt, red suspenders and a bow tie, was getting ready to open shop.

Juliet sighed and decided it was all quite spectacular and inviting, as well, right down to the little brass lanterns on each of the small conversation tables that surrounded the dance floor.

"What a job you've all done," she told Andrea and Reva, and everyone else within earshot.

Andrea nodded. "We certainly have. It helps to have a proper director, at last."

Juliet smiled a gracious thank-you. Then she pulled back her brass-buttoned cuff and glanced at her watch. It was seven-fifty, and the dance was scheduled to start at eight. People would begin arriving any minute now.

Juliet remembered her drum. "Is everything under control,

then?'' Reva and Andrea agreed that it was, and Juliet left them to collect the finishing touch of her costume.

Outside, it was still light, though the sun had slipped behind the rim of the mountains a few moments ago. She'd just swung the strap of her drum in place over her chest and locked her car door, when she spied the derelict in long johns coming toward her from the corner of Broad Street.

It took her several seconds to realize who it was: Cody, walking over from his restaurant. As soon as she recognized him, she burst into laughter. They'd both made a game of not telling the other what their costume would be. Leave it to Cody, the best-looking man in Emerald Gap, to get himself up like a vagrant prospector for the Gold Rush Ball.

He wore no pants over the grubby long johns. His boots looked like they'd been salvaged from a trash can. Around his waist, from a wide belt, he'd strung a gold pan and a small pickax. His hat, so battered and torn as to be truly pitiful, had a wide, floppy brim that shaded a face smeared with something gray and sooty, so that it looked as if it had been a long time since he'd shaved. When he got close enough to give her a wide grin, she saw that he'd blacked out a couple of teeth.

"Oh, Cody...."

"Gimme a kiss, woman," he demanded. He grabbed her, right there on the sidewalk, and bent her back over his arm, causing her drum to bang against the parking meter by her car.

"Unhand me, varlet." She giggled and pretended to struggle.

But the derelict prospector would not be refused. In the end, as best she could with a drum strapped across her chest, she gave him the kiss he'd demanded, though he did complain against her mouth that it was hard to believe she was really surrendering when she refused to stop laughing. Around them, as the first partygoers arrived, there were chuckles and shouts of encouragement.

At last, Cody released her and stepped back to study her costume. "Hmm. A soldier from Sutter's Fort?" Sutter's Fort, in Sacramento, was near where the first California gold had been discovered.

Juliet made a disgusted noise in her throat and held her arms out. "You happen to be looking at one of Lotta Crabtree's most beloved impersonations, The Drummer Boy."

Cody continued to look puzzled.

Juliet groaned. "It begins to look as if I won't be winning the Best Costume ribbon this year."

"Well, now, Julie...." He scratched his head through his pitiful hat.

She planted her hands on her hips. "'Well, now, Julie'? Is that all you can say? Do you have any idea how much I spent on this getup?"

He chucked her under the chin. "Settle down. So what if you're unrecognizable? You look terrific. Cutest little soldier I ever saw."

She looked down at herself, then doubtfully up at him. "Right."

"Come on, stop sulking. You're the boss of the party—it's not fair you should expect to win all the prizes, too."

"I just want..." she began, and then didn't finish.

"What?"

Tonight to be perfect, a memory to treasure. For the rest of my life, she thought. But she didn't say it. It sounded much too sad, somehow. And she didn't want to sound sad. She wanted to have a wonderful time.

"What is it, Julie?" His eyes were full of concern.

"It's nothing." Her voice was very bright.

"But, Julie—"

She didn't let him finish. "You're right. I was sulking. And I'm through sulking now." She took his arm and grinned up at him. "Shall we go in, sir?"

For a moment he just looked at her. Then he shrugged and fell in with her banter. "You bet, you little wildcat, you." He led her inside where Reva and Andrea were already busy taking tickets and the band had begun the first set.

Except for the fact that nobody recognized her costume, the first two hours of the dance were pure pleasure for Juliet. She beat on her drum and kicked up her heels, joining right in with the line dances even though she didn't know the steps.

Whenever a slow number started up, Andrea let her slip the drum beneath one of the ticket tables. Then Cody would lead her out on the floor and pull her into his arms and it was simply heaven. Not only was she close against his body, which she loved, but Cody was such a great dancer that he made even Juliet, who'd never had the opportunity to learn much about dancing, look like she knew what she was doing.

It wasn't until a little after ten, when the dance floor swarmed with costumed dancers and most of the tables on the sidelines were full, that things began to get rough.

First, there was a big commotion out in the lobby. When Juliet followed the problem to its source, she learned that someone—no one had seen who—had painted a purple moustache on a gold panner on one of the Rutger Dunlap murals. Burly Jones, now well into his seventies and costumed for the ball as the front half of a mule—Evan McMulch II being the other half—stood in the middle of the lobby ranting and raving and declaring, ''A priceless treasure has been defaced!''

With considerable effort, Juliet finally pushed her way through the growing group of gawkers to reach Burly's side.

''Mr. Jones—''

''Don't bother me, girl. A tragedy has occurred here! What has befallen our fair town, for such a thing to be allowed to happen, under the very noses of those of us that care the most! I ask you all, to what pass have we come?''

Juliet, who had smelled 80 proof when Burly turned to her, tried tugging on his arm, under which was tucked the mule head he had recently removed. ''Mr. Jones, if we could discuss this in private—''

''Private! Private, you say? I won't be silenced, never. I'll shout it to the rooftops. A sacred treasure has been defiled!''

''But, Mr. Jones, we *are* insured. All damages will be covered, I promise.''

Burly turned his rather bulging eyes on Juliet and released another fumy breath. "Money? You talk of mere money? This is *art* that has been destroyed here—our history, our past...."

Juliet almost gave in and left Burly Jones to rant and rave to his heart's content. But then she glanced to the side and saw Cody, an ironic grin on his face, giving her the lifted eyebrow that she knew meant, *Do you need some help?* She shook her head, reinforced by the simple knowledge that he was there.

This time, she took Burly firmly by the arm and began to walk. Though he continued to rant, he did go where she pulled him, which was through a side door into the small office at the front of the building. There, with no audience, he was at least willing to grudgingly listen as she promised that, though of course money couldn't replace the priceless mural, money *could* make certain that it was properly restored.

After Burly's feathers were effectively smoothed, Juliet returned to the lobby where all was now quiet. She then posted a volunteer guard on a folding chair to see that the murals received no further embellishments.

At last, near eleven, she reentered the hall to find Burt Pandley announcing the commencement of the competition for Best Costume, male and female. Andrea Oakleaf and Reva Reid, he explained, the two trusty ticket takers, had already acted as preliminary judges, since they'd seen everyone at least once when they came in the door.

At that point, Andrea and Reva were asked to step up onto the stage and, their feet in the aluminum creek, the two ladies took turns reading off their choices. Though she held out little hope of winning, Juliet grabbed her drum and drumsticks from beneath the ticket table anyway, so that she would be fully attired just in case a miracle happened and her name was called.

The miracle failed to occur. But Juliet found she didn't mind too much, especially when Cody was one of the finalists. She clapped and hooted with the best of them when he climbed up on the stage. He looked so totally absurd in his long johns and battered hat.

When all the nominees were named, there were four men and

four women contestants crammed up on the stage, as well as the master of ceremonies, Burt. Reva and Andrea had thoughtfully stepped down. Burt then held the microphone over each contender's head, gauging the success of the costume by the strength of the applause.

Cody lost out to Yardley Forbes, who'd got himself up as the doomed Maria Elena, in a dress that was a man-size duplicate of the one Yolanda Hughes wore in the revue, with a noose around his neck and a lot of blue face paint—so that he would look as if he'd already been hanged.

The woman who won—a redhead in a gorgeous dance hall-girl costume—looked familiar to Juliet. It wasn't until the woman grabbed Cody, who happened to be standing beside her when her victory was announced, and kissed him, that Juliet remembered her as the fiery-haired woman from McIntyre's the Wednesday before.

Cody pretended to reel from the woman's kiss, and then to recover himself enough to grin his black-toothed grin at the wave of hoots and catcalls that followed. Juliet, watching, knew he was only playing to the audience, not encouraging the beautiful redhead in the least. Still, seeing him kissing someone else touched her where she was most vulnerable.

The sadness she was trying to keep down rose up once more. It was Saturday night. Not much time left. Her fantasy was coming to an end. Midsummer Madness was almost over. Tomorrow night, she and Cody would talk about where they were going from here.

Up on the stage, Burt was pinning the blue ribbon to the beautiful redhead's silky bodice. The redhead was smiling seductively at Cody. The crowd hooted and stomped.

Juliet, who felt unwelcome tears rise to her eyes, began grimly reminding herself of the reality of the situation.

Cody was a wonderful person. He was kind, and he'd always looked out for her. But that didn't make him hers, not the way she wanted him to be.

He might handle Billy Butley for her. He might encourage her to dive off the high rock down at the South Fork swimming hole. He might do her the ultimate kindness and teach her the mysteries of passion and desire. He might even want her, for a brief time, before someone more beautiful, more self-assured, came along and stole him away.

But the reality was that Juliet Huddleston would never be able to hold a man like Cody McIntyre. She simply must make herself come to grips with that fact.

Beyond the press of people in front of her, the stage grew more blurry with each passing moment. Juliet dashed away the foolish tears. Then, adjusting the leather strap so that her drum hung behind her, she turned to make her way through the press of people to the lobby and the rest room. Once safely there, she could lock herself into a stall for a few minutes until her shaky emotions were back under control.

But she didn't make it, because halfway there, Andrea Oakleaf met up with her.

"There you are. We've got a little problem."

"Oh, Andrea...." She longed to just beg off, but then she remembered that, as the director of the festival, problems that others couldn't solve fell to her. She shifted the big drum to the side again, where it was more comfortable when she was standing still. "What is it?"

Andrea leaned toward her and spoke in a low voice. "When Reva and I were up on stage, Melda was watching the door for us...."

"Yes?"

"And somehow..."

"What? Tell me."

Andrea finally got it out. "Someone appears to have stolen one of the cashboxes."

"Oh, Lord."

"I know. It's terrible."

"How much was in it?"

"About half of tonight's take—and the fifty in change that we started with."

"Did anybody see anything?"

"Not that we can find out. Melda was just using the one box, while we were on the stage. She asked Evan McMulch to watch the other one, but he had had a lot to drink, and appears to have wandered off, leaving the box unguarded. Evidently, for several minutes, no one was paying any attention to the box."

Juliet considered. All told, the festival had been the biggest money-maker ever. And the ball was supposed to be the crowning glory of the ten days of fun. "Look. We can afford to lose the money better than we can afford to ruin the ball, don't you think?"

"Yes," Andrea said. "Yes, I agree."

"So let's get a few people together to look, but keep it low-key, fair enough?"

Andrea nodded. "Very wise, I would say."

However that was not to be, because poor Melda, in a dither over what had happened under her very nose, had mentioned the problem to more than one person before she reported it to Andrea and Reva. And, just as Juliet and Andrea agreed to keep things quiet, Burly Jones began decrying the theft from over near the entrance doors.

Juliet, grimly pushing her drum behind her again, turned to jostle her way through the crowd and deal with Burly one more time. She was just pulling on the arm that held the mule's head again, to lead Burly to the front office where she could calm him down, when there was a cry from out near the double doors to the street.

She glanced that way, through the hall doors and across the lobby, and there was Flat-nosed Jake, locked in a tussle with Evan McMulch II. Evan, still dressed as the back half of the mule to which Burly was the front, clutched the missing cashbox and whined piteously that he hadn't done anything wrong.

"My God," Burly breathed beside her. "It's Evan. Evan is the culprit. To what a pass has this world come?"

Juliet very calmly took off her drum and held it out to Burly. "Hold this, would you?"

For once Burly Jones was shocked enough to simply do as he was told. He took the big drum in his free hand and Juliet hurried across the lobby to help Flat-nosed Jake.

Fifteen minutes later, as midnight approached, Juliet finally felt she had the story straight. Melda had asked Evan to watch the spare cashbox for her, and Evan, feeling the call of nature, had taken the box with him to the men's room in the front of the building off the lobby. Once in the rest room, Evan had found that he was feeling a little ill—perhaps he'd had just one too many bourbons on the rocks, he was willing to admit—and so he'd sat down on the waste bin to wait for the room to stop whirling around. When he collected himself enough to venture out again, he'd been ruthlessly attacked by Flat-nosed Jake and accused of all manner of heinous crimes.

After the whole story was out, Juliet spent a while soothing Evan's hurt pride and reassuring Jake that he'd done the right thing. At last, everyone seemed to come down to earth and accept the fact that it had all been nothing more than a massive misunderstanding.

Praying that nothing else would go wrong with her "perfect" evening, Juliet returned to the ballroom just as the fiddle player was announcing the last waltz of the evening. "Grab your special lady, gents. Because this is it for the Gold Rush Ball for another year...."

Juliet, wanting the last waltz with Cody more than just about anything right then, scanned the crowded room for his disreputable hat. He saw her just as she saw him, and he started elbowing his way toward her through the throng. The smile of anticipation on his grimy face lifted her spirits and soothed her frazzled nerves. The ball might not have been exactly as she might have dreamed, but at least she would have the last waltz with Cody to remember when everything was done.

Cody was less than fifteen feet from her when the beautiful redhead in the dance hall-girl costume materialized out of nowhere and laid her slim hand on his arm. "How about the last dance, handsome?"

Cody smiled politely at her. "No, ma'am. I have a partner." He shook her hand off.

But too many strangers nearby had seen the redhead kiss Cody up there on the stage. The hoots and hollers began.

"Give the lady the last dance, you fool!"

"Don't turn down an offer like that!"

"What are you, man? Certifiable?"

Cody gently said no again and shrugged off the gibes. He kept coming toward Juliet. Jokingly, one man grabbed him, and then another joined in. "Dance with the lady," they demanded, caught up in the moment, and perhaps pushing the joke a little too far.

Cody was beginning to look angry. "Look, folks. Back off, okay?"

Juliet, who'd had enough hassles for one evening, decided it would be wiser to give in. She sent Cody a regretful look, then mouthed the words, "Dance with her. It's okay."

He narrowed his eyes at her and said again, "No."

"Please. Just do it."

He stared at her for a moment, an unreadable expression on his face, while the hecklers who held him badgered him some more. Then, finally, he shrugged. "Okay. Fine."

He was immediately released and pushed in the direction of the beautiful redhead. She gave him a come-hither smile. He held out his hand and led her out on the floor.

Juliet stood on the sidelines and watched them for a moment. Even with Cody wearing his silly costume, they were still the two most beautiful people in the room. They might have been made for each other.

"Share the last waltz with old Jake?" Flat-nosed Jake was grinning at her. Juliet smiled back at him and followed him out on the floor.

Soon enough, the dance ended. Jake gave her a courtly bow.

"That's all, folks. See you next year," the fiddle player announced. There was a round of applause, and then Burt took the microphone once again to remind everyone of the closing day picnic tomorrow and the final performance of the Midsummer Madness Revue tomorrow night.

Burt Pandley left the stage. The regular hall lights came up.

Juliet blinked at the sudden brightness, and when she opened her eyes, all the painted faces around her looked garish and haggard. Up on the stage, a couple of the trees had toppled, their pine stands naked and raw looking in the harsh light. The tinfoil stream, torn and trampled by too many high-heeled shoes, made a pathetic sight. Above, a lot of the looped foil had come loose and hung in sad tendrils all around the hall.

The Gold Rush Ball was over. Slowly the movement of the crowd toward the exits began.

Jake gave Juliet a quick peck on the cheek and murmured something about getting things straightened up enough to leave, then he was gone.

Juliet, feeling disoriented, tried to remember what she had to do next. Not much, really. Babe Allen would take care of the cashboxes, since she was treasurer of the festival this year. And Jake was responsible for locking up, while a volunteer cleanup crew would put the place to rights at nine the next morning.

Her drum. That was it. She had to get her drum from Burly Jones. Juliet turned to look for Burly—and came up short against Cody's hard chest.

"Hey, imagine running into you here." Cody laughed, a warm, masculine sound that, for some stupid reason, made Juliet want to cry all over again. She looked down, in a frantic effort to get her emotions back in control. "Julie?" Cody took her by the arms. "Julie, what the hell is bothering you?"

"Nothing. Nothing, really." She flashed him a blinding smile and wriggled free of his grip. "I have to get my drum. Burly's got it somewhere."

"Julie, wait...."

She was already moving away from him, calling over her shoulder. "I'll meet you at my car. Fifteen minutes, okay?"

She didn't hear his answer and right then it didn't matter. All she wanted was a little time, to get her feelings back in line. Then everything would be fine. She was sure of it. They'd have their final beautiful night together. Her last memory to treasure, for the rest of her days.

CHAPTER TEN

"LOOK, JULIE. I can't take this anymore. What the hell is going on?"

They'd just arrived at the ranch house after the dance and were standing in the big foyer at the foot of the stairs. It was past 2:00 a.m.

Cody had ridden home with her in her car. It had been a long, silent ride—except for the knocking sound from the engine, of course. Juliet, who had meant to put her sad feelings behind her, had not succeeded in the least.

All during the ride, she kept picturing Cody and the redhead, whirling across the dance floor in the last waltz. And the more she pictured them dancing, the more she had to admit that she was jealous of the redhead, though Cody had done absolutely nothing to encourage the woman. In fact, if anyone had encouraged the woman, it had been Juliet herself. Cody had been clearly unwilling; he'd wanted to dance with Juliet. But Juliet had turned him down. Under the pretext of avoiding trouble, she'd pushed him right into the other woman's arms.

Oh, she didn't understand her own actions lately. It was as if she were...falling apart. As if the new, assertive woman she'd thought she'd become was just a false shell, now cracking, to expose a forlorn real self who huddled, fearful and confused, inside.

"Julie, talk to me."

Juliet, utterly miserable, looked down at her black soldier's boots and said nothing.

"Damn it, look at me."

She forced herself to look in his eyes. "I...I can't talk about it right now, Cody. I don't understand it myself. Please...." Her voice trailed off. Please what? She didn't know.

The limit of Cody's patience was unquestionably within view. "Great. Terrific," he said, and skimmed off his ragged hat to send it sailing through the doorway to his right, into the living room, where it landed on a recliner. "At first, you won't talk to me until Sunday. And now, you say you *can't* talk to me. I don't get it. I don't get it at all."

He shook his head, making a low sound of frustration in his throat, and then he followed his hat into the living room, where he dropped to the big sectional sofa. Juliet, despising herself by then, just stayed in the foyer staring after him woefully. After a minute, he craned his head to look back at her. "Well? Are you going to stand in the hall all night or what?"

Juliet obediently trudged into the living room.

He gave her a pushed-to-the-limit look. "Sit down."

She dropped to a straight chair. Cody looked at her some more, waiting for her to say something. When she didn't, he asked, "Why have you been moping around all night, looking like you want to cry one minute, and then pasting on a big smile and swearing it's nothing when I ask you what's wrong?"

"Oh, Cody..."

"What?"

"I don't know."

"That's not good enough. Tell me what's wrong."

She didn't answer. It seemed pointless. She'd only be repeating what she'd said before.

"Then answer another question." He tried again. "Why in hell did you shove that redheaded woman at me for the last dance? Are you trying to tell me something here, is that it?"

She managed to mutter, "I just thought it would be better, to avoid trouble." It was a coward's lie. Her shame increased.

"Better in what way?" he demanded. "Better if I dance the last dance with some woman I don't even know?"

"No, no, of course not."

"Then what?"

"Oh, Cody...."

"Answer me."

"Cody, it was only a dance."

"'Only a dance.'" He repeated the words with a sneer. "You wanted that dance. At least, the way you looked at me said you wanted that dance. Did I read you wrong?"

"Okay. Yes, I wanted the dance. But there were just...all these hassles tonight. The mustache on the mural, and Evan McMulch and the cashbox. I didn't want another hassle."

"I wanted to dance with you, and you wanted to dance with me. All you had to do was step forward, and those idiots who were after me would have left it alone. But instead, you stepped back. Why, Julie? Why did you do that?" He stood up then and came to loom over her. "Answer me. Why?"

"I just..." She gazed up at him, desolate. He should have looked absurd, in his long johns with his blacked-out teeth. But he didn't. He looked so achingly handsome that it hurt just to look at him. So handsome. So far out of her league. "Please. Please, not now."

"When then?"

"Tomorrow night...."

"Oh," he said with heavy sarcasm. "That's right, tomorrow night. Tomorrow night's the big night when you'll finally talk to me."

"We agreed—"

He loosed an expletive. "*We* didn't do anything. *You* told me how it would be, and then anytime I wanted to make things different, you'd change the subject or suddenly have to be somewhere else."

Juliet looked at him, admitting to herself that he was right, and feeling ashamed. She knew exactly what she should do: start right now with honesty. She should tell him everything, from the love in her heart for him, to her absolute conviction that someday she would lose him to someone more desirable.

The room was very quiet. Outside, Kemo, who had been left on the porch, whined to get in.

"Cody...." Juliet began, determined at last to tell all. A single tear trickled from her lid and trailed down her cheek.

"Damn it, Julie," Cody muttered. He reached out and wiped the tear away, the touch infinitely gentle.

"Oh, Cody, I..." She sought the right words, the honest words, that would get it all out in the open for good and all.

But then she saw the tenderness in his face. The sight of her tears had softened him, made him more vulnerable. He'd lost track of his goal to get her to talk.

It was truly her moment of choice. She could go ahead and tell him the secrets of her heart. Or she could claim what was left of her final night of fantasy.

She lifted her arms, rising toward him. "Please, Cody. Hold me."

With a low growl, he enfolded her, pulling her against his hard body, and lowering his mouth to hers. Juliet kissed him eagerly, hungrily, all her unspoken love and longing expressed in the heat and hunger of her lips beneath his.

As the kiss spun out into eternity, Cody swung her up against his chest and headed for the stairs and his own wide bed.

In his room, he set her down long enough to slip the brass buttons of her uniform through their holes, and slide her jacket off, to strip her of her boots, push down her soldier's pants, to peel away every wisp of cloth that protected her from his sight. He was out of his own absurd costume in no time at all.

Then he lay her down upon the bed and made love to her with a fierceness and heat that burned her down to pure sensation and made her beg him hoarsely to never, ever stop.

When the time came that he rose up over her and poised to bury himself in her softness, she cried out and reached for him. He came down upon her. She welcomed him eagerly. Slowly at first, then with building momentum, their bodies began the ultimate dance of love.

When her fulfillment came, she gloried in it, thrashing wildly beneath him, so that he, too, lost himself in the final, spinning vortex of shared pleasure.

Afterward, they lay, sweating bodies entwined. And Juliet rubbed her moist cheek against his shoulder, kissed him and tried not to think that she had made the coward's choice.

But she had. She'd chosen her fantasy, her final night of passion, over the harsh purity of truth.

Morning came too soon. Juliet woke alone in Cody's bed. Groggy and bewildered, she called to him. But no answer came. She pulled on his robe that hung behind the door and went to look for him, but the rooms were all empty.

Apprehension filled her. Had something happened; was something wrong?

She returned to Cody's bedroom and dressed in her wrinkled soldier's costume. Then she went out to the front porch, where Kemo waited to be scratched behind the ear. She petted the dog.

Bud Southey, the caretaker, who lived in a small set of rooms behind the garage, was over by the pool. Wondering if he might know something, she called to him.

Bud crossed the driveway and stood at the foot of the steps. "Yes, ma'am," he said, when she asked if he knew where Cody had gone. "Left about an hour ago. Said to tell you he decided to go on into town by himself this morning. Drove his old pickup."

It took Juliet a moment to absorb that information. "But why?" she asked at last.

Bud shrugged. "Well, ma'am, I didn't see as how it was my place to ask." The words were courteous, but pointed.

"Oh," she said, feeling her face color a little. Bud had always been a quiet, self-contained sort of fellow. He wasn't the type to get involved in his boss's private affairs. "Yes, of course. I see. Thank you, Bud."

"Welcome, ma'am." Bud politely tipped his baseball cap at her and went back to the pool, where he picked up the long-poled strainer and began sweeping the surface of the clear water.

For a moment more, Juliet absently stroked Kemo's sleek coat and tried to push down her growing anxiety. Perhaps something had come up concerning the restaurant or the hardware store—perhaps a break-in or something like that.

But that didn't add up. She would have heard the phone by the bed if it had rung; she was sure of it.

At last, accepting the fact that she could learn nothing by standing on the porch worrying and wondering, she felt in her pocket for her car keys. Then she told Kemo to stay, went down the steps to her car and drove it back to her house.

There, she showered and dressed. She put on her makeup. She ate breakfast—an egg, toast, juice, and coffee. A busy day lay before her, and she needed the food, especially considering how little sleep she'd had.

Sipping her second cup of coffee, Juliet glanced at her watch. Nine o'clock. In half an hour, she was due at Pine Grove Park. Though Andrea was in charge of the picnic and had enlisted a crew of seven to meet her at the crack of dawn to get things set up, Juliet was expected to oversee the final steps of the process. She should get going very soon.

But what about Cody? She needed to talk to him, find out what was going on, why he'd gotten up from bed and vanished without a word, leaving her nothing but the caretaker's brief message.

She picked up the phone and dialed the hardware store. After two rings, a machine answered and Elma Lou Bealer's voice listed the store hours and urged her to leave a message after the beep.

"Cody," Juliet said into the phone. "Cody, are you there? It's me, Juliet...." She began to feel like a fool; Elma Lou would probably pick up the messages tomorrow morning, and hear the frustration and confusion in her voice. Juliet cleared her throat and said swiftly. "Please call me." Then she hung up.

Next, she tried the restaurant, but this time she planned what she would say in her message before she dialed. Once again, she got a recording, so she waited for the beep.

"Cody, it's Juliet. I must speak with you. I think I can find some time after I check in with Andrea at the park. So if you happen to get this, would you please just...stay there and wait for me?"

* . * . *

Cody, sitting at his desk in the office of his deserted restaurant and staring at the answering machine as it recorded Juliet's voice on the other end of the line, grunted.

"Um, thank you." From the machine, there was a click, a dial tone and then the sounds of the tape rewinding as the thing reset itself.

Cody shifted his focus from the source of Juliet's voice to his booted feet, which were crossed on his desk not far from the machine. Next to his boots steamed an untouched cup of coffee.

Cody was a man who rarely got mad. But he was mad now. Madder than hell. At Juliet Huddleston.

He'd awakened next to her at a little after seven. Sleeping, she had looked as innocent as a child. He'd smoothed a few strands of hair away from her face and kissed her once lightly. She'd smiled and stirred but hadn't opened her eyes.

Lying there against her, he'd thought about their lovemaking the night before and felt himself getting aroused all over again.

And then he'd remembered how the lovemaking had started. How he'd begged her to talk to him, and she'd put him off the way she always did. How she'd finally cried a little, to soften him up. And then put her arms around him, offering him her sweet kiss—and once again he'd learned nothing of what was bothering her.

That was why he'd left without a word this morning. He'd needed to be alone. So he could decide what the hell was going on here, not to mention what he was going to do about it.

Cody recrossed his boots and looked at them some more.

Okay, maybe he was being a callous jerk. Maybe he should have been more understanding of whatever was going on with her that she didn't trust him enough to explain. Maybe last night he shouldn't have pressured her so hard.

Cody swung his boots to the floor and picked up his coffee. He brought the cup to his lips—and then set it down without drinking and stared off toward the door with unseeing eyes.

And maybe this morning he should have kissed her awake and

held her tenderly and begged her one more time to tell him what the hell was going on in her head.

But he was getting damned tired of begging. And he wasn't going to feel guilty for the things he hadn't done, for not being more understanding last night, and not hanging around to try again this morning. Why the hell should he keep trying to get through to her, when he knew damn well what was bothering her and just didn't want to admit it to himself?

Cody grabbed the coffee again and blew on it to cool it.

Yeah, he knew what it was all right. He might as well face it. She was calling it off between them...tonight.

He was sure that was it. Why else would she have thrown some other woman at him, unless she was hoping the other woman might take him off her hands? It made depressing sense, if he just faced up to it. She'd been mooning around like a motherless calf all through the dance last night because she knew what she planned to do, and she dreaded hurting him.

That was how Julie was. She never wanted to hurt a soul—not even a man she was trying to get rid of.

Cody drank from his cup. The coffee scalded his lip, and he swore when he set the brew down.

He was mad as hell at her. She'd had her fantasy, just the way she'd wanted it, and now she was ready to get back to real life.

She was planning to dump him; he knew it. And she thought doing a lot of suffering over it would somehow make it okay. She probably expected, when she finally dropped the news on him, that he'd feel so sorry for her because she was so upset, he'd forget all about the fact that he was the one getting dumped.

Good old Cody McIntyre, he thought with considerable ire. A gentleman to the end. And, of course, he'd always been a gentleman before, with women. Julie, who'd known him all his life, would expect him to be the same with her.

But that was the point, he'd realized just now. It wasn't the same with her. Nothing, at all, was the same with her.

Cody swung his boots back up on his desk and stared at them

some more. She had a surprise coming, he decided. Because he wasn't going take this lying down.

And he wasn't going to be here waiting when she came looking for him, either. Let her have a little taste of her own medicine today. Let her try to talk to him and find just how busy *he* could be....

There was trouble at Pine Grove Park. The moment Juliet arrived, Andrea came rushing over to the car, her expression harried and her gray bun askew.

"Juliet. At last. I was beginning to think you'd never get here."

Juliet, who'd barely managed to climb from the car before Andrea descended on her, shut her door behind her and grimly accepted the fact that her plans for seeking out Cody might have to be changed. "What's wrong?"

"Everything. Only four of the seven on my setup crew showed up on time. Edna Coombes hasn't come yet. And she's supposed to bring the folding tables from the town hall. And you know Melda's second cousin from Roseville?"

"Our professional auctioneer for the pie auction?"

"The very one. He's begged off."

"Oh, no."

"Oh, yes. Melda just came over to tell me. Poor thing. She feels terrible. First, Evan staggered off with the cashbox when she was supposed to be in charge of it last night, and now her cousin backs out on her. She was almost in tears, and swore that that cousin of hers was never a person one could depend on— Heaven knows why she waited until now to say that, but I didn't have the heart to point that out. She looked mortified enough as it was."

"I understand," Juliet soothed. "Anything else?"

"We're still waiting for the complimentary meats and buns from Steerman's Grocery."

"And?"

"The paper products. The charcoal briquettes."

"Has *anything* arrived on time?"

Andrea sighed. "The tablecloths are here—too bad we don't have the tables to put them on."

"Okay," Juliet said. "How many vehicles do we have?"

Andrea quickly counted and told her, and Juliet began assigning errands to everyone with a car.

Juliet herself drove over to Steerman's Grocery to see what had happened to the meat and the buns. The assistant manager, on duty at the time, claimed he knew nothing about a contribution to the picnic. The manager was called, and the assistant manager had a very red face by the time he hung up the phone.

Steerman's delivery truck was immediately requisitioned and filled with every manner of hot dog and burger and bun imaginable. The truck followed Juliet directly to Pine Grove Park.

By then, the tables had arrived, and Andrea's crew was busy setting them up. Juliet was helping wherever she was needed when it suddenly occurred to her that Burt Pandley, with his experience as a disc jockey, might pinch-hit just fine as a pie auctioneer.

She got in her car again and drove to a pay phone. Burt was a late sleeper and she ended up getting him out of bed. But he came awake rather quickly when she asked for his help.

"You betcha. Be glad to. I can be there in an hour."

Juliet looked at her watch. It was eleven-thirty and the auction was slated for one. It would be close but better than nothing. She thanked Burt profusely before she said goodbye.

After she hung up, Juliet just stood there, her hand still on the phone. It was her first quiet moment since Andrea had come flying out to meet her at her car.

She thought of Cody and wondered again what had happened to make him leave her this morning without a word. But the picnic was officially starting in just half an hour. It was her job to be there, at least until things were effectively underway.

Since she had the phone, she called the restaurant, the hardware store and the ranch, too. Cody didn't answer any of the calls.

Well, she decided grimly, she'd done what she could for now. She had to get back for the beginning of the picnic. Then, maybe, she could steal a little time away. She'd track Cody down, and they'd talk.

But Cody surprised her. He was there, at the park, tied into a white apron and grilling the first round of burgers and hot dogs when Juliet returned.

Hesitantly, she approached him. "Cody?"

He turned those gray-green eyes on her and something in her midsection turned over and then melted. "Yeah?"

"I..."

"What?"

"Where did you go?"

"When?"

"This morning."

"I told Bud to tell you."

"Into town?"

"That's right." He turned back to the grill.

She stared at his profile for a moment, wondering what to do next. He was being so...uncommunicative about this, so unlike his usual kind, attentive self.

"But, Cody...." She tried again.

"Yeah?"

She glanced around at the other three grills where volunteers were flipping burgers, at the tables laden with food, and all the people nearby bustling to get things in order. She knew this was neither the time nor the place.

"Um," she began, "after things get going here...in an hour or so? Could you and I talk?"

He flipped a burger over, and then set a few buns to warm on the edge of the grill. Then, after what seemed like forever, he said, "What do you think? These look done to you?" He pointed with the grill spatula.

"Fine. Did you hear what I asked?"

He gave her another look, a brief, distant one, and then he turned back to the grill again. "What was that now?"

"I want to talk. Maybe after the pie auction, or whenever..." Her voice faded off the way it used to.

He looked at her again, then back at his burgers. "You want to talk?"

"Yes." She spoke more firmly. "Yes, I do."

"Sure, Julie. We'll talk."

"When?"

"As soon as I can find the time." He gestured at the grill. "Right now I'm busy."

"Well, I know, but—"

She didn't get to finish, because Babe Allen appeared and grabbed her arm. "Juliet. Andrea tells me it's been a *circus*. But you took care of it. We are so fortunate to have discovered you. Now, come here with me and take a look at these salads...."

Juliet was dragged without further hesitation to the long folding tables, where the potluck dishes of half the women in town were slowly being set out. She exclaimed, rather limply, over everything from Madge Wireman's Three Bean Delight to Lelah McMulch's Tropical Surprise.

After that, she was informed that the reporter from the *Sacramento Bee* had returned, to do a follow-up article on the final day of the festival. She spoke to him, answering all of his questions with a determined smile and then turning him over to Jake, who would stick by him and see that he was entertained for the rest of the day.

By then it was one o'clock, and Burt Pandley was up on the grandstand stage, auctioning off pies and telling corny jokes and doing a great job of it. Several people remarked that Burt was "at least as good as that no-show professional." Melda, who happened to be within earshot, burst into tears and ran for the alder grove by the pond.

Andrea, standing by Juliet, whispered in her ear. "It would mean more if you talked to her than anyone."

So Juliet went after Melda, who cried on her shoulder and declared that she'd nearly ruined the festival twice. Juliet calmed her, swearing it wasn't so, reminding her of the rousing success of her play about Maria Elena and pointing out that everything had worked out fine in the end.

At last, Melda allowed herself to be soothed. Juliet led her back to where the crowd was, and Andrea immediately took over, handing Melda a paper plate and ordering her to get in line for lunch.

After that, things seemed to be under control. Juliet looked around for Cody, but he had disappeared. Later, she saw him throwing horseshoes with Evan McMulch and Burly Jones. She approached and asked him quietly if they might talk now.

Burly, who'd just thrown a ringer, shot her a warning glare. "Don't go bothering him, girl. This here game will be played right through."

Cody gave her a remote smile. "Sorry, Julie. Haven't got the time just yet."

It was that way for the rest of the day. Either Cody was in the middle of something, or he was nowhere to be found. Juliet grew more frustrated as the hours passed, but it did no good. He remained unavailable. At the corner of her consciousness, she began to admit that the way he avoided her could mean only one thing; it was ending between them, as she'd always known it would.

That evening, at home, as she got dressed for the final night of the revue, she longed to just put on her pajamas, climb in her lonely bed, pull the covers over her head and indulge in a week-long crying jag.

But that was impossible. She had responsibilities to fulfill.

Somewhat defiantly, she donned her reddest dress—a snug-fitting knit with a strapless top and a bolero jacket to match. She wore the red high heels that Cody had sneered about that night he'd driven her home when her car wouldn't start, before they'd become lovers—a lifetime ago.

At the auditorium, before the curtain went up, she gave a final pep talk to the cast. Cody stood in the back, watching, looking distant and withdrawn. Juliet tried not to look at him, because just the sight of him made her ache inside.

The revue went off beautifully. Yolanda was in especially good form. There wasn't a dry eye in the house when she uttered her final goodbyes as Maria Elena and then gave herself up to be hung.

As they always did, the members of the audience went wild with enthusiasm during Cody's first song. Juliet managed to stand in her place at the back and listen to that one. But when he strummed the first notes of the haunting ballad he sang in the second act, she felt the dangerous tightness in her throat and quickly slipped out into the lobby before she disgraced herself and burst into tears.

She reentered the auditorium just as the Gap High Madrigals were finishing their closing number. After that, there was a standing ovation and a never-ending curtain call. But at last, the curtain came down on the final performance of the Midsummer Madness Revue. Then Babe Allen got up and thanked everyone who'd had anything even remotely to do with the festival.

Finally Babe announced, "And there's one person, in particular, without whom this year's tremendous success would not have been possible. Let's get her up here to say a few words.... Juliet, come on up!"

Juliet, standing in the back, watched as people craned around to look for the indispensable person that Babe Allen was talking about: herself. It was a moment she'd always dreamed of—a major acknowledgment for a job well done. She should be ecstatic.

But instead, she felt exhausted and bleak. She needed sleep badly. Midsummer Madness was ending; it was over between her and Cody. She didn't want to get up and be gracious before all these people. She just wanted to go home.

Reva Reid, who stood next to her by the door, nudged her and murmured, "Juliet, go on...."

"Juliet," Babe urged with a wave of her arm. "Get on up here!"

Reva gave her a gentle shove. Juliet, moving automatically, started down the aisle for the stage. All around her were staring faces. Tottering a little on her high heels, she mounted the stage from the side, stepped up to the microphone and opened her mouth.

"Th-thank you," she managed to murmur. A few people clapped, a signal of support.

A brief speech took shape in her mind, and she gave it. "It's been challenging, exciting, rewarding and most of all, fun. I honestly wish it would never end. But everything does, I know. I'll just look forward to next year—when we can do it all again!''

And that was enough. The audience burst once more into a rousing round of applause.

Relief flooded through her, surprising her with its force. Deep in her heart, she had feared that she wouldn't be able to speak, that a scene from her worst nightmare would unfold before her. That somehow she would discover that she'd lost the ability she'd worked so hard to gain, the ability to get up in front of a crowd and make herself heard.

But that had not happened. And that was good to know.

Bowing once graciously, she turned and walked off into the wings just as someone raised the curtain again and all the performers came back onstage for a final closing-night bow. Juliet stood on the sidelines, clapping heartily for the others one more time.

At last it was truly over. Except for her final thank-you to the cast and crew, which she gave in the dressing room before everyone went home. Cody, as before, stood in the back while she spoke, his beautiful face cold and expressionless. Glancing his way once was enough. She got the message; the long-awaited talk between them would not be taking place that night. It was over, and that was that.

Juliet looked away from Cody and finished her final speech of the night. ''Thank you all, for everything. And please try out again next year.''

''Hold it there, Juliet.'' Flat-nosed Jake spoke up from near the doorway.

Juliet felt a slight lifting of her spirits at the sound of her friend's voice. She smiled. ''What is it, Jake?''

''I want everyone to come on out to my place. I'm throwing a closing-night party. And you all better be there.''

A fresh wave of excitement passed through the group. Most of them were too keyed up to go home and sleep, anyway. Jake began distributing maps to his big cabin out in the woods.

Juliet herself longed only to go home. But in the milling confusion as everyone got ready to leave, more than one person urged her to go to the party. And when Jake caught her arm and demanded her presence, she found she couldn't bring herself to refuse, though she was tired to the bone.

Jake, who usually saw to locking up, asked Juliet if she would take care of it tonight so he could go early and get ready for the party. Juliet agreed and thus found herself leaving the auditorium after everyone else had already gone.

She anticipated a long, lonely ride out there. But that wasn't exactly how it turned out. Because just as she pulled out of the auditorium's deserted parking lot, Cody's pickup fell in behind her.

Juliet's tiredness and frustration redoubled. He wouldn't talk to her, he walked away whenever she came near, but now he was going to shadow her all the way out to Jake's. What was the matter with him? Had he no heart at all?

It would serve him right if she slammed on the brakes, jumped out of her car and marched back there to demand to know what he was up to. But she wouldn't. He'd only say she didn't own the highway, and then where would she be?

No, better to ignore him.

Juliet defiantly slipped a tape into the deck and cranked up the car stereo. She sang along so loudly that her throat was burning by the time she turned off the main road and onto the twisting, two-lane highway that eventually would take her to Jake's place.

She drove deeper into the woods, where the tall trees grew close to the highway, so dense in some places that the night sky could not be seen. Cody's headlights, behind her, were the only proof she was not totally alone. The thought that he was the only one besides herself for miles brought on a fresh onslaught of misery. He was right behind her—yet they might as well be on different planets, with the distance that lay between them now.

She cranked up the stereo another notch and continued to shout along.

Whenever she came to a fork in the road, she'd shift down to be ready in case it was a place the map said to turn. And every time she did that, Cody's black pickup would loom up very close behind her. Once, he even honked at her, impatiently, to let her know she was driving erratically. But what else could she do? The small, wooden signposts were hard to read through the blur of her tears.

She was about two-thirds of the way there and looking for the next turnoff, when she saw one coming up and shifted down. But it wasn't the turn shown on the map after all. She shifted back up to a higher gear, pressing the accelerator, getting up to speed once again.

Right at that moment, something awful happened to her car, something she could hear even over the blaring of her stereo. The noise under the hood went mad, as if someone had taken a crowbar and decided to beat the engine to death with it. There was a lot of crunching. Then a huge, cataclysmic clunk.

Her car stopped dead in the middle of the road. Cody, behind her, skidded to keep from hitting her, pulled to the left, and ended up on the shoulder.

In the silence after both vehicles had stopped, Juliet's car stereo continued to bray, playing that song about a woman with legs who knew how to use them. After a few moments of that, Juliet reached out and silenced it.

And then, suffused suddenly with the kind of dead calm that occurs at the eye of a storm, she leaned on her steering wheel and stared through the windshield at the crouching, close-growing trees that loomed above her.

"Put it in neutral." It was Cody's voice, coming in her side window.

Juliet slowly turned from her close study of the crouching trees to look at him. She was hoping, in a distant sort of way, that he might have grown ugly or something, that her heart wouldn't start its rapid, anticipatory pounding at the sight of him.

But her hopes were dashed. He was more beautiful than ever, and her silly heart was jumping around in her chest just like it always did lately.

"Did you hear what I said?" he demanded.

"No. No, I guess not."

"Damn it, Julie." He spoke gruffly. "We have to get this car out of the middle of the road. It's not safe."

"Oh." That made sense. "Yes. Of course."

"Shift into neutral and steer. I'll push."

She nodded. "Certainly. I will." She shifted, and then gave him a numb smile.

"Fine," he said, looking put out. "Now steer."

He got behind the car and pushed, while she steered the car to the side of the road in front of his pickup. Then she conscientiously set the parking brake.

"Flip the hood latch," he told her then.

She did as he instructed. He opened the hood and poked around in there with a flashlight he must have brought from his pickup. Finally, leaving the hood up, he came back to her side of the car.

"Well?" she asked.

"It's bad," he told her.

"How bad?"

"You've thrown a rod. Basically, your engine's blown."

"My engine?"

"Yeah. The truth is it'll probably cost you more to fix this piece of junk than the thing is worth now."

Something gave inside of Juliet then. Her spirit seemed to break. It was only a car—she knew that. But in a way, it also represented all the changes she'd made in her life. All the changes that had, one by one, gone sour.

Midsummer Madness was truly over. Real life loomed. She and Cody were through. She'd probably have to move out of the guest-house soon, say goodbye to Black Bart and Lucky and Kemo. And she'd have to buy a new car, a dependable car. Something brown, with four doors.

Cody was standing right beside her, so she couldn't get out. And she wanted to get out. She said very politely, "Excuse me, Cody."

He looked at her a little strangely, but he did step back. She got out of the car and closed the door behind her. "Thank you," she said to him, "for, um, pushing the car to the side, and for looking under the hood, and everything."

"Julie?" He was really giving her a deep look now. "Julie, are you all right?"

"Fine. Just fine. I just want to get started back, that's all."

"Back where?"

"Home. To town." He kept looking at her as if she wasn't making sense. And maybe she wasn't. What did it matter? She didn't have to make sense to him; they were through. She waved a hand in front of her face. "I'm going back, that's all," she told him. "Just back." She pointed down the dark road in the direction they had come. "That way."

She turned then, with great dignity, and began walking down the highway, into the dark heart of the night.

CHAPTER ELEVEN

CODY STARED after her as she walked away. Her slim back was very straight, her head high. She walked a little stiffly on those high-heeled shoes.

"Julie!" he called after a moment, as the total absurdity of what she was doing sank in. Was she planning to walk the fifteen miles to town in pitch darkness? That would be insane. "Julie, stop!"

She didn't even pause. She kept on walking. Soon she'd turn the bend and the darkness would swallow her; she'd be lost to his sight.

"Julie!"

She turned the bend.

Cody stood there, staring after her, watching the place where her scarlet dress had vanished—and understood how completely his plot to give her a taste of her own medicine had backfired. He felt a healthy surge of shame.

Hell, he realized, he didn't know a damn thing about working out problems with a woman. He'd never had to work when it came to women. They chased him, and he said yes to the ones he wanted. And if a woman left him, he always knew another would be along soon enough.

But there would never be another Julie—he knew that. He was desperate not to lose her, yet right now she was walking into the night, away from him.

Something was really bothering her. And instead of keeping after her to find out exactly what, he'd thrown up his hands and walked out on her, decided without asking her that she must be dumping him—and then tormented her all day.

Even in the darkness, he'd noticed that her eyes were red-rimmed from crying. Right now, she was probably thinking he could care less about her—when nothing could be further from the truth.

They had to talk, damn it. Now, tonight, as she'd always promised they would. But first he had to catch up with her.

"Julie!" he shouted out loud.

And then he took off at a run for the turn where she'd vanished.

Juliet heard him coming. He was pretty hard to tune out.

And the knowledge that he was coming after her pushed back the numbness a little. That was bad, because when the numbness went away, the tears returned. She could feel them, closing off her throat, blurring her sight—which was pretty minimal anyway, in the pitch darkness along the road.

"Julie, wait! Please, Julie...."

He was catching up to her. His voice was closer now. The tears spilled down her cheeks. She hated her own tears and didn't want him to see her cry.

Irrational now, frantic to get away, to salvage some scrap of pride at least, she began to run. It was a stilted, hobbled flight because of her impractical high heels.

"Julie, wait!"

She turned, saw him, a shadow looming ever nearer. She veered off the road and into the dense growth of the trees.

"Julie, stop!"

She tried to run faster, stumbling and tripping, feeling her way around the looming shapes of the trees.

But it was no use. He was right behind her, calling for her. She sobbed and stumbled on a rock, lifted her other foot to catch herself, and it caught on an exposed root. She pitched forward with a little scream, and felt her ankle turn, heard a gruesome cracking sound as something happened to the bone.

Pain sliced up her leg, like a knife slashing from the inside. She landed on the hard ground, moaning, and somehow managed to reach out and free her foot, though she nearly passed out from the pain when she did so.

There was, she realized dimly through the pain, a tree trunk behind her; she'd landed against it. She dropped her head back on the rough bark, her eyes pressed shut in agony, her breath coming in quick, frantic pants.

"Julie?"

She peered up, through the darkness, to see his dim face.

He dropped to his knees before her. "What is it? Your leg?" He reached for her injured ankle.

She let out a scream that was barely human. He jerked back.

And she shouted at him, as she'd never in her life shouted at anyone, "Get away from me! Leave me alone. You've already broken my heart. Isn't that enough?"

After that, there was silence, except for the labored sounds of her breathing and his. He remained, a shadowed shape, kneeling there not three feet away.

As the moments stretched out and the throbbing in her ankle became a mean, insistent agony, Juliet found she was perversely grateful for the pain. It more or less absorbed all her energy, took her mind off everything else.

Cody said softly, "Can you walk on it?"

"No." She bit her lip. "I'm pretty sure it's broken."

"I'll carry you, then."

He moved—slowly, like a man afraid of spooking a skittish animal—to her side. Then he slipped an arm behind her and one beneath her knees. She let out a low groan when he stood up.

"Easy, sweetheart," he crooned.

Juliet twined her arms around his neck and buried her head against his chest, soothed in an elemental way by the solid strength of him. He carried her back to the road and from there to his truck.

At Gap Memorial, her ankle was x-rayed and set. Cody, who hovered so close that the doctor had to ask him more than once to step back, was finally instructed to wait in the lounge. He went unwillingly, reminding a pale but staunch Juliet that he was there if she needed him.

It occurred to him, as he sat on an olive-green plastic couch across from a wild-eyed fellow who jumped every time the swinging doors to the main part of the hospital moved, that the cast and crew of the revue might become worried if he and Julie didn't show up. So Cody placed a call to Jake and told him that Juliet had tripped and broken her ankle.

After that, he sat and waited. And he thought about what she'd yelled at him out there in the woods.

You've already broken my heart. That was what she'd said. But how could he do that...unless she loved him?

Did Julie love him?

At the thought, Cody shot up from the plastic couch causing the wild-eyed man to jerk upright and let loose a frightened, wordless shout.

"Sorry," Cody murmured.

"It's okay," the man growled, and then subsided in his chair.

Cody paced back and forth on the linoleum floor. My God, he thought. Did Julie love him? And if she did, why all the suffering and moping around over the past few days?

Unless she thought he didn't love her....

Could that be it? Did Julie think he didn't love her?

Hell, come to think of it, *did* he love Julie? Was that what it was, what *she* was to him? The woman he loved?

The idea was novel to Cody. He just hadn't thought about *love* before.

He felt like she was part of him. He couldn't picture waking up in the morning without her beside him. He wanted to do what he could to help her lead a happy life—with him in it.

Was that love?

He stopped in midstride in his pacing, right in front of the wild-eyed man, who looked up at him warily. "You all right, buddy?" the man asked.

"Yeah." Cody looked down at him. The poor guy was a wreck, eyes bloodshot, hair standing on end. "What happened to you?"

"My wife's in there. Having our first. I passed out. They said I couldn't stay."

"Tough break," Cody sympathized. Since the man was there and looking at him, he then asked, "You know what love is?"

The man swallowed. "You don't ask the easy ones, do you?"

Just then a nurse poked her head in through the swinging doors to the functional side of the small hospital. "Mr. Hickleby?"

The expectant father jumped out of his chair. "Yeah? What? Is she okay?"

"Your wife is fine. You have a healthy baby girl. Follow me, please...."

"Oh my God, a girl. I have a girl." The man grabbed Cody's hand and pumped it heartily. He beamed. "Evelyn is fine."

"Great," Cody said. "Congratulations."

"Yeah, thanks. Gotta go." Wearing a dazed ear-to-ear grin, Mr. Hickleby followed the nurse through the doors.

And Cody sat and waited for Juliet and wondered about the meaning of love.

Eventually they rolled her out in a wheelchair. Her injured leg was stuck out in front of her, covered with a cast from midcalf to her toes.

She looked pale, but peaceful.

"Julie!"

She smiled up at him benignly. "Oh, Cody. There you are." She shifted her glance back over her head, to the orderly who was wheeling her. "It's Cody," she explained. "Cody always saves me. Forever and ever. Whenever I get in trouble. He's my hero, ever since we were kids."

Cody realized they must have given Julie something for the pain—something that had improved her attitude immensely. She blithely signed the papers the admissions clerk presented on a clipboard, and then Cody led the way to his pickup, with the orderly pushing Julie behind him.

He lifted her inside himself, signed for the rental of a wheelchair and crutches and then saw to the stowing of them in the bed behind the cab.

All the way to the ranch, Cody planned what he would say when they got to his place. He wanted to talk about this thing called love. He wanted to tell her all she meant to him, make her understand that without her there was a big hole in his life—a hole he hadn't known was there until she filled it.

Juliet, smiling blissfully, stared out the window and sang that song that had been playing on her tape deck when her car broke down—the one about the woman who had legs and knew how to use them.

When they reached the gate to his house, he swung in, tensing as he realized that she might insist he take her to her place. But he forgot all about how he'd deal with it if she refused to talk to him, because the wide, long driveway was packed with cars.

Julie stopped singing long enough to remark, "Hmm. Company."

All the downstairs lights were on. Kemo wasn't on the porch where he was supposed to be, ready to ward off intruders.

Swearing under his breath, Cody managed to ease the pickup around the other cars. By the garage, he turned it around and then stopped alongside the front of the porch facing the gate, so her door was nearest the house.

The door opened, and Bud Southey came out on the porch.

"What the hell is this?" Cody remarked.

Juliet went on humming her song.

Cody went around to her side, scooped her up against his chest and carried her up the steps. When he reached Bud, the caretaker started explaining, "I didn't know what else to do, Mr. McIntyre. The dog woke me from a sound sleep and when I went out to see what was going on, they were all sitting in their cars, afraid to come out with the dog growling at them and all. I got Miss Oakleaf to roll down her window and she explained about Miss Huddleston. I figured you would probably want me to let them in, because they said they'd wait on the porch otherwise."

"Great," Cody muttered trenchantly, still cradling a humming Juliet against his chest. He reached the door and kicked it back.

He stepped over the threshold. There, in the living room, sat his dog, happily panting, surrounded by most of the cast and crew of the Midsummer Madness Revue, not to mention all of Juliet's committee heads.

Andrea Oakleaf sprang forward, clucking, giving orders right and left. "Well, here she is. Don't just stand there...Cody, did you bring a chair for her?"

"Uh, in the pickup."

Andrea glanced at Jake, who was up and out the door in seconds flat. He brought it right in and opened it up. Cody lowered Juliet into it.

"We won't stay long," Babe Allen promised.

Melda added, "We just wanted to see that she was okay...."

"Why, she's been drugged," Andrea declared.

Juliet held up two fingers, smiling. "Two little white pills. I feel just fine."

Cody stood back as they surrounded her. Jake produced a present, one that he explained she was to have received at the party, had she managed to make it there. She peeled back the bright paper and opened the box, then brought out a china figurine of a small boy holding a lamb. Even Cody, who wasn't much on figurines, thought it charming.

She held it up, her eyes alight with more than the effect of her two little white pills. "Cody, look. My favorite Hummel. The shepherd boy and the lamb."

He smiled and nodded, as Babe explained that they'd kept it back at the raffle when Juliet said she liked it best. Juliet thanked them all. And then Andrea produced one more gift—a brass plaque inscribed To Our Fearless Leader. Babe explained that it was to commemorate Juliet's first—of many—years of directorship of the Midsummer Madness Festival.

Juliet kissed it, proclaimed it wonderful and reached out to everyone for a hug and a peck on the cheek. Cody remained on the sidelines, watching, remembering a shy mouse who had asked him a month ago if she could run Midsummer Madness this year.

At last, everyone admitted it was time to go. Cody saw them to the door, listening patiently to Andrea's admonitions that he take proper care of Juliet, see that she got plenty of rest and nourishing food.

"I promise," he said. "Good night." He shut the door.

Relieved, he turned back to the living room. The moment had

finally come when he and Julie were alone. All the things he planned to say chased each other through his head. He wanted to say this just right, he wanted to make it clear to her how it was for him, what they might have together, all they might share.

"Julie..." he began. And then said no more. She was asleep in her chair against the far wall near the fireplace.

Cody sighed. Then he propped a pillow behind her head and draped a light blanket over her lap. After that, he stretched out on the longest end of the sectional sofa to be there when she woke.

"Cody?"

Her soft voice reached him through his dreams. "Um? Yeah? What?"

"Cody..."

He opened an eye. Around the edges of the closed shutters, dawn light shone. He groaned a little, from sleeping in a cramped position on the too-short sofa. And then he pulled himself to a sitting position and raked his hair back with his hands.

He remembered. Julie. She'd been hurt. If it was morning, that meant her medication had probably worn off. He peered across the room, where she sat in the wheelchair, awake now, looking at him.

He jumped up. "They gave me your pills. I left them in the glove box. Are you hurting? I'll get you a couple."

"No." She stretched out a hand. "Wait."

"But, Julie—"

"Please. Come here."

He went to her, took the offered hand. It was slim and smooth in his. He wanted to hold it forever.

Close up, he could see the strain in her face. "You're hurting," he said. "Let me—"

She held tighter to his hand as he tried to leave her side, pulling him back. "No. In a few minutes. First, I want to talk. Now. While my head's clear."

"We can talk later."

She gave a low chuckle. "Later's finally here, Cody. It doesn't hurt that much. And I want to talk more than I want to wipe out the pain.''

''All right,'' he said, and dropped into a chair beside her, one close enough that he could keep hold of her hand. ''Can I talk first?''

She looked at him levelly, her expression somewhat grim. ''Okay. If you want.'' He was reasonably sure then that she more or less expected bad news.

He began. ''I love you, and I want to marry you. Will you? Marry me, I mean?''

Her mouth dropped open. She swallowed. ''What?''

He repeated himself. This time, he thought, with more feeling. ''I love you, Julie. Please marry me.''

''You...you want to marry me?''

He grinned. ''You bet.''

''But I thought—'' she sputtered.

''You should have *asked*,'' he advised.

She confessed, ''I was afraid....''

He understood. ''I know the feeling.''

''Oh, Cody....'' She reached out her other hand.

He stood and scooped her up and sat back down with her across his lap. His lips found hers. The kiss went on and on and Cody began to think about how they both had too many clothes on.

Then he remembered that her ankle was broken and giving her pain. Reluctantly, he ended the kiss. ''Now I'll get those pills.''

She clutched his shoulders. ''Wait. In a minute. There's something I want to say. I want you to understand, I want to tell you...how it's been for me.''

He sat still. ''Okay. Go ahead.''

She fiddled with a button on his shirt. ''I love you, too.''

''Good.''

''And I've known it since the first night, when we made love. But I couldn't bring myself to tell you because I was sure I was going to lose you to another woman someday, someone like the redhead at the ball, someone more beautiful, more sophisticated— more *everything* than me. I guess that's why I pushed you into her arms for the last dance. Some confused part of me reasoned that since I was going to lose you anyway, I might as well get it over with.''

He tried to speak. She put a finger on his lips. "Shh. Let me finish. I've spent thirty years of my life feeling like the invisible woman, Cody. It always seemed to me that other people—including men—never even knew I was there. And now I've made some changes, and people are taking notice. But I suppose a part of me is still expecting to wake up in the morning and have everybody—including you—looking right through me again.''

He laughed at the impossibility of that and kissed the top of her head. She burrowed in close to his heart. "But I realized last night,'' she said against his chest, "that my fears were only in my head. I couldn't help but see it, the way everyone turned up here, just to be sure that I was all right. I was so grateful, Cody. And a little ashamed that I'd had so little faith in myself and in them.'' She added softly, "And in you, too.''

"I did act like a jerk,'' he confessed.

She chuckled. "You, who've always made it a point *not* to act like a jerk.''

"Love caught me unprepared. But I'll do better. Give me forty or fifty years—the next forty or fifty years. Okay?''

She kissed him. "Could we just make it an even lifetime and leave it at that?''

"Agreed,'' he said gruffly. Then he took her by the shoulders and held her away enough that she had to look at him. "And now I have something I want *you* to understand.''

She looked a little apprehensive. "What?''

He said with great care, "I'm not looking through you, sweetheart. And I'm not looking at any other woman, either. I am now blind to every woman but you. I knew that the first night I kissed you, out there on the porch. But I was too stunned by what you did to me to get the words out then. I'll never look through you again, Juliet Huddleston. You're all the woman I ever wanted to see. Call it love, call it whatever you want. But as far as I'm concerned, there isn't and never will be any other woman for me.''

Her eyes looked very soft. "It's true? You really mean that?"

"I do. With all my heart."

She sighed and snuggled close to him, oblivious to the throbbing in her ankle, to her rumbling stomach that wanted breakfast soon, to everything but the feel of Cody's arms around her.

"Oh, Cody." She sighed. "It's like a dream. Me and you."

He chuckled. "More than a fantasy, you mean?"

"Absolutely. It's a dream to last a lifetime. And we've made it real." She lifted her mouth for another lingering kiss.

Out by the barn, Black Bart crowed. Kemo, on the floor, thumped his tail and yawned. Midsummer Madness was over for another year. But for Juliet and Cody, a lifetime of happiness had only begun.

TEMPESTUOUS REUNION
Lynne Graham

CHAPTER ONE

'MARRY you?' Luc echoed, his brilliant dark gaze rampant with incredulity as he abruptly cast aside the financial report he had been studying. 'Why would I want to marry you?'

Catherine's slender hand was shaking. Hurriedly she set down her coffee-cup, her courage sinking fast. 'I just wondered if you had ever thought of it.' Her restless fingers made a minute adjustment to the siting of the sugar bowl. She was afraid to meet his eyes. 'It was just an idea.'

'Whose idea?' he prompted softly. 'You are perfectly content as you are.'

She didn't want to think about what Luc had made of her. But certainly contentment had rarely featured in her responses. From the beginning she had loved him wildly, recklessly, and with that edge of desperation which prevented her from ever standing as his equal.

Over the past two years, she had swung between ecstasy and despair more times than he would ever have believed. Or cared to believe. This beautiful, luxurious apartment was her prison. Not his. She was a pretty songbird in a gilded cage for Luc's exclusive enjoyment. But it wasn't bars that kept her imprisoned, it was love.

She stole a nervous glance at him. His light intonation had been deceptive. Luc was silently seething. But not at her. His ire was directed at some imaginary scapegoat, who had dared to contaminate her with ideas, quite embarrassing ideas above her station.

'Catherine,' he pressed impatiently.

Under the table the fingernails of her other hand grooved sharp crescents into her damp palm. Skating on thin ice wasn't a habit of hers with Luc. 'It was my own idea and...I'd appreciate an answer,' she dared in an ironic lie, for she didn't really want that answer; she didn't want to hear it.

Had the Santini electronics empire crashed overnight, Luc could not have looked more grim than he did now, pierced by a thorn from a normally very well-trained source. 'You have neither the background nor the education that I would require in my wife. There, it is said,' he delivered with the decisive speed and the ruthlessness which had made his name as much feared as respected in the business world. 'Now you need wonder no longer.'

Every scrap of colour slowly drained from her cheeks. She recoiled from the brutal candour she had invited, ashamed to discover that she had, after all, nurtured a tiny, fragile hope that deep down inside he might feel differently. Her soft blue eyes flinched from his, her head bowing. 'No, I won't need to wonder,' she managed half under her breath.

Having devastated her, he relented infinitesimally. 'This isn't what I would term breakfast conversation,' he murmured with a teasing harshness that she easily translated into a rebuke for her presumption in daring to raise the subject. 'Why should you aspire to a relationship within which you would not be at ease…hmm? As a lover, I imagine, I am far less demanding than I would be as a husband.'

In the midst of what she deemed to be the most agonising dénouement of her life, an hysterical giggle feathered dangerously in her convulsed throat. A blunt, sun-browned finger languorously played over the knuckles showing white beneath the skin of her clenched hand. Even though she was conscious that Luc was using his customary methods of distraction, the electricity of a powerful sexual chemistry tautened her every sinew and the fleeting desire to laugh away the ashes of painful disillusionment vanished.

With a faint sigh, he shrugged back a pristine silk shirt cuff to consult the rapier-thin Cartier watch on his wrist and frowned.

'You'll be late for your meeting.' She said it for him as she stood up, for the very first time fiercely glad to see the approach of the departure which usually tore her apart.

Luc rose fluidly upright to regard her narrowly. 'You're jumpy this morning. Is there something wrong?'

The other matter, she registered in disbelief, was already forgotten, written off as some impulsive and foolishly feminine piece of nonsense. It wouldn't occur to Luc that she had deliberately saved that question until he was about to leave. She hadn't wanted to spoil the last few hours they would ever spend together.

'No...what could be wrong?' Turning aside, she reddened. But he had taught her the art of lies and evasions, could only blame himself when he realised what a monster he had created.

'I don't believe that. You didn't sleep last night.'

She froze into shocked stillness. He strolled back across the room to link confident arms round her small, slim figure, easing her round to face him. 'Perhaps it is your security that you are concerned about.'

The hard bones and musculature of the lean, superbly fit body against hers melted her with a languor she couldn't fight. And, arrogantly acquainted with that shivery weakness, Luc was satisfied and soothed. A long finger traced the tremulous fullness of her lower lip. 'Some day our paths will separate,' he forecast in a roughened undertone. 'But that day is still far from my mind.'

Dear God, did he know what he did to her when he said things like that? If he did, why should he care? In probably much the same fashion he cracked the whip over key executives to keep them on their toes. He was murmuring something smooth about stocks and shares that she refused to listen to. You can't buy love, Luc. You can't pay for it either. When are you going to find that out?

While his hunger for her remained undiminished, she understood that she was safe. She took no compliment from the desire she had once naïvely believed was based on emotion. For the several days a month which Luc allotted cool-headedly to the pursuit of light entertainment, she had every attention. But that Luc had not even guessed that the past weeks had been unadulterated hell for her proved the shallowness of the bond on his side. She had emerged from the soap-bubble fantasy she had started building against reality two years ago. He didn't love her. He hadn't suddenly woken up one day to realise that he couldn't live without her…and he never would.

'You'll be late,' she whispered tautly, disconcerted by the glitter of gold now burnishing the night-dark scrutiny skimming her up-turned face. When Luc decided to leave, he didn't usually linger.

The supple fingers resting against her spine pressed her closer, his other hand lifting to wind with cool possessiveness into the curling golden hair tumbling down her back. *'Bella mia,'* he rhymed in husky Italian, bending his dark head to taste her moistly parted lips with the inherent sensuality and the tormenting expertise which all along had proved her downfall.

Stabbed by her guilty conscience, she dragged herself fearfully free before he could taste the strange, unresponsive chill that was spreading through her. 'I'm not feeling well,' she muttered in jerky excuse, terrified that she was giving herself away.

'Why didn't you tell me that sooner? You ought to lie down.' He swept her up easily in his arms, started to kiss her again, and then, with an almost imperceptible darkening of colour, abstained long enough to carry her into the bedroom and settle her down on the tossed bed.

He hovered, betraying a rare discomfiture. Scrutinising her wan cheeks and the pared-down fragility of her bone-structure, he expelled his breath in a sudden sound of derision. 'If this is another result of one of those asinine diets of yours, I'm likely to lose my temper. When are you going to get it through your head that I like you as you are? Do you want to make yourself ill? I don't have any patience with this foolishness, Catherine.'

'No,' she agreed, beyond seeing any humour in his misapprehension.

'See your doctor today,' he instructed. 'And if you don't, I'll know about it. I'll mention it to Stevens on my way out.'

At the reference to the security guard, supposedly there for her protection but more often than not, she suspected, there to police her every move, she curved her cheek into the pillow. She didn't like Stevens. His deadpan detachment and extreme formality intimidated her.

'How are you getting on with him, by the way?'

'I understood that I wasn't supposed to get on with your security men. Isn't that why you transferred Sam Halston?' she muttered, grateful for the change of subject, no matter how incendiary it might be.

'He was too busy flirting with you to be effective,' Luc parried with icy emphasis.

'That's not true. He was only being friendly,' she protested.

'He wasn't hired to be friendly. If you'd treated him like an employee he'd still be here,' Luc underlined with honeyed dismissal. 'And now I really have to leave. I'll call you from Milan.'

He made it sound as if he were dispensing a very special favour. In fact, he called her every day no matter where he was in the world. And now he was gone.

When that phone did ring tomorrow, it would ring and ring through empty rooms. For tortured minutes she just lay and stared at the space where he had been. Dark and dynamic, he was hell on wheels for a vulnerable woman. In their entire association she had never had an argument with Luc. By fair means or foul, Luc always got his own way. Her feeble attempts to assert herself had long since sunk without trace against the tide of an infinitely more forceful personality.

He was now reputedly one of the top ten richest men in the world. At twenty-nine that was a wildly impressive achievement. He had started out with nothing but formidable intelligence in the streets of New York's Little Italy. And he would keep on climbing. Luc was always number one and never more so than in his own self-image. Power was the greatest aphrodisiac known to humanity. What Luc wanted he reached out and took, and to hell with the damage he caused as long as the backlash did not affect his comfort. And, having fought for everything he had ever got, what came easy had no intrinsic value for him.

'The lone wolf,' *Time* magazine had dubbed him in a recent

article, endeavouring to penetrate the mystique of a rogue among the more conventional herd of the hugely successful.

A shark was a killing machine, superbly efficient within its own restricted field. And wolves mated for life, not for leisure-time amusement. But Luc was indeed a land-based animal and far from cold-blooded. As such he was all the more dangerous to the unwary, the innocent and the over-confident.

Technical brilliance alone hadn't built his empire. It was the energy source of one man's drive combined with a volatile degree of unpredictability which kept competitors at bay in a cut-throat market. She could have told that journalist exactly what Luc Santini was like. And that was hard, cruelly hard with the cynicism, the self-interest and the ruthless ambition that was bred into his very bones. Only a fool got in Luc's path...only a very foolish woman could have given her heart into his keeping.

Her eyes squeezed shut on a shuddering spasm of anguish. It was over now. She would never see Luc again. No miracle had astounded her at the eleventh hour. Marriage was not, nor would it ever be, a possibility. Her small hand spread protectively over her no longer concave stomach. Luc had begun to lose her one hundred per cent loyalty and devotion from the very hour she suspected that she was carrying his child.

Instinct had warned her that the news would be greeted as a calculated betrayal and, no doubt, the conviction that she had somehow achieved the condition all on her own. Again and again she had put off telling him. In fear of discovery, she had learnt to be afraid of Luc. When he married a bride with a social pedigree, a bride bred to the lofty heights that were already his, he wouldn't want any skeletons in the cupboard. Ice-cold and sick with apprehensions that she had refused to face head on, she wiped clumsily at her swollen eyes and got up.

He would never know now and that was how it had to be. Thank God, she had persuaded Sam to show her how to work the alarm system. She would leave by the rear entrance. That would take care of Stevens. Would Luc miss her? A choked sob of pain escaped her. He would be outraged that she could leave him and he had not foreseen the event. But he wouldn't have any trouble replacing her. She was not so special and she wasn't beautiful. She never had grasped what it was about her which had drawn Luc. Unless it was the cold intuition of a predator scenting good doormat material downwind, she conceded shamefacedly.

How could she be sorry to leave this half-life behind? She had no friends. When discretion was demanded, friends were impossible. Luc had slowly but surely isolated her so that her entire existence revolved round him. Sometimes she was so lonely that she talked out loud to herself. Love was a fearsome emotion, she thought with a convulsive shudder. At eighteen she had been green as grass. Two years on, she didn't feel she was much brighter but she didn't build castles in the air any more.

'*Arrivederci*, Luc, *grazie tanto*,' she scrawled in lipstick across the mirror. A theatrical gesture, the ubiquitous note. He could do without the ego boost of five tear-stained pages telling him pointlessly that nobody was ever likely to love him as much as she did.

Luc, she had learnt by destructive degrees, didn't rate love any too highly. But he had not been above using her love as a weapon against her, twisting her emotions with cruel expertise until they had become the bars of her prison cell.

'What are you doing with my books?'

Catherine straightened from the cardboard box and clashed with stormy dark eyes. 'I'm packing them. Do you want to help?' she prompted hopefully. 'We could talk.'

Daniel kicked at a chair leg, his small body stiff and defensive. 'I don't want to talk about moving.'

'Ignoring it isn't going to stop it happening,' Catherine warned.

Daniel kicked moodily at the chair leg again, hands stuck in his pockets, miniature-tough style. Slowly Catherine counted to ten. Much more of this and she would scream until the little men in the white coats came to take her away. How much longer was her son going to treat her as the wickedest and worst mother in the world? With a determined smile, she said, 'Things aren't half as bad as you seem to think they are.'

Daniel looked at her dubiously. 'Have we got any money?'

Taken aback by the demand, Catherine coloured and shifted uncomfortably. 'What's that got to do with anything?'

'I heard John's mum telling Mrs Withers that we had no money 'cos if we had we would've bought this house and stayed here.'

Catherine could happily have strangled the woman for speaking so freely in Daniel's presence. He might be only four but he was precociously bright for his age. Daniel already understood far too much of what went on around him.

'It's not fair that someone can take our house off us and sell it to someone else when we want to live here forever!' he burst out without warning.

The pain she glimpsed in his over-bright eyes tore cruelly at her. Unfortunately there was little that she could do to assuage that pain. 'Greyfriars has never been ours,' she reminded him tautly. 'You know that, Daniel. It belonged to Harriet, and on her death she gave it to charity. Now the people who run that charity want to sell and use the money to—'

Daniel threw her a sudden seething glance. 'I don't care about those people starving in Africa! This is our house! Where are we going to live?'

'Drew has found us a flat in London,' she told him yet again.

'You can't keep a donkey in London!' Daniel launched at her fierily. 'Why can't we live with Peggy? She said we could.'

Catherine sighed. 'Peggy really doesn't have enough room for us.'

'I'll run away and you can live in London all on your own because I'm not going without Clover!' Daniel shouted at her in a tempestuous surge of fury and distress. 'It's all your fault. If I'd had a daddy, he could've bought us this house like everybody else's daddy does! I bet he could even have made Harriet well again... I hate you 'cos you can't do anything!'

With that bitter condemnation, Daniel hurtled out of the back door. He would take refuge in one of his hiding places in the garden. There he would sit, brooding and struggling to cope with harsh adult realities that entailed the loss of all he held dear. She touched the solicitor's letter on the table. She would be even more popular when he realised that their holiday on Peggy's family farm was no longer possible either.

Sometimes—such as now—Catherine had this engulfing sense of total inadequacy in Daniel's radius. Daniel was not quite like other children. At two he had taken apart a radio and put it back together again, repairing it in the process. At three he had taught himself German by listening to a language programme on television. But he was still too young to accept necessary sacrifices. Harriet's death had hit him hard, and now he was losing his home, a much-loved pet donkey, the friends he played with…in short, all the remaining security that had bounded his life to date. Was it any wonder that he was frightened? How could she reassure him when she too was afraid of the future?

The conviction that catastrophe was only waiting to pounce round the next blind corner had never really left Catherine. Harriet's sudden death had fulfilled her worst imaginings. With one savage blow, the tranquil and happy security of their lives had been shattered. And right now it felt as though she'd been cruelly catapulted back to where she had started out over four years ago…

Her life had been in a mess, heading downhill at a seemingly breakneck pace. She had had the promising future of a kamikaze pilot. And then Harriet had come along. Harriet, so undervalued by those who knew her best. Harriet…in his exasperation, Drew had once called her a 'charming mental deficient'. Yet Harriet had picked Catherine up, dusted her down and set her back on the rails again. In the process, Harriet had also become the closest thing to a mother that Catherine had ever known.

They had met on a train. That journey and that meeting had forever altered Catherine's future. While they had shared the same compartment, Harriet had tried repeatedly to strike up a conversation. When you were locked up tight and terrified of breaking down in public, you didn't want to talk. But Harriet's persistence had forced her out of her self-absorption, and before very long her over-taxed emotions had betrayed her and somehow she had ended up telling Harriet her life-story.

Afterwards she had been embarrassed, frankly eager to escape the older woman's company. They had left the train at the same station. Nothing poor Harriet had said about her 'having made the right decision' had penetrated. Like an addict, sick for a long-overdue fix, Catherine had been unbelievably desperate just to hear the sound of a man's voice on the phone. Throwing Harriet a guilty goodbye, she had raced off towards the phone-box she could see across the busy car park.

What would have happened had she made that call? That call that would have been a crowning and unforgivable mistake in a relationship which had been a disaster from start to finish?

She would never know now. In her mad haste to reach that phone, she had run in front of a car. It had taken total physical incapacitation to finally bring her to her senses. She had spent the following three months recovering from her injuries in hospital. Days had passed before she had been strong enough to recognise the soothing voice that drifted in and out of her haze of pain and disorientation. It had belonged to Harriet. Knowing that she had no family, Harriet had sat by her in Intensive Care, talking back the dark for her. If Harriet hadn't been there, Catherine didn't believe she would ever have emerged from the dark again.

Even before his premature birth, Daniel had had to fight for survival. Coming into the world, he had screeched for attention, tiny and weak but indomitably strong-willed. From his incubator he had charmed the entire medical staff by surmounting every set-back within record time. Catherine had begun to appreciate then that, with the genes her son carried to such an unmistakably marked degree, a ten-ton truck couldn't have deprived him of existence, never mind his careless mother's collision with a mere car.

'He's a splendid little fighter,' Harriet had proclaimed proudly, relishing the role of surrogate granny as only an intensely lonely woman could. Drew had been sincerely fond of his older sister but her eccentricities had infuriated him, and his sophisticated French wife, Annette, and their teenage children had had no time for Harriet at all. Greyfriars was situated on the outskirts of an

Oxfordshire village, a dilapidated old house, surrounded by untamed acres of wilderness garden. Harriet and Drew had been born here and Harriet had vociferously withstood her brother's every attempt to refurbish the house for her. Surroundings had been supremely unimportant to Harriet. Lame ducks had been Harriet's speciality.

Catherine's shadowed gaze roamed over the homely kitchen. She had made the gingham curtains fluttering at the window, painted the battered cupboards a cheerful fire-engine red sold off cheap at the church fête. This was their home. In every sense of the word. How could she persuade Daniel that he would be as happy in a tiny city flat when she didn't believe it herself? But, dear God, that flat was their one and only option.

A light knock sounded on the back door. Without awaiting an answer, her friend Peggy Downes breezed in. A tall woman in her thirties with geometrically cut red hair, she dropped down on to the sagging settee by the range with the ease of a regular visitor. She stared in surprise at the cardboard box. 'Aren't you being a little premature with your packing? You've still got a fortnight to go.'

'We haven't.' Catherine passed over the solicitor's letter. 'It's just as well that Drew said we could use his apartment if we were stuck. We can't stay here until the end of the month and the flat won't be vacant before then.'

'Hell's teeth! They wouldn't give you that extra week?' Peggy exclaimed incredulously.

As Peggy's mobile features set into depressingly familiar lines of annoyance, Catherine turned back to the breakfast dishes, hoping that her friend wasn't about to climb back on her soap-box to decry the terms of Harriet's will and their imminent move to city life. In recent days, while exuding the best of good intentions, Peggy had been very trying and very impractical.

'We have no legal right to be here at all,' Catherine pointed out.

'But morally you have every right and I would've expected a charitable organisation to be more generous towards a single parent.' Peggy's ready temper was rising on Catherine's behalf. 'Mind you, I don't know why I'm blaming them. This whole mess is your precious Harriet's fault!'

'Peggy—'

'Sorry, but I believe in calling a spade a spade.' That was an unnecessary reminder to anyone acquainted with Peggy's caustic tongue. 'Honestly, Catherine…sometimes I think you must have been put on this earth purely to be exploited! You don't even seem to realise when people are using you! What thanks did you get for wasting four years of your life running after Harriet?'

'Harriet gave us a home when we had nowhere else to go. She had nothing to thank me for.'

'You kept this house, waited on her hand and foot and slaved over all her pet charity schemes,' Peggy condemned heatedly. 'And for all that you received board and lodging and first pick of the jumble-sale clothes! So much for charity's beginning at home!'

'Harriet was the kindest and most sincere person I've ever known,' Catherine parried tightly.

And crazy as a coot, Peggy wanted to shriek in frustration. Admittedly Harriet's many eccentricities had not appeared to grate on Catherine as they had on other, less tolerant souls. Catherine hadn't seemed to notice when Harriet talked out loud to herself and her conscience, or noisily emptied the entire contents of her purse into the church collection plate. Catherine hadn't batted an eyelash when Harriet brought dirty, smelly tramps home to tea and offered them the freedom of her home.

The trouble with Catherine was… It was a sentence Peggy often began and never managed to finish to her satisfaction. Catherine was the best friend she had ever had. She was also unfailingly kind, generous and unselfish, and that was quite an accolade from a female who thought of herself as a hardened cynic. How did you criticise someone for such sterling qualities? Unfortunately it was exactly those qualities which had put Catherine in her present predicament.

Catherine drifted along on another mental plane. Meeting those misty blue eyes in that arrestingly lovely face, Peggy was help-lessly put in mind of a child cast adrift in a bewildering adult world. There was something so terrifyingly innocent about Catherine's penchant for seeing only the best in people and taking them on trust. There was something so horribly defenceless about her invariably optimistic view of the world.

She was a sucker for every sob-story that came her way and a wonderful listener. She didn't know how to say no when people asked for favours. This kitchen was rarely empty of callers, moth-ers in need of temporary childminders or someone to look after the cat or the dog or the dormouse while they were away. Catherine was very popular locally. If you were in a fix, she would always lend a hand. But how many returned those favours? Pre-cious few, in Peggy's experience.

'At the very least, Harriet ought to have left you a share of her estate,' Peggy censured.

Catherine put the kettle on to boil. 'And how do you think Drew and his family would have felt about that?'

'Drew isn't short of money.'

'Huntingdon's is a small firm. He isn't a wealthy man.'

'He has a big house in Kent and an apartment in central London. If that isn't wealthy, what is?' Peggy demanded drily.

Catherine suppressed a groan. 'Business hasn't been too brisk for the firm recently. Drew has already had to sell some property he owned, and though he wouldn't admit it, he must have been disappointed by Harriet's will. As building land this place will fetch a small fortune. He could have done with a windfall.'

'And by the time the divorce comes through Annette will prob-ably have stripped him of every remaining movable asset,' Peggy mused.

'She didn't want the divorce,' Catherine murmured.

Peggy pulled a face. 'What difference does that make? She had the affair. She was the guilty partner.'

Catherine made the tea, reflecting that it was no use looking to Peggy for tolerance on the subject of marital infidelity. Her friend was still raw from the break-up of her own marriage. But Peggy's

husband had been a womaniser. Annette was scarcely a comparable case. Business worries and a pair of difficult teenagers had
put the Huntingdon marriage under strain. Annette had had an
affair and Drew had been devastated. Resisting her stricken pleas
for a reconciliation, Drew had moved out and headed straight for
his solicitor. Funny how people rarely reacted as you thought they
would in a personal crisis. Catherine had believed he would forgive and forget. She had been wrong.

'I still hope they sort out their problems before it's too late,'
she replied quietly.

'Why should he want to? He's only fifty…an attractive man,
still in his prime…'

'I suppose he is,' Catherine allowed uncertainly. She was very
fond of Harriet's brother, but she wasn't accustomed to thinking
of him on those terms.

'A man who somehow can't find anything better to do than
drive down here at weekends to play with Daniel,' Peggy commented with studied casualness.

Unconscious of her intent scrutiny, Catherine laughed. 'He's at
a loose end without his family.'

Peggy cleared her throat. 'Has it ever occurred to you that Drew
might have a more personal interest at stake here?'

Catherine surveyed her blankly.

'Oh, for goodness' sake!' Peggy groaned. 'Do I have to spell
it out? His behaviour at the funeral raised more brows than mine.
If you lifted anything heavier than a teacup, he was across the
room like young Lochinvar! I think he's in love with you.'

'In love with me?' Catherine parroted, aghast. 'I've never heard
anything so ridiculous!'

'I could be wrong.' Peggy sounded doubtful.

'Of course you're wrong!' Catherine told her with unusual ve-
hemence, her cheeks hot with discomfiture.

'All right, calm down,' Peggy sighed. 'But I did have this little
chat with him at the funeral. I asked him why he'd dug up another
old lady for you to run after—'

'Mrs Anstey is his godmother!' Catherine gasped.

'And she'll see out another generation of downtrodden home-helps,' Peggy forecast grimly. 'When I ran you up to see the flat, that frozen face of hers was enough for me. I told Drew that.'

'Peggy, how could you? I only have to do her shopping and supply her with a main meal every evening. That isn't much in exchange for a flat at a peppercorn rent.'

'That's why I smell a big fat rat. However...' Peggy paused smugly for effect '...Drew told me that I didn't need to worry because he didn't expect you to be there for long. Now why do you think he said that?'

'Maybe he doesn't think I'll suit her.' /Thank you, Peggy for giving me something else to worry about, she thought wearily.

Peggy was fingering the solicitor's letter, a crease suddenly forming between her brows. 'If you have to move this week, you can't possibly come up home with me, can you?' she gathered frustratedly. 'And I was absolutely depending on you, Catherine. My mother and you get on like a house on fire and it takes the heat off me.'

'The news isn't going to make me Daniel's favourite person either,' Catherine muttered.

Unexpectedly, Peggy grinned. 'Why don't I take him anyway?'

'On his own?'

'Why not? My parents adore him. He'll be spoilt to death. And by the time we come back you'll have the flat organised and looking more like home. I've felt so guilty about not being able to do anything to help out,' Peggy confided. 'This is perfect.'

'I couldn't possibly let you—'

'We're friends, aren't we? It would make the move less traumatic for him. Poor little beggar, he doesn't half take things to heart,' Peggy said persuasively. 'He won't be here when you hand Clover over to the animal sanctuary and he won't have to camp out *en route* in Drew's apartment either. I seem to recall he doesn't get on too well with that housekeeper.'

Daniel didn't get on too terribly well with anyone who crossed him, Catherine reflected ruefully. He especially didn't like being babied and being told that he was cute, which, regrettably for him, he was. All black curly hair and long eyelashes and huge dark eyes. He was extremely affectionate with her, but not with anyone else.

'You do trust me with him?' Peggy shot at her abruptly.

'Of course I do—'

'Well, then, it's settled,' Peggy decided with her usual impatience.

The comment that she had never been apart from Daniel before, even for a night, died on Catherine's lips. Daniel loved the farm. They had spent several weekends there with Peggy in recent years. At least this way he wouldn't miss out on his holiday.

Six days later, Daniel gave her an enthusiastic hug and raced into Peggy's car. Catherine hovered. 'If he's homesick, phone me,' she urged Peggy.

'We haven't got a home any more,' Daniel reminded her. 'Africa's getting it.'

Within minutes they were gone. Catherine retreated indoors to stare at a set of suitcases and a handful of boxes through a haze of tears. Not much to show for four years. The boxes were to go into Peggy's garage. A neighbour had promised to drop them off at Drew's apartment next week. She wiped at her overflowing eyes in vexation. Daniel was only going to be away for ten days, not six months!

Drew met her off the train and steered her out to his car. He was a broadly built man with pleasant features and a quiet air of self-command. 'We'll drop your cases off at the apartment first.'

'First?' she queried.

He smiled. 'I've booked a table at the Savoy for lunch.'

'Are you celebrating something?' Catherine had lunched with Drew a dozen times in Harriet's company, but he had always taken them to his club.

'The firm's on the brink of winning a very large contract,' he divulged, not without pride. 'Unofficially, it's in the bag. I'm flying to Germany this evening. The day after tomorrow we sign on the dotted line.'

Catherine grinned. 'That's marvellous news.'

'To be frank, it's come in the nick of time. Lately, Huntingdon's has been cruising too close to the wind. But that's not all we'll be celebrating,' he told her. 'What about your move to London?'

'When will you be back from Germany?' she asked as they left his apartment again.

'Within a couple of days, but I'll check into a hotel.'

Catherine frowned. 'Why?'

Faint colour mottled his cheeks. 'When you're in the middle of a divorce you can't be too careful, Catherine. Thank God, it'll all be over next month. No doubt you think I'm being over-cautious, but I don't want anyone pointing fingers at you or associating you with the divorce.'

Catherine was squirming with embarrassment. She had gratefully accepted his offer of a temporary roof without thought of the position she might be putting him in. 'I feel terrible, Drew. I never even thought—'

'Of course you didn't. Your mind doesn't work like that.' Drew squeezed her hand comfortingly. 'Once this court business is over, we won't need to consider clacking tongues.'

She found that remark more unsettling than reassuring, implying as it did a degree of intimacy that had never been a part of their friendship. Then she scolded herself and blamed Peggy for making her read double meanings where no doubt none existed. She had inevitably grown closer to Drew since he had separated from Annette. He had become a frequent visitor to his sister's home.

In the bar they received their menus. Catherine made an elaborate play of studying hers, although she did have great difficulty with words on a printed page. The difficulty was because she was dyslexic, but she was practised at concealing the handicap.

'Steak, I think.' Steak was safe. It was on every menu.

'You're a creature of habit,' Drew complained, but he smiled at her. He was the sort of man who liked things to stay the same. 'And to start?'

She played the same game with prawns.

'I might as well have ordered for you,' he teased.

Her wandering scrutiny glanced off the rear-view of a tall black-haired male passing through the foyer beyond the doorway. At accelerated speed her eyes swept back again in a double-take, only he was out of sight. Bemusedly she blinked and then told herself off for that fearful lurch of recognition, that chilled sensation enclosing her flesh.

'Take one day at a time,' Harriet had once told her. Harriet had been a great one for clichés, and four years ago she had made it sound so easy. But a day was twenty-four hours and each of them broken up into sixty minutes. How long had it been before she could go even five minutes without remembering? How long had it been since she had lain sleepless in bed, tortured by the raw strength of the emotions she was forcing herself to deny? In the end she had built a wall inside her head. Behind it she had buried two years of her life. Beyond it sometimes she still felt only half-alive...

'Something wrong?'

Meeting Drew's puzzled gaze, she gave an exaggerated shiver. 'Someone walked over my grave,' she joked, veiling her too-expressive eyes.

'Now that you're in London, we'll be able to see each other more often,' Drew remarked tensely and reached for her hand. 'What I'm trying to say, not very well, perhaps, is...I believe I'm in love with you.'

Her hand jerked, bathing them both in sherry. With a muttered apology she fumbled into her bag for a tissue, but a waiter moved forward and deftly mopped up the table. Catherine sat, frozen, wishing that she were anywhere but where she was now, with Drew looking at her expectantly.

He sighed, 'I wanted you to know how I felt.'

'I...I didn't know. I had no idea.' It was all she could think to say, hopelessly inadequate as it was.

'I thought you might have worked it out for yourself.' There was a glimmer of wry humour in his level scrutiny. 'Apparently I haven't been as obvious as I thought I was being. Catherine, don't look so stricken. I don't expect anything from you. I don't believe there is an appropriate response for an occasion like this. I've been clumsy and impatient and I'm sorry.'

'I feel that I've come between you and Annette,' she whispered guiltily.

He frowned. 'That's nonsense. It's only since I left her that I began to realise just how much I enjoyed being with you.'

'But if I hadn't been around, maybe you would have gone back to her,' she reasoned tautly. 'You're a very good friend, but I'm...'

He covered her hand again with his. 'I'm not trying to rush you, Catherine. We've got all the time in the world,' he assured her evenly, and deftly flipped the subject, clearly registering that further discussion at that moment would be unproductive.

They were in the River Room Restaurant when she heard the voice. Dark-timbred, slightly accented, like honey drifting down her spine. Instantly her head spun on a chord of response rooted too deep even to require consideration. Her eyes widened in shock, her every sinew jerked tight. The blood pounded dizzily in her eardrums. With a trembling hand she set down her wine glass.

Luc.

Oh, God...Luc. It had been him earlier. It was him. His carved profile, golden and vibrant as a gypsy's, was etched in bold relief against the light flooding through the window behind him. One brown hand was moving to illustrate some point to his two male companions. That terrible compulsion to stare was uncontrollable. The lean, arrogant nose, the hard slant of his high cheekbones and the piercing intensity of deep-set dark eyes, all welded into one staggeringly handsome whole.

His gleaming dark head turned slightly. He looked straight at her. No expression. No reaction. Eyes golden as the burning heart of a flame. Her ability to breathe seized up. A clock had stopped ticking somewhere. She was sentenced to immobility while every primitive sense she possessed screamed for her to get up and run and keep on running until the threat was far behind. For a moment her poise almost deserted her. For a moment she forgot that he was very unlikely to acknowledge her. For a moment she was paralysed by sheer gut-wrenching fear.

Luc broke the connection first. He signalled with a hand to one of his companions, who immediately rose from his seat with the speed of a trained lackey, inclining his head down for his master's voice.

'I've upset you,' Drew murmured. 'I should have kept quiet.'

Her lashes dropped down like a camera shutter. The clink of cutlery and the buzz of voices swam back to her again. One thing hadn't changed, she acknowledged numbly; when she looked at Luc there was nothing and nobody else in the world capable of stealing her attention. Perspiration was beading her upper lip. Luc was less than fifteen feet away. They said that when you drowned your whole life flashed before you. Oh, for the deep concealment of a pool.

'Catherine—'

Belatedly she recalled the man she had been lunching with. 'I've got a bit of a headache,' she mumbled. 'If you'll excuse me, I'll get something for it.'

Up she got, on jellied knees, undyingly grateful that she didn't have to pass Luc's table. Even so, leaving the restaurant was like walking the plank above a gathering of sharks. An unreasoning part of her was expecting a hand to fall on her shoulder at any second. Feeling physically sick, she escaped into the nearest cloakroom and ran cold water over her wrists.

Drying her hands, she touched the slender gold band on her wedding finger. Harriet's gift, Harriet's invention. Everyone but Peggy thought she was a widow. Harriet had coined and told the lie before Catherine had even left hospital. She could not have publicly branded Harriet a liar. Even so, it had gone against the grain to pose as something she wasn't, although she was ruefully aware that, without Harriet's respectable cover-story, she would not have been accepted into the community in the same way.

Her stomach was still heaving. Calm down, breathe in. Why give way to panic? With Luc in the vicinity, panic made sense, she reasoned feverishly. Luc was very unpredictable. He threw wild cards without conscience. But she couldn't stay in here forever, could she?

'I think there must be a storm in the air,' she told Drew on her return, her eyes carefully skimming neither left nor right. 'I often get a headache when the weather's about to break.'

She talked incessantly through the main course. If Drew was a little overwhelmed by her loquacity, at least he wasn't noticing that her appetite had vanished. Luc was watching her. She could feel it. She could feel the hypnotic beat of tawny gold on her profile. And she couldn't stand it. It was like Chinese water-torture. Incessant, remorseless. Anger began to gain ground on her nerves.

Luc was untouched. It was against nature that he should be untouched after the scars he had inflicted on her. There was no justice in a world where Luc continued to flourish like a particularly invasive tropical plant. Hack it down and it leapt up again, twice as big and threatening.

And yet some day…somehow…some woman had to slice beneath that armour-plating of his. It had to happen. He had to learn what it was to feel pain from somebody. That belief was all that had protected Catherine from burning up with bitterness. She would picture Luc driven to his knees, Luc humanised by suffering, and then she would filter back to reality again, unable to sustain the fantasy.

Religiously she stirred her coffee. Clockwise, anti-clockwise, clockwise again, belatedly adding sugar. Her mind was in turmoil, lost somewhere between the past and the present. She was merely one more statistic on the long Santini casualty list. It galled her to acknowledge that demeaning truth.

'I've been cut dead.' Drew planted the observation flatly into the flow of her inconsequential chatter.

'Sorry?' she said, all at sea.

'Luc Santini. He looked right through me on the way out.'

She was floored by the casual revelation that Drew actually *knew* Luc. Yet why was she so surprised? Even if he was in a much smaller category, Drew was in the same field as Luc. Huntingdon's manufactured computer components. 'Is th-that important?' she stammered.

'It'll teach me not to get too big for my boots,' Drew replied wryly. 'I did do some business with him once, but that was years ago. I'm not in the Santini league these days. Possibly he didn't remember me.'

Luc had a memory like a steel trap. He never forgot a face. She was guiltily conscious that Luc had cut Drew because of her presence and for no other reason. And she wasn't foolish enough to pretend that she didn't know who Luc was. The individual who hadn't heard of Luc Santini was either illiterate or living in a grass hut on a desert island.

Drew sipped at his coffee, clearly satisfied that he had simply been forgotten. 'He's a fascinating character. Think of the risks he must have taken to get where he is today.'

'Think of the body-count he must have left behind him.'

'That's a point,' Drew mused. 'To my knowledge, he's only slipped once. Let me see, it was about four...five years ago now. I don't know what happened, but he damned near lost the shirt off his back.'

Obviously he had snatched his shirt back again and, knowing Luc, he had snatched someone else's simultaneously. On that level, Luc was unashamedly basic. An eye for an eye, a tooth for a tooth, and perhaps interest into the bargain. In remembrance she stilled a shudder.

As they left the hotel, Drew said in a driven undertone, 'I've made a bloody fool of myself, haven't I?'

'Of course you haven't,' she hastened to assure him.

'Do you want a taxi?' he asked stiffly. 'I'd better get back to the office.'

'I think I'll go for a walk.' She was ashamed that she hadn't handled the situation with greater tact, but the combination of his confession and Luc, hovering on the horizon like a pirate ship, had bereft her of her wits.

'Catherine?' Before she could turn away, Drew bent down in an almost involuntary motion and crushed her parted lips briefly with his own. 'Some day soon I'm going to ask you to marry me, whether you like it or not,' he promised with recovering confidence. 'It's nearly five years since you lost your husband. You can't bury yourself with his memory forever. And I'm a persistent man.'

A second later he was gone, walking quickly in the other direction. Tears lashed her eyes fiercely. Waves of delayed reaction were rolling over her, reducing her self-control to rubble. He was such a kind man, the essence of an old-fashioned gentleman, proposing along with the first kiss. And she was a fraud, a complete fraud. She was not the woman he thought she was, still grieving for some youthful husband and a tragically short-lived marriage. Drew had her on a pedestal.

The truth would shatter him. In retrospect, it even shattered her. For two years she had been nothing better than Luc Santini's whore, in her own mind. Kept and clothed in return for her eagerness to please in his bed. Luc hadn't once confused sex with love. That mistake had been hers alone. The polite term was 'mistress'. Only rich men's mistresses tended to share the limelight. Luc had ensured that she'd remained strictly off stage. He had never succumbed to an urge to take her out and show her off. She hadn't had the poise or the glitter, never mind the background or the education. Even now, the memories were like acid burns on her flesh, wounding and hurting wherever they touched.

Choices. Life was all about choices. Sometimes the tiniest choice could raise Cain at a later date. At eighteen Catherine had made a series of choices. At least, she had *thought* she was making them; in reality, they had most of them been made for her. Love was a terrifying leveller of pride and intelligence when a woman was an insecure girl. Before she had met Luc, she wouldn't have believed that it could be a mistake to love somebody. But it could be, oh, yes, it could be. If that person turned your love into a weapon against you, it could be a mistake you would regret for the rest of your days.

From no age at all, Catherine had been desperate to be loved. With hindsight she could only equate herself with a walking timebomb, programmed to self-destruct. Within hours of her birth, she had been abandoned by her mother and her reluctant parent had never been traced. Nor had anybody ever come forward with any information.

She had grown up in a children's home where she had been one of many. She had been a dreamer, weaving fantasies for years about the unknown mother who might eventually come to claim her. When that hope had worn thin in her teens, she had dreamt of a towering passion instead.

Leaving school at sixteen, she had worked as a helper in the home until it had closed down two years later. The Goulds had been related to the matron. A young, sophisticated couple, they had owned a small art gallery in London. Giving her a job as a receptionist, the Goulds had paid her barely enough to live on and had taken gross advantage of her willingness to work long hours. Business had been poor at the gallery and it had been kept open late most nights, Catherine left in charge on the many evenings that her employers went out.

Luc had strolled in one wet winter's night when she'd been about to lock up. His hotel had been near by. He had walked in off the street on impulse, an off-white trenchcoat carelessly draped round his shoulders, crystalline raindrops glistening in his luxuriant black hair and that aura of immense energy and self-assurance splintering from him in waves. She had made her first choice then, bedazzled and bemused by a fleeting smile...she had stopped locking up.

A silver limousine purred into the kerb several yards ahead of her now, penetrating her reverie. She hadn't even noticed where she'd been walking. Looking up, she found herself in a quiet side-street. The rear door of the car swung open and Luc stepped out on to the pavement, blocking her path. 'May I offer you a lift?'

CHAPTER TWO

CATHERINE focused on him in unconcealed horror, eyes wide above her pale cheeks. 'I'm...I'm not going anywhere—'

'You're simply loitering?' Luc gibed.

'That I would need a lift,' she completed jerkily. 'How did you know where I was?'

A beautifully shaped brown hand moved deprecatingly.

'How?' she persisted.

'I had you followed from the hotel.'

Oxygen locked in her throat. Had she really thought this second meeting a further coincidence? Had she really thought he would let her go without a single question? A car pulled up behind the limousine, two security men speedily emerging. Like efficient watchdogs, one of them took up a stance to Luc's rear, the other backing across the street for a better vantage point. For Catherine, there was an unreality to the scene. She was reminded of how vastly different a world she had inhabited over the past four years.

'Why would you want to do that?' she whispered tautly.

Black spiky lashes lowered over glittering dark eyes. 'Perhaps I wanted to catch up on old times. I don't know. You tell me,' he invited softly. 'Impulse? Do you think that is a possibility?'

Involuntarily she backed towards the railings behind her. 'You're not an impulsive person.'

'Why are you trembling?' He moved soundlessly closer, and her shoulders met wrought iron in an effort to keep the space between them intact.

'You come up out of nowhere? You gave me one heck of a fright!'

'You used to have the love of a child for surprises.'

'You might not have noticed, but I'm not a child any more!' It took courage to hurl the retort, but it was a mistake. Luc ran a raking, insolent appraisal over her, taking in the purple bullclip doing a haphazard task of holding up her silky hair, the lace-collared blouse and the tiered floral skirt cinched at her tiny waist with a belt. Modestly covered as she was, she still felt stripped.

'I see Laura Ashley is still doing a roaring trade,' he said drily.

He was so close now that she could have touched him. But she wouldn't raise her eyes above the level of his blue silk tie. He wore a dove-grey suit with an elegance few men could emulate. Superb tailoring outlined his lean length in the cloth of a civilised society. However, what she sensed in the atmosphere was far from civilised. It was nameless, frightening. A silent intimidation that clawed cruelly at her nerve-endings.

'We don't have anything to talk about after all this time.' The assurance left her bloodless lips in a rush, an answer to an unvoiced but understood demand.

Negligently he raised a hand and a fingertip roamed with taunting slowness from her delicate collarbone where a tiny pulse was flickering wildly up to the taut curve of her full lower lip. Her skin was on fire, her entire body suddenly consumed by a heat-wave.

'Relax,' he cajoled, carelessly withdrawing his hand a split second before she jerked her head back in violent repudiation of the intimacy. Flames danced momentarily in his dark eyes and then a slow, brilliant smile curved his hard mouth. 'I didn't intend to frighten you. Come…are we enemies?'

'I'm in r…rather a hurry,' she stammered.

'And you still don't want a lift? Fine. I'll walk along with you,' he responded smoothly. 'Or we could get into the car and just drive around for a while…even sit in a traffic jam. Believe me, I'm in an unusually accommodating mood.'

'Why?' Valiantly moving away from the hard embrace of the railings, Catherine straightened her shoulders. 'What do you want?'

'Well, I don't expect you to do what we used to do in traffic jams.' Slumbrous dark eyes rested unrepentantly on the tide of hot colour spreading beneath her fair skin. 'What do you think I might want? Surely, it's understandable that I should wish to satisfy a little natural curiosity?'

'What about?'

'About you. What else?' An ebony brow quirked. 'Do you think I am standing here in the street for my own pleasure?'

Catherine chewed indecisively at her lower lip. She could feel his temper rising. Time was when Luc would have said 'get in the car' and she would have leapt. He was smiling, but you couldn't trust Luc's smiles. Luc could smile while he broke you in two with a handful of well-chosen words. Without speaking, she reached her decision and bypassed him. Luc was exceptionally newsworthy and she could not afford to be seen with him, lest her past catch up with the present that Harriet had so carefully reconstructed for her.

A security man materialised at her elbow and opened the door of the limousine. Ducking her head, she slid along the cream leather upholstery to the far corner. The door slammed on them, sealing them into claustrophobic privacy.

'Really, Catherine…was that so difficult?' Luc murmured silkily. 'Would you like a drink?'

Her throat was parched. She fought for her vanished poise. 'Why not?'

Her palms smoothed nervously down over her skirt, rearranging the folds. Her skin prickled at his proximity as he bent forward to press open the built-in bar. For the longest moment of her existence, the black springy depths of his hair were within reach of her fingers. The mingled aroma of some elusive lotion and that indefinable but oh, so familiar scent that was purely him assailed her defensively flared nostrils. As he straightened again, she was disturbingly conscious of the clean movement of rippling muscles beneath the expensive fabric that sheathed his broad shoulders. And an ache and an agony were reborn treacherously within her.

Her hands laced tightly together. In the unrelenting silence, she believed she could hear her own heartbeat, speeding and pounding out the evidence of her own betrayal. She was horrified by the sensual imagery that had briefly driven every other thought from her mind. If her memory was playing tricks on her, her body was no less eager to follow suit.

Luc extended her glass, retaining hold of it long enough to force her to look at him. It was a power-play, a very minor one on Luc's terms but it made her feel controlled. She took several fast swallows of her drink. It hurt her tight throat and she hated the taste, but once she had been naïve enough to drink something she detested because she believed that was sophistication.

'Feel better now?' Luc enquired lazily, lounging back with his brandy in an intrinsically graceful movement. 'Do you live in London?'

'No,' she said hurriedly. 'I'm only here for the day. I live in…in Peterborough.'

'And you're married. That must be a source of great satisfaction to you.'

The ring on her wedding finger began to feel like a rope tightening round her vocal chords. She decided to overlook the sarcasm.

'When did you get married?'

'About four years ago.' She took another slug of her drink to fortify herself for the next round of whoppers.

'Shortly after—'

Her brain had already registered her error. 'It was a whirlwind romance,' she proffered in a rush.

'It must have been,' he drawled. 'Tell me about him.'

'It's all very pedestrian,' she muttered. 'I'm sure you can't really be interested.'

'On the contrary,' Luc contradicted softly. 'I am fascinated. Does your husband have a name?'

'Luc, I—'

'So, you remember mine? An unsought compliment…'

She stared down into her glass. 'Paul. He's called Paul.' Fighting the rigid tension threatening her, she managed a small laugh. 'Honestly, you can't want to hear all this!'

'Indulge me,' Luc advised. 'Are you happy living in…where was it? Peterhaven?'

'Yes, of course I am.'

'You don't look very happy.'

'It doesn't always show,' she retorted in desperation.

'Children?' he prompted casually.

Catherine froze, icicles sliding down her spine, and she could not prevent a sudden, darting, upward glance. 'No, not yet.'

Luc was very still. Even in the grip of her own turmoil, she noticed that. And then without warning he smiled. 'What were you doing with Huntingdon?'

The question thrown at her out of context shook her. 'I…I ran into him while I was shopping,' she hesitated and, with a stroke of what seemed to her absolute brilliance, added, 'My husband works for him.'

'You do seem to have enjoyed a day excessively full of coincidences.' Stunning golden eyes whipped over her flushed, heart-shaped face. 'The unexpected is invariably the most entertaining, isn't it?'

She set down her glass. 'I r…really have to be going. It's been…lovely meeting you again.'

'I'm flattered you should think so,' Luc murmured expressionlessly. 'What are you afraid of?'

'Afraid of?' she echoed unsteadily. 'I'm not afraid of anything!' She took a deep, shuddering breath. 'We have nothing to talk about.'

'I foresee a long day ahead of us,' Luc commented.

Catherine bent her head. 'I don't have to answer your questions,' she said tightly, struggling to keep a dismaying tremor out of her voice. Fight fire with fire. That was the only stance to take with Luc.

'Think of it as a small and somewhat belated piece of civility,' Luc advised. 'Four and a half years ago, you vanished into thin air. Without a word, a letter or a hint of explanation. I would like that explanation now.'

Stains of pink had burnished her cheeks. 'In a nutshell, getting involved with you was the stupidest thing I ever did,' she condemned.

'And telling me that may well prove to be your second.' Dark hooded eyes rested on her. 'You slept with me the night before you disappeared. You lay in my arms and you made love with me, knowing that you planned to leave...'

'H-habit,' she stammered.

Hard fingers bit into her wrist, trailing her closer without her volition. 'Habit?' he ground out roughly, incredulously.

Her tongue was glued to the dry roof of her mouth. Mutely she nodded, and recoiled from the raw fury and revulsion she read in his unusually expressive eyes. 'You're hurting me,' she mumbled.

He dropped her wrist contemptuously. 'My compliments, then, on an award-winning performance. Habit inspired you with extraordinary enthusiasm.'

She reddened to the roots of her hair, attacked by the sort of memories she never let out of her subconscious even on temporary parole. To remember was to hate herself. And that night she had known in her heart of hearts that she would never be with Luc again. With uncharacteristic daring, she had woken him up around dawn, charged with a passionate despair that could only find a vent in physical expression. Loving someone who did not love you was the cruellest kind of suffering.

'I don't remember,' she lied weakly, loathing him so much that she hurt with the force of her suppressed emotions. He made her a stranger to herself. He had done that in the past and he was doing it now. She was not the Catherine who understood and forgave other people's foibles at this moment. She had paid too high a price for loving Luc.

'Habit.' He said it again, but so softly; yet she was chilled.

Quite by accident, she registered, she had stung his ego, stirring the primitive depths of a masculinity that was rarely, if ever, challenged by her sex. She wasn't the only woman to make a fool of herself over Luc. Women went to the most embarrassing lengths to attract his attention. They went to even greater lengths to hold him. The reflection was of cold comfort to her.

Women were leisure-time toys for Luc Santini. Easily lifted, just as easily cast aside and dismissed. On the rise to the top, Luc had never allowed himself to waste an ounce of his single-minded energy on a woman. Women had their place in his life…of course they did. He was a very highly sexed male animal. But a woman never held the foreground in his mind, never came between him and his cold, analytical intelligence.

'I have to be going,' she said again and yet, when she collided with that gleaming gaze, she was strangely reluctant to move.

'As you wish.' With disorientating cool, he watched her gather up her bag and climb out of the car on rubbery legs, teetering dangerously for an instant on the very high heels she always wore.

Dragging wayward eyes from his dark, virile features, she closed the door and crossed the street. She felt dizzy, shell-shocked. All those lies, she thought guiltily; all those lies to protect Daniel. Not that Luc could be a threat to Daniel now, but she felt safer with Luc in ignorance. Luc didn't like complications or potential embarrassments. An illegitimate son would qualify as both.

A little dazedly, she shook her head. Apart from that one moment of danger, Luc had been so…so cool. She couldn't say what she had expected, only somehow it hadn't been that. In the Savoy, she could have sworn that Luc was blazingly angry. Obviously that had been her imagination. After all, why should he be angry? Four years was a long time, she reminded herself. And he hadn't cared about her. You didn't constantly remind someone you cared about that they were living on borrowed time. At least, not in Catherine's opinion you didn't.

Her mind drifted helplessly back to their first meeting. She had rewarded his mere presence at the gallery with a guided tour *par excellence*. She had never been that close to a male that gorgeous, that sophisticated and that exciting. Luc, bored with his own company and in no mood to entertain a woman, had consented to be entertained.

He had smiled at her and her wits had gone a-begging, making her forget what she was saying. It hadn't meant anything to him.

He had left without even advancing his name but, before he had gone, he said, 'You shouldn't be up here on your own. You shouldn't be so friendly with strangers either. A lot of men would take that as a come-on and you really wouldn't know how to handle that.'

As he'd started down the stairs, glittering golden eyes had glided over her one last time. What had he seen? A pretty, rounded teenager as awkward and as easily read as a child in her hurt disappointment.

In those days, though, she had been a sunny optimist. If he had happened in once, he might happen in again. However, it had been two months before Luc reappeared. He had walked in late on and alone, just as he had before. Scarcely speaking, he had strolled round the new pictures with patent uninterest while she'd chattered with all the impulsive friendliness he had censured on his earlier visit. Three-quarters of the way back to the exit, he had swung round abruptly and looked back at her.

'I'll wait for you to close up. I feel like some company,' he had drawled.

The longed-for invitation had been careless and last-minute, and the assumption of her acceptance one of unapologetic arrogance. Had she cared? Had she heck!

'I've been shut in all day. I'd enjoy a walk,' he had murmured when she'd pelted breathlessly back to his side.

'I don't mind,' she had said. He could have suggested a winter dip in the Thames and she would have shown willing. Taking her coat from her, he had deftly assisted her into it, and she had been impressed to death by his instinctive good manners.

As first dates went, it had been...different. He had walked her off her feet and treated her to a coffee in an all-night café in Piccadilly. She hadn't had a clue who he was and he had enjoyed that. He had told her about growing up in New York, about his family, the father, mother and sister who had died in a plane crash the previous year. In return she had opened her heart about her own background, contriving to joke as she invariably did about her unknown ancestry.

'Maybe I'll call you.' He had tucked her, alone and unkissed, into a cab to go home.

He hadn't called. Six, nearly seven agonising weeks had crawled past. Her misery had been overpowering. Only when she had abandoned all hope had Luc shown up again. Without advance warning. She had wept all over him with relief and he had kissed her to stop her crying.

He could have turned out to be a gangster after that kiss…it wouldn't have mattered; it wouldn't have made the slightest difference to her feelings. She was in love, hopelessly, crazily in love, and somewhere in the back of her mind she had dizzily assumed that he had to be too. How romantic, she had thought, when he presented her with a single white rose. Later she had bought a flower press to conserve that perfect bloom for posterity…

What utterly repellent things memories could be! Luc didn't have a romantic bone in his body. He had simply set about acquiring the perfect mistress with the same cool, tactical manoeuvres he employed in business. Step one, keep her off balance. Step two, convince her she can't live without you. Step three, move in for the kill. She had been seduced with so much style and expertise that she hadn't realised what was happening to her.

Pick an ordinary girl and run rings round her. That was what Luc had done to her. She might as well have tied herself to the tracks in front of an express train. Every card had been stacked against her from the start.

Glancing at her watch in a crowded street, she was stunned to realise how late it was. Lost in her thoughts she had wandered aimlessly through the afternoon. Without further ado, she headed for the bus-stop.

Drew's housekeeper, Mrs Bugle, was putting on her coat to go home when Catherine let herself into the apartment. 'I'm afraid I was too busy to leave dinner prepared for you, Mrs Parrish,' she said stiffly.

'Oh, that's fine. I'm used to looking after myself.' But

Catherine was taken aback by the formerly friendly woman's cold, disapproving stare.

'I want you to know that Mrs Huntingdon is taking this divorce very hard,' Mrs Bugle told her accusingly. 'And I'll be looking for another position if Mr Huntingdon remarries.'

The penny dropped too late for Catherine to speak up in her own defence. With that parting shot, Mrs Bugle slammed the front door in her wake. A prey to a weary mix of anger, embarrassment and frustration, Catherine reflected that the housekeeper's attack was the finishing touch to a truly ghastly day.

So now she was a marriage-wrecker, was she? The other woman. Mrs Bugle would not be the last to make that assumption. Annette Huntingdon's affair was a well-kept secret, known to precious few. Dear God, how could she have been so blind to Drew's feelings?

Harriet had been very much against her brother's desire for a divorce. She had lectured Drew rather tactlessly, making him more angry and defensive than ever at a time when he was already hurt and humiliated by his wife's betrayal.

Had she herself been too sympathetic in an effort to balance Harriet's well-meant insensitivity? When Drew chose to talk to her instead, had she listened rather too well? She had felt desperately sorry for him but she hadn't really wanted to be involved in his marital problems. All she had done was listen, for goodness' sake…and evidently Drew had read that as encouragement.

What she ought to be doing now was walking right back out of this apartment again! But how could she? After paying Mrs Anstey a month's rent in advance, she had less than thirty pounds to her name. Peggy had raged at her frequently for not demanding some sort of a wage for looking after Harriet, whose housekeeper had retired shortly after Catherine had moved in. However, Harriet, always ready to give her last penny away to someone more needy than herself and, let's face it, Catherine acknowledged guiltily, increasingly silly with what little money she did have, could not have afforded to pay her a salary.

And it hadn't mattered, it really hadn't mattered until Harriet had died. With neither accommodation nor food to worry about, Catherine had contrived to make ends meet in a variety of ways. She had registered as a child-minder, although, between Harriet's demands and Daniel's, that had provided only an intermittent income for occasional extras. She had grown vegetables, done sewing alterations, boarded pets...somehow they had always managed. But the uncertainties of their future now loomed over her like a giant black cloud.

As she unpacked, she faced the fact that she would have to apply to the Social Services for assistance until she got on her feet again. And when Drew returned from Germany, she decided, she would tell him about her past. If what he felt for her was the infatuation she suspected it was, he would quickly recover. Either way, she would lose a friendship she had come to value. When she fell off her pedestal with a resounding crash, Drew would feel, quite understandably, that he had been deceived.

The doorbell went at half-past six. She was tempted to ignore it, lest it be someone else eager to misinterpret her presence in the apartment. Unfortunately, whoever was pressing the bell was persistent, and her nerves wouldn't sit through a third shrill burst.

It was Luc. For a count of ten nail-biting seconds, she believed she was hallucinating. As she fell back, her hand slid weakly from the door. 'Luc...?' she whispered.

'I see you haven't made it back to Peterborough yet. Or was it Peterhaven?' Magnificent golden eyes clashed with startled blue. 'You didn't seem too sure where you lived. And you're a lousy liar, *cara*. In fact, you're so poor a liar, I marvel that you even attempted to deceive me. Yet you sat in that car and you lied and lied and lied...'

'Did I?' she gasped, in no state to put her brain into more agile gear.

'Do you know why I let you go this afternoon?' He sent the door crashing shut with one impatient thrust of his hand.

'N-no.'

'If you had told me one more lie in the mood I was in, I would have strangled you,' Luc spelt out. 'Where do you get the courage to lie to me?'

It was nowhere in evidence now. Helplessly she stared at him. He was so very tall and, in the confines of a hall barely big enough to swing the proverbial cat in, he was overpowering. He had all the dark splendour of a Renaissance prince in his arrogant bearing. And he was just as lethally dangerous. As he slid a sun-bronzed hand into the pocket of his well-cut trousers, pulling the fabric taut across lean, hard thighs, she shut her eyes tight on the vibrantly sensual lure of him.

But her mouth ran dry and her stomach clenched in spite of the precaution. Had she really expected to be quite indifferent? To feel nothing whatsoever for this man she had once loved, whose child she had once borne in fearful isolation? Now she knew why she had fled his car in such a state, both defying and denying the existence of responses she had fondly believed she had outgrown with maturity.

A woman met a male of Luc Santini's calibre only once in a lifetime if she was lucky. And forever after, whether she liked it or not, he would be the standard by which she judged other men. She was suddenly frighteningly aware that, in all the years since she had walked out of that Manhattan apartment, no other man had stirred her physically. It had been no sacrifice to ignore the sensuality which had in the past so badly betrayed her. Now she was recognising that facing Luc again had to be the ultimate challenge.

The silence went on and on and on.

'*Cristo, cara!*' The intervention was disturbingly low-pitched. 'What is it that you think of? You look as though you're about to fall down on your knees and pray for deliverance...'

Her lashes flew up. 'Do I?' It was called playing for time by playing dumb. What was he doing here? What did he want from her? Which lies had he identified as lies? Dear God, did he suspect that she had a child? How could he suspect? she asked herself. Even so, she turned white at the very thought of that threat.

Without troubling to reply, he strode past her to push open the kitchen door and glance in. In complete bewilderment, she watched him repeat the action with each of the remaining doors, executing what appeared to be an ordered search of the premises. What was he looking for? Potential witnesses? Her mythical husband? Or a child? Her flesh grew clammy with fear. In the economic market, Luc was famed for his uncanny omniscience. He noticed what other people didn't notice. He could interpret what was hidden. If he had ever taken the time to focus that powerful intelligence on her disappearance, he would have grasped within minutes that there was a strong possibility that she was pregnant.

'Did you enjoy yourself trailing my security men all over town for three hours this afternoon?' Luc enquired dulcetly, springing her from her increasingly panic-stricken ruminations.

'Trailing your...?' As she registered his meaning, her incredulity spoke for her.

'Zero for observation, *cara*. You don't change. You wander around in a rosy dream-state like an accident waiting to happen.' He strolled fluidly into the lounge, his wide mouth compressing as he took open stock of his surroundings. 'No verdant greenery, not a floral drape or a frill or a flounce anywhere in sight. Either you haven't lived here very long or he has imposed his taste on yours. *Dio*, he had more success than I...'

The last was an aside, as disorientating as the speech which had preceded it. Unwittingly, she went pink as she recalled scathing comments about her preference for nostalgia as opposed to the abrasively modern décors he favoured. It was an unfortunate reference, summoning up, as it inexplicably did, stray and rebellious memories of baths by candlelight and an over-the-top lace-strewn four-poster bed...

The vast differences between them even on that level were almost laughable. Two more radically differing personalities would have been hard to find. Her dreams had been the ordinary ones of love and marriage and children.

But Luc hadn't had dreams. Dreams weren't realistic enough to engage his attention. He lived his life by a master plan of self-aggrandisement. He achieved one goal and moved on to the next.

The possibility of failure never occurred to him. It was, after all, unthinkable that Luc would ever settle for less than what he wanted. As she thought unavoidably of how much less than her dreams she had settled for, bitterness coalesced into a hard, unforgiving stone inside her.

'Feel free to make yourself at home.' Her sarcasm was so out of character that Luc whipped round in surprise to stare at her.

'Don't talk to me like that,' he breathed almost tautly.

'I'll talk to you whatever way I want!' she dared.

'Be my guest,' Luc invited. 'You won't do it more than once.'

'Want to bet?' Her ability to defy him was gathering steam on the awareness that neither Daniel nor any trace of him could betray her in this apartment.

'If I were you, I wouldn't risk it,' Luc responded. 'You have this appalling habit of backing the wrong horse. And the odds definitely aren't in your favour.'

Courageously, she lifted her chin. 'I am not afraid of you.'

'You ought to be.'

Her Joan of Arc backbone suffered a sudden jolt in confidence. 'Are you trying to threaten me?' she asked shakily.

'To my knowledge, I've never *tried* to threaten anyone.' It was an assertion backed by immovable cool.

She bent her head. 'I've got nothing to say to you.'

'But I have plenty to say to you.'

'I don't want to hear it.' Jerkily she crossed her arms to conceal the fact that her hands were shaking, and moved over to the window, her back protectively turned on him.

'When I talk to people, I prefer them to look at me,' Luc imparted with irony.

'I don't want to look at you.' She was dismayed to realise that she was perilously close to tears. If wishes were horses, she would have been a thousand miles from this confrontation.

'Since I arrived, I've been having a marvellous conversation with myself.' The sardonic criticism of her monosyllabic responses drove much-needed colour into her cheeks. 'Perhaps I should approach this from a different angle.'

Taking a deep breath, she spun back to him. 'I want you to leave.'

An ebony brow elevated. 'The carpet or me?'

She flung her head back, sharp strain etched into every delicate line of her features, but she said nothing, could not trust her voice to emerge levelly or her gaze to meet directly with his.

'May we dispense with the imaginary husband, whose name you have such difficulty in recalling?' Luc murmured very quietly. 'I don't believe he exists.'

'I don't know where you get that idea.' Wildly disconcerted by the question thrown at her without warning, she was dismally conscious that her reply lacked sufficient surprise or annoyance to be convincing.

'I won't play these games with you.' The victim of that hooded dark stare holding her by sheer force of will, she felt cornered. 'I play them everywhere else in my life, but not with you. I saw you with Huntingdon outside the hotel. No doubt you believe that that ring lends a certain spurious respectability to your present position in his life. It doesn't,' he concluded flatly.

Desperation was beginning to grip her. 'You misunderstood what you saw.'

'Did I? I don't think so,' Luc murmured. 'Relax, he's still all in one piece…but he's halfway to Germany in pursuit of a contract he's not going to get.'

Her lower lip parted company with the upper. 'I b-beg your pardon?'

'You are not, I believe, hard of hearing.'

Unbearable tension held her unnaturally still. 'What have you got to do with that contract?'

'Influence alone,' Luc delivered. 'And influence will be sufficient.'

'But why? I mean, Drew?' she whispered strickenly.

'Unfortunately for him, this is his apartment.' Luc sent her a glittering glance, redolent of unashamed threat. 'And when a man trespasses on my territory, it must hurt. If it does not, who will respect the boundaries I set? Surely you do not expect me to reward him for bedding my woman?'

CHAPTER THREE

CATHERINE went white. Luc was hitting her with too much all at once. It was as if she were drowning and unable to breathe. Shock was reverberating with paralysing effect all the way down from her brain to her toes.

Luc surveyed her without a tinge of remorse. And this time she could sense the savage anger he was containing. A dark aura that radiated violent vibrations into the thickening atmosphere. It was an insidiously intimidating force, for Luc had never lost his temper with her before. Luc rarely unleashed his emotions. People who let anger triumph invariably surrendered control of the situation. Luc would not be guilty of such a gross miscalculation. Or so she had once believed...

She tried and failed to swallow. The tip of her tongue nervously crept out to moisten her dry lips. 'I am not your woman,' she said unsteadily.

Black spiky lashes partially screened a blaze of gold. 'For two years you were mine, indisputably mine, as no other woman ever has been. Some things don't change. In the Savoy, you couldn't take your eyes off me.'

Catherine was so appalled by the accusation that she momentarily forgot the threat to Drew. 'That's nonsense!'

'Is it?' She was reminded of a well-fed tiger indulgently watching his next meal at play. His brilliant gaze was riveted to her. 'I don't believe it is. And why should we argue about it? You have the same effect on me. I'm not denying it. A certain *je ne sais quoi*, unsought and, on many occasions since, unwelcome, but still in existence after six and a half years. Doesn't that tell you something?'

A furrow between her brows, Catherine was struggling to follow what he was telling her, but every time she came close to comprehension she retreated from it in disbelief.

'Plenty of marriages don't last that long,' Luc pointed out smoothly. 'I want you back, Catherine.'

In the bottomless pit of the silence he allowed to fall, she was sure she could hear her own heartbeat thundering fit to burst behind her breastbone. Her throat worked convulsively but no sound emerged, and that was hardly surprising when he had deprived her of the power of speech. Shock had gone into counter-shock, and her capacity to think straight had gone into cold storage.

'You have to be the most incredibly modest woman of my acquaintance. Do you really think I would go to these lengths for anything less?' Strolling over to the table, Luc uncapped one of the decanters, lifted a glass off the tray and poured a single measure of brandy.

'I can't believe that you can say that to me,' she mumbled.

'Console yourself with the reflection that I have not said one quarter of what I would like to say.' Luc slotted the glass between her nerveless fingers, cupped them helpfully round to clasp it, the easy intimacy of his touch one more violently disorientating factor to plague her. 'I feel sure that you are grateful for my restraint.'

Dimly she understood how a rabbit felt, mesmerised by headlights on the motorway. Those golden eyes could be shockingly compelling. The brandy went down in one appreciative gulp and she gasped as fire raced down her throat. It banished her paralysis, however, and retrieved her wits. 'You…you actually think that Drew is keeping me?' she demanded with a shudder of distaste. 'Is that what you're insinuating?'

'I rarely insinuate, *cara*. I state.'

'How dare you?' Catherine exclaimed.

Luc dealt her an impassive look. 'I find it particularly unsavoury that he should be a married man, old enough to be your father.'

Restraint, she acknowledged, was definitely fighting a losing battle. Fierce condemnation accompanied that final statement. 'There's nothing unsavoury about Drew!' she protested furiously. 'He's one of the most decent, honourable men I've ever met!'

'Only not above cheating on his wife with a woman half his age,' Luc drawled in biting conclusion. 'A little word of warning, *cara*. After tonight, I don't ever wish to hear his name on your lips again.'

Catherine was too caught up in an outraged defence of Drew to listen to him. 'He wouldn't cheat on his wife. He's been separated from her for almost a year. He'll be divorced next month!'

'I know,' Luc interposed softly, taking the wind from her sails. 'He should have stayed home with his wife. It would have been safer for him.'

'Safer?' she whispered, recalling what he had said some minutes earlier. 'You threatened him—'

'No. I delivered a twenty-two-carat-gold promise of intent.' The contradiction was precise, chilling.

'But you didn't mean it, you couldn't have meant it!' she argued in instinctive appeal.

Dark eyes lingered on her reflectively and veiled. 'If you say so.' A broad shoulder lifted in a very Latin shrug of dismissal. 'We have more important things to discuss.'

Her stomach executed a sick somersault. Under that exquisitely tailored suit dwelt a predator of Neanderthal proportions, ungiven to anything as remote as an attack of conscience. 'It's absolutely none of your business,' she conceded tightly, 'but I'm not having an affair with Drew.'

'Everything that concerns you is my business.'

It went against the grain to permit that to go past unchallenged, but she was more concerned about Drew. 'Why should you want to damage Huntingdon Components? What has he ever done to you?'

'You ask me that?' It was a positive snarl of incredulity. 'You live in his apartment and you ask me that?'

'It's not what it seems.'

'It is exactly what it seems. Cheap, nasty.' His nostrils flared as he passed judgement.

'Like what I had with you?' She couldn't resist the comparison.

'*Cristo!*' He threw up both hands in sudden lancing fury. 'How can you say that to me? In all my life, I never treated a woman as well as I treated you!'

The most maddening quality of that assurance was its blazing, blatant sincerity. He actually believed what he was saying. Her teeth ground together on a blistering retort.

'And what did I receive in return? You tell me!' he slashed at her rawly, rage masking his dark features. 'A bloody stupid scrawl on a mirror that I couldn't even read! I trusted you as though you were my family and you betrayed that trust. You stuck a knife in my back.'

She should have been better prepared for that explosion, but she wasn't. His legendary self-control had evaporated right before her stricken eyes, revealing the primitive depth of the anger she had dared to provoke. 'Luc, I—'

'Stay where you are!' The command cracked like a whiplash across the room, halting her retreat in the direction of the door. 'You were with me two years, Catherine. Two years,' he repeated fiercely, anger vibrating from every tensed line of his lean, powerful physique. 'And then you vanish into thin air. In nearly five years, what do I get? Hmm? Not so much as a postcard! So, I look for you. I wonder if you're starving somewhere. I worry about how you're managing to live. I think maybe you've had an accident, maybe you're dead. And where do I find you?' he grated in soaring crescendo. 'In the Savoy with another man!'

Her feet were frozen to the carpet under that searing onslaught. She had never seen Luc betray that much emotion. Dazedly, she watched him swing away from her, ferocious tension etched into the set of his broad shoulders and the angle of his hard, taut profile. She could not quite credit the evidence of what she was seeing, never mind what he had said.

He had worried about her? He had actually worried about her? In her mind she fought to come to terms with that revelation. When she had left him, sneaking cravenly out of the service entrance like a thief, she had foreseen his probable response to her departure. Disbelief...outrage...contempt...acceptance. The idea of his worrying about her, looking for her, had never once occurred to her.

In a strange way which she could not understand, she found the idea very disturbing, and it was in reaction to that that she chose to say nothing in her own defence. One fact had penetrated. Luc had no suspicion of Daniel's existence. That fear assuaged, she could only think of Drew.

'Leave Drew alone,' she said. 'He needs that contract.'

'Is that all you have to say to me?' There was a formidable chill in his dark eyes.

She swallowed hard. 'Losing that contract could ruin him.'

A grim smile curved his lips. 'I know.'

'If you're angry with me, take it out on me. I can't believe you really want to harm Drew,' she confided.

'Believe it,' Luc urged.

'I mean…' she made a helpless movement of her small hands, eloquent of her confusion '…you walk in here and you say…you say you want me back, but there's absolutely no question of that,' she completed shakily.

'No?'

'No! And I don't understand why you're doing this to me!' she cried.

'Maybe you should try.'

She refused to look at him. He had hurt her too much. In Luc's presence she was as fearfully wary as a child who had once put her hand in the fire. The memory of the pain was a persistent barrier. 'I won't try,' she said with simple dignity. 'You're an episode which I put behind me a long time ago.'

'An episode?' he derided incredulously. 'You lived with me for two years!'

'Nineteen months, and every month a mistake,' Catherine corrected, abandoning her caution by degrees.

'*Madre de Dio.*' A line of colour demarcated his high cheekbones. 'Hardly a one-night stand.'

Visibly she flinched. 'Oh, I don't know. I often used to feel like one.'

'How can you say that to me? I treated you with respect!' he ground out.

'That was respect?' A chokey laugh escaped her. She felt wild in that instant. If she had been a tigress, she would have clawed him to death in revenge. Her very powerlessness taunted her cruelly. 'When I look at you now, I wonder why it took me so long to come to my senses.'

'Since I arrived, you have looked everywhere but at me,' Luc said drily, deflatingly.

'I hate you, Luc. I hate you so much that if you dropped dead at my feet I'd dance on your corpse!' she vented in a feverish rush.

'The near future promises to be intriguing.'

'There isn't going to be one for us!' Catherine had never lost her head with anyone before, but it was happening now. As if it were not bad enough that he should stand there with the air of someone handling an escaped lunatic with enviable cool, he was ignoring every word she said. 'I'm not about to fall into line like one of your employees! Come back to you? You have to be out of your mind! You used me once, and I'd sooner be dead than let you do it again! I loved you, Luc. I loved you much more than you deserved to be loved—'

'I know,' he interposed softly.

A hectic flush carmined her cheeks, fury running rampant through her every skin-cell. 'What do you mean...you know? Where do you get the nerve to admit that?'

Unreadable golden eyes arrowed into her and lingered intently. 'I thought it might be in my favour.'

'In your favour? It makes what you did to me all the more unforgivable!' Catherine ranted in a fresh burst of outrage. 'You took everything I had to give and tried to pay for it, as though I were some tramp you'd picked up on a street-corner!'

His jawline clenched. 'I might have made one or two unfortunate errors of judgement,' he conceded after a very long pause. 'But, if you were dissatisfied with our relationship, you should have expressed that dissatisfaction.'

'I beg your pardon? Expressed it?' Catherine could hardly get the words out, she was so enraged. 'God forgive you, Luc, because I never will! Let me just make one little point. You can go out there and you can buy anything you want, but you can't buy me. I'm not available. I'm not up for sale. There's no price-tag attached, so what are you going to do?'

Trembling violently, she turned away from him, emotion still storming through her in a debilitating wave. She had never dreamt that she could attack Luc like that, but somehow it had simply happened. Yet in the aftermath she experienced no sense of pleasure; she felt only pain. A tearing, desperate pain that seemed to encompass her entire being. Just being in the same room with him hurt. She had sworn once that she would not let him do this to her. She would not let hatred poison the very air she breathed. But that wall inside her head was tumbling down brick by brick, and the vengeful force of all the feelings she had buried behind it was surging out of control. With those feelings came memories she fiercely sought to blank out...

That day he had given her the rose, he had escorted her down to a limousine. Cinderella had never had it so good. There had been no glass slipper to fall off at midnight. He had swept her off her feet into a world she had only read about in magazines. He had revelled in her wide eyes, her innocence, her inability to conceal her joy in merely being with him. For five days, she had been lost in a breathless round of excitement. Fancy night-clubs where they danced the night away, intimate meals in dimly lit restaurants...and his last evening in London, of course, in his hotel suite.

But even then Luc hadn't been predictable. When he had reduced her to the clinging, mindless state in his arms after dinner, he had set her back from him with a pronounced attitude of pious self-denial. 'I'm spending Christmas in Switzerland. Come with me,' he had urged lazily as though he were inviting her to merely cross the road.

She had been staggered, embarrassed, uncertain, but she had always been hopelessly sentimental about the festive season. Initially she had said no, uneasy about the prospect of letting Luc pay her way abroad.

'I don't know when I'll be back in London again.' A lie, though she hadn't known it then, as carefully processed as she had been by the preparation of two-month absences between meetings. What Luc didn't know about giving a woman withdrawal symptoms hadn't yet been written.

Convinced that she might lose him forever by letting old-fashioned principles come between them, she had caved in. She had been so dumb that she had expected them to be staying in a hotel in separate rooms. Even in the grip of the belief that she would walk off the edge of the world if he asked her to, she hadn't felt that she had known him long enough for anything else. He had returned to New York. Elaine Gould had been stunned to see a photo of her with Luc in a newspaper the next day. Elaine had tried to reason with her in a curt, well-meaning way. Even her landlady, breathlessly hung on the latest instalment of her romance, had given the thumbs-down to Switzerland. But she had been beyond the reach of sensible advice.

Six hours in an isolated Alpine chalet had been enough to separate her from a lifetime of principles. No seduction had ever been carried out more smoothly. No bride could have been brought to the marital bed with greater skill and consideration than Luc had employed. And, once Luc had taken her virginity, he had possessed her body and soul. She hadn't faced the fact that she knew about as much about having an affair as Luc knew about having a conscience. The towering passion had been there, the man of her dreams had been there, but the wedding had been nowhere on the horizon. She had given up everything for love…oh, you foolish, reckless woman, where were your wits?

'Catherine.' As she sank back to the present, she shivered. That accent still did something precarious to her knees.

'What were you thinking about?'

Blinking rapidly against the sting of tears, she breathed unsteadily, 'You don't want to know.'

'If you come back to me,' Luc murmured expressionlessly, 'I'll let Huntingdon have the contract.'

'Dear God, you can't bargain with a man's livelihood!' she gasped in horror.

'I can and I will.'

'I hate you! I'd be violently ill if you laid a finger on me!' she swore. Her legs were wobbling and she couldn't drag her eyes from his dark, unyielding features.

Unexpectedly, a smile curved his sensual mouth. 'I'll believe that when it happens.'

'Luc, please.' When it came down to it, she wasn't too proud to beg. She could not stand back and allow Drew to suffer by association with her. She could not disclaim responsibility and still live with herself. Luc did not utter idle threats. 'Please think of what you're doing. This is an ego-trip for you…'

A dark brow quirked. 'I've seldom enjoyed a less ego-boosting experience.'

'I can't come back to you, Luc…I just can't. Please go away and forget you ever saw me.' The wobble in her legs had spread dismayingly to her voice.

He drew closer. 'If I could forget you, I wouldn't be here, *cara*.'

Catherine took a hasty step backward. 'Don't you remember all those things I used to do that annoyed you?' she exclaimed in desperation.

'They became endearing when I was deprived of them.'

'Stay away from me!' Hysteria was creeping up on her by speedy degrees as he advanced. 'I'll die if you touch me!'

'And I'll die if I don't. I ought to remind you that I'm a survivor,' Luc drawled almost playfully, reaching for her, golden eyes burning over her small figure in a blaze of hunger. 'You won't remember his name by tomorrow.'

She lunged out of his reach and one of her stiletto heels caught in the fringe of the rug, throwing her right off balance. Her feet went out from under her and she fell, her head bouncing painfully off the edge of something hard. As she cried out, darkness folded in like a curtain falling and she knew no more.

*   *   *

'You can see the area I'm referring to here.' The consultant indicated the shading on the X-ray. 'A previous injury that required quite major surgery. At this stage, however, I have no reason to suspect that she's suffering from anything more than concussion, but naturally she should stay in overnight so that we can keep an eye on her.'

'She's taking a hell of a long time to come round properly.'

'She's had a hell of a nasty bump.' Meeting that narrowed, fierce stare, utterly empty of amusement, the older man mentally matched his facetious response to a lead balloon.

The voices didn't make any sense to Catherine, but she recognised Luc's and was instantly soothed by that recognition. A shard of cut-glass pain throbbed horribly at the base of her skull and, as she shifted her head in a pointless attempt to deaden it, she groaned, her eyes opening on bright light.

Luc swam into focus and she smiled. 'You're all fuzzy,' she mumbled.

A grey-haired man appeared at the other side of the bed and tested her co-ordination. Then he asked her what day it was. She shut her eyes again and thought hard. Her brain felt like so much floating cotton wool. Monday, Tuesday, Wednesday…take your pick. She hadn't a clue what day it was. Come to think of it, she didn't even know what she was doing in hospital.

The question was repeated.

'Can't you see that she's in pain?' Luc demanded in biting exasperation. 'Let her rest.'

'Catherine.' It was the doctor's voice, irritatingly persistent, forcing her to lift her heavy eyelids again. 'Do you remember how you sustained your injury?'

'I've already told you that she fell!' Luc intercepted him a second time. 'Is this interrogation really necessary?'

'I fell,' Catherine whispered gratefully, wishing the doctor would go away and stop bothering her. He was annoying Luc.

'How did you fall?' As he came up with a third question, Luc expelled his breath in an audible hiss and simultaneously the sound of a beeper went off. With a thwarted glance at Luc, the consultant said, 'I'm afraid I'll have to complete my examination in the morning. Miss Parrish will be transferred to her room. Perhaps you'd like to go home, Mr Santini?'

'I'll stay.' It was unequivocal.

Catherine angled a sleepy smile over him, happily basking in the concern he was showing for her well-being. Letting her lashes lower again, she felt the bed she was lying on move. Nurses chattered above her head, complaining about what a wet evening it was, and one of them described some dress she had seen in Marks. It was all refreshingly normal, even if it did make Catherine feel as though she were invisible. Without meaning to, she drifted into a doze.

Waking again, she found herself in a dimly lit, very pleasantly furnished room that didn't mesh with her idea of a hospital. Luc was standing staring out of the window at darkness.

'Luc?' she whispered.

He wheeled round abruptly.

'This may seem an awfully stupid question,' she muttered hesitantly. 'But where am I?'

'This is a private clinic.' He approached the bed. 'How do you feel?'

'As though someone slugged me with a sandbag, but it's not nearly as bad as it was.' She moved her head experimentally on the pillow and winced.

'Lie still,' Luc instructed unnecessarily.

She frowned. 'I don't remember falling,' she acknowledged in a dazed undertone. 'Not at all.'

Luc moved closer, looking less sartorially splendid than was his wont. His black hair was tousled, his tie crumpled, the top two buttons of his silk shirt undone at his brown throat. 'It was my fault,' he said tautly.

'I'm sure it wasn't,' Catherine soothed in some surprise.

'It was.' Dark eyes gleamed down at her almost suspiciously. 'If I hadn't tried to pull you into my arms when you were trying to get away from me, it wouldn't have happened.'

'I was trying to get away from you?' Nothing in her memory-banks could come to terms with that startling concept.

'You tripped over a rug and went down. You struck your head on the side of a table. *Madre de Dio, cara*...I thought you'd broken your neck!' Luc relived with unfamiliar emotionalism, a tiny muscle pulling tight at the corner of his compressed mouth. 'I thought you were dead...I really thought you were dead.' The repetition was harsh, not quite steady.

'I'm sorry.' A vaguely panicky sensation was beginning to nudge at her nerve-endings. If Luc hadn't been there, it would have swallowed her up completely. Yet his intent stare, his whole demeanour was somehow far from reassuring. Other little oddities, beyond her inability to recall her fall, were springing to mind. 'The nurses...that doctor...they were English. Are we in England?' she demanded shakily.

'Are *we*—?' He put a strange stress on her choice of pronoun, his strong features shuttered, uncommunicative. 'We're in London. Don't you know that?' he probed very quietly.

'I don't remember coming to London with you!' Catherine admitted in a stricken rush. 'Why don't I remember?'

Luc appraised her for a count of ten seconds before he abandoned his stance at a distance and dropped down gracefully on to the side of the bed. 'You've got concussion and you're feeling confused. That's all,' he murmured calmly. 'Absolutely nothing to worry about.'

'I can't help being worried—it's scary!' she confided.

'You have nothing to be scared of.' Luc had the aspect of someone carefully de-programming a potential hysteric.

Her fingers crept into contact with the hand he had braced on the mattress and feathered across his palm in silent apology. 'How long have we been in London?'

Luc tensed. 'Is that important?' As he caught her invasive fingers between his and carried them to his mouth, it suddenly became a matter of complete irrelevance.

Watching her from beneath a luxuriant fringe of ebony lashes, he ran the tip of his tongue slowly along each individual finger before burying his lips hotly in the centre of her palm. A quiver of weakening pleasure lanced through her and an ache stirred in her pelvis. It was incredibly erotic.

'Is it?' he prompted.

'Is…what?' she mumbled, distanced from all rational thought by the power of sensation.

Disappointingly, he laid her hand back down, but he retained a grip on it, a surprisingly fierce grip. 'What is the last thing you remember?'

With immense effort, she relocated her thinking processes and was rewarded. Remembering the answer to that question was as reassuringly easy as falling off the proverbial log. 'You had the flu,' she announced with satisfaction.

'The flu.' Black brows drew together in a frown and then magically cleared again. '*Si*, the flu. That was nineteen eighty—'

She wrinkled her nose. 'I do know what year it is, Luc.'

'*Senz'altro*. Of course you do. The year improves like a good vintage.' As she looked up at him uncomprehendingly, he bent over her with a faint smile and smoothed a stray strand of wavy hair from her creased forehead.

'It seems so long ago, and, when I think about it, it seems sort of hazy,' she complained.

'Don't think about it,' Luc advised.

'Is it late?' she whispered.

'Almost midnight.'

'You should go back to the hotel…are we in a hotel?' she pressed, anxious again.

'Stop worrying. It'll all come back,' Luc forecast softly. 'Sooner or later. And then we will laugh about this, I promise you.'

His thumb was absently stroking her wrist. She raised her free hand, powered by an extraordinarily strong need just to touch him, and traced the stubborn angle of his hard jawline. His dark skin was blue-shadowed, interestingly rough in texture. He had mesmeric eyes, she reflected dizzily, dark in shadow or dissatisfaction, golden in sunlight or passion. Vaguely she wondered why he wasn't kissing her.

In that department, Luc never required either encouragement or prompting. When he came back from a business trip, he swept through the door, snatched her into his arms and infrequently controlled his desire long enough to reach the bedroom. And when he was with her it sometimes seemed that she couldn't cook or clean or do anything without being intercepted.

It made her feel safe. It made her feel that where there was that much passion, surely there was hope. Only of late she had listened less willingly to another little voice. It was more pessimistic. It told her that expecting even the tiniest commitment from Luc where the future was concerned was comparable with believing in the tooth-fairy.

'I've only forgotten a few weeks, haven't I?' she checked, hastily pushing away those uneasy thoughts which made her so desperately insecure.

'You have forgotten nothing of import.' Brilliant eyes shimmered over her upturned face, meeting hers with the zap of a force-field, and yet still, inconceivably to her, he kept his distance.

'Luc—' she hesitated '—what's wrong?'

'I'm getting very aroused. *Dio*, how can you do this to me just by looking at me?' he breathed with sudden ferocity. 'You're supposed to be sick.'

She didn't know which of them moved first but suddenly he was as close as she wanted him to be and her fingers slid ecstatically into the springy depths of his hair. But, instead of the forceful assault his mood had somehow led her to anticipate, he outlined her parted lips with his tongue and then delved between, tasting her with a sweet, lancing sensuality again and again until her head was spinning and her bones were melting and a hunger more intense than she had ever known leapt and stormed through her veins.

With an earthy groan of satisfaction, Luc dragged her up into his arms and, although the movement jarred her painfully, she was more than willing to oblige him. Thrusting the bedding impatiently away from her, he lifted her and brought her down on his hard thighs without once removing his urgent mouth from hers.

Excitement spiralled as suddenly as summer lightning between them. Wild, hot and primeval. His hand yanked at the high neck of the white hospital gown, loosening it, drawing it away from her upper body. Cooler air washed her exposed skin as he held her back from him, lean hands in a powerful grip on her slender arms. A dark flush over his hard cheekbones, he ran raking golden eyes over the fullness of her pale breasts, the betraying tautness of the pink nipples that adorned them.

Reddening beneath that unashamed, heated appraisal, she muttered feverishly, 'Take me back to the hotel.'

Luc shook her by saying something unrepeatable and closing his eyes. A second later, he wrenched the gown back up over her again, stood up and lowered her into the bed. Tucking the light covers circumspectly round her again, he breathed, '*Chiedo scusa.* I'm sorry. You're not well.'

'I'm fine,' she protested. 'I don't want to stay here.'

'You're staying.' He undid the catch on the window and hauled it up roughly, letting a cold breeze filter into the room. 'You're safer here.'

'Safer?'

'Do you believe in fate, *cara*?'

Her lashes fluttered in bemusement and she turned her head on the pillow. Luc, who had been aghast and then vibrantly amused by her devotion to observing superstitions such as not walking under ladders, avoiding stepping on black lines...Luc was asking her about fate? He looked deadly serious as well. 'Of course I do.'

'One shouldn't fight one's fate,' Luc mused, directing a gleaming smile at her. 'You believe that, don't you?'

She had never had an odder conversation with Luc and she was so exhausted that it was an effort to focus her thoughts. 'I think it would be almost impossible to fight fate.'

'I've no intention of fighting it. It's played right into my hands, after all. Go to sleep, *cara*,' he murmured softly. 'We're flying to Italy in the morning.'

'I-Italy?' she parroted, abruptly shot back into wakefulness.

'Don't you think it's time we regularised our situation?'

Catherine stared at him blankly, one hundred per cent certain that he couldn't mean what she thought he meant.

Luc strolled back to the bed and sank down in the armchair beside her, fixing dark glinting eyes on her. 'I'm asking you to marry me.'

'Are you?' She was so staggered by the assurance that it was the only thing she could think to say.

He scored a reflective fingertip along the line of her tremulous bottom lip. 'Say something?' he invited.

'Have you been thinking of this for long?' she managed jerkily, praying for the shock to recede so that she could behave a little more normally.

'Let's say it crept up on me,' he suggested lightly.

That didn't sound very romantic. Muggers crept up on you; so did old age. A paralysing sense of unreality assailed her. Luc was asking her to marry him. That meant she had been living with a stranger for months. That meant that every disloyal, ungenerous thought she had ever had about him had been wickedly unjustified. Tears welled up in her eyes. Lines of moisture left betraying trails down her pale cheeks.

'What did I say? What didn't I say?' Luc demanded. 'OK, so this is not how you imagined me proposing.'

'I never imagined you proposing!' she sobbed.

With a succinct expletive, he slid his hands beneath her very gently and tugged her on to his lap, hauling off the light bedspread and wrapping it round her. She sniffed and sucked in oxygen, curving instinctively in the heat of him. 'I'm so h-happy,' she told him.

'You have a very individual way of being happy, but then,' a caressing hand smoothed through her silky, tumbled hair, 'you have an individual way of doing most things. We'll get married in Italy. And now that we've decided to do it, we don't want to waste time, do we?'

She rested her head against his chest as he lounged back into a more comfortable position to accommodate her. He was being so gentle and once she had honestly believed that he didn't know how to be. Had her fall given him that much of a shock? Certainly something had provoked an astonishing alteration in Luc's attitude to her...or had she really never understood Luc at all? Did it matter if she couldn't understand him? She decided it didn't.

Luc was planning the wedding. The royal 'we' did not mislead her. She could have listened to him talk all night, but the kind of exhaustion that was a dead weight on her senses was slowly but surely dragging her towards sleep.

CHAPTER FOUR

THE sapphire-blue suit was unfamiliar but it had 'bought to please Luc' stamped in its designer-chic lines. The shoes? Catherine grimaced at the low heels which added little to her diminutive height. She must have been in a tearing hurry when she chose them. They weren't her style at all, but they were a perfect match for the suit. Since co-ordinating her wardrobe had never been one of her talents, she was surprised by the discovery. Luc must have ransacked her luggage to pull off such a feat.

He had been gone when she'd woken, securely back within her bed. Her clothes had arrived after breakfast. Although the effort involved had left her weak, she had been eager to get dressed. A nurse had lightly scolded her for not asking for assistance, adding that Mr Ladwin, the resident consultant, would be in to see her shortly. Catherine couldn't help hoping that Luc arrived first. The prospect of a barrage of probing questions which she wouldn't be able to answer unnerved her.

So, a few weeks had sort of got lost, she told herself bracingly. A few weeks didn't qualify as a real loss of memory, did it? Subduing the panicky sensation threatening, she sat down in the armchair. Of course it would come back and, as Luc had pointed out, it wasn't as though she had forgotten anything important.

Even so, the silliest little things kept on stirring her up. When had she had her hair cut to just below her shoulders? And it was a mess, a real mess! Heaven knew when she had last had a trim. Then there were her hands. She might have been scrubbing floors with them! And there was this funny little dent on her wedding finger, almost as if she had been wearing a ring, and she never put a ring on that finger...

She didn't even recognise the contents of her handbag. She had hoped that something within its capacious depths might jog her memory. She had hoped in vain. Even the purse had been unfamiliar, containing plenty of cash in both dollars and sterling but no credit cards and no photos of Luc. Even the cosmetics she presumably used every day hadn't struck a chord. And where was her passport?

Luc's proposal last night already had a dream-like quality. Luc hadn't been quite Luc as she remembered him. That was the most bewildering aspect of all.

When she had broken an ankle in Switzerland last year, Luc had been furious. He said she was the only person he knew who could contrive to break a limb in the Alps without ever going near a pair of skis. He had stood over her in the casualty unit, uttering biting recriminations about the precarious height of the heels she favoured. The doctor had thought he was a monster of cruelty, but Catherine had known better.

Her pain had disturbed him and he had reacted with native aggression to that disturbance in his usually well-disciplined emotions. Telling her that he'd break her neck if he ever saw her in four-inch stilettos again had been the uncensored equivalent of a major dose of sympathetic concern.

But last night, Luc hadn't been angry...Luc had asked her to marry him. And how could that seem real to her? Her wretched memory had apparently chosen to block out a staggeringly distinct change in her relationship with Luc. Her very presence in London with him when he always jetted about the world alone fully illustrated that change in attitude. But what exactly had brought about that change?

She could not avoid a pained recall of the women Luc had appeared with in newsprint in recent months. Beautiful, pedigreed ladies, who took their place in high society without the slightest doubt of their right to be there. Socialites and heiresses and the daughters of the rich and influential. Those were the sort of women Luc was seen in public with—at charity benefits, movie premières, Presidential dinners.

'I don't sleep with them,' Luc had dismissed her accusations, but still it had hurt. She had looked into the mirror that day and seen her own inadequacy reflected, and she had never felt the same about herself since. It was agonising to be judged and found wanting without ever being aware that there had been a trial.

The door opened abruptly. Luc entered with the consultant in tow. Sunk within the capacious armchair, tears shimmering on her feathery lashes, she looked tiny and forlorn and defenceless in spite of her expensive trappings.

Luc crossed the room in one stride and hunkered down lithely at her feet, one brown hand pushing up her chin. 'Why are you crying?' he demanded. 'Has someone upset you?'

If someone had, they would have been in for a rough passage. Luc was all Italian male in that instant. Protective, possessive, ready to do immediate battle on her behalf. Beneath the cool façade of sophistication, Luc was an aggressively masculine male with very unliberated views on sexual equality. His golden eyes were licking flames on her in over-bright scrutiny. 'If someone has, I want to know about it.'

'I seriously doubt that any of our staff would be guilty of such behaviour.' Mr Ladwin bristled at the very suggestion.

Luc dropped a pristine handkerchief on her lap and vaulted upright. 'Catherine's very sensitive,' he said flatly.

Catherine was also getting very embarrassed. Hastily wiping at her damp cheeks, she said, 'The staff have been wonderful, Luc. I'm just a little weepy, that's all.'

'As I have been trying to explain to you for the past half-hour, Mr Santini,' the consultant murmured, 'amnesia is a distressing condition.'

'And, as you also explained, it lies outside your field.'

Catherine studied the two men uneasily. The undertones were decidedly antagonistic. Ice had dripped from every syllable of Luc's response.

Mr Ladwin looked at her. 'You must feel very confused, Miss Parrish. Wouldn't you prefer to remain here for the present and see a colleague of mine?'

The threat of anything coming between her and the wedding

Luc had described so vividly filled Catherine with rampant dismay. 'I want to leave with Luc,' she stressed tautly.

'Are you satisfied?' Luc enquired of the other man.

'It would seem that I have to be.' Scanning the glow that lit Catherine's face when she looked at Luc Santini, the older man found himself wondering with faint envy what it felt like to be loved like that.

Mr Ladwin shook hands and departed. Luc smiled at her. 'The car's outside.'

'I can't find my passport,' she confided abruptly, steeling herself for the disappearance of that smile. Luc got exasperated when she mislaid things.

'Relax,' he urged. 'I have it.'

She sighed relief. 'I thought I'd lost it...along with my credit cards and some photos I had.'

'You left them behind in New York.'

She smiled at the simplicity of the explanation. Her usual disorganisation appeared to be at fault.

'Why were you crying?'

She laughed. 'I don't know,' she said, but she did. 'Has someone upset you?' he had demanded with a magnificent disregard for the obvious. Nobody could hurt her more than Luc and, conversely, nobody could make her happier. Loving Luc put her completely in his power and, for the first time in a very long time, she no longer felt she had to be afraid of that knowledge.

A brown forefinger skimmed the vulnerable softness of her lower lip. 'When I'm here, you don't have to worry about anything,' he censured.

Since meeting Luc, worry had become an integral part of her daily existence. The sharp streak of insecurity ingrained in her by her rootless childhood had been roused from dormancy. But it wasn't going to be like that any more, she reminded herself. As Luc's wife, she would hold a very different position in his scheme of what was important. Depressingly, however, when she struggled to picture herself in that starring role, it still felt like fantasy.

'Why do you want to marry me?' Her hands clenched fiercely together as she forced out that bald enquiry in the lift.

'I refuse to imagine my life without you.' He straightened the twisted collar of her silk blouse and tucked the label out of sight with deft fingers. 'Do you think we could save this very private conversation for a less public moment?' he asked lazily.

Catherine made belated eye-contact with the smiling elderly couple sharing the lift with them and reddened to her hairline. She had been too bound up in her own emotions to notice that they had company. Catherine Santini. Secretly she tasted the name, savoured it, and the upswell of joy she experienced was intense.

'Life doesn't begin with "once upon a time", *cara*, and end "and they all lived happily ever after", Luc had once derided. But, regardless, Luc had just presented her with her dream, gift-wrapped and tagged. Evidently if you hoped hard enough and prayed hard enough, it could happen.

As she crossed to the limousine, the heat of the sun took her by surprise. Her eyes scanned the climbing roses in bloom at the wall bounding the clinic's grounds and her stomach lurched violently. 'It's summer,' she whispered. 'You had the flu in September.'

With inexorable cool, Luc pressed her into the waiting car. Her surroundings were then both familiar and reassuring, but still she trembled. Luc hadn't said a word. Of course, he had known. He had known that she had lost more than a few weeks, had seen no good reason to increase her alarm. Everything now made better sense. No wonder Mr Ladwin had been reluctant to see her leave so quickly. No wonder she didn't recognise her clothes or her hairstyle or the change in Luc. She had lost almost a year of her life.

'Luc, what's happening to me?' she said brokenly. 'What's going on inside my head?'

'Don't try to force it.' His complete calm was wondrously soothing. 'Ladwin advised me not to fill in the blanks for you. He said you should have rest and peace and everything you wanted within reason. Your memory will probably come back naturally, either all at once or in stages.'

'And what if it doesn't?'

'We'll survive. You didn't forget me.' Satisfaction blazed momentarily in his stunning eyes before he veiled them.

The woman who could forget Luc Santini hadn't been born yet. You could love him passionately, hate him passionately, but you couldn't possibly forget him. Hate him? Her brow creased at that peculiar thought and she wondered where it had come from.

'Are you thinking of putting off the wedding?' she asked stiffly. It was the obvious thing to do, the sensible thing to do. And what she most feared was the obvious and the sensible.

'Is that what you want?'

Vehemently she shook her head, refusing to meet his too perceptive gaze. How could she still be so afraid of losing him? He had asked her to marry him. What more could he do? What more could she want?

He didn't love her, he still didn't love her. If she was winning through, it was by default and staying power. She wasn't demanding or difficult, spoilt or imperious. She was loyal and trustworthy and crazy about children. She had had no other lovers. Luc would have a problem coming to terms with a woman who had a past to match his own. And in the bedroom…her skin heated at the acknowledgement that she never said no to him, could hardly contain her pleasure when he touched her. Most importantly of all, perhaps, she loved him, and he was content to be loved as long as she never asked for more than he was prepared to give. All in all, he wasn't so much marrying her as promoting her and, though her pride warred against that reality, it was better than severance pay.

'The wedding will take place within a few days,' Luc drawled casually and, picking up the phone, he began the first of several calls. Finding himself the focus of her attention, a smile of almost startling brilliance slashed his hard mouth and he extended a hand, drawing her under the shelter of his arm. 'You look happy,' he said approvingly.

Only a woman who was fathoms deep in love could lose a year of her life and still be happy. Kicking off her shoes, she rested blissfully back into the lean heat of him, thinking she had to be the luckiest woman alive. Maybe if she worked incredibly hard at being a perfect wife, he might fall in love with her.

'We're in a traffic jam,' she whispered teasingly, tugging at the end of his tie, feeling infinitely more daring than she had ever felt before. The awareness that they would soon be married was dissolving her usual inhibitions.

Luc tensed into sudden rigidity and stumbled over what he was saying. Leaning over him, bracing one hand on a taut thigh, Catherine reached up and loosened his tie, trailing it off in what she hoped was a slow, seductive fashion.

'Catherine…what are you doing?'

Luc was being abnormally obtuse. Colliding with golden eyes that had a stunned stillness, she went pink and, lowering her head, embarked on the buttons of his shirt. Hiding a mischievous smile, she understood his incredulity. Undressing Luc was a first. Initiating lovemaking was also a first. She ran caressing fingertips over warm golden skin roughened by black curling hair. His audible intake of oxygen matched to the raw tension in his muscles encouraged her to continue.

There was so much pleasure in simply touching him. It was extraordinary, she thought abstractly, but, although sanity told her it couldn't be possible, she felt starved of him. As she pressed her lips lovingly to his vibrant flesh and kissed a haphazard trail of increasing self-indulgence from his strong brown throat to his flat muscular stomach, he jerked and dropped the phone.

'Catherine…' he muttered, sounding satisfyingly ragged.

Her small hand strayed over his thigh. As she touched him he groaned deep in his throat and a sense of wondering power washed over her. He was trembling, his dark head thrown back, a fevered flush accentuating his hard bone-structure. All this time and it was this easy, she reflected, marvelling at the sheer strength of his response to her.

'Catherine, you shouldn't be doing this.' He was breathing fast and audibly, the words thick and indistinct.

'I'm enjoying myself,' she confided, slightly dazed by what she was doing, but telling the truth.

'*Per amor di Dio*, where's my conscience?' he gasped as she ran the tip of her tongue along his waistband.

'What conscience?' she whispered, lost in a voluptuous world all of her own as she inched down his straining zip.

'*Cristo*, this is purgatory!' Taking her by surprise, Luc jack-knifed out of reach at accelerated speed. 'We can't do this. We're nearly at the airport!' he muttered unsteadily.

'We're in a traffic jam.' In an agony of mortification more intense than any she had ever known, she stared at him, her hauntingly beautiful eyes dark with pain.

With a succinct swear-word, he dragged her close, taking her mouth with a wild, ravishing hunger that drove the breath from her lungs and left her aching for more. Every nerve-ending in her body went crazy in that powerful embrace. Plastered to every aroused line of his taut length, the scent of him and the taste of him and the feel of him went to her head with the potency of a mind-blowing narcotic.

Dragging his mouth from hers, he buried his face in her tumbled hair. The sharp shock of separation hurt. His heart was crashing against her crushed breasts. She could literally feel him fighting to get himself back under control. A long, shuddering breath ran through him. 'You're not strong enough for this, Catherine. You're supposed to be resting,' he reminded her almost roughly. 'So, have a little pity, hmm? Don't torture me.'

'I'm not ill. I feel great.' She ignored the throbbing at the base of her skull.

With a hard glance of disagreement, he set her back on the seat. 'You're quite capable of saying that because you think that's what I want to hear. How could you feel great? You must feel lousy, and, the next time I ask, lousy is what I want to hear! Is that clear?'

'As crystal.' Bowing her head, she fought to suppress the silent explosion of amusement that had crept up on her unawares. Why was she laughing? Why the heck was she laughing? Her body was shrieking at the deprivation he had sentenced them both to suffer. It wasn't funny, it really wasn't funny, but if she went to her dying day she would cherish the look of disbelief on his dark features when she, and not he, took the initiative for a change.

She had shocked Luc, actually shocked him. Who would ever have dreamt that she could possess that capability? It made her feel wicked…it made her feel sexy…and his reaction had made her feel like the most wildly seductive woman in the world. And wasn't it sweet, incredibly sweet of her supremely self-centred Luc to embrace celibacy for her benefit?

Once, she was convinced, Luc would have taken her invitation at face value, satisfying his own natural inclinations without further thought. That he *had* thought meant a great deal to her. That brand of unselfish caring was halfway to love, wasn't it? In a state of bliss, Catherine listened to him reeling off terse instructions to some unfortunate, no doubt quailing at the other end of the phone line. She wanted to smile. She knew why Luc was in a bad mood.

They traversed the airport at speed in a crush of moving bodies, security men zealously warding off the reporters and photographers Luc deplored. He guarded his privacy with a ferocity that more than one newspaper had lived to regret.

'Who's the blonde, Mr Santini?' someone shouted raucously.

Without warning, Luc wheeled round, his arm banding round Catherine in a hold of steel. 'The future Mrs Santini,' he announced, taking everyone by surprise, including Catherine.

There was a sudden hush and then a frantic clamour of questions, accompanied by the flash of many cameras. Luc's uncharacteristic generosity towards the Press concluded there.

They were crossing the tarmac to the jet when it happened. Something dark and dreadful loomed at the back of her mind and leapt out at her. The sensation frightened the life out of her and she froze. She saw an elderly woman with grey hair, her kindly face distraught. 'You mustn't do it…you mustn't!' she was pleading. And then the image was gone, leaving Catherine white and dizzy and sick with only this nameless, irrational fear focused on the jet.

'I can't get on it!' she gasped.

'Catherine.' Luc glowered down at her.

'I can't...I can't! I don't know why, but I can't!' Hysteria blossoming, she started to back away with raised hands.

Luc strode forward, planted powerful hands to her narrow waist and swung her with daunting strength into his arms. In the grip of that incomprehensible panic, she struggled violently. 'I can't get on that jet!'

'It's not your responsibility any more.' Luc held her with steely tenacity. 'I'm kidnapping you. Think of it as an elopement. Good afternoon, Captain Edgar. Just ignore my fiancée. She's a little phobic about anything that flies without feathers.'

The pilot struggled visibly to keep his facial muscles straight. 'I'll keep it smooth, Mr Santini.'

Luc mounted the steps two at a time, stowed Catherine into a seat and did up the belt much as though it were a ball and chain to keep her under restraint. He gripped her hands. 'Now breathe in slowly and pull yourself together,' he instructed. 'You can scream all the way to Rome if you like but it's not going to get you anywhere. Think of this as the first day of the rest of your life.'

Gasping in air, she stared at him, wide-eyed. 'I saw this woman. I remembered something. She said I mustn't do it...'

'Do what?'

'She didn't say what.' Already overwhelmingly aware of the foolishness of her behaviour, her voice sank to a limp mumble. 'I had this feeling that I shouldn't board the jet, that I was leaving something behind. It was so powerful. I felt so scared.'

'Do you feel scared now?'

'No, of course not.' She flushed. 'I'm sorry. I went crazy, didn't I?'

'You had a flashback. Your memory's returning.'

'Do you think so?' She brightened, was faintly puzzled by his cool tone and the hard glitter of his gaze. 'Why was I so scared?'

'The shock and the suddenness of it,' he proffered smoothly. 'It couldn't have been a comforting experience.'

The flight lasted two hours. They were not alone. There was the steward and the stewardess, the two security men, a sleek executive type taking notes every time Luc spoke, and a svelte female secretary at his elbow, passing out files and removing them and relaying messages. And the weird part of it all was that if Catherine looked near any of them they hurriedly looked away as if she had the plague or something.

Sitting in solitary state, she beckoned the stewardess. 'Could I have a magazine?'

'There are no magazines or newspapers on board, Miss Parrish. I'm so sorry.' The woman's voice was strained, her eyes evasive. 'Would you like lunch now?'

'Thanks.' It was quite peculiar that there shouldn't even be a magazine on board. Still, she would only have flicked through it. Sooner or later, she would have to tell Luc that she was dyslexic. She cringed at the prospect. She had never expected to be able to fool Luc this long. But somehow he had always made it so easy for her.

If there was a menu in the vicinity, he ordered her meals. He accepted that she preferred to remember phone messages rather than write them down for him, and was surprisingly tolerant when she forgot the details. He never mentioned the rarity with which she read a book. Occasionally she bought one and left it on display, but he never asked what it was about. And why did she go to all that trouble?

She remembered how often she had been called stupid before the condition was diagnosed at school. She remembered all the potential foster parents who had backed off at the very mention of dyslexia, falsely assuming that she would be more work and trouble than any other child. She also remembered all the people who had treated her as though she were illiterate. And if Luc realised he was taking on a wife to whom the written word was almost a blur of disconnected images, he might change his mind about marrying her.

When they landed in Rome, he told her that they were completing their journey by helicopter. 'Where will we be staying?' she prompted.

'We won't be staying anywhere,' he countered. 'We're coming home.'

'Home?' she echoed. 'You've bought a house?'

Luc shifted a negligent hand. 'Wait and see.'

'I haven't been there before, have I? It's not something else that I've forgotten, is it?'

'You've never been in Italy before,' he soothed.

She hated the helicopter and insisted on a rear seat, refusing the frontal bird's-eye view that Luc wanted her to have. The racket of the rotors and her sore head interacted unpleasantly, upsetting her stomach. She kept her head down, only raising it when they touched down on solid ground again.

Luc eased her out into the fresh air again, murmuring, 'Lousy?'

'Lousy,' she gulped.

'I should've thought of that, but I wanted you to see Castelleone from the air.' Walking her way from the helipad, he carefully turned her round. 'This is quite a good vantage point. What do you think?'

If he hadn't been supporting her, her knees would have buckled at the sight which greeted her stunned eyes. Castelleone was a fairy-tale castle with a forest of towers and spires set against a backdrop of lush, thickly wooded hills. Late-afternoon sunlight glanced off countless gleaming windows and cast still reflections of the cream stone walls on the water-lily-strewn moat. She should have been better prepared. She should have known to think big and, where Luc was concerned, think extravagant. He might have little time for history but with what else but history could he have attained a home of such magnificence and grandeur?

'It wasn't for sale when I found it, and it wasn't as pretty as it is now...'

'Pretty?' she protested, finding her tongue again. 'It's beautiful! It must have cost a fortune.'

'I've got money to burn and nothing else to spend it on.' Idle fingertips slid caressingly through her hair. 'It's a listed building, which is damnably inconvenient. The renovations had to be restorations. Experts are very interfering people. There were times when I wouldn't have cared if those walls came tumbling down into that chocolate-box moat.'

'You're joking!' she gasped.

'Am I? Have you ever lived with seventeenth-century plumbing, *cara*? It was barbaric,' Luc breathed above her head. 'The experts and I came to an agreement. The plumbing went into a museum and I stopped threatening to fill in the moat. We understood each other very well after that.'

'You said it wasn't for sale when you first saw it.'

'For everything there is a price, *bella mia*.' With a soft laugh, he linked his arms round her. 'The last owner had no sentimental attachment to the place. It had been a drain on his finances for too long.'

'Did you ever tell me about it?'

'I wanted to surprise you.' He guided her towards the elaborate stone bridge spanning the moat. Tall studded doors stood wide on a hall covered with exquisitely painted frescoes.

'I've never seen anything so beautiful,' she whispered.

'Admittedly not everyone has a foyer full of fat cherubs and bare-breasted nymphs. I'll concede that if I concede nothing else,' Luc said mockingly. 'The original builder wasn't over-endowed with good taste.'

'If you don't like it, why did you buy it?' she pressed, struggling to hold back her tiredness.

He moved a broad shoulder. 'It's an investment.'

'Does that mean you plan to sell it again?' Her dismay was evident.

'Not if you feel you can live with all those naked women.'

'I can live with them!'

'Somehow,' he murmured softly, 'I thought you would feel like that.'

Luc appraised her pallor, the shadows like bruises below her eyes, and headed her to the curving stone staircase. 'Bed, I think.'

'I don't want to go to bed. I want to see the whole castle.' If it was a dream that Luc should want to marry her and live in this glorious building, she was afraid to sleep lest she wake up.

'You've had all the excitement you can take for one day.' Luc whipped her purposefully off her feet when she showed signs of straying in the direction of an open doorway. 'Why are you smiling like that?'

'Because I feel as though I've died and gone to heaven and—' she hesitated, sending him an adoring look '—I love you so much.'

Dark blood seared his cheekbones, his jawline hardening. Unconcerned, she linked her arms round his throat. 'I'm not a plaster saint,' he breathed.

'I can live with your flaws.'

'You'll have to live with them,' he corrected. 'Divorce won't be one of your options.'

She winced, pained by that response. 'It isn't very romantic to talk about divorce before the wedding.'

'Catherine...as you ought to know by now, I'm not a very romantic guy. I'm not poetic, I'm not sentimental, I'm not idealistic,' he spelt out grimly.

'You make love in Italian,' she said in a small voice.

'It's the first language I ever spoke!'

For some peculiar reason, he was getting angry. She decided to let him have his own way. If he didn't think sweeping her off to a castle in Italy and marrying her within days was romantic, he had a problem. It might be wise, she decided, to share a little less of her rapture. But it was very difficult. Feeling weak and exhausted didn't stop her from wanting to pin him to the nearest horizontal surface and smother him with grateful love and kisses.

At the top of that unending staircase, Luc paused to introduce her to a little man called Bernardo, who rejoiced in the title of major-domo. Catherine beamed at him.

'Do you think you could possibly pin those dizzy feet of yours back to mother earth for a while?' Luc enquired sardonically.

'Not when you're carrying me,' she sighed.

Thrusting open a door, he crossed a large room and settled her down on a bed. It was a four-poster, hung with tassels and fringes and rich brocade. She rested back with a groan of utter content-ment, lifted one leg and kicked off a shoe, repeated the action with the other. It was definitely her sort of bed.

His expressive mouth quirked. 'I've arranged for a doctor to see you in half an hour. Do you think you could manage to look less as though you've been at the sherry?'

'What do I need another doctor for?'

A smile angled over her. 'Amnesia is a distressing condition, or so the story goes. I've never seen you like this…at least,' he paused, 'not in a long time.'

'You've never asked me to marry you before,' she whispered shyly.

'A serious oversight. You've never tried to seduce me in the back of a limousine before, either.' Golden eyes rested on her intently and then, abruptly, he took his attention off her again. 'I don't think you'll find Dr Scipione too officious. He believes that time heals all.' He strolled back to the door, lithe as a leopard on the prowl. 'Bernardo's wife will come up and help you to get into bed.'

'I don't need—'

'Catherine,' he interrupted, 'one of the minor advantages of being my wife is being waited on hand and foot, thus saving your energy for more important pursuits.'

Her eyes danced. 'And one of the major ones?'

Hooded dark eyes wandered at a leisurely pace over her, and heat pooled in her pelvis, her stomach clenching. 'I'll leave that to your imagination, active as I know it to be. *Buona sera, cara.* I'll see you tomorrow.'

'Tomorrow?' She sat up in shock.

'Rest and peace.' Luc made the reminder mockingly and shut the door.

She stared up at the elaborately draped canopy above her. You were flirting with him, a little voice said. What was so strange about that? She couldn't ever recall doing it before. As a rule, she guarded and picked and chose her words with Luc in much the same fashion as one trod a careful passage round a sleeping volcano. Only at the beginning had she been naïve enough to blurt out exactly what was on her mind.

But she wasn't conscious of that barrier now, hadn't been all day or even last night. She was no longer in awe of Luc. When had that happened? Presumably some time during this past year. And yet Luc had said he had never seen her like this in a long time. What was this? This, she conceded, hugging a pillow dripping lace and ribbons to her fast-beating heart, was being wonderfully, madly and utterly without restraint…happy.

CHAPTER FIVE

THE rails of clothing in the dressing-room bedazzled Catherine. Encouraged, the little maid, Guilia, pressed back more doors: day-wear, evening-wear, leisure-wear, shelves of cobwebby, gorgeous lingerie and row upon row of shoes, everything grouped into tiny bands of colour. Co-ordination for the non-colour-clever woman, she thought dazedly. Luc had bought her an entire new wardrobe.

Such an extensive collection could not have been put together overnight. Overwhelming as the idea was, she could only see one viable explanation—Luc must have been planning to bring her to Italy for months! As her fingertips lingered on a silk dress, Guilia looked anxious and swung out a full-length gown, contriving to be very apologetic about the suggested exchange.

'*Grazie*, Guilia.'

'*Prego, signorina.*' With enthusiasm, Guilia whipped out lin-gerie and shoes and carried the lot reverently through to the bed-room. Catherine recognised a plant when she saw one. Guilia was here to educate her in the nicest possible way on what to wear for every possible occasion. Luc excelled on detail. Guilia had prob-ably been programmed to bar the wardrobe doors if presented with a pretty cabbage-rose print.

It was eight in the evening. She had slept the clock round, slumbering through her first day at Castelleone. Last night, Bernardo's wife, Francesca, had fussed her into bed with the warmth of a mother hen. Dr Scipione had then made his début, a rotund little man with a pronounced resemblance to Santa Claus and an expression of soulful understanding.

Only when he had gone had she realised that she had chattered her head off the whole time he was there. He had only made her uneasy once by saying, 'Sometimes the mind forgets because it wants to forget. It shuts a door in self-protection.'

'What would I want to protect myself from?' she laughed.

'Ask yourself what you most fear and there may well lie the answer. It could be that when you fully confront that fear your mind will unlock that door,' he suggested. 'I suspect that you are not ready for that moment as yet.'

What did she most fear? Once it had been losing Luc, but since Luc had asked her to marry him that old insecurity had been banished forever. And the truth was that a little hiccup in her memory-banks did not currently have the power to alarm her—despite a nagging anxiety which she resolutely banished.

Attired in the fitting cerise-hued sheath, which was tighter over the fullness of her breasts than Guilia seemed to have expected, judging by the speed with which she had whipped out a tape-measure, Catherine sat down at the magnificent Gothic-styled dressing-table and smiled at the familiarity of the jewellery on display there. Her watch, stamped with the date she had first met Luc; clasping it to her wrist, she marvelled at how long it seemed since she had worn it. A leather box disclosed a slender diamond necklace and drop earrings; a second, a shimmering delicate bracelet. Christmas in Switzerland and her birthday, she reflected dreamily.

Leaving the bedroom, she peered over the stone balcony of the vast circular gallery. Bernardo's bald-spot was visible in the hall far below. She hurried downstairs and said in halting Italian, 'Buona sera, Bernardo. Dov'é Signor Santini?'

Bernardo looked anguished. He wrung his hands and muttered something inaudible. Abruptly she turned, her eyes widening. Raised voices had a carrying quality in the echoing spaces around them.

One of the doors stood ajar. A tall black-haired woman, with shoulder-pads that put new meaning into power-dressing, was ranting, presumably at Luc, who was out of view. Or was she pleading? It was hard to tell.

Catherine tensed. She had no difficulty in recognising Rafaella

Peruzzi. She was the only person Catherine knew who could argue with Luc and still have a job at the end of the day. She inhabited a nebulous grey area in Luc's life, somewhere between old friend and employee. She was also Santini Electronics' most efficient hatchet-woman. She lived, breathed, ate and slept profit...and Luc.

She had grown up with him. She had modelled herself on him. She was tough, ruthless and absolutely devoted to his interests. At some stage she had also shared a bed with Luc. Nobody had told Catherine that. Nobody had needed to tell her. Rafaella was a piece of Luc's past, but the past was a hopeful present in her eyes every time she looked at him. The women who blazed a quickly forgotten trail through his bedroom didn't bother Rafaella. Catherine had.

'You've got six weeks left. Enjoy him while you can,' she had derided the first time Catherine met her. 'With Luc, it never lasts longer than three months, and, with the clothes-sense you've got, honey, another six weeks should be quite a challenge for him.'

Luc was talking very quietly now. Rafaella vented a strangled sob and spat back in staccato Italian. Catherine moved away, ashamed that she hadn't moved sooner, and uneasily certain of the source of the drama. Yesterday, Luc had publicly announced his marital plans. Rafaella was reeling. Her pain seared Catherine with a strange sister pain. There but for the grace of God go I.

Luc was the sun round which Rafaella revolved. She could not resist that pull even when it scorched her; she could not break free. Though she knew that she was overstepping the boundaries that Luc set, she would still interfere. That was Rafaella. Stubborn, persistent, remorseless in enmity. Sometimes what disturbed Catherine most about Rafaella was her similarity to Luc. By the law of averages, she had thought uneasily more than once, Luc and Rafaella ought to have been a match made in heaven.

A door slammed on its hinges with an almighty crash. Bernardo had made himself scarce. Catherine wasn't quick enough. Rafaella stalked across the hall and circled her like a killer shark drawn by a lump of raw meat, rage and hatred splintering from her diamond-hard stare.

'You bitch!' She launched straight into attack. 'He wouldn't believe me when I told him, but I'll be back when I can prove it. And when I get the evidence you'll be out with the garbage, because he'll never forgive you!'

'Rafaella.' Luc was poised fifty feet away, lithe and sleek as a panther about to spring, his features savagely set.

She shot him a fierce, embittered glance. 'I wanted a closer look at the only truly honest woman you've ever met! She must be on the endangered species list. And, *caro*,' she forecast on her passage to the door, 'you're in for a severe dose of indigestion.'

Bernardo reappeared out of nowhere and surged to facilitate her exit. Catherine slowly breathed again. Rafaella, out of control and balked of her prey, was an intimidating experience. And she was astounded by her threats. What wouldn't Luc believe? What did Rafaella intend to prove? What would Luc never forgive her for?

'What on earth was she talking about?' she whispered tautly.

Smouldering tension still vibrated from Luc. She could read nothing in the steady beat of his dark eyes. For an instant it seemed to her that that stare both probed and challenged, but she dismissed the idea when a faintly sardonic smile lighted his expression. 'Nothing that need concern you.'

But it *did* concern her, she reasoned frustratedly as he curved a possessive arm to her slim shoulders and guided her into the magnificently proportioned *salone*. 'And Rafaella need not concern you either,' he completed.

'Why?' she prompted uncertainly.

'As of now, she no longer works for me,' Luc drawled with a chilling lack of sentiment.

Catherine was immediately filled with guilt. Rafaella lived for her career. If she hadn't been hanging about in the hall, the incident which had so enraged Luc would never have occurred. 'She was terribly upset, Luc. Shouldn't you make allowances for that?' she muttered after a long pause, resenting the ironic twist of fate that had set her up as the brunette's sole defender.

'What is wrong with you?' Luc demanded, abrasive in his incredulity. 'In the same position, she'd slit your throat without a second's hesitation. She walks into my home, she insults me, she insults you…and you expect me to take that lying down? I don't believe this!'

'She lost her head and it wouldn't have happened if…if…' she fumbled awkwardly beneath his piercing scrutiny '…she didn't love you.'

'Love like that I can do without,' he responded, unmoved.

'Sometimes,' she whispered, 'you can be very unfeeling, Luc.'

His superb bone-structure clenched, something more than irritation leaping through him now. 'Which translates to a ruthless, insensitive bastard, does it not?' he sizzled back at her.

Nobody criticised Luc. Rafaella might argue with him, but she would not have dreamt of criticising him. From being an infant prodigy in a very ordinary, poorly educated family in awe of his intellectual gifts, Luc had stalked into early adulthood, unfettered by any need or demand to consider anyone but himself. But he was in the wrong and she was helplessly tempted to tell him that plainly, had to bite back the words. He could not treat Rafaella as an old friend one moment and a humble employee the next. It had not been a kindness to keep Rafaella so close when he was aware of her feelings for him. It had only encouraged her to hope.

'I didn't say that,' she said tightly. 'Don't shout me down.'

'I am not shouting you down. You fascinate me. You belong up on a cloud with a harp!' he derided with acid bite. 'You haven't the slightest conception of what makes other human beings tick.'

Catherine lifted her chin. 'I only said that Rafaella deserves a little compassion—'

'Compassion? If you were bleeding to death by the side of the road, she'd sell tickets!' he grated. 'She's out because I don't trust her any more. I understand her too well. The first opportunity she gets, she'll stick a knife in your back, even if it costs her everything she has.'

Her flesh chilled involuntarily at the deadly certainty with which he voiced that belief.

'The subject is now closed. Are you coming to dinner?' he concluded drily.

'Will you give her a reference?'

There was a sharp little silence. Luc spun back, clashed with the hauntingly beautiful blue eyes pinned expectantly to him. '*Per amor di Dio*...all right, if that's what you want!' he gritted, out of all patience.

He wasn't built to recognise compromise. Compromise was a retrograde step towards losing, and losing didn't come gracefully to Luc. Catherine tucked into her dinner with unblemished appetite. Luc poked at his appetiser, complained about the temperature of the wine, sat tapping his fingers in tyrannical tattoo between courses and cooled down only slowly.

'What did you think of Dr Scipione?' he enquired over the coffee.

'He was very kind. Is he the local doctor?'

An ebony brow quirked. 'He lives in Rome. He's also one of the world's leading authorities on amnesia.'

'Oh.' Catherine almost choked on her dismay. 'I treated him as if he was just anybody!'

'Catherine, one of your greatest virtues is the ability to treat everyone from the lowliest cleaning-lady up in exactly the same way,' he murmured, unexpectedly linking his fingers with hers, a smile curving the formerly hard line of his lips. 'Let us at least agree that your manners are a great deal better than mine. By the way, I have some papers for you to sign before we can get married. We should take care of them now.'

She accompanied him into the library where he had been with Rafaella earlier. It was packed with books from floor to ceiling, and a massive desk sat before the tall windows. Fierce discomfiture gripped her when she saw the sheaf of documents he lifted. Forms to fill in...bureaucracy. With Luc present, her worst nightmare had full substance.

'This is the...' Luc handed her a pen but she didn't absorb his explanation. There was a thunderbeat of tension in her ears. 'You sign here.' A brown forefinger indicated the exact spot and stayed there.

The paper was a grey and white blur. Covertly she bent her

head. 'I just s-sign?' she stammered, terrified that there was some-thing else to do that he wasn't mentioning because he would nat-urally assume that she could easily see it and read it for herself.

'You just sign.'

She inscribed her signature slowly and carefully. Luc whipped the document away and presented her with a second. 'And here.'

More hurriedly, less carefully, she complied. 'Is that it?' Strug-gling to conceal her relief at his nod of confirmation, she lifted the document. 'You once told me never to sign anything I couldn't read,' she joked unsteadily.

'I was more obtuse than I am now.' He studied her. The strain etched in her delicate profile was beginning to ease but her hand was shaking perceptibly. 'It's in Italian, *cara*,' he told her very gently.

'I wasn't really looking at it.' Clumsily she put it down again.

Before she could turn away, lean hands came down to rest on her tense shoulders, keeping her in front of him where he lounged on the edge of the polished desk. 'I believe it's more than that,' he countered quietly. 'Don't you think it's time that we stopped playing this game? Whether you realise it or not, it's caused a lot of misunderstanding between us.'

Her face had gone chalk-white. 'G-game?'

He sighed. 'Why do you think I choose your meals for you when we dine out?'

'I...I dither; it saves time,' she muttered, making an abrupt move to walk away, but he was impervious to the hint.

'And I'm just naturally insensitive to what you might choose for yourself?' he chided. 'Catherine, I've been aware that you have trouble reading since the first week I spent with you in London. I saw through all those painfully elaborate little stratagems and, I have to admit, I was pretty shocked.'

Her stricken gaze veiled as tears lashed her eyelids in a blis-tering surge. She wanted the ground to open up and swallow her. His deep voice, no matter how calm and quiet it was, stung like a whip on her most vulnerable skin. Her throat was convulsing and she couldn't speak. All she wanted to do was get away from him, but his arms banded round her slim waist like steel hawsers.

'We are going to have this all out in the open,' Luc informed her steadily. 'Why didn't you tell me right at the beginning that you were dyslexic? I didn't realise that. You were ashamed of it and I didn't want to hurt your feelings, so I pretended as well. I ignored it but, in my ignorance of the true situation, I hoped very much that you would do something about it.'

'I can't!' she gasped. 'They did all they could for me at school but I'll never be able to read properly!'

'Do you think I don't know that now? Will you stop trying to get away from me?' he demanded, subduing her struggles with determined hands. 'I know that you're dyslexic, but I didn't know it then. I thought—'

'You thought I was just illiterate!' she sobbed in agonised interruption. 'I'll never forgive you for doing this to me!'

'You're going to listen to me.' He held her fast. 'I was at fault as well. I took the easy way out. What I didn't like, I chose not to see. I should have tried to help you myself. Had I done that, I would have realised what was really wrong. But you should have told me,' he censured.

'Let go of me!' she railed at him, shaken by tempestuous sobs of humiliation.

'Don't you understand what I'm trying to tell you?' He gave her a fierce little shake that momentarily roused her from her distress. 'If I had known, if I had understood, I wouldn't have been angry when you made no effort to improve your situation! I'm not getting through to you, am I?'

'You're ashamed of me!' she accused him despairingly.

Sliding upright, he crushed her into his arms and laced one hand into the golden fall of her hair to tip her head back. 'No, I'm not,' he contradicted fiercely. 'There is nothing to be ashamed of. Einstein was dyslexic, da Vinci was dyslexic. If it was good enough for them, it's good enough for you!'

'Oh, Luc!' A laugh somewhere between a hiccup and a sob

escaped her as she looked up at him. 'Good enough? I probably have it worse than they did.'

'I don't know how I could have been so blind for so long,' he admitted. 'You have no sense of direction, you can't tell left from right, the tying of a bow defeats you, and sometimes you're just a little forgetful.' There was a teasing, soothing quality to that concluding statement.

She was still shaking. Her distress had been too great to ebb quickly. She buried her face in his jacket, weak and uncertain, but beyond that there was this glorious sense of release from a pretence that had frequently lacerated her nerves and kept her in constant fear of discovery.

'You don't mind, you really don't mind?' she muttered.

'All that I mind is that you didn't trust me enough to tell me yourself, but, now I know, we can speak to an educational specialist—I'm sure you can be helped.' Tipping her head back, he produced a hanky and automatically mopped her up, smiling down at her, and something about that smile made her heart skip an entire beat. 'It wasn't brave to suffer in silence, it was foolish. I would have understood your difficulties. We live in a world in which the capacity to interpret the written word is taken for granted. How did you manage to work in the art gallery? I've often wondered that,' he confided.

'Elaine taped the catalogue for me.'

He finger-combed her hair back into a semblance of order. 'Secrets,' he said, 'create misunderstandings.'

'That's the only one I have,' she sighed. 'You're always tidying me up and putting me back together again.'

'Maybe I enjoy doing it. Have you thought of that?' he teased, his husky voice fracturing slightly as she stared up at him.

All the oxygen in the air seemed to be used up without warning. Desire clutched at her stomach in a lancing surge. Her breasts felt constrained within their silken covering as her sensitive flesh swelled and her nipples peaked into tight aching buds. The sensations were blindingly physical, unnervingly powerful, and she trembled.

He withdrew his hand from her hair and stepped back. 'It's late. You should go to bed,' he muttered harshly. 'If you don't, I'll take you here.'

A heady flush lit her cheeks. She backed away obediently on cotton-wool legs. She couldn't drag her eyes from his dark-golden beauty. The view was spiced by her intrinsic awareness of the savage sexual intensity contained below that surface calm and control. She wanted him. She wanted him so much that it scared her. In her memory there was nothing to equal the force of the hunger she was experiencing now. It confused her, embarrassed her.

'I'm expecting an important call,' he added, and, as she looked at him in surprise, said succinctly, 'Time zones.'

She couldn't picture Luc sitting up to take a phone call, no matter how important it was. People called at his convenience, not their own. Still watching him, she found the door more by accident than design and fumbled it open. 'I really am feeling marvellous,' she assured him in a self-conscious rush before she ducked out into the hall.

Although she had bathed earlier, Catherine decided to have a refreshing shower. Fifteen minutes later, liberally anointed with some of the scented essences she had found on a shelf in the *en suite* bathroom, she donned the diaphanous peach silk nightdress lying across the bed and slid between the sheets to lie back in a breathless state of anticipation and wait for Luc.

The minutes dragged past. She amused herself by thinking lovingly of how reassuring he had been about her dyslexia. He was right. She should have confided in him a long time ago. He would have understood. She saw that now, regretted her silence and subterfuge, and felt helplessly guilty about misjudging him so badly.

Somewhere in the midst of these ruminations, she dozed off and dreamt. It was the strangest dream. She was writing on a mirror, sound-spelling 'Ah-ree-va'...and she was crying while she did it, reflections of what she was writing and her own unhappy face making the task all the more difficult. There was so much pain in that image that she wanted to scream with it, and she woke up with a start in the darkness, tears wet on her cheeks.

Somebody had switched the light out. She made that connection, bridging the gap between a piece of the past she had forgotten and the present. She slumped back against the pillows, clinging to the dream, but there was so little of it to hold on to and build on. It was the pain she recalled most, a bewildered, frantic sense of pain and defeat.

Padding into the bathroom, she splashed her face and dried it. Who had switched the light off? It must have been Luc. He had come to her and she had been fast asleep. She lifted a weak hand to her forehead where the pounding in her temples was only slowly steadying. It was impossible to stifle a sudden, desperate, tearing need to be with him.

She approached the door in her bedroom which she assumed connected with his. Finding it locked, she frowned and crept out on to the gallery, dimly wondering what time it was. The bedroom itself was in darkness when she entered, but a triangle of light was spilling from the open bathroom door. She could hear a shower running and she smiled. It couldn't be that late. She scrambled into the turned-back bed as quietly as a mouse.

The shower went off and the light almost simultaneously. A second or two later the bedroom curtains were drawn back. Luc unlatched one of the windows and stood there in the moonlight, magnificently naked, towelling his hair dry.

He was asking to catch his death of cold but the urge to announce her presence dwindled. Whipcord muscles flexed taut beneath the smooth golden skin of his back. Her mouth ran dry. Feeling mortifyingly like a voyeur, she closed her eyes. The mattress gave slightly with his weight and three-quarters of the sheet was wrenched from her.

As he rolled over, punching a pillow and narrowly missing her head, he came into sudden contact with her. *'Dio!'* Jerking semi-upright, he lunged at the light above the bed before she could prevent him.

One hand braced tautly on the carved headboard, he stared down at her in shock. 'Catherine?'

She could feel one of those ghastly beetroot blushes crawling in a tide over her exposed skin. Somehow his tone implied that the very last place he expected to find her was in his bed. 'I couldn't sleep.'

He slid lower on the mattress, surveying her intently, his cheekbones harshly accentuated. 'No more could I. Come here.' He reached out with a determined hand and brought her close, not giving her time to respond to what was more of a command than a request. 'I want you,' he admitted roughly. 'Do you have any idea how much I want you?'

'I'm here,' she whispered, suddenly shy of him.

Bending his dark head, he muttered something ferocious in Italian and crushed her lips apart with a savage urgency that took her very much by surprise. His tongue ravished the tender interior of her mouth. She might have been a life-saving draught to a male driven to the edge of madness by thirst. He bruised her lips and drank deep and long until her head swam and she couldn't breathe. Fire as elemental as he was leapt through her veins.

Her hands found his shoulders. He was burning up as though he had a fever, his skin hot and dry, his long, hard body savagely tense against hers. Lean fingers fumbled with an unusual lack of dexterity at the silk that concealed her from him. With a stifled growl of frustration, he drew back and tore the whisper-fine fabric apart with impatient hands.

'Luc!' Catherine surfaced abruptly from a drowning well of passion and fixed shocked eyes on him as he knelt over her, trailing the torn remnants from her and tossing them carelessly aside. As she made an instinctive attempt to cover herself from his devouring scrutiny, he caught at her wrists and flattened them to the bed.

'Please.' It was a word he very rarely employed and there was a note in that roughened plea that stabbed at her heart and made her ache.

Brilliant golden eyes ran over her in a look as physical as touch, exploring the burgeoning swell of her breasts, the smoothness of her narrow ribcage, the feminine curve of her hips and the soft curls at the juncture of her thighs.

'*Squisita…perfetta,*' he muttered raggedly as he drew her towards him, and his mouth swooped down to capture a taut nipple.

Her back arched as a whimper of formless sound was torn from her throat. He suckled her tender flesh with an intensely erotic enjoyment that drove her wild. He bit with subtle delicacy, his hand toying with the neglected twin, shaping, tugging, exciting until she was writhing beneath his ministrations. She wanted his weight on her and he denied her, lifting his head only to trail the tip of his tongue teasingly down between her breasts, traversing the pale skin of her ribs and dipping into the hollow of her navel.

Her hands dug into his hair and tightened in immediate protest as he strung a line of wholly determined kisses from the bend of her knee to the smooth inner skin of her thigh, tensing tiny muscles she didn't know she possessed. And then her neck extended and her head fell back on the pillows. A cry fled her lips, all thought arrested as she sank into the seduction of pure sensation and was lost in the frantic clamour of her own body.

At the peak of an excitement more of agony than pleasure, Catherine cried out his name, and his hands curved hard to her hips as he rose above her, silencing her with the tormenting force of his mouth. Against her most tender flesh, he was hot and insistent. For a split second he stared down at her, desire and demand stamped in his dark, damp features, and then he moved, thrusting deep as a bolt of lightning rending the heavens.

Pain clenched her, unexpected enough to dredge her briefly from the driving, all-enveloping hunger for satisfaction that he had induced. He stilled, dealt her a look in which tenderness and triumph blazed, more blatant than speech, and pressed a fleeting benediction of a kiss to her brow. He muttered something about doubting her and never doubting her again.

She was in no condition to absorb what he was saying. With tiny, subtle, circling movements of his hips, he was inciting her to passion again, accustoming her to his fullness. All conscious thought was suspended. She was lost in the primal rhythm of giving all and taking everything, driven mindless and powerless towards that final shattering release. When it came in wave after wave of unbelievable pleasure, it was sublime.

His harsh groan of masculine satisfaction still echoing in her ears, she let her hands rove possessively over his sweat-dampened skin. Obtrusive questions licked at the corners of her mind. Had it ever been that profound, that overwhelming before? She remembered excitement, but not an excitement that swept her so quickly into oblivion. She remembered his hunger, but not a hunger that threatened to rage out of control in its raw intensity. She remembered the sweet joy of fulfilment, but not a fulfilment that stole her very soul with its fiery potency.

And she also remembered...sadly...that Luc was invariably halfway to the shower by now, shunning with that essential detachment of his the aftermath of passion when she had so desperately wanted him to stay in her arms.

He was holding her now as if at any moment she might make a break for freedom, and the awareness provoked a deep rush of tenderness within her. She rubbed her cheek lovingly against a strong brown shoulder. He shifted languorously like a sleek cat stretching beneath a caress, as unashamedly physical in his enjoyment as any member of the animal kingdom.

'I had a very strange dream.' She broke the silence hesitantly, afraid that the magic might escape. 'I don't know if it was a memory.'

Tension snaked through his relaxed length. 'What was it?'

'You'll probably laugh.'

'I promise I won't. Tell me.'

'I was writing on a mirror,' she whispered. 'Can you imagine that? I never write anything but my name unless I can help it, and there I was, writing on this mirror!'

'Amazing,' he murmured softly.

'It wasn't. It felt scary,' she muttered, half under her breath. 'It probably has nothing to do with my memory at all. What do you think?'

'I think you're talking too much.' Rolling over, he carried her with him on to a cool spot on the bed. 'And I would much rather make love, *bella mia*.' He nipped teasingly at the velvet-soft lobe of her ear and forged an erotic path along the slender arch of her throat as she involuntarily extended it for his pleasure. Her hair splayed out across the pillow and he studied the chopped ends wryly and looked down at her. 'You've been using scissors to hack at your hair again.'

'I can't think why,' she confessed with a slight frown. 'I'll go and get it cut tomorrow.'

'Someone can come here to take care of it,' he countered.

'I want to see Rome.'

'Bumper-to-bumper traffic and unbelievable heat and noise and pollution. Not to mention the tourists.' He extracted a long lingering kiss before she could protest, and then he started to make love to her again. This time he was incredibly gentle and seductive, utilising every art to enthrall her. Pleasure piled on pleasure in layers of ever-deepening delight. Incredibly, it was even more exciting than the first time.

A single white rose lay on the pillow when she opened her eyes. She discovered it by accident, her hand feeling blindly across the bed in automatic search for Luc. Instead she found a thorn and, with a yelp, she reared up, sucking her pricked finger. And there it was. The rose. She wanted to cry, but that was soppy. The dew still dampened the petals. She tried to picture her supremely elegant Luc clambering through a rosebed and failed utterly. A gardener had undoubtedly done the clambering. Luc wouldn't be caught dead in a flowerbed. All the same, it was the thought which counted and, for an unromantic guy, he really was trying very hard to please. In the end, it was that reflection rather than the rose that flooded her eyes with tears.

CHAPTER SIX

THE heat had reduced Catherine to a somnolent languor. She heard footsteps, recognised them. The cool of a large parasol blocked out the sun and shadowed her. She turned her head, rested her chin on her elbow and watched Luc sink down on the edge of the lounger beside her. In an open-necked short-sleeved white shirt and fitting black jeans that accentuated slim hips and long, lean thighs, he looked stunning enough to stop an avalanche in its tracks. A sun-dazed smile tilted her soft lips. He also looked distinctly short-tempered.

Since wedding fervour had hit Castelleone, the peace, the privacy and the perfect organisation which Luc took for granted had been swept away by a chattering tidal wave of caterers and florists and constantly shrilling phones. Luc's enthusiasm had waned with almost comical speed once he'd realised what throwing a reception for several hundred people entailed.

'I feel like throwing them all out,' he admitted grimly.

'You wanted a big splash,' she reminded him with more truth than tact.

'I thought it was what you expected!' he condemned.

'A couple of witnesses and a bunch of flowers would have done me,' she confided, feeling too warm and lazy to choose her words.

He threw up expressive hands. 'Now she tells me!'

The rattle of ice in glasses interrupted them. Luc leapt up and carefully intercepted Bernardo before he could come any closer. Catherine absorbed this defensive exercise with hidden amusement. Anyone would have been forgiven for thinking that her bare back was the equivalent of indecent exposure. Yesterday, a low-flying light plane had provoked an embargo on topless sunbathing and a no doubt fierce complaint to the local airfield. She wondered why it had taken her all this time to notice just how shockingly old-fashioned Luc could be about some things.

He cast her a sardonic glance. 'I love the way you lie out here as though there's nothing happening.'

'Bernardo knows exactly what he's doing.' With an excess of tact, she did not add that if Luc stopped wading in to interfere and organise, imbuing everyone with the feeling that their very best wasn't good enough, the last-minute arrangements would be proceeding a lot more smoothly. Having given the intimidating impression that he intended to supervise and criticise every little detail, he was not receiving a moment's peace.

Tomorrow, she reflected blissfully. Tomorrow, she would be Luc's wife. The 'died and gone to heaven' sensation embraced her again. Whole days had slid away in a haze of hedonistic pleasure since her arrival in Italy. Never had she enjoyed such utter relaxation and self-indulgence. Her sole contribution to the wedding had been two dress-fittings. Her gown, fashioned of exquisite handmade lace, was gorgeous. It was wonderful what could be achieved at short notice if you had as much money as Luc had.

'Tomorrow, I'll be rich,' she mused absently.

After an arrested pause, Luc flung back his gleaming dark head and roared with laughter. 'You're probably the only woman in the world who would dare to say that to me *before* the wedding.'

She gave him an abstracted smile. Luc? Luc was wonderful, fantastic, beautiful, incredible, divine… With unwittingly expressive eyes pinned to him, she ran out of superlatives, and he sent her a glittering look that made her toes curl. That detachment which had once frozen her out when she got too close was steadily becoming a feature of the past.

Last night, Luc had actually talked about his family. And he never talked about them. The death of his parents and sister in that plane crash had shattered him but he had never actually come close to admitting that fact before. And she was quite certain that he would never admit the guilt he had suppressed when they died. On the rise to the top, Luc had left his family behind.

He had given them luxury, but not the luxury of himself. Business had always come first. He had sent them off on an expensive vacation in apology for yet another cancelled visit and he had never seen them alive again. When he had talked about them last night, it had been one of those confiding conversations that he could only bring himself to share with forced casualness in the cloaking darkness of the bedroom. Until now, she had never understood just how very difficult it was for Luc to express anything which touched him deeply.

Sliding up on her knees, she lifted her bikini top. His dark eyes travelled in exactly the direction she had known they would, lingering on the unbound curves briefly revealed. A heady pink fired her cheeks but, as she arched her back to do up the fastener, the all-male intensity of his appraisal roused an entirely feminine satisfaction as old as Eve within her.

'You like me looking at you,' he commented, lazily amused.

She bent her head, losing face and confidence. 'You're not supposed to notice that.'

'I can't help noticing it when you look so smug.'

Leaning lithely forward, he scooped her bodily across the divide between the loungers with that easy strength of his that melted her somewhere deep down inside. He laced an idle hand into her hair and claimed her mouth in a provocative sensual exploration. The world lurched violently on its axis and went into a spin, leaving her light-headed and weak. It didn't matter how often he touched her, it was always the same. There had always been this between them, this shatteringly physical bond.

And once it had scared her. In her innocence, she had believed it one-sided, had assumed that Luc could, if he wanted, discover the same pleasure with any other woman. She was not so quick to make that assumption now. In the long passion-drenched hours which had turned night into day and day into night, the depth of Luc's hunger had driven her again and again to the brink of exhaustion.

He released her mouth with reluctance. 'You make me insatiable.' The sexy growl to that lancing confession did nothing to cool her fevered blood and she rested her head on his shoulder. 'Somehow, I doubt,' he murmured, 'that it'll take that long for you to become pregnant.'

'Pregnant?' she squeaked, jerking back from him, her first reaction one of shock and, curiously, fear.

His hands steadied her before she could overbalance and he nuzzled his lips hotly into the hollow of her collarbone where a tiny pulse beat out her tension. 'Don't tell me you believed in the stork story,' he teased. 'Believe it or not, what we've been doing in recent days does have another more basic purpose above and beyond mere pleasure.'

She was trembling. 'Yes, but—'

'And we haven't been taking any steps to forestall such a result,' he reminded her with complete calm.

That awareness was only hitting Catherine now. It shook her that a matter which had once been shrouded with such importance could have slipped her mind so entirely. There had been no contraceptive pills in her possession. Evidently she was no longer taking them. Remembering to take them had once been the bane of her existence, invoking horrid attacks of panic when she realised that she had forgotten one or two. If Luc realised just how many near misses they had had, he would probably feel very much as she did now.

That background hadn't prepared her very well for Luc's smoothly talking about having a baby as if it was the most natural thing in the world. Which of course it was…if you were married. In the circumstances, she decided that her initial sense of panic at his comment had been quite understandable. Where reproduction was concerned, she had to learn a whole new way of thinking.

Seemingly impervious to the frantic readjustments he had set in train, Luc ran a caressing hand down her spine and eased her closer. 'Didn't you notice that omission?' he said softly.

'No,' she muttered with instinctive guilt.

'I want children while I'm young enough to enjoy them.'

It crossed her mind that he might just have mentioned that before taking the decision right over her head, as it were. But equally fast came a seductive image of carrying Luc's baby and she was overcome by the prospect and quite forgot to be annoyed with him. 'Yes,' she agreed wistfully.

Engaged on cutting a sensual path across her fine-boned shoulder, Luc murmured huskily, 'I knew you'd agree with me. Now, instead of rushing to look into every baby carriage that passes by, you can concentrate on your own.'

'Do I do that?' she whispered.

'You do,' he said wryly.

Once anything to do with babies had left Luc arctic-cold. Naturally she couldn't help but be surprised that he should want a child with such immediacy. But when she thought about it for a minute or two, it began to make sense. Luc was entering marriage much as he entered a business deal, armed with expectations. He wanted an heir, that was all. You couldn't empire-build without a dynasty. But still she couldn't summon a smile to her face and she couldn't shake off that irrational fear assailing her.

Common sense ought to have reasoned it away. She loved Luc. She loved children. Where was the problem? Yet still the feeling persisted and her temples began to throb. When the phone buzzed on the table and Luc reached for it impatiently, she was starting to feel distinctly shaky and sick into the bargain.

Luc was talking in Japanese with the languid cool of someone fluent in a dozen languages. A frown pleating his dark brows, he sighed as he replaced the phone. 'Business,' he said. 'I have to go inside to make a few calls. I'll be as quick as I can.'

Sunlight played blindingly on the surface of the pool several feet away. As a faint breeze sent a glimmering tide of ripples across the water, the effect was almost hynotic. Catherine's head ached too much to think. She wondered ruefully if she had had too much sun.

A sound jerked her out of an uneasy doze. A child emerged from below the trees. His stubby little legs pumped energetically in pursuit of the ball he was chasing. As it headed directly for the water, Catherine flew upright, consumed by alarm. But he caught the ball before it reached the edge, and as he did so one of the maids came racing down the slope from the castle.

'Scusi, signorina, scusi!' she gasped in frantic apology for the intrusion as she scooped the child up into her arms. He gave a wail of protest. As he was hurried away, still clutching his ball, Catherine stopped breathing.

The thumping behind her forehead had for a split second become unbearable, but now it receded. She didn't even notice the fact. She was in a benumbed state that went beyond shock into incredulous horror. Daniel...Daniel! The sybaritic luxury of the pool with its marble surround vanished as she unfroze.

Snatching up the phone, she pressed the button for the internal house line. A secretary answered. 'This is Miss Parrish.' She had to cough to persuade her voice to grow from a thread into comprehensible volume. 'I want you to get me a number in England and connect me. It's urgent,' she stressed, straining to recall Peggy's maiden name and the address of her home and finally coming up with them.

Shaking like the victim of an accident, she sat down before her legs gave out beneath her. What sort of a mother could forget about her son? Oh, dear God, please let me wake up, please don't let this nightmare be real, she prayed with fervour.

The phone buzzed and she leapt at it.

'Hello? Hello?' Peggy was saying.

'It's Catherine. Is Daniel there?'

'He's out bringing in the hay. I cried off to make refreshments,' Peggy chattered. 'Our phone was out for a couple of days and we didn't realise. Have you been frantic, trying to get through?'

'Well—'

'I thought you would've been,' Peggy interrupted with her usual impatience. 'I tried to ring you a few times from the call-box in the village but I always struck out. I suppose you've been out scouring the pavements in search of a job if you've decided against working for Mrs Anstey.'

'I—'

'Daniel's having a fabulous time. The weather's been terrific. We were planning to camp out tonight but, of course, if you want to speak to him...'

'No, that's OK.' I've been kidnapped. I'm in Italy. I'm getting married tomorrow. The revelations went unspoken. Peggy would think she was a candidate for the funny farm. In any case, she would be home before they were back in London. Nobody need ever know, she thought in that first frantic flush of desperation.

'Catherine, somebody's just driven into the yard. Wow, fancy car. Can I ring you back?'

'No...no, I'm out...I mean, I'm ringing from somewhere else. Give my love to Daniel.' She dropped the phone as though it burnt, and tottered backwards on to the lounger.

The hideous, absolutely inexcusable events of the past week were suddenly all crowding in on her. She flinched and she shrank and she cringed over the replay. Humiliation scored letters of fire into her soul. From rock-bottom there was only one way to go, and that was up, as she relived what Luc had done to her.

And really, there wasn't anything that Luc *hadn't* done. While she was in no condition to know what was happening to her, he had moved in for the kill. Plotting and intrigue were a breath of fresh air to that Borgia temperament of his. It had been as easy as stealing candy from a baby. Baby. *Baby*! She blenched and recoiled from that terrifying train of thought, completely unable to deal with it on top of everything else.

For a week she had been unaware that she was living four years in the past. He had left nothing within her possession that might jog her memory. Not a newspaper or a television set or a calendar had been allowed anywhere within a mile of her.

Every detail had been bloodlessly, inhumanly precise. It had Luc stamped all over it. He hadn't made a single error. She had been baited, hooked and landed like a fish. Only even a fish would have had more sense of self-preservation. A fish wouldn't have scrambled up the line, thrown itself masochistically on to the gutting knife and looked forward to the heat of the grill...but she had.

What Luc wanted, he took. Scruples didn't come into it. Costs didn't come into it. The end result was all that interested him. He had believed that she had planned to marry Drew and, with Drew's freedom so close, time had been a luxury Luc hadn't had. No doubt if she had thrown herself gratefully at his feet that night marriage would never have been mentioned. But in resisting Luc, she had challenged Luc. And he could not resist a challenge.

Her teeth ground together and her stomach heaved. That degrading fish image wouldn't leave her alone. Her small hands clenched into fists. Rage shuddered through her; rage that knew no boundaries; rage so powerful that it boiled up in a violent physicality she had not known she could experience.

At that precise moment, Luc appeared, striding down the steps set into the slope, and she remembered the episode in the back of the limousine and death would have been too quick a release for him to satisfy her. Springing upright, she grabbed up a glass and threw it at him. As it smashed several feet to the left of him, he stilled.

'You filthy, rotten, cheating, conniving swine!' she railed at him, snatching up the second glass and hurling it with all her might. 'You rat!' she ranted, and the phone went in the same direction. 'You louse!' she launched, bending in a frenzy to take off a shoe, her rage only getting more out of control at her failure to hit a fixed target. 'Bastard!' She broke through her loathing for that particular word and punctuated it with her other shoe. 'I want to kill you!'

'Poison would be a better bet than a gun.' Luc spread a speaking glance over the far-flung positions of the missiles, entire and smashed. 'Marksmanship wouldn't appear to be one of your hidden talents.'

Her rage reached explosive, screaming proportions. 'Is that all you've got to say?'

'It seems fairly safe to assume that you've retrieved your memory,' he drawled. 'I'm not sure it would be safe to assume anything else.'

'No, it wouldn't be!' His complete cool was maddening her even more. 'If you were dying of thirst, I wouldn't give you a drink! If you were starving, I wouldn't feed you! If you were the only man left alive on this earth and I was the only woman, the human race would grind to a halt! You deserve to be horse-whipped and keelhauled and hung, and if I was a man I'd do it!'

'And if you were a man, you wouldn't be in this situation,' Luc input helpfully as she paused to catch her breath.

'I'm going to report you to the police!' Catherine blazed at him, satisfied to have at last found a realistic threat.

Luc angled his dark head back, piercing golden eyes resting on her. 'What for?'

'W-what for?' she stammered an octave higher. 'What for? You kidnapped me!'

'Did I drug you? Physically abuse you? Have you witnesses to these events?'

'I'll make it up; I'll lie!' she slashed back at him.

'But why did you stand so willingly at my side at the airport when I announced our marriage plans?' Luc enquired with the same immovable, incredibly outrageous cool.

'You've kept me a prisoner here all week!' In desperation, she set off on another tack, determined to nail him down to a crime on the statute books.

An ebony brow quirked. 'With locked doors? I don't recall refusing to let you go anywhere.'

'Physical abuse, then!' Catherine slung through gnashing teeth. 'I'll get you on that!'

Luc actually smiled. 'What physical abuse?'

Catherine drew herself up to her full five feet and one quarter inch and shrieked. 'You know very well what I'm talking about! While I…while I was not in my right mind, you took disgusting advantage of me!'

'Did I?' he murmured. 'Catherine, it is my considered opinion that over the past week you've been more in your right mind than you've been for almost five years.'

'How dare you?' she screamed at him, fit to be tied. 'How dare you say that to me?'

A broad shoulder shifted in an elegantly understated shrug. 'I say it because it is the truth.'

'The truth according to who?' she shouted ferociously. 'You take that back right now!'

'I have not the slightest intention of withdrawing that statement,' he informed her with careless provocation. 'When you calm down, you will realise that it is the truth.'

'When I calm down?' she yelled. 'Do I look like I'm about to calm down?'

Luc ran a reflective appraisal over her. 'If you could swim a little better, I would drop you in the pool.'

'You're not even sorry, are you?' That was one reality that was sinking in. It did nothing to reduce her fury.

He sighed. 'Why would I be sorry?'

'Why? Why?' She could hardly get the repetition out. 'Because I'm going to make you sorry! I should have known you wouldn't have a twinge of conscience about bringing me here!'

'You're quite right. I haven't.'

'You act as though I'm some sort of a thing, an object you can lift and lay at will!' As his wide mouth curled with amusement, she understood why people committed murder.

His lashes screened his expressive eyes. 'If you are an object to me, then I am an object to you in the same way.'

For a second she glared at him uncomprehendingly and then caught his meaning. 'I'm not talking about sex!' she raged.

'No,' he conceded. 'I had noticed that once the charge of physical abuse was withdrawn—'

'I didn't withdraw it!' she interrupted.

'You were careful to change the subject,' he countered. 'You want me every bit as much as I want you.'

'You conceited jerk! I was sick! I hate you!'

'You'll get over that,' he assured her.

'I'm not going to get over it! I'm leaving, walking out, departing...' she spelt out tempestuously.

'A fairly typical response of yours when the going threatens to get rough, but you're not doing a vanishing act this time.'

'I'm leaving you!' she shouted wildly.

'Watch the glass!' Luc raked at her rawly.

But it was too late. A sharp pain bit into her foot and she vented a gasp. Striding forward, Luc wrenched her off her feet, moved over to the nearest seat and literally tipped her up, a lean hand retaining a hold on one slender ankle. 'Stay still!' he roared at her. 'Or you'll push the glass in deeper.'

Sobbing with thwarted temper and pain, she let him withdraw the sliver and then she cursed him.

'I knew you would do that.'

'Let go of me!' she screeched.

'With all this broken glass around? You just have to be kidding,' he gibed, wrapping an immaculate hanky round her squirming foot. 'When did you last have a tetanus jab?'

'Six months ago!' she spat, infuriated beyond all bearing by the ignominy of her position. 'Did you hear what I said? I'm leaving!'

'Like hell you are.' Jerking up the sarong that had fallen on the ground, he proceeded to her utter disbelief to wrap it round her much as if she were a doll to be dressed.

She thrust his hands away. 'Don't you dare touch me! What do you mean—"Like hell you are"? You can't keep me here!'

Casting the sarong aside, he took her by surprise by lifting her and, when she fought tooth and nail with every limb flailing, he flung her over his shoulder.

'Let me go!' she shrieked, hammering at his back with her fists. 'What do you think you're doing?'

'Putting you under restraint for your own good. You're hysterical,' he bit out. 'And I've had enough.'

'*You've* had enough?' Her voice broke incredulously. 'Put me down!'

'*Sta' zitta*. Be quiet,' he ground out.

Gravity was threatening the bra of her bikini. She became more occupied with holding it in place than thumping any part of him she could reach. He was heading for the stone staircase that led up to the french doors on the first-floor gallery. 'I hate you!' she sobbed, tears of mortification, unvented fury and frustration flooding her eyes without warning.

A minute later Luc dumped her on her bed with about the same level of care as a sack of potatoes might have required. 'And hating me isn't making you happy, is it?' he breathed derisively. '*Per dio*, doesn't that tell you something?'

'That you're the most unscrupulous primitive I've ever come across!' she spat through her tears. 'And I'm leaving!'

'You're not going anywhere.'

'You can't stop me!' And you certainly can't make me marry you!' she asserted with returning confidence, wriggling off the bed and hobbling over to a chair to pull on the flimsy négligé lying there, suddenly feeling very exposed in what little there was of the bikini. 'And, now that Drew's got his precious contract, you can't hold that over me any more!'

'He signs for it one hour after the wedding.'

Catherine was paralysed in her tracks. Jerkily she turned round. Shimmering golden eyes clashed with hers in an almost physical assault. 'I had foreseen the possibility that this might occur.'

'He...he hasn't got it yet?' She could hardly get the stricken question past her lips.

'I'm such a conniving bastard, I'm afraid,' Luc purred like a tiger on the prowl.

'You can't want me when I don't want you!' she gasped.

'I've already disproved that fallacy,' he said drily. 'And, when we reach our destination in England tomorrow, I have no doubt that you will be in a more receptive frame of mind.'

All Catherine caught was that one magical word. 'England?' she repeated. 'You're taking me back to England after the wedding?'

'A change of scene is usual.'

Evidently he believed that, once that ring was on her finger, it would have the same effect as a chain holding a skeleton to a dungeon wall. But, once she was back in England, he couldn't hold her. While she was here, he had her passport and she wouldn't have liked to bet on her chances of escape from a walled estate patrolled by security staff, aided in their task by an impressive range of electronic devices.

If she didn't go through with the wedding, Drew would suffer.

She shuddered with inner fury at that unavoidable conclusion. The seductive fantasy of leaving Luc without a bride on his much-publicised wedding-day faded. She should have known better than to think it could be that easy. All the same, the prospect of being back in England tomorrow was immensely soothing. He could hardly force her to stay with him.

'Catherine,' Luc drawled. 'Don't even think it.'

'I have nothing to say to you,' she muttered tightly. 'I've already said it all.'

'We have to talk.' A knock sounded on the door. He ignored it. 'I won't allow you to spoil the wedding.'

A gagged and bound bride might raise an eyebrow or two, she reflected fiercely as the knock on the door was repeated.

'*Avanti!*' Luc called in exasperation.

Bernardo appeared, a secretary just visible behind him. 'Signorina Peruzzi.' He gestured with the cordless phone apologetically. 'She says it is a matter of great urgency that she speak with you, *signor*.'

'I will not take a call from her,' Luc dismissed. 'Leave us, Bernardo.'

The door shut again.

'He speaks English,' Catherine realised. 'Only you must've told him not to around me.'

'The staff are under the illusion that the request was made because you are keen to improve your Italian.'

She covered her face with shaking hands, what composure she had retained threatening all of a sudden to crumble. 'I loathe you!'

'You are angry with me,' he contradicted steadily. 'And I suppose you have some reason for that.'

'You suppose?' Wild-eyed, she surveyed him over the top of her white-boned fingers. Reaction was setting in.

'You belong with me, Catherine. Use the brain God gave you at birth.' The advice was abrasive. 'You have been happy, happier than I have ever known you to be, here.'

'I was living in the past!'

'But why did you choose to return to that particular part of the past?' His sensual mouth twisted. 'Ask yourself that.'

'I didn't choose anything!' she protested. 'And what I ended up with isn't real!'

'It can be as real as you want it to be.'

The sense of betrayal was increasing in her. He had betrayed her. But, worst of all, she had betrayed herself. She had betrayed everything she believed in, everything that she was, everything that she had become after leaving him. In one week she had smashed four years of self-respect. In one week she had destroyed every barrier that might have protected her.

'Can you turn water into wine as well?' she demanded wildly, choking on her own humiliation. 'You must have been laughing yourself sick all week at just how easy it was to make a fool of me!'

A muscle pulled tight at his hard jawline. 'That is not how it has been between us.'

'That's how it's always been between us!' she attacked shakily. 'You plot and you plan and you manipulate and you make things happen just as you want them to happen.'

'I didn't plan for you to lose your memory.'

'But you didn't miss a trick in making use of it!' she condemned. 'And I've been through all this before with you. When we came back from Switzerland, my employers had mysteriously vacated their flat and shut down the art gallery, leaving me out of a job! Coincidence?' she prompted. 'I don't think so. You made that happen as well, didn't you?'

A faint darkening of colour flared over his cheekbones, accentuating the brilliance of his dark eyes. 'I bought the building,' he conceded in a driven tone.

'And it made it so much easier for you to persuade me to come to New York.' Her breath caught like a sob in her throat.

'I wanted you very much. And I was impatient.' He looked at her in unashamed appeal. 'I am what I am, *bella mia*, and I'm afraid I don't have the power to change the past.'

'But I had. Don't you understand that?' Moisture was hitting her eyes in a blinding, burning surge and she could not bear to let him see her cry. 'I had!' she repeated in bitter despair.

'Catherine…what do you want me to say in answer?' he demanded. 'If you want me to be honest, I will be. All that I regret in the past is that I lost you.'

'You didn't lose me…you drove me away!' she sobbed.

He spread eloquent, beautifully shaped hands. 'All right, if semantics are that important, I drove you away. But you might try to see it from my point of view for a change. You shoot a crazy question at me out of the blue one morning over breakfast—'

'Yes, it was crazy, wasn't it?' she cut in tremulously. 'Absolutely crazy of me to think that you might actually condescend to marry me!'

'I didn't know there was going to be no court of appeal!' he slashed back at her fiercely. 'So I said the wrong thing. It was cruel, what I said. I admit that. If you want an apology, you should have stayed around to get it because I don't feel like apologising for it now! I came back to the apartment an hour and a half after I left it that morning. I didn't go to Milan. And where were you?'

She was shattered by the news that he had returned that morning. It shook her right out of her incipient hysteria.

'Yes, where were you?' Luc pressed remorselessly. 'You'd gone. You'd flounced out like a prima donna, leaving everything I'd ever given you, and if you wanted your revenge you got it then in full!'

With a stifled sob, she fled into the bathroom and locked the door, folding down on to the carpet behind it to bury her face in her hands and cry as though her heart was breaking. The past and the present had merged and she could not cope with that knowledge.

CHAPTER SEVEN

WHAT a fool Catherine had been, what a blind, besotted fool! The instant Luc had asked her to marry him, her wits had gone walkabout. So many little things had failed to fit but she had suppressed all knowledge of them, trusting Luc and determined to let nothing detract from her happiness. If it had been his intent to divert her from her amnesia, he could not have been more successful.

How dared he suggest that she had somehow chosen to return to a period of the past when they had still been together? That night in Drew's apartment, Luc had trapped her between two impossible choices. Either she sacrificed Drew or Daniel. With every fibre of her being she would have fought to keep Daniel from Luc.

But Drew also had a strong hold on her loyalty, both in his own right and in his sister's right as well. She owed Harriet a debt she could never repay for helping her when she had hit rock-bottom. How could she have chosen between Daniel and Drew? Faced with the final prospect of telling Luc that he had a son, she had shut her mind down on Daniel to protect him.

Luc poisoned all that he touched. And if he was prepared to marry her simply to ensure her continuing presence in his bed, why shouldn't he accept Daniel as well? Luc, she sensed fearfully, would want his son. Five years ago, Daniel would have been a badly timed, unwelcome complication. Luc had not over-valued her precise importance to him. She was convinced that he would have expected her to have an abortion. But times had changed...

Daniel was innocent and vulnerable, a little boy with a lion-sized intellect often too big for him to handle. Once Luc had been a little boy like that...and look how he had turned out. Hard as diamonds. Cold, calculating and callous. Did she want to risk that happening to Daniel? Daniel already had too many of Luc's traits. They had been doled out to him in his genes at birth.

He was strong-willed, single-minded and, if left to his own devices unchecked, exceedingly self-centred. Catherine had spent four and a half years endeavouring to ensure that Daniel grew up as a well-rounded, normal child rather than a remote, hot-house-educated little statistician, divorced by his mental superiority from childish things.

She hated Luc, oh, God, how she hated him! Enshrouded in lonely isolation, she clung ferociously to the hatred that was her only strength. She squashed the sneaking suspicion that Luc was not as callous and cold as she had once believed he was, tuned out the little voice that weakly dared to hint that Luc might have changed. Anger and self-loathing warred for precedence inside her as she cried.

So what if she had to go through the wedding first? As soon as they landed in London, she would leave him. She had done it before; she would to it again, and this time she wouldn't be so dumb. She would take her jewellery with her and sell it. With the aid of that money, she could make a new life for herself and Daniel. She would do it for Daniel's sake.

Misery crept over her with blanket efficiency. It hadn't been real; none of it had been real. She had been living out a fantasy. The background had been so cruelly perfect. A castle for the little girl who had once dreamt about being a princess. A white wedding for the teenager who had once believed in living happily ever after. But, for the woman she was now, there was nothing, less than nothing. And wasn't that her own fault? A grown woman ought to have been able to tell the difference between fantasy and reality.

A certain *je ne sais quoi*, he had called it. A certain three-letter word would have been less impressive but more accurate. Sex. Luc's fatal flaw and probably his only weakness. A certain *je ne sais quoi*, unsought and on many occasions since unwelcome, he had admitted. And you really couldn't blame him for feeling like that, could you? It must be galling to acquire that much wealth and power and discover that you still lusted after a very ordinary little blonde with none of the attributes necessary to embellish your image.

'Catherine? Are you OK?' Luc demanded, startling her.

'You b-bloody snob!' she flared on the back of another sob.

Silence stretched.

'What the hell are you talking about?' he blazed from the other side of the door. 'If you don't come out of there, I'll smash the lock!'

'Force is your answer to everything, isn't it?' Abruptly galvanised into action by the mortifying awareness that he had been listening to her crying, she stood up, stripped off, and walked into the shower, hoping the sound of it would make him go away.

Sex, she thought, loathing him. The lowest possible common denominator. And, after a five-year drought, her value had mushroomed. In fact it had smashed all known stock-market records. In return for unlimited sex, Luc was graciously ready to lower his high standards and marry her. Well, bully for him, and wasn't she a lucky girl?

Little wonder he didn't understand what all the fuss was about. He was sensationally attractive, super-rich and oversexed. Nine out of ten women would contrive to live with his flaws. Unfortunate that she was the tenth. Unfortunate for him, that was!

He might get a bride, but he wasn't getting a wife. He would live to regret forcing her to go through with the wedding. When she took off within hours of it, the public embarrassment would be colossal. Then she could stamp the long-overdue account 'paid in full'. Getting mad got her nowhere; getting even would restore her self-respect. Luc might have set her up, but he had set himself up as well.

Pay-back time was here. She would go down in history as the woman of principle who had rejected one of the world's most eligible bachelors. It was perfect, she decided, the old adrenalin flowing again. Shame she wouldn't be able to stay around to take advantage of the publicity. She could see the headlines. Why I couldn't live with Luc Santini.

Tying a towelling robe round her, she abandoned the entrancing imagery with regret and padded back to the bedroom, a woman with a mission now, a woman set on revenge and nobody's victim.

A cork exploded from a bottle like a pistol shot. His dark head thrown back as he let the excess champagne foam down into his mouth, Luc was a blaze of stunning black and gold animal vibrancy in the strong sunlight. He straightened and poured the mellow golden liquid expertly into a pair of glasses, white teeth flashing against brown skin as a brilliant smile curved his mouth. 'Force is not my answer to everything.' Magnificent lion-gold eyes skimmed over her. 'You look like a lobster. You've been in there so long, you must have used up all the hot water in the castle.'

She hadn't expected him to still be waiting for her. The filthy look she gave him ought to have withered him. Naturally it didn't. It drifted impotently off him like a feather trying to beat up a rock. Crossing the carpet with feline grace, he pressed a glass into her hand. 'You're not in love with Huntingdon,' he drawled. 'If you were, you would have slept with him.'

Just looking at him drained her. Her nerves were suddenly in shreds again. Her hands weren't steady. It was an unequal contest. She wasn't ready for another confrontation and he knew it, conniving and ruthless swine that he was! She marvelled at his arrogance in believing that he could bring her back to heel within the next twenty-four hours. That was, of course, what he was banking on.

'You wouldn't understand a man like Drew if you lived to be a thousand.' Her cheeks had gone all hot, and she tossed back the champagne in the hope of cooling down her temperature.

'He attracts you because he's a loser. You feel sorry for him.'

Her teeth gritted. 'Drew is not a loser.'

'He's run a healthy family firm off its feet with a series of bad business decisions,' Luc traded succinctly.

'And any day of the week, he's still a finer man than you'll ever be!' she launched shakily.

The superb bone-structure hardened. 'You're in a privileged

position, *cara*. I would allow no one else to say that to me with impunity.'

The chill she had invoked was intimidating. A shiver ran down her backbone. She felt like a reckless child rebuked for embarrassing the adults. But his contempt for Drew deeply angered her. Yet, at heart, she knew he was right. Drew had never been ambitious or hungry enough to become successful. He had allowed his family to live at a level beyond their means, draining the firm of capital that should have been reinvested for the future. However, those facts didn't lower Drew in her estimation. He was not a born wheeler-dealer and he never would be. When she thought of the dreadful week of worry Drew had had to endure waiting for that contract, she tasted the full threat of Luc's savagery. No…no, she reflected tautly, she would never have cause to regret concealing Daniel's existence from Luc.

'You've hurt Drew,' she whispered, thinking that, once she was gone, Drew would be safe from all interference. She saw no reason to disabuse Luc of his conviction that she had had a relationship with Drew. It infuriated her that Luc should believe he had the right to stare at her with such chilling censure. 'And you don't own me.'

Confusingly, his wide mouth curled into a sudden, almost tender smile. 'I don't need to own you. You are mine, body and soul. So, you strayed a little, got lost, but you didn't stray as far as I'd feared, and now you are back where you belong.'

Seething temper gripped her. 'I don't belong with you!'

'Why do you fight me?' he demanded softly. 'Why do you fight yourself?'

As she collided unwarily with ebony-fringed dark eyes, a squirming helpless sensation kicked at her stomach. It was hard to withstand that burning, blatant self-assurance of his. 'I'm not fighting myself.'

'Come here,' he invited very quietly. 'And prove it.'

The magnetic force of his will was concentrated on her. Her body shivered, though she was not cold, her heart raced, though she was not exerting herself, in reaction to the sheer physical pull he could exert. It crossed her mind crazily that he ought to be banned like a dangerous substance.

He strolled closer and refilled her glass in the throbbing silence. 'You're afraid to,' he noted. 'Indeed, you behave as though you are afraid of me. I don't like that. I don't want a little white ghost with fear in her eyes in my bed tomorrow night. I want that scatty, loving, happy creature you've been all week.'

He was so close now she couldn't breathe. 'I don't love you.'

'If I weren't so certain that you loved me, I wouldn't be marrying you.'

She backed off hastily from his proximity. 'I wouldn't have thought it would have mattered a damn to you either way!'

'If you take refuge in the bathroom again, I'll break the door down,' he delivered conversationally. 'You started this and I'll finish it. I want to know why you're putting up barriers again.'

'Why?' she echoed breathlessly. 'Why? After what you've done?'

A brown hand inscribed a graceful arc. 'What have I done? I spend all these years looking for you and, the moment I find you again, I ask you to marry me. Isn't that a compliment?'

'A c-compliment?'

'It is certainly not an insult, *bella mia*.'

'But I don't want to marry you!'

'I'm becoming fascinated by what must go on in your subconscious mind,' he confessed huskily.

God, he was incredibly attractive. He could talk his way round a lynch mob, she conceded in panic. What she was experiencing right now came down to hormones. That was all. Luc was turning up the heat, stalking her like the pure-bred predator he was. If she lost her head for a second, she would be flat on her back on that bed. Somehow he contrived to say the most outrageous things charmingly. Or maybe it was just that her brain had packed up in disgust at her own frailty.

'You can't persuade me differently with sex either!' she asserted, her spine meeting unexpectedly with a wall that concluded her retreat.

Dancing golden eyes, alight with mockery, arrowed over her. He took her glass from her hand and set it aside. 'We don't have sex, we have intensely erotic experiences,' he countered, his wine-dark voice savouring the syllables.

'Sex!' She hurled the reiteration like a forcefield behind which she might hide. 'And I'm not some tramp... Are you listening to me?'

'I might listen if you say something I want to hear, but you've been rather remiss in that department this afternoon.' Instead of moving closer, he stayed where he was, confusing her. 'And I'm not about to make it easy for you by persuading you into bed.'

She straightened from the wall jerkily, no longer under threat, pink flying into her cheeks. 'You couldn't persuade me.'

'I wouldn't try. I'm saving you up for an intensely erotic experience tomorrow night,' he murmured softly, before closing the door behind him.

She darted after him and turned the key. Then she slumped. Heavens, he was so modest, such a shrinking violet. Wiping her damp forehead, she lay down on the bed, acknowledging, now that he was gone, just how much the past hours of stormy emotion had taken out of her. She had time for a nap before dinner.

She was terribly hot and sticky and thirsty when she woke up. Filling a glass to the brim with flat champagne, she drank it down much as she would have treated lemonade. Had someone been banging on the door a while ago, or was that her imagination?

Nobody's victim, eh? Her earlier fighting thoughts came back to haunt her. Luc had walked the last round. He had switched back to the intimate playful mood of the last few days and she hadn't expected that; she hadn't been prepared. He was in for a heck of a shock when she took her leave at the airport. He hadn't given serious consideration to a single thing she said. Her temper sparked again.

It maddened her to have to admit it, but hating Luc did not make her immune to his physical attraction. It was a hangover from the bad old days—what else could it be? Once she had believed he was a bit like the measles. If you caught him once, you couldn't catch him again.

Evidently the chemistry didn't work like that. Here she was, in full possession of her senses, no longer the doormat *doppelgänger* of recent days, and still she was vulnerable. It enraged her. When he had taken that glass from her and she had thought...she had been in the act of melting down the wall in anticipation.

Pacing about the room in a temper, she helped herself to more champagne. When she had loved Luc, she had just about been able to live with the effect he had on her. When she didn't even like him, never mind love him, it was inexcusable. And as for him—what he deserved was a cheap little tramp, the sort of female prepared to barter sexual favours for his bank balance, the sort of female he ought to understand. That was exactly what he deserved...

She was rifling the dressing-room when the banging on the door interrupted her. Opening it a crack, she found Guilia, for some reason backed by Bernardo, who was holding a large bunch of keys. Her maid looked all hot and flushed and anxious.

'I won't be needing any help tonight. *Grazie*, Guilia.'

'But *signorina*—'

'Dinner will be served in one half-hour,' Bernardo said with a look of appeal.

'I'm sorry, but dinner will have to wait.' Catherine shut the door again. Didn't they all speak great English? When she recalled the sign language she had been reduced to using several times during the week, she cursed Luc. Why had Bernardo looked so shattered at the idea of dinner's having to be held back?

Luc would probably create. Well, so what? It would do him no harm to cool his heels for once. He would appreciate her appearance all the more when she did wander in. Dinner, she decided fiercely, would be fun...fun...fun! However, lest the staff receive the blame for her tardiness, she would be as quick as she possibly could be.

The shimmering tunic top of a black evening suit was extracted from the wardrobe first. It would just cover her hips and, if she wore it back to front, the neckline would be equally abbreviated. Sheer black stockings, no problem. She had every colour of the rainbow. A very high pair of black court shoes were withdrawn next and finally a pair of long black gloves.

Dressed, she walked a slightly unsteady line into the bathroom to go to town on her face. Sapphire and violet outlined her eyes dramatically. Putting on loads of blue mascara, she dabbed gold glitter on her cleavage and traced her lips with strawberry pink. She was starting to enjoy herself. Having moussed her hair into a wild, messy tangle, she went through her jewellery.

She had three diamond bracelets. One went on an ankle, the other two on her wrists over the gloves. A necklace and earrings completed the look. Sort of Christmassy. It was astonishing how cheap diamonds could look when worn to excess. And her wardrobe, shorn of Guilia, had far more adventurous possibilities than Luc could ever have dreamt. The reflection that greeted her in the mirror was satisfyingly startling.

She picked a careful passage down the staircase, aware that she had been a little free with the champagne. Bernardo literally couldn't take his eyes from her as she crossed the hall. He froze, stared, tugged at his tie.

'Evening, Bernardo,' she carolled on her way past. 'It's a hot night, isn't it?'

And it's about to get hotter, she forecast with inner certainty. Abruptly, Bernardo flashed in front of her, spreading wide both doors of the salon. 'Signorina Parrish.'

Why on earth was he announcing her? Did he think Luc wouldn't recognise her under all this gloop? Have her thrown out as a gatecrasher? Taking a deep breath, she launched herself over the threshold. A whole cluster of faces looked back at her, some standing, some sitting. Horror-stricken, she blinked, stage fright taking over. The outfit had been for private viewing only. Behind her, Bernardo was subduing a fit of coughing.

Now that she came to think of it—and thinking was exceedingly difficult at that moment—Luc had mentioned something casual about some close friends coming to stay the night before the wedding. The minute she had shown her nerves at the prospect, he had dropped the subject. Right now, he was undoubtedly wishing he hadn't. Right now, he was remembering that she had a head like a sieve. Right now, as his long lean stride carried him towards her, his eyes were telling her that he wanted to kill her, inch by painful inch, preferably over a lengthy period. And that he intended to enjoy every minute of it when he got the chance.

'Say, I thought it was fancy dress,' she muttered and attempted to sidle out again, but Luc snaked out a hand and cut off her escape.

'She's so avant-garde,' a youthful female voice gasped. 'Mummy, why can't I wear stuff like that?'

'Designer punk,' someone else commented. 'Very arresting.'

'And I wouldn't mind being arrested with her.' A tall, very good-looking blond man sent her a sizzling smile. 'Luc, I begin to understand why you kept this charming lady under wraps until the very last moment. I'm Christian...Christian Denning.'

Catherine shook his hand with a smile. He had bridged an awkward silence. A whirl of introductions took place. There were about thirty people present, an even mix of nationalities, fairly split between the business élite and the upper crust. It was a relief when she finally made it into a seat to catch her breath.

'You have the most fabulous legs.' Christian dropped down on to the arm of her sofa. 'Why do I have the feeling that Luc would rather have kept the view an exclusive one?'

'Have you known Luc for long?' she asked in desperation.

'About ten years. And I saw you at a distance once in Switzerland, seven years ago,' he confided in an undertone. 'That was as close as I was allowed to get.'

A wave of heat consumed her skin. This was someone who had to have a very fair idea of what her former association with Luc had been. 'Was it?' She tried to sound casual.

'Luc's very possessive,' he responded mockingly. 'But he must have snatched you right out of your cradle. I must remember to tease him about that.'

Luc strolled over. 'Enjoying yourself, Christian?'

'Immensely. There isn't a man in the room who doesn't envy me. Why did I have to wait this long to meet her?'

'Perhaps I foresaw your reaction.' Luc reached for Catherine's hand. It was time to go into dinner. 'Everybody likes you,' he breathed, pressing his mouth with fleeting brevity to her bare shoulder, fingertips skating caressingly down her taut spinal cord. 'You forgot they were coming, didn't you?' He was smiling at her, she registered dazedly. '*Cara*, if you had seen your face when you realised what you had done! But in this gathering you don't look quite as shocking as you no doubt thought you would.'

On that point, he was correct. There was no conventional garb on display. At this level, the women were more interested in looking different from each other. She might look startling to her own eyes and to those of anyone who knew her, but nobody was likely to suspect that she had deliberately dressed up as some sort of pantomime hooker. Had it been her intent to embarrass Luc in company, she would not have succeeded and, since that had not been her intent, she was relieved until it occurred to her that he would endure more than embarrassment when she walked out on him at the airport. A sneaking twinge of guilt assailed her. Immediately she was furious with herself. Luc had set the rules and she was playing by *his* rules now. He had given her no other choice. What transpired, therefore, was of his own making.

A middle-aged woman with a beaky nose took a seat to the left of her at the dining-table and asked, 'Do you hunt?'

'Only when I lose something,' Catherine replied abstractedly.

Someone hooted with amusement as though she had said something incredibly witty. A wry smile curved Luc's mouth. 'Catherine's not into blood sports.'

'She must be planning to reform you, then,' a blonde in cerise silk said with smiling sarcasm. 'Blood sports are definitely your forte.'

'And yours, sister, dear,' Christian interposed drily.

The long meal was not the ordeal she had expected but it was impossible for her to relax. Luc was in an exceptionally good mood, which somehow had made her feel uncomfortable. She was flagging by the time the Viennese coffee was served in the *salone*. Christian's sister settled down beside her and she struggled to recall her name. Georgina, that was it.

'I didn't see you with Luc in Nice last week,' Georgina remarked.

'I wasn't there.'

Georgina contrived to look astonished. 'But he was with Silvana Lenzi. Naturally, I assumed... Oh, dear, have I said something I oughtn't?'

'You've said exactly what you intended to say, young lady,' the kindly woman with the beaky nose retorted crisply, and changed the subject.

Across the room, Lùc was laughing with a group of men. Catching her eye, he gave her a brilliant smile. Hurriedly, she glanced away. Her nails dug into the soft flesh of her palm. She really couldn't understand why she should feel so shattered. Luc had not spent the past four and a half years without a woman in his bed. Celibacy would come no more naturally to him than losing money.

The South American film actress was notorious for her passionate affairs. He certainly hadn't been boldly going where no man had gone before, Catherine thought with a malice that shook her. She was speared by a Technicolor picture of that beautiful, lean, muscular, suntanned body of his engaged in intimate love-play with the gorgeous redhead. It made her feel sick. She felt betrayed.

Obviously she had had too much to drink. It had unsettled her stomach, confused her thoughts. If she felt betrayed, it was only because she had been the chosen one this week and the awareness was bound to distress her. Really, she didn't care if he had been throwing orgies in Nice. His womanising habits were a matter of the most supreme indifference to her.

A few minutes later, Luc interceded to conclude her evening. She was tired. He was sure everyone would excuse her. With his usual panache, he swept her out of the *salone*. She shook off his arm with distaste.

'It's ten minutes to midnight.' Impervious to hints, he was

reaching for her. 'Isn't it supposed to be bad luck for me to see you after midnight?' he teased, glittering golden eyes tracking over her in the most offensively proprietorial way.

Without even thinking about it, Catherine lifted her arm and slapped him so hard across one cheekbone that she almost fell. 'That's for Nice!' she hissed, stalking up the staircase. 'And if I see you after midnight, it won't be just bad luck, it'll be a death-trap!'

'*Buona notte, carissima,*' he said softly, almost amusedly.

Incredulous at the response, she halted and turned her head.

He stared up at her and smiled. 'You're crazy, but I like it.'

'What's the matter with you?' she snapped helplessly.

He checked his watch. 'You have six minutes to make it out of my sight. If you start talking, you'll never make it.'

Her fingermarks were clearly etched on one high cheekbone. The sight of her own handiwork filled her with sudden shame. She really didn't know what had come over her. 'I'm sorry. I shouldn't have done that,' she conceded.

'I'd forgive you for anything tonight. Even keeping me awake,' he advanced huskily.

That did it. She raced up to her room as though all the hounds in hell were pursuing her.

The beautiful breakfast brought to Catherine on a tray couldn't tempt her. The hair-stylist arrived, complete with retinue, followed by the cosmetics consultant and then the manicurist. The constant female chatter distanced her from the proceedings. As the morning moved on, she felt more and more as if she were a doll playing a part. She had nothing to do. Everyone else did it for her. And finally they stood back, hands were clapped, mutually satisfied smiles exchanged and compliments paid...the doll was dressed.

It wasn't real, not really real, she told herself repeatedly and stole another glance at her reflection, for it so closely matched that teenage dream. Certainly she had never before looked this good. No wonder they were all so pleased with themselves.

The little church was only a mile from the castle. It had been small and plain and dark when she had seen it earlier in the week.

Today it was ablaze with flowers that scented the air heavily. She was in a daze. She went down the short aisle on the arm of a Spanish duke she had only met the night before. It's five years too late, five years too late; this doesn't mean anything to me now, she reasoned at a more frantic pitch as Luc swung round to take a long unashamed look at her. But somehow from that moment she found it quite impossible to reason at all.

'The most beautiful bride I've ever seen.' Luc brushed his lips very gently across hers and the combination of a rare compliment and physical contact sent her senses reeling dizzily.

Sunlight was warming her face, glinting off the twist of platinum on her finger next, and Christian was dropping a kiss on her brow, laughingly assuring her that Luc had said her mouth was out of bounds.

In the limousine, he caught her to him and took her mouth with all the hunger he had earlier restrained. Her bouquet dropped from her fingers, fell forgotten to the floor, and her arms went round his neck, her unsteady fingers linking in an unbroken chain to hold him to her.

CHAPTER EIGHT

VIOLINS were thrumming in Catherine's bloodstream. She drifted round the floor in a rosy haze of contentment.

'Catherine?'

'Hmm?' she sighed dreamily into Luc's shoulder, opening her eyes a chink and vaguely surprised to recognise that the light, cast by the great chandeliers above, was artificial. In her mind she had been waltzing out under the night stars. 'Candles would have been more atmospheric,' she whispered, and then, 'You're thinking of the fire hazard and the smoke they would have created.'

'I'm trying very hard not to. I know what's expected of me,' Luc confessed above her head, and she gave a drowsy giggle. A lean hand tipped her face back, lingered to cup her chin. 'It's time for us to leave.'

'L-leave?' she echoed, jolted by the announcement.

His thumb gently eased between her parted lips and rimmed the inviting fullness of the lower in a gesture that was soul-shatteringly sensual. A heady combination of drowning feminine weakness and excitement spread burning heat through her taut-ening muscles. He might as well have thrown a high-voltage switch inside her. Dark eyes shaded by ebony lashes glimmered with gold. 'Leave,' he repeated, the syllables running together and merging. 'Fast,' he added as an afterthought.

'Everybody's still here.' She trembled as the hand resting at her spine curved her into contact with the stirring hardness of his thighs. 'Oh.'

'As you say, *cara*...oh,' he murmured softly. 'Our guests will dance quite happily to dawn without me. I have other ambitions.'

Her body was dissolving in the hard circle of his arms. She would have gone anywhere, done anything to stay there. The very thought of detaching herself long enough to get changed scared her. She was waking up out of the dream-like haze which had floated her through the day. And waking up was absolutely terrifying.

Had she really been stubborn enough to cling to the conviction that she hated him? It hadn't been hatred she'd felt when she saw him at the altar. It wasn't hatred she felt when he touched her. It was love. Love. She was blitzed by that reality. Her emotions had withstood the tests of pain and disillusionment, time and maturity. Why? But she knew why; scarcely had to answer the question. And in the beginning there was Luc...and there ended her story.

He steered her out of the ballroom, quite indifferent to the conversational sallies of several cliques in their path. In the shadow of the great staircase, he moulded her against him, his mouth hard and urgent, long fingers framing her cheekbones as he kissed her, at first roughly, then lingeringly with a slow, drugging sexuality that devastated her.

A low-pitched wolf-whistle parted them. Hot-cheeked, still trembling with the force of the hunger Luc had summoned up, she let her hands slide down from his shoulders, steadying herself.

Christian was regarding them from several feet away, a smile of unconcealed amusement on his face. Dealing him an unembarrassed glance, Luc directed her upstairs with the thoughtful precision of someone who doubted her ability to make it there without assistance. Guilia was waiting to help her out of her gown.

Dear God, Catherine thought in numbed confusion, was there a strong streak of insanity in her bloodline? Nothing less than madness could excuse her behaviour over the past twenty-four hours. Did all women lie to themselves as thoroughly as she had? Luc knew her better than she knew herself. He knew her strengths and insecurities, her likes and dislikes, even, it seemed, her craven habit of avoiding what she couldn't handle and denying what she was afraid of...

Why did she deceive herself this way? She had been like a child with an elaborate escape-plan, a child who secretly wanted to be caught before she did any real damage. Almost seven years ago she had given her heart without the slightest encouragement, and that heart was still his. And that love was something she couldn't change, something that was simply a part of her, something that it was quite useless to fight. Luc was her own personal self-destruct button. But leaving him less than five years ago had still been like tearing her heart from her body.

'I need you,' he had said once in the darkness of the night in Switzerland. The admission had turned her over and inside out. She would have walked on fire for him just for those three little words. But he had never said them again, never even come close to saying them once he had been secure in the knowledge that she adored him.

It hadn't been very long before he'd begun to smoothly remind her that what they had wouldn't last forever. He had hurt her terribly. He had taught her to walk floors at night, to feel sick at a careless word or oversight, to panic if a phone call was late...to live from day to day with this dreadful nagging fear of losing him always in the background. Inside, where it didn't show, he had killed her by degrees.

'He was very bad for you,' Harriet had scolded. 'You're not cut out to cope with someone like that. But you did what you had to do. You protected Daniel. Be proud that you had that much sense.'

Whenever she had wavered, as waver she had for far longer than she wanted to recall, Harriet had been the little Dutch boy, sticking her finger in the dam-wall of her emotions, preventing the leak from developing into a torrent that might prompt her into some foolish action. Oh, yes, she had thought about phoning him times without number. She had always chickened out. Once she had even stood in the post office a couple of days before his birthday, crazy enough to consider sending him a card because she knew that since his family's death there was nobody else but her to remember. Harriet had had her work cut out and no mistake. That first year keeping her away from Luc had been a full-time occupation.

But Catherine had been lucky enough to have had Daniel on

whom to target her emotions. How could anyone understand what Daniel meant to her? The first time she held him in her arms she had wept inconsolably. Nobody but Harriet had understood. Daniel had been the first living person she had ever seen to whom she was truly related. Between them, Daniel and Harriet had become the family she had never had.

Why had she planned to leave Luc again? This time she was honest with herself about her most driving motivation. She was terrified of telling him about Daniel, as terrified as she had been when she had realised she was pregnant. Luc did not have and clearly never had had the smallest suspicion that she might have been pregnant.

It was all so horribly complicated and she had so much to lose. Daniel believed his father was dead. He had asked very few questions and she really hadn't understood that he actually resented not having a father until that day at Greyfriars when he had raged at her, naïvely sharing his secret belief that his father, had he still been alive, would have been able to work miracles.

Daniel would accept Luc with very little encouragement. How Daniel would react to the discovery that his mother had lied to him was another question entirely. And could she trust Luc with Daniel? Daniel was very insecure right now, very breakable. If Luc could not accept him wholeheartedly, Daniel would know it. In addition, he was illegitimate. That couldn't be hidden and, sooner or later, it would hit the newspapers. Luc would find that intolerable.

And on what basis did she dare to assume that Luc saw their marriage as a permanent fixture? Luc was so unpredictable. Did she turn Daniel's life upside-down in the hope that Luc could come to terms with the decision she had made five years ago, and the fact that he had a four-year-old son?

Yesterday she had believed she had a choice. Today she accepted that she had merely talked herself into taking the easy way out and running away again. It wouldn't work this time. And the irony was that she didn't want it to work anyway. She loved Luc. She wanted to hope. She wanted to trust. She wanted to believe that somehow all this could be worked out. And that meant telling Luc about Daniel.

There was no time to be lost. The day after tomorrow, Peggy would be driving down to London. How did she tell him? The enormity of the announcement she had to make sunk in on her, another razor edge to hone her nerves. She would tell him on the flight to London…it wouldn't be very private, though. She would tell him whenever they arrived at their destination, wherever that was. But the more she dwelt on the coming confrontation, the more panic-stricken she became at the prospect.

'You're very pale.'

In the limousine, she didn't feel up to that narrowed, probing gaze. How would Luc react? That was all she could think about. Yesterday she had been telling herself that he was cold, callous and calculating in an effort to shore up her reluctance to tell him about Daniel. Yesterday she had been determined to hate him, determined to see him as a threat to Daniel. Now she had come down out of the clouds again, but the view was no more encouraging. She had deceived him. She had lied by omission. Those who crossed Luc lived to regret the miscalculation. Since she had never put herself in that position before, how could she possibly predict how he would react?

'And very quiet,' Luc continued.

She gulped. 'I was just thinking.'

'About what?'

'Nothing in particular.' She veiled her troubled eyes in case he did what he had done before and read her mind. Do it now, do it now, she urged herself. You know what you're like. The longer you leave it, the bigger mess you'll make of it. 'What time do we arrive in London?'

'Didn't I tell you? The air-traffic controllers in Rome are having a twenty-four-hour stoppage,' he imparted with the utmost casualness. 'We fly to London early tomorrow morning.'

'We're not going to the airport?' she gasped.

'A friend has offered us the use of his villa overnight.'

Her hands clenched convulsively together. Reprieve, the coward in her thought. An opportunity to be alone with him and tell him, her conscience insisted. The limousine was already turning through tall gates.

A housekeeper greeted them on the steps. When Luc refused the offer of supper, they were shown upstairs to a bedroom suite. It was full of mirrors and exotic silks and the most enormous bed. This was her wedding night, she reflected in despair. How could she tell him tonight? It would ruin the whole day, she reasoned weakly.

He came up behind her and buried his mouth hotly against the soft, sensitive spot where her shoulder met her throat, and her knees buckled. 'We should have supper,' she managed shakily.

'Are you hungry?'

'Well—'

'Supper wouldn't satisfy my hunger either,' he breathed approvingly. Slowly, heart-stoppingly, he turned her round. 'What's wrong with you?' he enquired, completely without warning.

'W-wrong?'

'You have the look of a murderer caught burying the body,' he murmured thoughtfully. 'Or is that my imagination?'

'Your imagination.' Avoiding his far too perceptive eyes, she tried to sidetrack him by reaching up and starting to undo his tie.

'My imagination rarely plays tricks on me.' He watched her struggling with his tie. With an expressive sigh, he covered her small shaking hands with one of his. 'You don't trust me, do you? I won't hurt you ever again, *bella mia*. I promise you that.'

Unbearably touched and suddenly rent with guilt, her eyes clouded over.

'I was only twenty-seven when I met you.' He ran a questing fingertip along the taut curve of her cheek. 'And I didn't want to meet someone like you. I set out to get you on my terms and I knew it wasn't what you wanted or what you deserved. You loved me too much, *cara*. You let me get away with murder. So, I took you for granted.' His superb bone-structure was prominent beneath his suntanned skin, his eyes very dark. 'I thought you would always be there. And then one day you were gone and I realised that even you had your breaking point. I realised that a little too late for it to make any difference.'

'Luc, I—'

He brushed his fingers in a silencing motion against her lips. 'I don't want to talk about the past now. It casts shadows. Maybe tomorrow, maybe the next day, hmm?' he cajoled. 'But not to-night.'

She turned her mouth involuntarily into the warm palm of his hand, tears wet on her cheeks. He appealed to her for understanding and Luc was not given to appeals. Strain clenched his dark features. The break with the tradition of keeping his own counsel hurt.

He trailed his tie off, shed his jacket with a lithe twist of his shoulders and pulled her into his arms, emanating now all the raw self-assurance that came so naturally to him. 'I scarcely slept last night,' he admitted softly. 'And I intend to keep you awake all night as punishment.'

His breath warmed her cheek and then his tongue slid between her lips, thrusting them apart to explore the moist interior she so freely offered him. The floor under her feet seemed to fall away, and she clung to him while he took her mouth again and again with a stormy intensity that stirred a dulled ache in the pit of her stomach. Her silk dress pooled on the carpet without her even being aware that he was expertly removing it. Lean fingers slid caressingly over her hip, encountering lace, and, disregarding the fragile barrier, he made her jerk and moan beneath his marauding mouth.

He laughed soft and deep in his throat, ceasing the provocation only to pick her up and carry her over to the bed, following her down in fluid motion, reacquainting her with every sleek line of his lean body. His shirt had come adrift and she ran her hands up over his smooth brown back, feeling every muscle tauten to her reconnaissance. He ground his hips sensuously slowly into hers, and for mindless seconds she was ruled by the hunger he could evoke and completely lost.

He looked down at her, dark eyes aflame with gold satisfaction and desire. 'Remember that first night in Switzerland?' he whispered huskily. 'You were so exquisitely shy.' He strung a line of kisses across her delicate collarbone. 'So innocent. I was a bastard, *bella mia*. It should have been our wedding night.'

'I pretended it was.'

A faint flush of colour irradiated the high cheekbones that intensified his raw attraction. He captured the fingers lacing into his black silky hair and pressed them to his lips, dense lashes concealing his gaze. 'I'd never made love to a virgin before. I wanted it to be special for you. That's why I took you to Switzerland.'

'It was special,' she managed unsteadily. 'Very special.'

'*Grazie…grazie tanto, cara,*' he teased. 'It was so special for me that I had to keep you all to myself, being of a naturally selfish disposition.'

She had never seen him so relaxed, not this last week, not ever. But for a split second he reminded her so powerfully of Daniel. The same beautiful dark eyes, the same wide mouth that could yank at her heart-strings with the faintest smile. Her breath caught in her throat, but he was brushing aside the lace cups of her bra, letting his tongue and then his mouth circle the taut pink nipples he had uncovered, and her mind became a complete blank, her fingers clenching together as sensation began to build, drawing every tiny muscle tight beneath his ministrations.

There was a mirror above the bed. She blinked bemusedly and then the imagery of his brown hands on her paler skin and his dark head bent so intimately over her took over. 'There's a mirror up there,' she whispered.

'How shocking.' His voice was indistinct, abstracted. 'Tell Christian he has outrageous bad taste next time you see him.'

'This is his villa?'

Luc eased back from her reluctantly, rolled off the bed and proceeded to strip. She couldn't take her eyes from him. Wide shoulders tapered down to a narrow waist, lean hips and long, muscular thighs. He was very aroused, superbly male, supremely beautiful.

'Looking at me like that does nothing for my self-control.' He came down beside her again, dispensed with the wispy lingerie and curved her into his arms. The dark hair hazing his chest rubbed against her tender breasts, one lean thigh hooking over hers as he stared down at her, so much unashamed hunger in his probing appraisal that she was breathless. 'You wouldn't have done it.'

'Done what?'

'Walked away at the airport.' A wry smile challenged her shock. 'I wouldn't have let you go. Did you think I didn't know? Sometimes I know what you think before you think it.'

Having devastated her, he took advantage by ravishing her swollen mouth with a fierce, driving sweetness. Time and thought were banished. She got drunk on the taste of him. The warm masculine scent of him flooded her, making her even more light-headed. She could feel herself sliding out of control. Breathing hurt her lungs. Tiny sounds she was barely conscious of broke from her lips, and when his hand touched her where she most ached for fulfilment, she went wild, writhing with his burning caresses, hungrily searching out for herself the compulsive heat of his mouth.

It was agony and ecstasy but he wouldn't give her what she sought as she blindly arched her hips in a silent expression of need as old as time. She was twisting in the heat of a fire that demanded assuagement. Her fingernails raked his back in torment and protest. And then, in the shuddering, explosive tension of his body, she felt the flames leap and scorch through him as well. Suddenly he was all aggressor, all savage demand, spreading her out like a sacrifice to some primitive god and falling on her, hands bruising her thighs as he took her with all the strength he possessed in a driving surge of passionate intensity.

It went on and on and on, more and then incredibly more until she was sobbing her pleasure out loud, lost to everything but the remorseless demands of her own body. The release came in a frenzied explosion of exquisite sensation that left her awash with the bliss of satiation.

'*Dio!*' he groaned in harsh satisfaction, shuddering in the possessive circle of her arms, burying his damp face in her hair. '*Te amo,*' he muttered, almost crushing her beneath his weight. '*Te amo.*'

She stilled. I love you. I love you, he had said.

'*Scusi.*' He rolled over and sprawled back in an indolent tangle of sun-darkened limbs against the white percale sheeting. 'Now I finally know what it's like to be a sex object,' he sighed without particular concern in the winging smile he angled at her. 'You made me lose control. That's my department.'

She smiled, a fat-cat-got-the-cream smile. He probably didn't even know he'd said it. That was fine. The last thing she wanted to do was to make an issue out of it. She had lived off 'I need you' for almost two years once. She could manage a good decade on 'I love you'. Moving over, she scattered a trail of kisses across a sweat-slicked broad shoulder. 'I love you...I love you...I love you,' she whispered feverishly.

He caught a hand into her tousled hair. 'I know, I know, I know,' he said playfully.

He hadn't bitten the bait. When did he? She was too impatient. If he had meant it, he would tell her in his own good time. If? It didn't help to be aware that such a confession at the height of sexual excitement was recorded the world over as a statutory and meaningless phrase. But didn't she have rather more to worry about right now? Daniel rose like Mount Everest in the back of her mind.

'Luc...how do you feel about children?'

He tugged her down on top of him, claimed a kiss, clearly not very focused on the concept of dialogue. 'I never thought of them until recently.'

'Do...do you like them?'

'Like them?' Ebony brows slashed together in a frown. 'What sort of a question is that? I expect I will like my own. I have no real interest in other people's.'

It wasn't very encouraging. She made no demur when his hands started to roam lazily over her again. Indeed, she needed that closeness, that hunger of his to control the fear that was steadily rising inside her. Luc would be furious. But what frightened her most was the unknown quantity of how he would react after the fury.

'You can sleep during the flight.' Luc smiled down into her heavy eyes, satisfaction and amusement mingling in his scrutiny.

They were about to leave the VIP lounge when a small grey-haired man, closely followed by a security guard, came in.

'Antonio?' Luc crossed the room to greet him with pleated brows.

The low-pitched exchange of Italian had an odd edge of urgency that made Catherine glance in their direction. The older man gave something to Luc, withdrew a handkerchief to mop his perspiring brow and, by his manner, was clearly apologising. He looked as though he was reporting a death. She stifled a yawn, and her attention slewed away again.

'Who was that?' she asked as they boarded the jet.

'One of my lawyers.' His intonation was curiously clipped.

She hated take-off; always had. She didn't open her eyes until they were airborne. Luc wasn't beside her. On the other side of the cabin, he was scanning a single sheet of paper. As she watched he scrunched it up between his fingers and snatched up the newspaper lying on the desk in front of him. He signalled to the steward with a snap of his fingers. A large whiskey arrived pronto. Draining it in one long, unappreciative gulp, he suddenly sprang up, issuing a terse instruction to the steward who left the cabin at speed.

'Catherine...come here.' He moved a hand in an oddly constrained arc.

Releasing her belt, she got up. His set profile was dark, brooding. He indicated the seat opposite. 'Sit down.'

When she collided with his eyes her heart stopped beating and her mouth ran dry. The suppressed violence that sprang out at her from that hawk-like stare of intimidation was terrifying.

'I will not lose my head with you,' he asserted in a controlled undertone. 'There must be an explanation. I still have faith, but it hangs by a thread.'

'You're scaring me.'

He continued to study her, a kind of flagellating stare that threatened to strip the skin from her facial bones. 'Last week, Rafaella told me something I refused to believe. After your disappearance five years ago, she stayed in the apartment we shared for some weeks. I didn't want it to be empty if you phoned or chose to return.'

Uncertainly she nodded.

'And last week she informed me that during her stay a call came from some doctor's surgery, asking why you hadn't been back for a check-up.'

She bent her head and studied the desk-top, gooseflesh prickling at the nape of her neck, an impending sense of doom sliding over her.

'From that call and certain trivia she subsequently uncovered in the apartment,' Luc continued in the same murderously calm tone, 'Rafaella deduced that you were pregnant at the time of your departure.'

She flinched, froze, watched the desk-top blur.

'She assumed—that is, if her story is true—that you had decided on an abortion. She told me that at the time she saw no good reason to share this knowledge with me. So she cultivated a short memory.'

Catherine wanted God to pluck her out of the sky and put her somewhere out of Luc's reach. Her vocal cords were in arrest. Her brain had stopped functioning.

'Naturally her assumption was that, if there was a child, it was not mine. Halston figured largely as the culprit,' he extended, his tone quieter and quieter, every word slow and precise and measured. 'Perhaps you can now understand why I was so angry with her. After this length of time the story struck me as fantastic and wholly incredible. I didn't believe a word of it. I defended you.'

The weight of the world's sins seemed to sit on her bowed shoulders. She was shrinking inwardly and outwardly.

'This is now your cue to tell me that not a word of her story is true. You see, Rafaella is persistent. When I refused her calls, she communicated with one of my lawyers in Rome, giving him the details of what she apparently discovered in England,' he spelt out. 'Antonio spent a most troubled night before rousing the courage to bring those facts to me. He was hastened to a decision when an article purporting to relate to you was printed in an English newspaper.'

'I...I didn't think of it coming out like this!' she burst out strickenly. 'I intended to tell you when we arrived in England...' Her voice trailed away.

'Look at me.' He ground out the command fiercely. 'Are you telling me it is true? That you were pregnant? That there is a child?'

Like a puppet she nodded twice, shorn of speech by the violent incredulity splintering from him in waves.

'And...you...married...me?' He was rising slowly from behind the desk, having trouble in getting the question past his compressed lips.

'What did you expect me to do?' she muttered frantically.

'What did I expect? What did I expect?' he roared at her, a hand like a vice closing round her wrist to trail her bodily out of her seat.

'You're hurting me!'

'He'd better not be mine!' he bit down at her rawly.

The tension broke her and she sobbed, 'Of course he is. Of course he's yours. Why would you want anything else?'

He punched a fist into the palm of his other hand with a sickening thud and swung violently away from her. Barbaric fury throbbed from every tensed line of his long, taut body. 'If I touch you, I'll kill you. *Cristo*, get out of my sight before I lose control!'

'Luc, please,' she said brokenly.

He spun back to her, fluid as a cat on his feet even in rage. 'If he hadn't been mine, maybe...just maybe I could have forgiven you, because then at least I could have understood why you ran away. But this!' He spread brown hands eloquently wide in a slashing movement. 'This I don't understand at all!'

'If you would just calm down,' she interposed pleadingly.

'Calm down? I find out I have a son of almost five whom I don't know and I never even dreamt existed, and you ask me to calm down?'

'I should have told you last night.'

'Last night?' he grated in disbelief. 'Last night, while you were playing the whore in my arms, I'd definitely have strangled you! I don't give a damn about last night or last week! I'm talking about five years ago when you were pregnant!'

The brutality of his attack on her behaviour the night before cut with the efficacy of a knife through her heart. 'S-stop shouting—'

'If I don't shout I'll get physical! And I've never struck a woman in my life and I will not start now,' he shot at her furiously.

It took immense will-power for her to drag her thoughts into order. The sheer force of his rage had shattered her, and his contention that he would have preferred to learn that Daniel was another man's child was quite incomprehensible to her.

'Why didn't you tell me five years ago?' The repetition scorched back at her.

'I meant to...I tried to—'

'I don't remember you trying,' he cut in ruthlessly.

She sucked in air convulsively. 'I was afraid to tell you.'

He uttered a succinct swear-word he had never used in her presence before. It blazed with his derision.

'All right,' she whispered, and, mustering the tattered shreds of her composure, she mastered herself sufficiently to continue. 'You won't like what I'm about to say...'

'I don't like you,' he breathed with chilling effect. 'Nothing that you could say could be any worse than the revulsion I feel now.'

Unintentionally she burst into tears, hating herself for the weakness, but she felt as if she were an animal caught in a trap.

'I couldn't bring myself to tell you,' she formulated shakily, 'because I knew you wouldn't want him and I was scared that I would let you talk me into getting rid of him.'

'You dare to foist the blame on me!' he raked back at her with contempt.

In a benumbed state, she moved her head back and forth. 'You always made it so obvious that you didn't want to commit yourself to me in any way. I honestly believed that you would see a termination as the only practical solution.'

'Where my own flesh and blood is concerned, I am not practical! And what does commitment to you have to do with commitment to my unborn child?' he demanded. 'And what do you know of my feelings about abortion? When did we ever discuss the subject?'

'I...I made an assumption,' she conceded, no longer able to look at him.

'You made one hell of an assumption!'

'At the time, I believed it was the right one,' she whispered.

'And shall I tell you why you made that assumption? Look at me!' he commanded fiercely, and she did, fearfully, sickly, wondering where the axe could possibly fall next. 'I never knew what a temper you had. I never dreamt there could be such bitterness and obstinacy behind that angel face. But I know it now, and I don't need your interpretation, for I have my own! Let me tell you how it was: if I wasn't going to marry you, I would pay for that with the loss of my child!'

'No!' she cried. 'It wasn't like that!'

'It was exactly like that. No ring, no child. I was playing Russian roulette over that breakfast table and I didn't know it!' He looked at her with hatred. 'To think that I tortured myself over what I said to you that day! You had no right to conceal the truth from me. It was my right to know that you were carrying my child. *Cristo*, did you hate me so much that you couldn't even give me a chance?'

Her legs were shaking. She sank down in the nearest seat and covered her face with damp hands. 'I loved you. I loved you so much.'

'*That* was love?' He emitted a harsh laugh of incredulity. 'I lash out at you once. In nearly two years, I lose my temper with you once! Once! And I've been paying for it ever since. It was revenge you took, and I understand revenge very well.'

'I don't think like you,' she said in defeat.

'If you thought like me, you'd have been my wife five years ago! *Si*, I'd have married you.' Lancing dark eyes absorbed her white face with a kind of grim satisfaction. 'I probably wouldn't have done it with the best of grace, but I'd have married you.'

She shrank in retrospect from such a fate. Luc, forced into marriage shotgun-style. It would have been a nightmare. 'I wouldn't have wanted you to marry me feeling like that.'

'*Dio!* What would your feelings or my feelings have had to do with it with a child on the way?'

'I couldn't have lived with you under those circumstances,' she muttered limply.

His mouth twisted chillingly. 'The only truly honest woman I ever met—that's what I told Rafaella about you. It's a wonder she didn't laugh in my face! But then, she has one virtue you don't have. She's loyal even when I turn on her as I did last week.'

'Daniel and I will go away.' Hardly knowing what she was saying, Catherine spoke the thought out loud. 'You won't hear from us again.'

CHAPTER NINE

'YOU'RE not taking him anywhere!'

'You don't want him. You didn't even want him to be yours. That has to be the sickest, cruellest thing you've ever said to me.' Catherine's voice wobbled alarmingly on the contention.

'Sick?' Luc thundered. 'I've lost five years of his life! He's illegitimate. What will he suffer in later years? Don't you realise that all this will hit the papers? Did you think you'd be able to shelter behind the fallacy that you were a widow with a child for the rest of your days? It will come out...of course it will, and how will the child feel then? About you? About me? That is why my first wish was that he should not be mine. For *his* sake, not my own. The papers are already sifting what few facts they have, already hinting that all is not as it appears. Why else was he left in England?'

'The papers?' She was ghost-pale, paralysed by the sheer force of the condemnation coming her way.

'Surely you didn't believe that you could step from nowhere into the life that I lead and conceal the truth? If it hadn't been for Rafaella, his face would already have been splashed all over the gutter Press! When she tracked him down to your friend's home in the Lake District, she got him out before the paparazzi could make a killing.'

'Got him out? To take him where?' she pressed feverishly, registering that the threat of Press interest had been roused far more swiftly than she had naïvely expected.

'She persuaded your friend to bring him south before the Press arrived. They're waiting for us at the house.'

'What house?' she mumbled dazedly.

His strong jawline clenched, a tiny muscle tugging at the hardened line of his mouth. 'I bought it for you as a wedding present. Five years ago...five long, wasted years ago!' he vented rawly.

In the state she was in, it took a little while for the significance of that admission to sink in. 'Five years ago?'

Smouldering dark eyes black as pitch bit into her. 'I was such a fool. I, who prided myself on my superior judgement! Haven't you worked it out yet, *cara*? I was in love with you.'

'F-five years ago?' It was a shattered gasp.

'I didn't know it myself until you had gone.' His inflexion, his whole demeanour, was chillingly cold and harsh. 'The last laugh really was on me. I believed you would return...phone...send a postcard with "x marks the spot" on it...something, anything! I couldn't believe you would stay away forever. I could not have done that to you.' That confession appeared to awaken another scorching tide of anger. His teeth gritted as he stared at her. 'I spent a fortune trying to trace you. In an excess of conscience-stricken self-reproach, I intended to marry you as soon as I found you! So much for the fresh start!'

Slow tears brimmed up in her eyes and rolled down her cheeks. She swallowed back her sobs in the seething silence that throbbed and tortured and taunted. But Luc was not finished with her.

'And when I find you, I close my eyes to the evidence of what you are. I make excuses for you. I cling to an illusion that probably never existed anywhere outside my own imagination. Why?' A savage bitterness stamped his dark taut features. 'It can only be because you're the best lay I've ever had. That is all I will ever allow it to be now.'

'Don't,' she begged brokenly, sensing his destructive determination to smash the bonds between them...or had she already done that for herself?

'You did this to me before. I will never let you do it to me again.' The assurance carried all the lethal conviction of an oath.

'What did I do?' she whispered.

'Five years ago I trusted you more than anyone else in this world, Catherine. And you betrayed that trust,' he delivered contemptuously. 'You spent all night in my arms, telling me how much you loved me and then you walked out...'

'I was saying goodbye the only way I could.' It was a dulled murmur.

'Of course, it would not occur to you that one of the reasons I was so angry with you the next morning was that I felt that I had been set up!'

'How could you feel that?'

'How could I fail to feel that? And then I didn't want to marry you, I didn't want to marry anyone. My parents did not give me a very entrancing view of the married state. They hated the sight of each other!'

She looked up in shock at that grated revelation. 'You never told me that!'

'You have so many illusions about happy family life, I could never bring myself to tell you the truth.' His dark gaze was unrelentingly grim. 'My parents married because they had to marry. My mother was pregnant. They didn't love each other. They didn't even like each other. They lived together all those years in absolute misery. And the only thing they ever wanted from me was money. As long as the money came, they hadn't the slightest interest in what I was doing. But it took me a long while to face that reality. When that plane went down, the only things I lost were a sister and two parents who never wanted to be parents in the first place.'

Shutting her eyes tightly, she lowered her head. 'I always thought your family loved you.'

'They loved what I could give them,' he contradicted fiercely. 'And you're not so very different, are you? Ten days ago, you were sitting in Huntingdon's apartment ready to marry him. Miraculously, you converted to me!'

'He asked me to marry him that day you saw us. There was never anything between us before that. At least not on my side. I should have been honest about that sooner,' she conceded uncertainly.

'Honest?' he gritted. 'You don't know the meaning of the word.

I look forward to you telling my son in another few years that the reason for my late appearance in his life lies with your fear of my intentions towards him before he was even born!'

She flinched at the image he projected.

'What have you told him about me?'

She might as well have been hanging from a cliff by her fingernails. One by one, he was breaking them, loosening their hold, bringing the jagged rocks of retribution closer and closer. She chose to jump. 'Nothing,' she admitted shakily.

'Nothing?' he exclaimed. 'You must have told him something about his father!'

She broke into a faltering explanation of Harriet's cover-story. She could not have said that he absorbed the details. He zoomed in on only one, cutting her short in another surge of shuddering rage when he realised that Daniel thought his father was dead. The last straw had broken the camel's back. That Luc should not know he had had a son was bad enough. But that Daniel should not know about him was unforgivable.

She was desperately confused by what he had told her in anger, confidences which she sensed that in his present mood would never have been made otherwise. He had said that he loved her five years ago. All else receded before that single stated fact. The love she had longed to awaken had been there. And she had been too blind and too insecure to even suspect its existence for herself.

Why had she listened to Harriet? Why, oh, why? But it wasn't fair to blame Harriet. Harriet had judged Luc on the evidence of what Catherine herself had told her. Harriet had influenced her only in so far as she had confirmed what Catherine had already believed. And Luc had just brought down the convictions that had sustained her through the years like a pack of cards.

Enormous guilt weighted her now. She had run away when she should have stood her ground, stayed away when she should have returned. A little voice said that what Luc said so impressively now with the benefit of hindsight was no very good guide to how he might have reacted to her pregnancy without having sustained the shock of first losing her. That voice was quashed because the guilt was greater. Luc would have married her. Daniel would have had a father. Daniel would have had many things and many advantages which she had not had the power to give him.

Luc was right on one count. She had not given him a chance. In her own mind, the result had been a foregone conclusion. Then, she had to admit, it had been easier to run away than face a confrontation. In those days, she had been out of her depth with Luc, unable to hold her own. She could not have dreamt then that Luc could be so bitter or indeed that losing her could have brought him so much pain. For it had been pain that powered that bitterness, that fierce conviction that she had betrayed him for the second time. Luc viewed her response to his lovemaking last night in the same light as he had viewed that long-ago last night in New York.

And she understood facets of his temperament which she had not understood before. The heat in the bedroom, the coolness beyond it. Recently he had begun to break out of that pattern. But he must have learnt early in life not to show his emotions. And he must have been hurt. His parents, by all accounts, had not encouraged or sought his affection. The financial generosity, which in the past had made her feel like an object to be bought, was shown now in a different light. Luc had had a long history before her of giving to those closest to him. It had been expected of him. When his family had died, he had simply continued the same habit with her.

There was so much fear trapped inside her. Luc was more than disappointed in her: Luc was embittered and disillusioned. Five years ago, whether she knew it or not, she had thumped the last nail into her coffin. It had never occurred to Luc that she might have been pregnant because it had equally never occurred to him that, if she was, she might go to such lengths to conceal the fact from him.

But what a disaster it would have been had Luc felt forced to marry her, repeating what he surely would have believed to be his parents' mistake. He had not been ready to make such a commitment of his own free will. It wouldn't have worked, it couldn't have worked, but Luc could not see that. No, at this moment Luc saw only Daniel, and he was already demonstrating a voracious appetite for knowledge of his son. He wanted Daniel. Right now, he did not want Daniel's mother.

Anger was within him still, anger dangerously encased in ice which could shatter again. When Luc came to terms with the awareness that he was a father, how would he feel about her then? He had trusted her. He had blamed himself entirely for her defection in the past. He had wanted to put the clock back, make everything right...she could see that now. And now he had learnt that that wasn't possible. It was very probable, she registered strickenly, that the driving determination of his to take what he wanted had resulted in a too hasty marriage.

'I love Daniel very much,' she murmured tightly.

'You have a fine way of showing it,' he censured. 'You dump him in the back of beyond with some seething feminist—'

'Don't you dare call Peggy that!' Catherine interrupted hotly. 'She's a university lecturer and she's written three books. She's also a very good friend.'

But possibly Peggy wouldn't be a friend any more in the midst of this nightmare that had erupted. Kept in the dark about Luc's identity, railroaded from her family home by Rafaella, and told goodness knew what, Peggy was sure to be furious as well.

Catherine's wedding present was an Elizabethan country house. It wasn't enormous, it wasn't ostentatious and it would have stolen her heart had she been in a less wretched mood...and had Rafaella not been emerging from the front entrance, wreathed in welcoming smiles...

'Not bad as a pressie, not bad at all.' Hands on her slim hips, Peggy scanned the house in the early-evening sunshine, her wryly admiring scrutiny glossing over manicured lawns, a stretch of woodland and the more distant glimmer of a small lake. 'Strewth, Catherine, it's incredibly hard not to be impressed by all this.'

Catherine glanced at her watch helplessly again.

Too observant to miss the betraying gesture, Peggy frowned. 'They'll show up again sooner or later. Stop worrying. Daniel will come round. It's my fault,' she sighed. 'I shouldn't have left him alone with Rafaella for a second. The woman's poisonous.'

Catherine thought back reluctantly to their arrival. Luc had gone straight to greet Rafaella. Catherine had no idea what had passed between them but the brunette had been smiling and laughing, switching on to the ultra-feminine mode she invariably employed around Luc. Then, with a pretty little speech about not wanting to intrude, she had climbed into her car, no doubt smugly aware that she was leaving bedlam in her wake between husband and wife...and mother and son.

Daniel had been sitting like a solemn little old man in one of the downstairs rooms. Her attempt to put her arms round him had been fiercely rejected. 'You tol' me my daddy was dead!' Daniel had condemned and, from that point on, the reunion had gone from bad to worse.

Rafaella had done her work well. Daniel might be a very clever child but his grasp of adult relationships was no greater than any other four-year-old's. He understood solely that his mother had lied to him. Hurt and confused, terribly nervous of meeting this father Rafaella had described in over-impressive terms, Daniel had taken the brunt of his conflicting emotions out on Catherine.

Luc had taken over the same second he chose to join them, crouching down on his son's diminutive level to engage his attention. 'I don't know anything about being a father,' he had confided cleverly. 'I'll probably make mistakes. You'll have to help me.'

'I don't want a daddy who bosses me around all the time,' Daniel had traded in a small voice, but quick as a flash with the return.

'I wouldn't either,' Luc had agreed smoothly.

'I'm not sure I want one,' Daniel had admitted less argumentatively.

'I can understand that, but I am very sure that I want you to be my son.'

'Have you got any other ones?' Daniel asked innocently.

'Only you. That is what makes you so special.'

Catherine had hovered like a third wheel, watching without

great surprise as Daniel had responded to Luc. Luc had put in a performance of unsurpassed brilliance, quieting all of Daniel's fears. It had gone on for ages. A series of extremely subtle negotiations on Luc's side and of blossoming confidence and curiosity on Daniel's.

Luc hadn't moved too far, too fast. A mutual sizing-up had been taking place. After an hour, Daniel had been chattering confidingly, flattered by Luc's interest in him, relaxed and unthreatened by his manner. Clover had been mentioned. It had taken Luc precisely five seconds to recognise that the retrieval of an elderly donkey from an animal sanctuary would do much to cement his new relationship with his son. And never let it be said that Luc would look a gift horse or, in this case, a gift donkey in the mouth. A phone call had established that Clover was still in residence.

'I think we should go and get her now, don't you?' Luc had suggested with the innate cool of a master tactician, and Daniel had been so overcome with tears, excitement and gratitude that he had flung himself at Luc, breaking the no-physical-contact barrier he had until that moment rigidly observed.

They had departed before lunch. 'He's a beautiful child,' Luc had murmured, choosing then to notice Catherine for the first time since their arrival. 'And I am very proud that he is mine.'

She still wasn't sure whether that had been a compliment, a veiled apology, a mere acknowledgement of Daniel's attractions or a concealed criticism that he had had to wait this long to meet his own son.

'You should have gone with them,' Peggy told her.

'I wasn't invited. Anyway,' she sighed, 'I needed to talk to you. I thought you'd be furious over all that's happened.'

'Are you kidding? The last two days have been excitement all the way!' Peggy laughed. 'I was staggered when Rafaella showed me that picture of you with Luc at the airport and by that time the first reporter was ringing. Someone in the village must have tipped them off. Lots of people knew I was taking Daniel up to my parents' place. When I go back, I can bask in your reflected glory...'

'There's not a lot of it around at the moment. You'll catch a chill,' Catherine warned ruefully. 'When all of this comes out—'

'When all of what comes out? Don't exaggerate,' Peggy scolded. 'You lived with him, it broke down, and now you're married to him. You can't get a lot of scandalous mileage out of that. Daniel's his, end of story.'

'It's not that simple—'

'Neither was the amount of information you contrived to leave out when you once briefly discussed Daniel's father with me,' Peggy interposed. 'I've met him for about ten minutes now and I'm not sure I'm very much the wiser. Mind you, he has three virtues not to be sneezed at. One, he's generous. I won't add that he can afford to be. Two, he has to be the best-looking specimen I've ever seen live off a movie-screen. That's a sexist observation, Catherine, but, shamefully, that *was* my first reaction. Three, anyone capable of charming Daniel out of a tantrum that fast is worthy of respect.'

'Anything else?'

'When he breezed off with Daniel and left you behind like faithful Penelope, I found myself hoping that Clover would be in a more than usually anti-social state of mind when he has to get close and enthuse. I bet he's never been within twenty feet of a donkey before!'

That so matched Catherine's thoughts that she burst out laughing, but her amusement was short-lived. She sighed. 'If I hadn't lost my memory, I'd have had to tell him about Daniel last week. That wouldn't have been quite so bad.'

'If you ask me, and you won't, so I'll give it to you for free,' Peggy murmured, 'where Daniel's concerned, Luc got what he deserved. If he hadn't made you so insecure you'd have trusted him enough to tell him. And it strikes me that he's bright enough to work that one out for himself.'

If he *wants* to work it out, Catherine reflected unhappily. And nothing Luc had said earlier in the day had given her the impression that he intended to make that leap in tolerant understanding.

She walked Peggy back to her car, both dreading and anticipating Luc's return.

Clover arrived first, as irascible as ever, snapping at the gardener, who was detailed to take her to the paddock. Catherine was interrupted in the midst of her thanks to the lady who ran the animal sanctuary and had taken the trouble to deliver Clover back, and was informed with an embarrassed smile that Luc had made a most handsome donation to the sanctuary. Ironically, that irritated her. Why were things always so easy for Luc?

He strolled in after ten with Daniel fast asleep in his arms. On the brink of demanding to know where they had been all day, she caught herself up. The cool challenge in Luc's gaze informed her that he was prepared for exactly that kind of response. Moving forward, she took Daniel from him instead. 'I'll put him to bed.'

She carted her exhausted son up to the bedroom where he had slept for the previous two nights. He stirred while she was undressing him, eyes flying open in sudden panic. 'Where's Daddy?'

'Downstairs.'

'I thought I dreamt him.' Daniel gave her a sleepy, beguiling smile. 'He doesn't know anything about kids but he knows a lot about computers,' he said forgivingly, submitting to a hug and winding his arms round her neck. 'I'm sorry I was bad.'

Her eyes stung. 'I'll forgive you this once.'

'Daddy s'plained everything. It's all his fault we got split up,' he whispered, drifting off again.

From the bottom of her heart, she thanked Luc for that at least. He had put Daniel's needs before his own anger, healing the breach between Catherine and her son before it could get any wider. As it could have done. Catherine was well aware that, for the foreseeable future, Luc would occupy centre stage with Daniel. Luc had had the power to swerve him even further in that direction. But he hadn't used it.

She went down to the drawing-room. For all its size, it had a cosy aspect of comfort, decorated as it was with the faded country-house look she had always admired. The interior lacked a lived-in quality, though. The housekeeper, Mrs Stokes, had gone to considerable trouble with flower arrangements in empty spaces, but it was so obvious that nobody had lived here in years. Mrs Stokes had told her quite casually that Luc had never even spent a night below this roof before.

And he had bought this house for her, had scarcely come near it after the first few months. Luc had had faith in her, she registered painfully. Luc had been convinced that she would return. What she had forced him to face today was that she had not had a corresponding faith in him. She had asked for nothing, expected nothing and, not surprisingly, nothing was what she had received.

'Is he asleep?' Luc paused on the threshold, leashed vitality vibrating from his poised stance. His veiled dark gaze was completely unreadable.

She cleared her dry throat. 'He went out like a light. You must have tired him out. That doesn't often happen.'

Luc moved a fluid shoulder. 'He doesn't have enough stimulation. He was on his very best behaviour with me, but I suspect displays of temper such as I witnessed earlier are not infrequent.'

'He was upset,' she said defensively.

'He's an extremely bright child. He should start school as soon as possible.'

She paled in dismay. 'I don't want him sent away.'

Luc raised a brow. 'Did I suggest that? He does not have to board. Rome has an excellent school for gifted children. The opportunity to compete with equals would benefit Daniel.' He took a deep breath, cast an almost wary look at her, but she wasn't looking at him. Tight-mouthed, she was staring at the floor. 'He's a little old to be throwing tantrums. That surplus energy could be better employed.'

'You're very critical!' she snapped.

'That wasn't my intention. He's an infinitely more well-balanced child than I was at the same age, but he needs more to occupy him. Unless you plan to continue letting him educate himself from the television set.'

Catherine reddened fiercely but she didn't argue, uneasily conscious that he had some grounds for that comment. 'I did my best.'

'He's basically a very happy, very confident child. I think you did a marvellous job, considering that you were on your own and, as Daniel assured me repeatedly, very short of money.'

The compliment only increased her tension. Luc was so distant, so controlled. She didn't recognise him like this. He was unnerving her. She stole a covert under-the-lashes glance at the vibrancy of his dark golden features, desperate to know how he felt now that he had had time to cool down.

'Was what you said to me this morning true? Or a fabrication of the moment?' he prompted very quietly. 'Did you really believe that I would have demanded that you have an abortion?'

The colour drained from her complexion. 'Put like that, it sounds so—'

'Cruel? Inhuman? Selfish?' he suggested, his beautiful eyes running like flames of dancing gold over her distressed face. 'Presumably that is how you saw me then.'

In bewilderment she shook her head at this incorrect assertion. 'I didn't...when something gets in your way, you get rid of it,' she stumbled, conscious that she was not expressing herself very well. 'I just felt that if that was what you wanted, I mightn't have been able to stand up to you. That was what I was most afraid of. I might have let you persuade me...'

Every angle of his strong bone-structure was whip-taut. '*Per amor di Dio*, what did I do to give you such an image of me?'

The scene wasn't working in the way she had hoped it would. Luc was dwelling with dangerously precise intensity on the jumbled mess of imprecise emotions and fears which had guided her almost five years ago. 'It wasn't like that. Can't you understand that the longer I kept quiet about it, the harder it was for me to tell you?'

'What I understand is that you were very much afraid of me and that you were convinced that I would kill my unborn child for convenience. Yet even when I didn't know that I loved you, I cared for you,' he murmured with flat emphasis. 'And even if I hadn't loved you, I still couldn't have chosen such a course of action.'

Tears lashed the back of her eyes. She blinked rapidly. 'I'm sorry.' It was a cry from the heart.

A grim curve hardened his mouth. 'I think it is I who should be sorry. I appear to have reaped what I sowed. And you had no more faith in me yesterday when you married me. You still couldn't summon up the courage to tell me about Daniel.'

'I'm a frightful coward...you ought to know that by now.' It was an uneasy joke that was truth. 'And anyway, I didn't want to spoil the wedding,' she muttered, not looking at him, too aware that it was a pathetic excuse.

The silence stretched, dragging her nerves unbearably tight.

'How much of a chance is there that this last week will threaten to extend the family circle?' he asked tautly.

As his meaning sank in, she licked her dry lips nervously, conscious that she would very soon have confirmation one way or another. 'Very little chance,' she proffered honestly, strangely, ridiculously embarrassed all of a sudden by the subject. Luc's attitude was a far cry from his attitude that day at the pool, and that day seemed so long ago now.

If he wasn't quite tactless enough to heave a loud sigh of relief at the news, he wasn't capable of concealing that she had alleviated a fairly sizeable apprehension. The most obvious aspects of his strong tension dissolved. 'I want you to know that I didn't think of repercussions either those first few days that we were together. I am not that unscrupulous,' he asserted, even managing a faint smile. 'I didn't plan to make you pregnant.'

'That's OK.' Catherine gave a jerky shrug, couldn't have got another word out, she was so desperately hurt by his reaction. The idea of another child had taken surprising root, she discovered belatedly. She saw Luc's withdrawal of enthusiasm as the ultimate rejection. It was only a tiny step further to the belief that he no longer saw their marriage as a permanent fixture. A second child would only have complicated matters.

'I was very careless,' he remarked.

Catherine wasn't listening to him. She was on the edge of bursting into floods of tears and bitter recriminations. A strategic retreat was called for. She cut a wide passage round him. 'I'm tired. I'm going to bed.'

'I won't disturb you.'

It was no consolation at all to discover that Luc's possessions had been removed from the main bedroom at some stage of the evening. He hadn't even given her the chance to throw him out! Grabbing a pillow, she punched it and then thrust her face in it to muffle her sobs.

CHAPTER TEN

'CAN I get you anything else, Mrs Santini?'

Catherine surveyed her plate guiltily. One croissant, shredded into about fifteen pieces, not a toothmark on one of them. 'No, thanks.' She forced a smile. 'I'm not very hungry.'

Her appetite was no more resilient than her heart. Luc had taken Daniel to Paris with him very early this morning. They would be back by evening. In Daniel's hearing, Luc had smoothly suggested that she might like to accompany them. Her refusal had been equally smoothly accepted. The invitation had clearly been for Daniel's benefit alone.

The past four days, she conceded numbly, had been hell upon earth. She had learnt the trick of shortening them. She went to bed early and slept late. Yet she could not fault Luc's behaviour. He was being scrupulously polite and considerate. Indeed, he was making a very special effort. It didn't come naturally to him. She could feel the raw tension behind the cool front. She could taste it in the air. He couldn't hide it from her.

He didn't love her. How could she ever have been foolish enough to believe that he might? Then again, she had a talent for dreaming, for believing what she wanted to believe, she conceded with bitter self-contempt. Luc had chased an illusion for almost five years and he had suddenly woken up to the truth. Daniel had been the catalyst, but even if Daniel hadn't existed Luc would inevitably have realised that he had made a mistake.

In her absence, Luc must have built her up to be something more exciting than she was. When he'd found her again, her reluctance and the challenge of apparently taking her away from another man had provoked that dark, savage temperament of his.

All that mattered to him was winning. Having won, he'd found that the battle had not proved to be worth the prize.

He was in a quandary now. It would look exceedingly strange if their marriage broke up too soon. There was also Daniel to be considered. At least, however, there would be no other child. She sat rigidly in the dining chair, a tempest of emotion storming through her slight body.

She was not carrying his child. The proof had come that very night when she had abandoned herself to grief. There would be no other baby, no further tie by which she might hold him. Her sane mind told her that was fortunate, but more basic promptings rebelled against that cooler judgement.

She could not picture life without Luc again. That terrified her. The more distant he was, the more desperate she felt. She couldn't eat, she couldn't sleep, she couldn't do anything. What was there now? she asked herself. What had he left her? Daniel adored him. Daniel could hardly bear Luc out of his sight.

Her future stretched emptily before her. Daniel would start school in Rome. Initially she would be there as well but, little by little, the marriage that had never quite got off the ground would shift into a separation. Luc would make lengthy business trips and she would no doubt do what was expected of her and make regular visits back to England. Certainly it would be impossible for her to withstand continual exposure to Luc as he was now.

It was torture to be so close and yet so far, to shake with wanting him in the loneliness of her bed at night, to exhaust herself by day keeping up a pretence that she was quite happy with things as they were. Damp-eyed, she lifted her head high. She would not let Luc see how much he was hurting her. Pride demanded that she equal his detachment and make no attempt to break it.

Not that she thought she was managing to be totally convincing. In between all the pleases and thank-yous she had never heard so many of before, she occasionally encountered searching stares. His tension spoke for itself. Luc wanted her to let go with finesse. He was willing her not to force some melodramatic scene. Rage and despair constrained her in an iron yoke of silence, creating an inner conflict that threatened to tear her apart. Why couldn't he have left her alone? Why had he had to thrust his way back into her life? Why had he laid a white rose on her pillow? Why had he had to force her to admit that, far from hating him, she loved him? Why? Why? Why?

Angered by her own desperation, she stood up, determined not to spend another day wandering about like a lost soul. For starters, it was time she saw Drew, time she stopped avoiding that issue. After all, she had already contacted his godmother. Mrs Anstey had ranted down the phone at her, refusing her apologies and telling her with satisfaction that she had given the flat to a great-niece, who would be far more suitable. Catherine had taken the verbal trouncing in silence. It had lightened her conscience.

She didn't expect her meeting with Drew to be quite so straight-forward. Did she tell him that she was responsible for the nerve-racking experiences he must have endured in Germany? Or did he already know? Would he even want to see her now?

It was early afternoon when she entered the compact offices that housed Huntingdon Components. Drew's secretary phoned through an announcement of her arrival. Drew emerged from his office, his pleasant features stiff and almost expressionless. 'This is a surprise.'

'I felt I had to see you.'

'I'm afraid I don't know quite how to greet Mrs Luc Santini.'

She tilted her chin. 'I'm still Catherine,' she murmured steadily.

He stood at the window, his back half turned to her. 'I tried to call you from Germany. My housekeeper told me that you'd cleared out without even staying the night. She said the bedroom was so tidy that she wasn't too sure you'd been in it at all.'

Catherine bent her head. Luc's security staff were thorough.

'Then I saw that photo of you at the airport with Santini. It was in every newspaper,' he sighed. 'Daniel is the image of him. Harriet lied about your background. I put that together for myself.'

'I'm sorry that I couldn't tell you the truth.'

'It was none of my business when I first knew you. But I preferred competing with a ghost,' he admitted wryly, and hesitated. 'To take off with him like that, you have to be crazy about him...'

Her vague idea of explaining what had really happened died there. Somehow she felt it would be disloyal to Luc. Drew had no need of that information. 'Yes,' she agreed, half under her breath, and then, looking up, asked, 'Did you get your contract?'

Unexpectedly, he smiled widely. 'Not the one I went out for. Quite coincidentally, an even more promising prospect came up. It's secured the firm's future for a long time to come. What's that saying? Lucky at cards, unlucky in love?'

Her eyes clouded over, but she was shaken to realise that Drew was quite unaware that his firm had been under threat and had ultimately profited from the change in contracts. He had undergone no anxiety, and the news that he had achieved that second contract through Luc's influence would not be welcome.

He cleared his throat awkwardly. 'I've agreed to go to counselling with Annette, but I don't know if it will change anything.'

A smile chased the tension from her soft mouth. 'I'm glad,' she said sincerely.

'I still think you're pure gold, Catherine.' His mouth twisted. 'I just hope that he appreciates how lucky he is.'

Not so's you'd notice, she repined helplessly as she climbed back into the limousine. A male, punch-drunk on his good fortune, did not willingly vacate the marital bed and avoid all physical contact. Quite obviously, Luc couldn't bring himself to touch her. The white-hot heat of his hunger had died along with the illusion. But it hadn't died for her. Her love had never been an illusion. She had never been blind to Luc's flaws or her own. She still ached with wanting him. And soon she would despise herself again for that weakness.

It was wrong to let Luc do this to her. It was undignified, degrading...cowardly. Their marriage had been a mistake. Continuing it purely for the sake of appearances demanded too high a cost of her self-respect. Nor could she sacrifice herself for Daniel's sake. Daniel was like Luc. Daniel would survive. It was her own survival that was at risk. She couldn't afford to sit back and let events overtake her as she had done so often in the past. A clean break was the only answer and it was for her to take the initiative.

Dazed by the acknowledgement, she wandered round Harrods in the afternoon. The heavens were falling on her. The ground was suddenly rocking beneath her feet. It was over…over. She had felt this way once before and she had never wanted to feel like this again.

The chauffeur was replacing the phone when she returned to the car. 'Mr Santini's back from Paris, madam. I said we'd be back within two hours, allowing for the traffic.'

Dear heaven, for someone who didn't give two hoots about her, Luc certainly kept tabs on her! She was suddenly very reluctant to go home. It would be better, she reasoned, if Daniel was in bed when she returned.

'We'll be later,' she said. 'I want to stop somewhere for a meal.'

She selected a hotel. She spent ages choosing from the chef's recommendations, chasing each course round the plate and deciding what she would say to Luc, how she would say it and, more importantly, how she would look when she said it. Cool, calm and collected. Not martyred, not distressed, not apologetic. When she told Luc that she wanted an immediate separation, she would do it with dignity.

She was tiptoeing up the stairs, deciding that she would feel fresher and more dignified in the morning, when Luc strode out of the drawing-room. 'Where the hell have you been?' he demanded, making her jump with fright.

'Out.' Carefully not sparing his lean, dark physique a single visually disturbing glance, she murmured, 'I want a separation, Luc.'

'*Prego?*' It was very faint. She studied him then, unable to resist the temptation. The lights above shed cruel clarity on the sudden pallor defining his hard bone-structure. For some reason, he looked absolutely shattered by her announcement. It also occurred to her that he had lost weight over the last few days.

'We can talk about it tomorrow.' Consumed by raging misery, she lost heart in her prepared speeches about incompatability.

'We talk about it now. You've been with Huntingdon!' The condemnation came slamming back at her with ferocious bite as he mounted the stairs two at time.

He was seething, she registered bemusedly.

'You go slinking back to him the instant my back's turned. I won't let you go,' he swore fiercely. 'I'll kill him if he comes near you!'

'I can't think why. After all—'

'After all *nothing*,' he cut in wrathfully. 'You're my wife.'

Gingerly, she pressed open her bedroom door. 'Your room's next door, I seem to recall,' she reminded him for want of anything better to say.

'I was a fool to take that lying down! How dare you put me out of your bed?' he ground out between clenched white teeth, following her in, slamming the door with a resounding crash.

She blinked. 'I didn't—'

'I should never have stood for it. You played on my guilt!'

Catherine was frowning. 'Mrs Stokes must have moved your luggage. I remember her asking me how many bedrooms Castelleone had. We talked a lot about bedrooms but I really wasn't paying much attention—'

'Is this a private conversation or can anyone join in? I don't know what you're talking about!'

'She must have realised we had separate bedrooms in Italy and she probably assumed we wanted the same set-up here.' She smiled at him sunnily. 'You thought I was responsible?'

A dark flush had risen over his cheekbones. 'I came in very quietly and you were asleep that night. My clothes had gone.'

'I thought you'd told her to move them.' She could hardly credit that a mistake on the housekeeper's part had led to such a misunderstanding. 'Why didn't you say something?'

He looked ever so slightly sheepish. 'I didn't know what to say. All that day I was in shock at what you said to me on the jet.' He shifted a beautifully shaped brown hand in a movement of frustration. 'It only happens with you,' he breathed tautly.

She watched him move fluidly across the room like a restive cat night-prowling on velvet paws. 'What only happens with me?'

His jawline clenched. 'I lose my temper and I say things I don't mean.' Long fingers balled into a fist and then vanished into the pocket of his well-cut trousers. Discomfiture was written all over him. 'But that you should distrust me to such an extent...it...it hurt.'

So did saying it. She longed to reach out and put her arms round him, but sensed how unwelcome it would be. He was so proud, so defensive and ill-at-ease with words that came so easily to her. He was fluent in every other mood but this one, where deeper emotions intruded. And he was only talking now because anger had spurred him to the attempt.

'I was very insecure when I was pregnant,' she said uncertainly. 'You were breaking me up, Luc. Emotionally I was in a mess. I just didn't have the courage to face you with a complication you didn't want. It never occurred to me that you might choose to insist on marrying me or want to take any responsibility for the child I was expecting...'

The muscles in his strong brown throat worked. 'You don't have to justify your decision. I don't blame you for what you did,' he said almost indistinctly. 'I had to lose you before I could appreciate what you meant to me.'

He hadn't vacated the marital bed. He understood what she had done five years ago. He wasn't holding it against her as if she had failed him. He was accepting that, whether he liked it or not, it had been inevitable.

'Actually, if I hadn't been hit by that car,' she muttered, 'I would have phoned you.'

He paled. 'What car?'

She told him about the accident in the car park and the months she had spent in hospital. He was visibly appalled and shaken, but he didn't take her into his arms as she had secretly hoped. He wandered over to the window and looked back at her with glittering dark eyes. 'The first time I saw you, you reminded me of a Christmas-tree angel. Very fragile, not intended for human handling. You were wearing a hideous dress covered with roses and you were so tiny, it wore you. When I smiled at you you lit up like an electric light and you chattered non-stop for fifteen solid minutes,' he extended very quietly. 'You got lost in the middle of sentences. You didn't hear the phone ringing. You didn't notice that a woman came in and walked round while I was there. You were so dizzy, you fascinated me. I'd never met anyone like you before. You want to hear that I was ravished at first glance but I wasn't.'

'I never thought you were.' Her cheeks were hot enough to light a fire.

'That night I didn't think of you in a sexual way,' he was scrupulously careful to tell her.

'Nostalgia's not your thing,' she muttered fiercely.

'But I'd never met anyone with so much natural warmth. Being with you was like standing in the sunshine. When I walked away, I felt as though I'd kicked a puppy...'

Her nails ploughed furrows into her palms.

'It was surprisingly hard to walk away,' he confided in an undertone. 'Over the next two months, you kept drifting into my mind at the oddest times. I slept with another woman and then I would think about you. It was infuriating.'

'I'm not overcome by it either!' she snapped.

'When I was next in London, I didn't intend to look you up again. In fact, I had a woman with me on that trip. I deliberately went to a different hotel that was nowhere near the gallery.'

'Am I supposed to *want* to hear this?'

Tense dark eyes flickered over her and veiled. 'I never slept with her. She got on my nerves and I sent her back to New York. I was callous about it. I was callous in most of my dealings with women in those days. But I found I couldn't be callous with you. You had incredible pulling-power, *cara*. I was back at the gallery the second she left for the airport.'

'Why?' Involuntarily, she was finding that this was compulsive listening, a window on to a once blank wall.

'I didn't know why then. You were so extravagantly pleased to see me, it was as though you'd been waiting for me. Or as though you knew something I didn't. And perhaps you did.' An almost tender smile softened his mouth. 'It was unsettling. It threw me. I haven't asked a woman to go for a walk since I was thirteen. I was in a foul mood and you talked me out of it. You were so painfully honest about yourself and so agonisingly young, but somehow…' he hesitated '…you made me feel ten feet tall.'

'I made you feel so good it took you another two months to show up again!' she protested.

He released his breath in a hiss. 'You were only eighteen. You didn't belong in my world. I didn't want to hurt you. I also never wanted to make love to anyone as badly as I wanted you that night. I was twenty-seven, but I felt like a middle-aged lecher!' he gritted abruptly. 'I didn't plan to see you ever again.'

'Have you any idea how many nights I sat up, waiting for you to call?'

'I knew it.' He sounded grimly fatalistic. 'I could feel you waiting and I couldn't get you out of my head. I also found that I couldn't stay away from you. I believed that once I went to bed with you I would be cured.'

'That's disgusting!' she gasped.

'*Per Dio*, what do you want? The truth or a fairy-tale?' he slashed back at her in sudden anger. 'You think it is easy for me to admit these things? The lies I told to myself? That first night in Switzerland—how is it you describe euphoria? You thought you'd died and gone to heaven? Well, so did I, the first time I made love to you!'

The shocked line of her mouth had softened into a faint smile.

'But naturally I assured myself that I only felt that way because it was the best sex I'd ever had.'

Her smile evaporated like Scotch mist.

'I was in love with you but I didn't want to accept that fact,' he admitted harshly. 'I hated being away from you but I didn't want to take you abroad with me. The papers would have got hold of you then.'

'Would that have mattered?'

'Seven years ago, *cara*, you couldn't have handled a more public place in my life.' He shrugged in a jerky motion. 'And I didn't want to share you with anyone. I didn't want other women bitching at you. I didn't want gossip columnists cheapening what we had.'

She lowered her head. 'And perhaps you didn't want anyone realising that I had a literacy problem.'

'Yes. That both embarrassed and angered me.' He had to force out the admission. 'But I wouldn't have felt like that had I known you were dyslexic. I could have been open about that. In spite of that, wherever you were was home for me. If something worried me, I forgot about it when I was with you. I didn't realise until you had gone just how much I relied on you.'

She was trying very hard not to cry. He pulled her rigid figure into his arms very slowly, very gently. 'I have few excuses for what I did five years ago. But, if it is any consolation to you, I paid; *Dio*...' he said feelingly, 'I paid for not valuing you as I should have done. If only I'd intercepted you before you left the apartment that morning! I must have missed you by no more than an hour.'

She bowed her head against his broad chest, drowning in the warm masculine scent of him, feeling weak, shivery and on the brink of melting. 'I hated leaving you.'

'For a while, *bella mia*, I too hated you for leaving.' The hand smoothing through her hair was achingly gentle. 'It was the one and only time I lost interest in making money. I hit the bottle pretty hard...'

She was shocked. 'You?'

'Me. I felt unbelievably sorry for myself. I let everything slide.'

Her brow indented. 'Drew told me that you almost lost the shirt off your back a few years ago. Was that true?'

'It was.'

'Over me?' she whispered incredulously.

'I needed you,' he said gruffly. 'I missed you. I felt very alone.'

Tears swimming in her eyes, she wrapped her arms tightly round him, too upset by the image he invoked to speak.

'I picked myself up again because I believed you would come back,' he shared. 'When I saw you in the Savoy two weeks ago there was nothing I would not have done to get you back.'

'No?' She positively glowed at the news.

'It was not, however, how I pictured our reconciliation. You shouldn't have been with another man. You should have looked pleased to see me, instead of horror-stricken. I'm afraid I went off the rails that day,' he breathed tautly.

'Did you?' She smiled up at him, unconcerned.

He frowned down at her. 'I threatened you. I took advantage of your amnesia to practically kidnap you. You could have been madly in love with Huntingdon and I was determined that you would get over it. When you came round in the clinic and smiled at me, I was lost to all conscience. When I realised you'd lost your memory, all I could think about was getting you out of the country.'

'You were always quick to recognise a good opportunity,' she sighed approvingly.

Long fingers cupped her cheekbones. 'Catherine, what I did was wrong. This week, after I learnt about Daniel and cooled down, which I did very quickly, I felt very ashamed of what I had done. It was completely unscrupulous of me.'

'If you say so.' She wound her arms round his neck, stretching up on tiptoe. 'Personally I think it was thrilling. I waited twenty-four and a half years to be spirited off to an Italian castle, and I wouldn't have missed it for the world.'

'Be serious.' He was alarmingly set on contrition. In fact, the more forgiving she became, the more grim he looked. 'Be honest with me. Can you forgive me for what I have said and done?'

'I forgive you freely, absolutely and forever. Do you want to know why?' she whispered teasingly. 'You're crazy about me...aren't you?' She drew back to stare up at him, suffering a sudden lurch in overwhelming confidence.

Brilliant golden eyes shimmered almost fiercely over her anxious face. 'Only a lunatic would behave the way I did if I wasn't,' he grated. 'Of course I love you!'

'I don't want a separation...I don't even want a separate bedroom,' she swore.

'Relax—you weren't getting either. What I have, I hold.' He lifted her with wonderful ease off her feet. 'But I should never have made love to you before you regained your memory. Unfortunately that night I found you in my bed,' his voice thickened betrayingly, 'I could not resist you.'

'I can't resist you, either.' She sank small determined hands into his black hair and drew his mouth down to hers. He lowered her to the bed without breaking the connection. It was some minutes before she remembered to breathe again.

'It's been torture to stay away from you,' he admitted roughly. 'But I believed that was what you wanted. I went to all that trouble arranging to go to Paris, thinking that you would be tempted to come, and you said no.'

'Serves you right for being so casual about it.'

He shuddered beneath the caressing sweep of her hands. 'Don't do that,' he groaned, pinning her provocative hands to the mattress. 'When you do that, I react like a teenager.'

'Why do you think I do it?' she murmured wickedly.

'*Dio*, I want you so much,' he said raggedly, removing her dress with more speed than expertise. Abruptly he stopped dead, staring down at her. 'It isn't safe, is it? I could make you pregnant.'

'The best things in life are dangerous. It's your choice,' she whispered.

'You wouldn't mind?' He looked dazed. 'By the pool that day, you weren't very enthusiastic about the idea. That's why I worried that it was too late.'

She ran a loving fingertip across his sensual mouth. 'I'm afraid all those intensely erotic experiences in Italy were unproductive.'

He nipped at her fingertip with his teeth, a brilliant smile curving his lips. 'Give me a month's trial.'

'You're so modest.' She blushed under raking golden eyes, heat striking her to the very centre of her body, making her tremble deliciously. He started to kiss her slowly and deeply and hungrily until conversation was the last thing on either of their minds.

What followed was wild, passionate and incredibly sweet. And afterwards he told her how much he loved her in Italian and English and French.

'You've got a certain *je ne sais quoi*,' Catherine conceded against a damp brown shoulder, letting the tip of her tongue slide teasingly across his smooth skin.

Luc's tousled dark head lifted, a sudden lancing grin flashing across his darkly handsome features. 'I understood that I was a habit.'

'You are,' she sighed with a voluptuous little wriggle of glorious contentment. 'An addictive one. Didn't I mention that?'

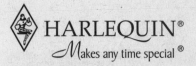

Three of romance's most talented craftsmen
come together in one special collection.

New York Times bestselling authors

Jayne Ann Krentz
Tess Gerritsen

National bestselling author

Stella Cameron

in

Stolen Memories

With plenty of page-turning passion and dramatic
storytelling, this volume promises many memorable
hours of reading enjoyment!

Coming to your favorite retail outlet in February 2002.

TRUEBLOOD, TEXAS

Coming in February 2002…

HOT ON HIS TRAIL
by
Karen Hughes

Lost:

Her so-called life. After being sheltered by her mother for years, Calley Graham hopes to sign on as a full-time investigator for Finders Keepers.

Found:

One tough trail boss. Matt Radcliffe doesn't have time during his cattle drive for a pesky investigator who insists on dragging him back to Pinto, Texas.

But Calley is one determined woman—so she volunteers as camp cook on Matt's drive, hoping to keep her job…and maybe the cowboy, too!

Finders Keepers: bringing families together

HARLEQUIN®
Makes any time special ®

Visit us at www.eHarlequin.com

TBTCNM6-TR